CRITICAL ACCLAIM FOR
FOUNDATION'S FEAR

"[Benford] brings out the complexities of a galactic empire that Asimov never filled out . . . the first book stands well on its own."

—*Denver Post*

"[Benford] took on the huge task of answering questions [raised in the original], and difficult as it may sound, he pulled it off with style. . . . Rest assured, Asimov's work is in good hands."

—Craig E. Engler
Editor and Publisher
of *Science Fiction Weekly*

"A richly rewarding delight . . . Benford writes up to his usual high standard and excels in bringing Asimovian concepts . . . to vivid, visually compelling life."

—*Publishers Weekly*
(starred review)

"Intriguing and engrossing . . . [a] curious blend of reinventions and retrospective criticism."

—*Kirkus Reviews*
(starred review)

THE SECOND FOUNDATION TRILOGY

Foundation's Fear
by Gregory Benford

Foundation and Chaos
by Greg Bear

The Secret Foundation*
by David Brin

BY ISAAC ASIMOV

Gold: The Final Science Fiction Collection
Magic: The Final Fantasy Collection

Isaac Asimov's History of I-Botics

Isaac Asimov's I-Bots: Time Was*
by Steve Perry and Gary A. Braunbeck

Published by HarperPrism

*coming soon

THE SECOND

FOUNDATION TRILOGY

◆

Foundation's Fear

◆

GREGORY BENFORD

HarperPrism
A Division of HarperCollinsPublishers

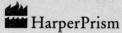 HarperPrism

A Division of HarperCollinsPublishers
10 East 53rd Street, New York, N.Y. 10022-5299

This is a work of fiction. The characters, incidents, and dialogues are products of the author's imagination and are not to be construed as real. Any resemblance to actual events or persons, living or dead, is entirely coincidental.

ISBN 0-06-105638-3

HarperCollins®, ®, and HarperPrism® are trademarks of HarperCollins*Publishers* Inc.

Cover illustration © 1997 by Jean Targete

A hardcover edition of this book was published in 1997 by HarperPrism

First paperback printing: March 1998

Printed in the United States of America

Visit HarperPrism on the World Wide Web at http://www.harperprism.com

❖ 10 9 8 7 6 5 4 3 2 1

To Greg Bear and David Brin
fellow voyagers on strange seas

RENDEZVOUS

◆

R. Daneel Olivaw did not look like Eto Demerzel. That role he had already cast aside.

This Dors Vanabili expected, though it was unsettling to her. She knew that through millennia he had discarded the skin and shape of countless guises.

Dors studied him in the cramped, dingy room two Sectors away from Streeling University. She had followed a convoluted route to get here and the site was protected by elaborate, overlapping security measures. Robots were outlaws. They had lived for millennia in the deep shadow of taboo. Though Olivaw was her guide and mentor, she saw him seldom.

Yet as a humaniform robot she felt a tremor of mingled fear and reverence at this ancient, partly metallic form before her. He was nearly twenty millennia old. Though he could appear human, he did not truly wish to be human. He was inexpressibly greater than that now.

She had lived happily as a pseudo-person for so long now. Even a reminder of who and what she was came like cold fingers along her spine. "The recent increasing attention paid to Hari . . ."

"Indeed. You fear you will be detected."

"The newest security measures are so invasive!"

He nodded. "You are correct to be concerned."

"I need more help in protecting Hari."

"Adding another of us to his close associates would double the danger of detection."

"I know, I know, but . . ."

Olivaw reached out and touched her hand. She blinked back tears and studied his face. Small matters, such as consistent movement of his Adam's apple when he swallowed, had long ago been perfected. To ease himself in this meeting, he had omitted these minor computations and movements. He obviously enjoyed even momentary freedom from such taxation.

"I am constantly fearful," she admitted.

"You should be. He is much threatened. But you are designed to function best with a high level of apprehension."

"I know my specifications, yes, but—take this latest move of yours, involving him in Imperial politics at the highest level. It imposes severe strain on my task."

"A necessary move."

"It may distract him from his work, from psychohistory."

Olivaw shook his head slowly. "I doubt that. He is a certain special kind of human—driven. He once remarked to me, 'Genius does what it must and talent does what it can'—thinking that he merely had talent."

She smiled ruefully. "But he is a genius."

"And like all such, unique. Humans have that—rare, great excursions from the mean. Evolution has selected them for it, though they do not seem to realize that."

"And we?"

"Evolution cannot act on one who lives forever. In any case, there has not been time. We can and do develop ourselves, however."

"Humans are also murderous."

"We are few; they are many. And they have deep animal spirits we cannot fathom, in the end, no matter how we try."

"I care about Hari, first."

"And the Empire, a distant second?" He gave her a thin smile. "I care for the Empire only so far as it safeguards humanity."

"From what?"

"From itself. Just remember, Dors: this is the Cusp Era, as anticipated by ourselves for so long. The most critical period in all of history."

"I know the term, but what is the substance? Do we have a theory of history?"

For the first time Daneel Olivaw showed expression, a rueful grimace. "We are not capable of a deep theory. For that, we would have to understand humans far better."

"But we have something . . . ?"

"A different way of viewing humanity, one now badly strained. It caused us to shape this greatest of humanity's creations, the Empire."

"I do not know of this—"

"No need for you to. We now require a more profound view. That is why Hari is so important."

Dors frowned, troubled for reasons she could not quite express. "This earlier, simpler theory of . . . ours. It tells you that humanity now must have psychohistory?"

"Exactly. We know this, from our own crude theory. But only this."

"For more, we rely on Hari alone?"

"Alas, yes."

PART 1

PART 1

*MATHIST
MINISTER*

HARI SELDON — ... *though it is the best existing authority on the details of Seldon's life, the biography by Gaal Dornick cannot be trusted regarding the early rise to power. As a young man, Dornick met Seldon only two years before the great mathist's death. By then, rumor and even legend had already begun to grow about Seldon, particularly regarding his shadowy period of large-scale authority within the fading Imperium.*

How Seldon became the only mathist in all Galactic history to ascend to political power remains one of the most intractable puzzles for Seldon scholars. He gave no sign of ambitions beyond the building of a science of "history"—all the while envisioning not the mere fathoming of the past, but in fact the prediction of the future. (As Seldon himself remarked to Dornick, he early on desired "the prevention of certain kinds of futures.")

Certainly the mysterious exit of Eto Demerzel as First Minister was the opening act in a play of large proportions. That Cleon I immediately turned to Seldon suggests that Demerzel hand-picked his successor. Yet why go to Seldon? Historians are divided about the motivations of the central players in this crucial moment. The Empire had entered a period of challenge and disruption, coming especially from what Seldon termed the "chaos worlds." How Seldon adroitly maneuvered against powerful opponents, despite no recorded experience in the political arena, remains an active but vexing area of research ...

—ENCYCLOPEDIA GALACTICA[1]

[1]All quotations from the *Encyclopedia Galactica* here reproduced are taken from the 116th edition, published 1,020 F.E. by the Encyclopedia Galactica Publishing Co., Terminus, with permission of the publishers.

1.

◆

He had made enough enemies to acquire a nickname, Hari Seldon mused, and not enough friends to hear what it was.

He could feel the truth of that in the murmuring energy in the crowds. Uneasily he walked from his apartment to his office across the broad squares of Streeling University. "They don't like me," he said.

Dors Vanabili matched his stride easily, studying the massed faces. "I do not sense any danger."

"Don't worry your pretty head about assassination attempts—at least, not right away."

"My, you're in a fine mood today."

"I hate this security screen. Who wouldn't?"

The Imperial Specials had fanned out in what their captain termed "an engaging perimeter" around Hari and Dors. Some carried flash-screen projectors, capable of warding off a full heavy-weapons assault. Others looked equally dangerous bare-handed.

Their scarlet-and-blue uniforms made it easy to see where the crowd was impinging on the moving security boundary as Hari walked slowly across the main campus square. Where the crowd was thickest, the bright uniforms simply bulled their way through. The entire spectacle made him acutely uncomfortable. Specials were not noted for their diplomacy and this was, after all, a quiet place of learning. Or had been.

Dors clasped his hand in reassurance. "A First Minister can't simply walk around without—"

"I'm not First Minister!"

"The Emperor has designated you, and that's enough for this crowd."

"The High Council hasn't acted. Until they do—"

"Your friends will assume the best," she said mildly.

"These are my friends?" Hari eyed the crowd suspiciously.

"They're smiling."

So they were. One called, "Hail the Prof Minister!" and others laughed.

"Is that my nickname now?"

"Well, it's not a bad one."

"Why do they flock so?"

"People are drawn to power."

"I'm still just a professor!"

To offset his irritation, Dors chuckled at him, a wifely reflex. "There's an ancient saying, 'These are the times that fry men's souls.'"

"You have a bit of historical wisdom for everything."

"It's one of the few perks that come with being an historian."

Someone called, "Hey, Math Minister!"

Hari said, "I don't like that name any better."

"Get used to it. You'll be called worse."

They passed by the great Streeling fountain and Hari took refuge in a moment of contemplating its high, arching waters. The splashes drowned out the crowd and he could almost imagine he was back in his simple, happy life. Then he had only had to worry about psychohistory and Streeling University infighting. That snug little world had vanished, perhaps forever, the moment Cleon decided to make him a figure in Imperial politics.

The fountain was glorious, yet even it reminded him of the vastness that lay beneath such simplicities. Here the tinkling streams broke free, but their flight was momentary. Trantor's waters ran in mournful dark pipes, down dim passages scoured by ancient engineers. A maze of fresh water arteries and sewage veins twined through the eternal bowels. These bodily fluids of the planet had passed through uncountable trillions of kidneys and throats, had washed away sins, been toasted with at marriages and births, had carried off the blood of murders and the vomit of terminal agonies. They flowed on in their deep night, never knowing the clean vapor joy of unfettered weather, never free of man's hand.

They were trapped. So was he.

Their party reached the Mathist Department and ascended. Dors rose through the traptube beside him, a breeze fluttering her hair amiably, the effect quite flattering. The Specials took up watchful, rigid positions outside.

Just as he had for the last week, Hari tried again with the captain. "Look, you don't really need to keep a dozen men sitting out here—"

"I'll be the judge of that, Academician sir, if you please."

Hari felt frustrated at the waste of it. He noticed a young Specialman eyeing Dors, whose uni-suit revealed while still covering. Something made him say, "Well then, I will thank you to have your men keep their eyes where they belong!"

The captain looked startled. He glared at the offending man and stomped over to reprimand him. Hari felt a spark of satisfaction. Going in the entrance to his office, Dors said, "I'll try to dress more strictly."

"No, no, I'm just being stupid. I shouldn't let tiny things like that bother me."

She smiled prettily. "Actually, I rather liked it."

"You did? Me being stupid?"

"Your being protective."

Dors had been assigned years before to watch over him, by Eto Demerzel. Hari reflected that he had gotten used to that role of hers, little noticing that it conflicted in a deep, unspoken way with her also being a woman. Dors was utterly self-reliant, but she had qualities which sometimes did not easily jibe with her duty. Being his wife, for example.

"I will have to do it more often," he said lightly.

Still, he felt a pang of guilt about making trouble for the Specialmen. Their being here was certainly not their idea; Cleon had ordered it. No doubt they would far rather be off somewhere saving the Empire with sweat and valor.

They went through the high, arched foyer of the Mathist Department, Hari nodding to the staff. Dors went into her own office and he hurried into his suite with an air of an animal retreating into its burrow. He collapsed into his airchair, ignoring the urgent-message holo that hung a meter from his face.

A wave erased it as Yugo Amaryl came in through the connecting e-stat portal. The intrusive, bulky portal was also the fruit of Cleon's security order. The Specials had installed the shimmering weapons-nulling fields everywhere. They lent an irksome, prickly smell of ozone to the air. One more intrusion of Reality, wearing the mask of Politics.

Yugo's grin split his broad face. "Got some new results."

"Cheer me up, show me something splendid."

Yugo sat on Hari's broad, empty desk, one leg dangling. "Good mathematics is always true and beautiful."

"Certainly. But it doesn't have to be *true* in the sense that ordinary people mean. It can say nothing whatever about the world."

"You're making me feel like a dirty engineer."

Hari smiled. "You were once, remember?"

"Don't I!"

"Maybe you'd rather be sweating it out as a heat-sinker?"

Hari had found Yugo by chance eight years ago, just after arriving on Trantor, when he and Dors were on the run from Imperial agents. An hour's talk had shown Hari that Yugo was an untutored genius at trans-representational analysis. Yugo had a gift, an unconscious lightness of touch. They had collaborated ever since. Hari honestly thought he had learned more from Yugo than the other way around.

"Ha!" Yugo clapped his big hands together three times, in the Dahlite manner of showing agreeable humor. "You can grouse about doing filthy, real-world work, but as long as it's in a nice, comfortable office, I'm in paradise."

"I shall have to turn most of the heavy lifting over to you, I fear." Hari deliberately put his feet up on his desk. Might as well look casual, even if he didn't feel that way. He envied Yugo's heavy-bodied ease.

"This First Minister stuff?"

"It is getting worse. I have to go see the Emperor again."

"The man wants you. Must be your craggy profile."

"That's what Dors thinks, too. I figure it's my disarming smile. Anyway, he can't have me."

"He will."

"If he forces the ministership on me, I shall do such a lousy job, Cleon will fire me."

Yugo shook his head. "Not wise. Failed First Ministers are usually tried and executed."

"You've been talking to Dors again."

"She *is* a historian."

"Yes, and we're psychohistorians. Seekers of predictability." Hari threw up his hands in exasperation. "Why doesn't that count for anything?"

"Because nobody in the citadels of power has seen it work."

"And they won't. Once people think we can predict, we will never be free of politics."

"You're not free now," Yugo said reasonably.

"Good friend, your worse trait is insisting on telling me the truth in a calm voice."

"It saves knocking sense into your head. That would take longer."

Hari sighed. "If only muscles helped with mathematics. You would be even better at it."

Yugo waved the thought away. "You're the key. You're the idea man."

"Well, this font of ideas hasn't got a clue."

"Ideas, they'll come."

"I never get a chance to work on psychohistory anymore!"

"And as First Minister—"

"It will be worse. Psychohistory will go—"

"Nowhere, without you."

"There will be some progress, Yugo. I am not vain enough to think everything depends on me."

"It does."

"Nonsense! There's still you, the Imperial Fellows, and the staff."

"We need leadership. Thinking leadership."

"Well, I could continue to work here part of the time . . ."

Hari looked around his spacious office and felt a pang at the thought of not spending every day here, surrounded by his tools, tomes, and friends. As First Minister he would have a minor palace, but to him it would be mere empty, meaningless extravagance.

Yugo gave him a mocking grin. "First Minister is usually considered a full-time job."

"I know, I know. But maybe there's a way—"

The office holo bloomed into full presentation a meter from his head. The office familiar was coded to pipe through only high-priority messages. Hari slapped a key on his desk and the picture gave the gathering image a red, square frame—the signal that his filter-face was on. "Yes?"

Cleon's personal aide appeared in red tunic against a blue background. "You are summoned," the woman said simply.

"Uh, I am honored. When?"

The woman went into details and Hari was immediately thankful for the filter-face. The personal officer was imposing, and he did not want to appear to be what he was, a distracted professor. His filter-face had a tailored etiquette menu. He had automatically thumbed in a suite of body-language postures and gestures, tailored to mask his true feelings.

"Very well, in two hours. I shall be there," he concluded with a small bow. The filter would render that same motion, shaped to the protocols of the Emperor's staff.

"Drat!" He slapped his desk, making the holo dissolve. "My day is evaporating!"

"What's it mean?"

"Trouble. Every time I see Cleon, it's trouble."

"I dunno, could be a chance to straighten out—"

"I just want to be left alone!"

"A First Ministership—"

"*You* be First Minister! I will take a job as a

computational specialist, change my name—" Hari stopped and laughed wryly. "But I'd fail at that, too."

"Look, you need to change your mood. Don't want to walk in on the Emperor with that scowl."

"Ummm. I suppose not. Very well—cheer me up. What was that good news you mentioned?"

"I turned up some ancient personality constellations."

"Really? I thought they were illegal."

"They are." He grinned. "Laws don't always work."

"Truly ancient? I wanted them for calibration of psychohistorical valences. They have to be early Empire."

Yugo beamed. "These are *pre*-Empire."

"Pre—impossible."

"I got 'em. Intact, too."

"Who are they?"

"Some famous types, dunno what they did."

"What status did they have, to be recorded?"

Yugo shrugged. "No parallel historical records, either."

"Are they authentic recordings?"

"Might be. They're in ancient machine languages, really primitive stuff. Hard to tell."

"Then they could be . . . sims."

"I'd say so. Could be they're built on a recorded underbase, then simmed for roundness."

"You can kick them up to sentience?"

"Yeah, with some work. Got to stitch data languages. Y'know, this is, ah . . ."

"Illegal. Violation of the Sentience Codes."

"Right. These guys I got it from, they're on that New Renaissance world, Sark. They say nobody polices those old Codes anymore."

"It's time we kicked over a few of those ancient blocks."

"Yessir." Yugo grinned. "These constellations, they're the oldest anybody's ever found."

"How did you . . . ?" Hari let his question trail off. Yugo had many shady connections, built on his Dahlite origins.

"It took a little, ah, lubrication."

"I thought so. Well, perhaps best that I don't hear the details."

"Right. As First Minister, you don't want dirty hands."

"Don't call me that!"

"Sure, sure, you're just a journeyman professor. Who's going to be late for his appointment with the Emperor if he doesn't hurry up."

2.

◆

Walking through the Imperial Gardens, Hari wished Dors was with him. He recalled her wariness over his coming again to the attention of Cleon. "They're crazy, often," she had said in a dispassionate voice. "The gentry are eccentric, which allows emperors to be bizarre."

"You exaggerate," he had responded.

"Dadrian the Frugal always urinated in the Imperial Gardens," she had answered. "He would leave state functions to do it, saying that it saved his subjects a needless expense in water."

Hari had to suppress a laugh; palace staff were undoubtedly studying him. He regained his sober manner by admiring the ornate, towering trees, sculpted in the Spindlerian style of three millennia before. He felt the tug of such natural beauty, despite his years buried in Trantor. Here, verdant wealth stretched up toward the blazing sun like outstretched arms. This was the only open spot on the planet, and it reminded him of Helicon, where he had begun.

He had been a rather dreamy boy in a laboring district of Helicon. The work in fields and factories was easy enough that he could think his own shifting, abstract musings while he did it. Before the Civil Service exams changed his life, he had worked out a few simple theorems in number theory and later was crushed to find that they were already known. He lay in bed at night thinking of planes and vectors and trying to envision dimensions larger than three, listening to the distant bleat of the puff-dragons who came drifting down the mountain sides in search of prey. Bioengineered for some ancient purpose, probably hunting, they were revered beasts. He had not seen one for many years. . . .

Helicon, the wild—that was what he longed for. But his destiny seemed submerged in Trantor's steel.

Hari glanced back and his Specials, thinking they were summoned, trotted forward. "No," he said, his hands pushing air toward them—a gesture he was making all the time these days, he reflected. Even in the Imperial Gardens they acted as though every gardener was a potential assassin.

He had come this way, rather than simply emerge from the grav lifter inside the palace, because he liked the gardens above all else. In the distant haze a wall of trees towered, coaxed upward by genetic engineering until they obscured the ramparts of Trantor. Only here, on all the planet, was it possible to experience something resembling the out of doors.

What an arrogant term! Hari thought. To define all of creation by its lying outside the doorways of humanity.

His formal shoes crunched against gravel as he left the sheltered walkways and mounted the formal ramp. Beyond the forested perimeter rose a plume of black smoke. He slowed and estimated distance, perhaps ten klicks. Some major incident, surely.

Striding between tall, neopantheonic columns, he felt a weight descend. Attendants dashed out to welcome him, his Specials tightened up behind, and they made a little procession through the long corridors leading to the Vault of Audience. Here the accumulated great artworks of millennia crowded each other, as if seeking a constituency in the present to give them life.

The heavy hand of the Imperium lay upon most official art. The Empire was essentially about the past, its solidity, and so expressed its taste with a preference for the pretty. Emperors favored the clean straight lines of ascending slabs, the exact parabolas of arcing purple water fountains, classical columns and buttresses and arches. Heroic sculpture abounded. Noble brows eyed infinite prospects. Colossal battles stood frozen at climactic moments, shaped in glowing stone and holoid crystal.

All were entirely proper and devoid of embarrassing challenge. No alarming art here, thank you. Nothing "disturbing" was even allowed in public places on Trantor which the Emperor might visit. By exporting to the periphs all hint of the unpleasantness and smell of human lives, the Imperium achieved its final state, the terminally bland.

Yet to Hari, the reaction against blandness was worse. Among the galaxy's twenty-five million inhabited planets endless variations appeared, but there simmered beneath the Imperial blanket a style based solely on rejection.

Particularly among those Hari termed "chaos worlds," a smug avant-garde fumbled for the sublime by substituting for beauty a love of terror, shock, and the sickeningly grotesque. They used enormous

scale, or acute disproportion, or scatology, or discord
and irrational disjunction.

Both approaches were boring. Neither had any airy
joy.

A wall dissolved, crackling, and they entered the
Vault of Audience. Attendants vanished, his Specials
fell behind. Abruptly Hari was alone. He padded
over the cushiony floor. Baroque excess leered at him
from every raised cornice, upjutting ornament, and
elaborate wainscoting.

Silence. The Emperor was never waiting for anyone, of course. The gloomy chamber gave back no
echoes, as though the walls absorbed everything.

Indeed, they probably did. No doubt every
Imperial conversation went into several ears. There
might be eavesdroppers halfway across the Galaxy.

A light, moving. Down a crackling grav column
came Cleon. "Hari! So happy you could come."

Since refusing a summons by the Emperor was traditionally grounds for execution, Hari could barely suppress a wry smile. "My honor to serve, sire."

"Come, sit."

Cleon moved heavily. Rumor had it that his
appetite, already legendary, had begun to exceed
even the skills of his cooks and physicians. "We have
much to discuss."

The Emperor's constant attendant glow served to
subtly enhance him with its nimbus. The contrast
was mild, serving to draw him out from a compara-
tive surrounding gloom. The room's embedded intelligences tracked his eyes and shed added light where
his gaze fell, again with delicate emphasis, subtly
applied. The soft touch of his regard yielded a radiance which guests scarcely noticed, but which acted
subconsciously, adding to their awe. Hari knew this,
yet the effect still worked; Cleon looked masterful,
regal.

"I fear we have hit a snag," Cleon said.

"Nothing you cannot master, I am sure, sire."

Cleon shook his head wearily. "Now don't you, too, go on about my prodigious powers. Some . . . elements—" he drew the word out with dry disdain "—object to your appointment."

"I see." Hari kept his face blank, but his heart leaped.

"Do not be glum! I *do* want you for my First Minister."

"Yes, sire."

"But I am not, despite commonplace assumption, utterly free to act."

"I realize that many others are better qualified—"

"In their own eyes, surely."

"—and better trained, and—"

"And know nothing of psychohistory."

"Demerzel exaggerated the utility of psychohistory."

"Nonsense. He suggested your name to me."

"You know as well as I that he was exhausted, not in his best frame of—"

"His judgment was impeccable for decades." Cleon eyed Hari. "One would almost think you were trying to avoid appointment as First Minister."

"No, sire, but—"

"Men—and women, for that matter—have killed for far less."

"And been killed, once they got it."

Cleon chuckled. "True enough. Some First Ministers do get self-important, begin to scheme against their Emperor—but let us not dwell upon the few failures of our system."

Hari recalled Demerzel saying, "The succession of crises has reached the point where the consideration of the Three Laws of Robotics paralyzes me." Demerzel had been unable to make choices because there were no good ones left. Every possible move hurt someone, badly. So Demerzel, a supreme intelligence, a clandestine humaniform robot, had suddenly left the scene. What chance did Hari have?

"I will assume the position, of course," Hari said quietly, "if necessary."

"Oh, it's necessary. If *possible*, you mean. Factions on the High Council oppose you. They demand a full discussion."

Hari blinked, alarmed. "Will I have to debate?"

"—and then a vote."

"I had no idea the Council could intervene."

"Read the Codes. They do have that power. Typically they do not use it, bowing to the superior wisdom of the Emperor." A dry little laugh. "Not this time."

"If it would make it easier for you, I could absent myself while the discussion—"

"Nonsense! I want to use you to counter them."

"I haven't any ideas how to—"

"I'll scent out the issues; you advise me on answers. Division of labor, nothing could be simpler."

"Um." Demerzel had said confidently, "If he believes you have the psychohistorical answer, he will follow you eagerly and that will make you a good First Minister." Here, in such august surroundings, that seemed quite unlikely.

"We will have to evade these opponents, maneuver against them."

"I have no idea how to do that."

"Of course you do not! I do. But you see the Empire and all its history as one unfurling scroll. You have the *theory*."

Cleon relished ruling. Hari felt in his bones that he did not. As First Minister, his word could determine the fate of millions. That had daunted even Demerzel.

"There is still the Zeroth Law," Demerzel had said just before they parted for the last time. It placed the well-being of humanity as a whole above that of any single human. The First Law then read, *A robot may not injure a human being, or through inaction, allow a human being to come to harm, unless this would violate the Zeroth Law.* Fair enough, but how was Hari to carry out a job which not even Demerzel could do? Hari realized that he had been silent for too long, and that Cleon was waiting. What could he say?

"Um, who opposes me?"

"Several factions united behind Betan Lamurk."

"What's his objection?"

To his surprise, the Emperor laughed heartily. "That you aren't Betan Lamurk."

"You can't simply—"

"Overrule the Council? Offer Lamurk a deal? Buy him off?"

"I didn't mean to imply, sire, that you would stoop to—"

"Of course I would 'stoop,' as you put it. The difficulty lies with Lamurk himself. His price to allow you in as First Minister would be too high."

"Some high position?"

"That, and some estates, perhaps an entire Zone."

Turning an entire Zone of the Galaxy over to a single man . . . "High stakes."

Cleon sighed. "We are not as rich, these days. In the reign of Fletch the Furious, he bartered whole Zones simply for seats on the Council."

"Your supporters, the Royalists, they can't outmaneuver Lamurk?"

"You really must study current politics more, Seldon. Though I suppose you're so steeped in history, all this seems a bit trivial?"

Actually, Hari thought, he was steeped in mathematics.

Dors supplied the history he needed, or Yugo. "I will do so. So the Royalists—"

"Have lost the Dahlites, so they cannot muster a majority coalition."

"The Dahlites are that powerful?"

"They have an argument popular with a broad audience, plus a large population."

"I did not know they were so strong. My own close assistant, Yugo—"

"I know, a Dahlite. Watch him."

Hari blinked. "Yugo is a strong Dahlite, true. But he is loyal, a fine, intuitive mathist. But how did you—"

"Background check." Cleon waved his hand in airy dismissal. "One must know a few things about a First Minister."

Hari disliked being under an Imperial microscope, but he kept his face blank. "Yugo is loyal to me."

"I know the story, how you uplifted him from hard labor, bypassing the Civil Service filters. Very noble of you. But I cannot overlook the fact that the Dahlites have a ready audience for their fevered out-pourings. They threaten to alter the representation of Sectors in the High Council, even in the Lower Council. So—" Cleon jabbed a finger "—watch him."

"Yes, sire." Cleon was getting steamed up about nothing, as far as Yugo was concerned, but no point in arguing.

"You will have to be as circumspect as the Emperor's wife during this, ah, transitional period."

Hari recalled the ancient saying, that above all the Emperor's wife (or wives, depending upon the era) must keep her skirts clean, no matter what muck she walks above. The analogy was used even when the Emperor proved to be homosexual, or even when a woman held the Imperial Palace. "Yes, sire. Uh, 'transitional' . . . ?"

Cleon looked off in a distracted way at the towering, shadowy art forms looming around them. By now Hari understood that this pointed to the crux of why he had been summoned. "Your appointment will take a while, as the High Council fidgets. So I shall seek your advice . . ."

"Without giving me the power."

"Well, yes."

Hari felt no disappointment. "So I can stay in my office at Streeling?"

"I suppose it would seem forward if you came here."

"Good. Now, about those Specials—"

"*They* must remain with you. Trantor is more dangerous than a professor knows."

Hari sighed. "Yes, sire."

Cleon lounged back, his airchair folding itself about him elaborately. "Now I would like your advice on this Renegatum matter."

"Renegatum?"

For the first time, Hari saw Cleon show surprise. "You have not followed the case? It is everywhere!"

"I am a bit out of the main stream, sire."

"The Renegatum—the Society of Renegades. They kill and destroy."

"For what?"

"For the pleasure of destruction!" Cleon slapped his chair angrily and it responded by massaging him, apparently a standard answer. "The latest of their members to 'demonstrate their contempt for society' is a woman named Kutonin. She invaded the Imperial Galleries, torch-melted art many millennia old, and killed two guards. Then she peacefully turned herself over to the officers who arrived."

"You shall have her executed?"

"Of course. Court decided she was guilty quickly enough—she confessed."

"Readily?"

"Immediately."

Confession under the subtle ministrations of the Imperials was legendary. Breaking the flesh was easy enough; the Imperials broke the suspect's psyche, as well. "So sentence can be set by you, it being a high crime against the Imperium."

"Oh yes, that old law about rebellious vandalism."

"It allows the death penalty and any special torture."

"But death is not enough! Not for the Renegatum crimes. So I turn to my psychohistorian."

"You want me to . . . ?"

"Give me an idea. These people *say* they're doing it to bring down the existing order and all that, of course. But they get immense planet-wide coverage, their names known by everyone as the destroyers of time-honored art. They go to their graves *famous*. All the psychers say that's their real motivation. I can kill them, but they don't care by that time!"

"Um," Hari said uncomfortably. He knew full well he could never comprehend such people.

"So give me an idea. Something psychohistorical."

Hari was intrigued by the problem, but nothing came to mind. He had long ago learned to deliberately not concentrate on a vexing question immediately, letting his subconscious have first crack. To gain time he asked, "Sire, you saw the smoke beyond the gardens?"

"Um? No." Cleon gave a quick hand signal to unseen eyes and the far wall blossomed with light. A full holo of the gardens filled the massive space. The oily black plume had grown. It coiled snakelike into the gray sky.

A soft, neutral voice spoke in midair. "A breakdown, with insurrection by mechanicals, has caused this unfortunate lapse in domestic order."

"A tiktok riot?" This sort of thing Hari had heard about.

Cleon rose and walked toward the holo. "Ah yes, another recalcitrant riddle. For some reason the mechanicals are going awry. *Look* at that! How many levels are burning?"

"Twelve levels are aflame," the autovoice answered. "Imperial Analysis estimates a death toll of four hundred thirty-seven, within an uncertainty of eighty-four."

"Imperial cost?" Cleon demanded.

"Minor. Some Imperial Regulars were hurt in subduing mechanicals."

"Ah. Well then, it is a small matter." Cleon watched as the wall close-upped. The view plunged down a smoking pit. To the side, like a blazing layer cake, whole floors curled up from the heat. Sparks shot between electrical boosters. Burst pipes showered the flames but had little effect.

Then a distant view, telescoping up into orbit. The program was giving the Emperor an eyeful, showing off its capabilities. Hari guessed that it didn't often get the chance. Cleon the Calm was one derisive nickname for him, for he seemed bored with most matters that moved men.

From space, the only deep green was the Imperial Gardens—just a splotch amid the grays and browns of roofs and roof-agriculture. Charcoal-black solar collectors and burnished steel, pole to pole. The ice caps had dissipated long ago and the seas sloshed in underground cisterns.

Trantor supported forty billion people in a world-wrapping single city, seldom less than half a kilometer deep. Sealed, protected, its billions had long grown used to recycled air and short perspectives, and feared the open spaces a mere elevator ride away.

The view zoomed down into the smoky pit again.

Hari could see tiny figures leaping to their deaths to escape the flames. *Hundreds dying . . .* Hari's stomach lurched. In crowded stacks of humanity, accidents took a fearsome toll.

Still, Hari calculated, there were on average only a hundred people in a square kilometer of the planet's surface. People jammed into the more popular Sectors out of preference, not necessity. With the seas pumped below, there was ample room for automated factories, deep mines, and immense, cavernous growing pods, where raw materials for food emerged with little direct human labor needed. These wearisome chores the tiktoks did. But now they were bringing mayhem to the intricacy that was Trantor, and Cleon fumed as he watched the disaster grow, eating away whole layers with fiery teeth.

More figures writhed in the orange flames. These were *people*, not statistics, he reminded himself. Bile rose in his throat. To be a leader meant that sometimes you had to look away from the pain. Could he do that?

"Another puzzle, my Seldon," Cleon said abruptly. "Why do the tiktoks have these large-scale 'disorders' my advisers keep telling me about? Ah?"

"I do not—"

"There must be *some* psychohistorical explanation!"

"These tiny phenomena may well lie beyond—"

"Work on it! Find out!"

"Uh, yes, sire."

Hari knew enough to let Cleon pad pointlessly around the vault, frowning at the continuing wall-high scenes of carnage, in utter silence. Perhaps, Hari thought, the Emperor was calm because he had seen so much calamity already. Even horrendous news palls. A sobering thought; would the same happen to the naïve Hari Seldon?

Cleon had some way of dealing with disaster, though, for after a few moments he waved and the scenes vanished. The vault filled with cheerful music and the lighting rose. Attendants scampered out with bowls and trays of appetizers. A man at Hari's elbow offered him a stim. Hari waved it away. The sudden shift in mood was heady enough. Apparently it was commonplace, though, for the Imperial Court.

Hari had felt something tickling at the back of his mind for several minutes now, and the quiet moments had given him a chance to finally pay attention to it. As Cleon accepted a stim, he said hesitantly, "Sire, I—?"

"Yes? Have one, ah?"

"Nossir, I, I had a thought about the Renegatum and the Kutonin woman."

"Oh, my, I'd rather not think about—"

"Suppose you erase her identity."

Cleon's hand stopped with a stim halfway to his nose. "Ah?"

"They are willing to die, once they've attracted attention. They probably think they will live on, be famous. Take that away from them. Permit no release of their true names. In all media and official documents, give them an insulting name."

Cleon frowned. "Another name . . . ?"

"Call this Kutonin woman Moron One. The next one, Moron Two. Make it illegal by Imperial decree to ever refer to her any other way. Then she as a person vanishes from history. No fame."

Cleon brightened. "Now, that's an idea. I'll try it. I not merely take their lives, I can take their *selves*."

Hari smiled wanly as Cleon spoke to an adjutant, giving instructions for a fresh Imperial Decree. Hari hoped it would work, but in any case, it had gotten him off the hook. Cleon did not seem to notice that the idea had nothing to do with psychohistory.

Pleased, he tried an appetizer. They were startlingly good.

Cleon beckoned to him. "Come, First Minister, I have some people for you to meet. They might prove useful, even to a mathist."

"I am honored." Dors had coached him on a few homilies to use when he could think of nothing to say and he trotted one out now. "Whatever would be useful in service to the people—"

"Ah, yes, the people," Cleon drawled. "I hear *so* much about them."

Hari realized that Cleon had spent a life listening to pat, predictable speeches. "Sorry, sire, I—"

"It reminds me of a poll result, assembled by my Trantorian specialists." Cleon took an appetizer from a woman half his size. "They asked, 'To what do you attribute the ignorance and apathy of the Trantorian masses?' and the most common reply was 'Don't know and don't care.'"

Only when Cleon laughed did Hari realize this was a joke.

3.

He woke with ideas buzzing in his head.

Hari had learned to lie still, facedown in the gossamer e-field net that cradled his neck and head in optimum alignment with his spine . . . to drift . . . and let the flitting notions collide, merge, fragment.

He had learned this trick while working on his thesis. Overnight his subconscious did a lot of his work for him, if he would merely listen to the results in the morning. But they were delicate motes, best caught in the fine fabric of half-sleep.

He sat up abruptly and made three quick notes on his end table. The squiggles would be sent to his primary computer, for later recall at the office.

"Rooowwwrr," Dors said, stretching. "The intellect is already up."

"Um," he said, staring into space.

"C'mon, before breakfast is body time."

"See if you disagree with this idea I just had. Suppose—"

"I am not inclined, Academician Professor Seldon, to argue."

Hari came out of his trance. Dors threw back the covers and he admired her long, slim legs. She had been sculpted for strength and speed, but such qualities converged in an agreeable concert of surfaces, springy to the touch, yielding yet resisting. He felt himself jerked out of his mood and into— "Body time, yes. You are inclined for other purposes."

"Trust a scholar to put the proper definition to a word."

In the warm, dizzying scuffle that followed there was some laughter, some sudden passion, and best of all, no time to think. He knew this was just what he needed, after the tensions of yesterday, and Dors knew it even better.

He emerged from the vaporium to the smell of kaff and breakfast, served out by the autos. The news flitted across the far wall and he managed to ignore most of it. Dors came out of her vaporium patting her hair and watched the wall raptly. "Looks like more stalling in the High Council," she said. "They're putting off the ritual search for more funding in favor of arguments over Sector sovereignty. If the Dahlites—"

"Not before I ingest some calories."

"But this is just the sort of thing you must keep track of!"

"Not until I have to."

"You know I don't want you to do anything dangerous, but for now, not paying attention is foolish."

"Maneuvering, who's up and who's down—spare me. Facts I can face."

"Fond of facts, aren't you?"

"Of course."

"They can be brutal."

"Sometimes they're all we have." He thought a moment, then grasped her hand. "Facts, and love."

"Love is a fact, too."

"Mine is. The undying popularity of entertainments devoted to romance suggests that to most people it is not a fact but a goal."

"An hypothesis, you mathematicians would say."

"Granted. 'Conjecture,' to be precise."

"Preserve us from precision."

He swept her suddenly into his arms, cupped her rump in his hands and, with some effort he took trouble to conceal, lifted her. "But this—this is a fact."

"My, my." She kissed him fiercely. "The man is not all mind."

He succumbed to the seductive, multisensic news as he munched. He had grown up on a farm and liked big breakfasts. Dors ate sparingly; her twin religions, she said, were exercise and Hari Seldon—the first to preserve her strength for the second. He thumbed his own half of the wall to the infinitesimal doings of markets, finding there a better index of how Trantor was doing than in the stentorian bluster of the High Council.

As a mathist, he liked following the details. But after five minutes of it he slapped the table in frustration.

"People have lost their good sense. No First Minister can protect them from their own innocence."

"My concern is protecting you from them."

Hari blanked his holo and watched hers, an ornate 3D of the factions in the High Council. Red tracers linked factions there with allies in the Low Council, a bewildering snake pit. "You don't think this First Minister thing is going to work, do you?"

"It could."

"They're absolutely right—I'm not qualified."

"Is Cleon?"

"Well, he has been reared to do the job."

"You're ducking the question."

"Exactly." Hari finished his steak and began on the egg-quhili soufflé. He had left the e-stim on all night to improve his muscle tone and that made him hungry. That, and the delightful fact that Dors viewed sex as an athletic opportunity.

"I suppose your present strategy is best," Dors said thoughtfully. "Remain a mathist, at a lofty remove from the fray."

"Right. Nobody assassinates a guy with no power."

"But they do 'erase' those who might get in the way of *their* taking power."

Hari hated thinking of such things so early. He dug into the soufflé. It was easy to forget, amid the tastes specially designed to fit his own well-tabulated likes, that the manufacturum built their meal from sewage. Eggs that had never known the belly of a bird. Meat appeared without skin or bones or gristle or fat. Carrots arrived without topknots. A food-manfac was delicately tuned to reproduce tastes, just short of the ability to actually make a live carrot. The minor issue of whether his soufflé tasted like a real one, made by a fine chef, faded to unimportance compared with the fact that it tasted good to him— the only audience that mattered.

He realized that Dors had been talking for some moments about High Council maneuverings and he had not registered a word. She had advice on how to handle the inevitable news people, on how to receive calls, on everything. Everyone did, these days. . . .

Hari finished, had some kaff, and felt ready to face the day as a mathist, not as a minister. "Reminds me of what my mother used to say. Know how you make God laugh?"

Dors looked blank, drawn out of her concentration. "How to . . . oh, this is humor?"

"You tell him your plans."

She laughed agreeably.

Outside their apartment they acquired the Specials again. Hari felt they were unnecessary; Dors was quite enough. But he could scarcely explain that to Imperial officials. There were other Specials on the floors above and below as well, a full-volume defense screen. Hari waved to friends he saw on the way across the Streeling campus, but the presence of the Specials held them at too great a distance to speak.

He had a lot of Mathist Department business to tend to, but he followed his instinct and put his calculations first. Briskly he retrieved his ideas from the bedside notepad and stared at them, doodling absently in air, stirring symbols like a pot of soup, for over an hour.

When he was a teenager the rigid drills of schooling had made him think that mathematics was just felicity with a particular kind of minutiae, *knowing things*, a sort of high-grade coin collecting. You learned relations and theorems and put them together.

Only slowly did he glimpse the soaring structures above each discipline. Great spans joined the vistas of topology to the infinitesimal intricacies of differentials, or the plodding styles of number theory to the shifting sands of group analysis. Only then did he see mathematics as a landscape, a territory of the mind to rove and scout.

To traverse those expanses he worked in mind time—long stretches of uninterrupted flow when he could concentrate utterly on problems, fixing them like flies in timeless amber, turning them this way and that to his inspecting light, until they yielded their secrets.

Phones, people, politics—all these transpired in real time, snipping his thought train, killing mind time. So he let Yugo and Dors and others fend off the world throughout the morning.

But today Yugo himself snipped his concentration. "Just a mo," he said, slipping through the crackling door field. "This paper look right?"

He and Yugo had developed a plausible cover for the psychohistory project. They regularly published research on the nonlinear analysis of "social nuggets and knots," a subfield with an honorable and dull history. Their analysis applied to subgroups and factions in Trantor, and occasionally on other worlds.

The research was in fact useful to psychohistory, serving as a subset of equations to what Yugo insisted on calling the full "Seldon Equations." Hari had given up being irked at this term, even though he wished to keep a personal distance from the theory.

Though scarcely a waking hour passed without his thinking about psychohistory, he did not want it to be a template for his own worldview. Nothing rooted in a particular personality could hope to describe the horde of saints and rascals revealed by human history. One had to take the longest view possible.

"See," Yugo said, making lines of print and symbols coalesce on Hari's holo. "I got all the analysis of the Dahlite crisis. Neat as you please, huh?"

"Um, what's the Dahlite crisis?"

Yugo's surprise was profound. "We're not bein' represented!"

"You live in Streeling."

"Once a Dahlan, you're always one. Just like you, from Helical."

"Helicon. I see, you don't have enough delegates in the Low Council?"

"Or the High!"

"The Codes allow—"

"They're out of date."

"Dahlites get a proportional share—"

"And our neighbors, the Ratannanahs and the Quippons, they're schemin' against us."

"How so?"

"There're Dahlans in plenty other Sectors. They don't get represented."

"You're spoken for by our Streeling—"

"Look, Hari, you're a Helical. Wouldn't understand. Plenty Sectors, they're just places to sleep. Dahl is a *people*."

"The Codes set forth rules for accommodating separate subcultures, ethnicities—"

"They're not workin'."

Hari saw from Yugo's jutting jaw that this was not a point for graceful debate. He did know something of the slowly gathering constitutional crisis. The Codes had maintained a balance of forces for millennia, but only by innovative adaptation. Little of that seemed available now. "We agree on that. So how does our research bear upon Dahl?"

"See, I took the socio-factor analysis and—"

Yugo had an intuitive grasp of nonlinear equations. It was always a pleasure to watch his big hands cut the air, slicing through points and pounding objections to pulp. And the calculations were good, if a bit simple.

The nuggets-and-knots work attracted little attention. It had made some in mathematics write him off as a promising young man who had never risen to his potential. This was perfectly all right with Hari. Some mathists guessed that his true core research went unpublished; these he treated kindly but gave no hint of confirmation.

"—so there's a pressure-nugget buildin' in Dahl, you bet," Yugo finished.

"Of course, glancing at the news holos shows that."

"Well, yeah—but I've proved it's justified."

Hari kept his face composed; Yugo was really worked up about this. "You've shown one of the factors. But there are others in the knot equations."

"Well, sure, but everybody knows—"

"What everybody knows doesn't need much proof. Unless, of course, it's wrong."

Yugo's face showed a rush of emotions: surprise, concern, anger, hurt, puzzlement. "You don't support Dahl, Hari?"

"Of course I do, Yugo." Actually, the truth was that Hari didn't care. But that was too bald a point to make, with Yugo seeming wounded. "Look, the paper is fine. Publish."

"The three basic knot equations, they're yours."

"No need to call them that."

"Sure, just like before. But your name goes on the paper."

Something tickled Hari's mind, but he saw the right answer now was to reassure Yugo. "If you like."

Yugo went on about details of publication, and Hari let his eyes drift over the equations. Terms for representation in models of Trantorian democracy, value tables for social pressures, the whole apparatus. A bit stuffy. But reassuring to those who suspected that he was hiding his major results—as he was, of course.

Hari sighed. Dahl was a festering political sore. Dahlites on Trantor mirrored the culture of the Dahl

Galactic Zone. Every powerful Zone had its own Sectors in Trantor, for influence-peddling and general pressuring.

But Dahl was minor on the scale that he wanted to explore—simple, even trivial. The knot equations which described High Council representation were truncated forms of the immensely worse riddle of Trantor.

All of Trantor—one teeming world, baffling in its sheer size, its intricate connections, meaningless coincidences, random juxtapositions, sensitive dependencies. His equations were still terribly inadequate for this shell which housed forty billion bustling souls.

How much worse was the Empire!

People, confronting bewildering complexity, tend to find their saturation level. They master the easy connections, local links, and rules of thumb. They push this until they meet a wall of complexity too thick and high and hard to grasp, to climb.

There they stall. Gossip, consult, fret—and finally, gamble.

The Empire of twenty-five million worlds was a problem greater even than understanding the whole rest of the universe—because at least the galaxies beyond did not have humans in them. The blind, blunt motions of stars and gas were child's play, compared to the convoluted trajectories of people.

Sometimes it wore him down. Trantor was bad enough, eight hundred Sectors with forty billion people. What of the Empire, with twenty-five million planets of average four billion souls apiece? One hundred quadrillion people!

Worlds interacted through the narrow necks of wormholes, which at least simplified some of the economic issues. But culture traveled at the speed of light through wormholes, information without mass, zooming across the Galaxy in destabilizing waves. A farmer on Oskatoon knew that a duchy had fallen on the other side of the Galactic disk a few hours after the blood on the palace floor started turning brown.

How to include *that*?

Clearly, the Empire extended beyond the Complexity Horizon of any person or computer. Only sets of equations which did not try to keep track of every detail could work.

Which meant that an individual was nothing on the scale of events worth studying. Even a million made about as much difference as a single raindrop falling in a lake.

Suddenly Hari was even more glad that he had kept psychohistory secret. How would people react if they knew that he thought they didn't matter?

"Hari? Hari?"

He had been musing again. Yugo was still in the office. "Oh, sorry, just mulling over—"

"The department meeting."

"What?

"You called it for today."

"Oh, no." He was halfway through a calculation. "Can't we delay . . . ?"

"The whole department? They're waiting."

Hari dutifully followed Yugo into the assembly room. The three traditional levels were already filled. Cleon's patronage had filled out an already high-ranked department until it was probably—how could one measure such things?—the best on Trantor. It had specialists in myriad disciplines, even areas whose very definitions Hari was a bit vague about.

Hari took his position at the hub of the highest level, at the exact center of the room. Mathists liked geometries which mirrored realities, so the full professors sat on a round, raised platform, in airchairs with ample arms.

Forming a larger annulus around them, a few steps lower, were the associate professors—those with tenure, but still at the middle rank in their careers. They had comfortable chairs, though without full computing and holo functions.

Below them, almost in a pit, were the untenured professors, on simple chairs of sturdy design. The oldest sat nearest the room's center. In their outer ranks were the instructors and assistants, on plain benches without any computer capabilities whatever. Yugo rested there, scowling, plainly feeling out of place.

Hari had always thought it was either enraging or hilarious, depending on his mood, that one of the most productive members of the department, Yugo, should have such low status. This was the true price of keeping psychohistory secret. The pain of this he tried to soothe by giving Yugo a good office and other perks. Yugo seemed to care little for status, since he had already ascended so far. And all without the Civil Service exams, too.

Today, Hari decided to make a little mischief. "Thank you, colleagues, for attending. We have many administrative matters to engage. Yugo?"

A rustle. Yugo's eyes widened, but he stood up quickly and climbed up to the speaker's platform.

He always had someone else chair meetings, even though as chairman he had called them, chosen the hour, fixed the agenda. He knew that some regarded him as a strong personality, simply by dint of knowing the research agenda so deeply.

That was a common error, mistaking knowledge for command. He had found that if he presided, there was little dissent from his own views. To get open discussion demanded that he sit back and listen and take notes, intervening only at key moments.

Years ago Yugo had wondered why he did this, and Hari waved away the problem. "I'm not a leader," he said. Yugo gave him a strange look, as if to say, *Who do you think you're kidding?*

Hari smiled to himself. Some of the full professors around him were muttering, casting glances. Yugo launched into the agenda, speaking quickly in a strong, clear voice.

Hari sat back and watched irritation wash over some of his esteemed colleagues. Noses wrinkled at Yugo's broad accent. One of them mouthed to another, *Dahlite!* and was answered, *Upstart!*

About time they got "a bit of the boot," as his father had once termed it. And for Yugo to get a taste of running the department.

After all, this First Minister business could get worse. He could need a replacement.

4.

◆

"We should leave soon," Hari said, scribbling on his notepad.

"Why? The reception doesn't start for ages." She smoothed out her dress with great care, eyes critical.

"I want to take a walk on the way."

"The reception is in Dahviti Sector."

"Humor me."

She pulled on the sheath dress with some effort. "I wish this weren't the style."

"Wear something else, then."

"This is your first appearance at an Imperial affair. You'll want to look your best."

"Translation: you look your best and stand next to me."

"You're just wearing that Streeling professorial garb."

"Appropriate to the occasion. I want to show that I'm still just a professor."

She worked on the dress some more and finally said, "You know, some husbands would enjoy watching their wives do this."

Hari looked up as she wriggled into the last of the clingy ensemble in amber and blue. "Surely you don't want to get me all excited and then have to endure the reception that way."

She smiled impishly. "That's exactly what I want."

He lounged back in his airchair and sighed theatrically. "Mathematics is a finer muse. Less demanding."

She tossed a shoe at him, missing by a precise centimeter.

Hari grinned. "Careful, or the Specials will rush to defend me."

Dors began her finishing touches and then glanced at him, puzzled. "You are even more distracted than usual."

"As always, I fit my research into the nooks and crannies of life."

"The usual problem? What's important in history?"

"I'd prefer to know what's not."

"I agree that the customary mega-history approach, economics and politics and the rest, isn't enough."

Hari looked up from his pad. "There are some historians who think that the little rules of a society have to be counted, to understand the big laws that make it work."

"I know that research." Dors twisted her mouth doubtfully. "Small rules and big laws. How about simplifying? Maybe the laws are just all the rules, added up?"

"Of course not."

"Example," she persisted.

He wanted to think, but she would not be put off. She poked him in the ribs. "Example!"

"All right. Here's a rule: Whenever you find something you like, buy a lifetime supply, because they're sure to stop making it."

"That's ridiculous. A joke."

"Not much of a joke, but it's true."

"Well, do you follow this rule?"

"Of course."

"How?"

"Remember the first time you looked in my closet?"

She blinked. He grinned, recalling. She had been subtly snooping, and slid aside the large but featherlight door. In a rectangular grid of shelves were clothes sorted by type, then color. Dors had gasped. "Six blue suits. At least a dozen padshoes, all black. And shirts!—off-white, olive, a few red. At least fifty! So many, all alike."

"And exactly what I like," he had said. "This also solves the problem of choosing what to wear in the morning. I just reach in at random."

"I thought you wore the same clothes day after day."

He had raised his eyebrows, aghast. "The same? You mean, dirty clothes?"

"Well, when they didn't change . . ."

"I change every day!" He chuckled, remembering, and said, "Then I usually put on the same outfit the next day, because I *like* it. And you will not find *any* of those available in the stores again."

"I'll say," she said, fingering the weave on his shirts. "These are at least four seasons out of fashion."

"See? The rule works."

"To me, a week is twenty-one clothing opportunities. To you, it's a chore."

"You're ignoring the rule."

"How long did you dress that way?"

"Since I noticed how much time I spent making decisions about what to wear. And that what I really liked to wear wasn't in the stores very often. I generalized a solution to both problems."

"You're amazing."

"I'm simply systematic."

"You're obsessional."

"You're judging, not diagnosing."

"You're a dear. Crazy, but a dear. Maybe they go together."

"Is that a rule, too?"

She kissed him. "Yes, professor."

The inevitable Special screen formed about them the instant they left their apartment. By now he and Dors had trained the Specials to at least allow them the privacy of a single wedge in the drop tube.

The grav drop was in fact no miracle of gravitational physics; it came from advanced electromagnetics. Each instant over a thousand electrostatic fields supported him through intricate charge imbalances. He could feel them playing in his hair, small twinges skating across his skin, as the field configurations handed him off to each other, each lowering his mass infinitesimally down the chute.

When they left the wedge, thirteen floors higher, Dors passed a charge-programmed comb through her hair. It crackled and snapped obediently into its style: "smart" hair.

They entered a broad passageway lined with shops. Hari liked being in a place where he could see farther than a hundred meters.

Movement was quick because there was no cross traffic for any conveyance. A slidewalk ran at the center, going their way, but they stayed near the shop windows and browsed as they ambled.

To move laterally, one simply went up or down a level by elevator or escalator, then stepped on a moving belt or entered a robopod. In the corridors to both sides the slideway ran opposite. With no left or right turns, traffic mishaps were rare. Most people walked wherever was practical, for the exercise and for the indefinable exhilaration of Trantor itself. People who came here wanted the constant stimulation of humanity, ideas, and cultures rubbing against each other in productive friction. Hari was not immune to it, though it lost some savor if overdone.

People in the squares and park-hexagons wore fashions from the twenty-five million worlds. He saw self-shaping "leathers" from animals who could not possibly have resembled the mythical horse. A man sauntered by with leggings slit to his hip, exposing blue-striped skin that bunched and slid in a perpetual show. An angular woman sported a bodice of open-mouthed faces, each swallowing ivory-nippled breasts; he had to look twice to believe they weren't real. Girls in outrageously cut pomp-vestments paraded noisily. A child—or was it a normal inhabitant of a strong-grav world?—played a photozither, strumming its laser beams.

The Specials fanned out and their captain came trotting over. "We can't cover you well here, Academician sir."

"These are ordinary people, not assassins. They had no way of predicting that I'd be here."

"Emperor says cover you, we cover you."

Dors rapped back smartly, "I'll handle the close-in threats. I'm able, I assure you."

The captain's mouth twisted sourly, but he gave himself a moment before saying, "I heard something about that. Still—"

"Have your men use their range detectors vertically.

A shaped charge on the layers below and above could catch us."

"Uh, yes'm." He trotted off.

They passed by the jigsaw walls of the Farhahal Quadrant. A wealthy ancient had become obsessed with the notion that as long as his estate was unfinished, he would not himself finish—that is, die. Whenever an addition neared completion, he ordered up more. Eventually the tangle of rooms, runways, vaults, bridges and gardens became an incoherent motley stuck into every cranny of the original, rather simple design. When Farhahal eventually did "finish," a tower half built, bickering by his heirs and lawyerly plundering of the estate for their fees brought the quadrant low. Now it was a fetid warren, visited only by the predatory and the unwary.

The Specials pulled in tight and the captain urged them to get into a robo. Hari grudgingly agreed. Dors had the concentrated look that meant she was worried. They sped in silence through shadowy tunnels. There were two stops and in the brilliantly lit stations Hari saw rats scurrying for shelter as the pod eased to a halt. He silently pointed them out to Dors.

"Brrrr," she said. "One would think that at the very center of the Empire we could eliminate pests."

"Not these days," Hari said, though he suspected the rats had thrived even at the height of Empire. Rodents cared little for grandeur.

"I suppose they've been our eternal companions," Dors said somberly. "No world is free of them."

"In these tunnels, the long-distance pods fly so fast that occasionally rats get sucked into the air-breathing engines."

Dors said uneasily, "That could damage the engines, even crash the pods."

"No holiday for the rat, either."

They passed through a Sector whose citizens

abhorred sunlight, even the wan splashes which came down through the layers by radiance tubes. Historically, Dors told him, this had arisen from fears of its ultraviolet component, but the phobia seemed to go deeper than a mere health issue.

Their pod slowed and passed along a high ramp above open, swarming vaults. No natural light shafts brought illumination, only artificial phosphor glows. The Sector was officially named Kalanstromonia, but its citizens were known worldwide as Spooks. They seldom traveled, and their bleached faces stood out in crowds. Gazing down at them, they looked to Hari like swarms of grubs feeding on shadowy decay.

The Imperial Zonal Reception was inside a dome in the Julieen Sector. He and Dors entered with the Specials, who then gave way to five men and women wearing utterly inconspicuous business dress. These nodded to Hari and then appeared to forget him, moving down a broad rampway and chatting with each other.

A woman at the grand doorway made too much of his entrance. Music descended around him in a sound cloud, an arrangement of the Streeling Anthem blended subtly with the Helicon Symphony. This attracted attention from the crowds below—exactly what he did not want. A protocol team smoothly took the handoff from the door attendants, escorting him and Dors to a balcony. He was happy for the chance to look at the view.

From the peak of the dome the vistas were startling. Spirals descended to plateaus so distant he could barely make out a forest and paths. The ramparts and gardens there had drawn millennia of spectators, including, a guide told him, 999,987 suicides, all carefully tabulated through many centuries.

Now that the number approached a million, the guide went on with relish, attempts occurred nearly every hour. A man had been stopped just short of leaping that very day, wearing a gaudy holosuit programmed to flash I MADE THE MILLION after he struck.

"They seem so *eager*," the guide concluded with what seemed to Hari a kind of pride.

"Well," Hari remarked, trying to get rid of the man, "suicide is the most sincere form of self-criticism."

The guide nodded wisely, unperturbed, and added, "Also, it does give them *some*thing to contribute to. That must be a consolation."

The protocol team had, all planned out for him, an orbit through the vast reception. Meet X, greet Y, bow to Z.

"Say nothing about the Judena Zone crisis," an aide insisted. This was easy, since he had never heard of it.

The appetite-enhancers were excellent, the food that followed even better (or seemed so, which was the point of the enhancers), and he took a stim offered by a gorgeous woman.

"You could get through this entire evening just nodding and smiling and agreeing with people," Dors said after the first half hour.

"It's tempting to do just that," Hari whispered as they followed the protocol lieutenant to the next bunch of Zonal figures. The air in the vast, foggy dome was freighted with negotiations advanced and bargains struck.

The Emperor arrived with full pomp. He would pay the traditional hour's tribute, then by ancient custom leave before anyone else was permitted to. Hari wondered if the Emperor ever wanted to linger in the middle of an interesting conversation. Cleon was well schooled in emperorhood, though, so the issue probably never came up. Cleon greeted Hari effusively, kissed Dors' hand, and then seemed to lose interest in them within two minutes, moving on with his entourage to another circle of expectant faces.

Hari's next group proved different. Not the usual mix of diplomats, aristos, and anxious brownclad assistants, his lieutenant told him, but high figures. "People with *punch*," the man whispered.

A large, muscular man was holding forth at the center of a circle, a dozen faces raptly following his every word. The protocol lieutenant tried to whisk them past, but Hari stopped her. "That's . . ."

"Betan Lamurk, sir."

"Knows how to hold a crowd."

"Indeed, sir. Would you like a formal introduction?"

"No, just let me listen."

It was always a good idea to size up an opponent before he knew he was being watched. Hari's father had taught him that trick, just before his first matheletic competition. Such techniques had not managed to save his father, but they worked in the milder groves of academe.

Black hair invaded his broad brow like a pincer attack, two pointed wedges reaching down to nearly the end of his eyebrows. His hooded eyes were widely spaced and blazed intently from a rigging of mirth wrinkles. A slender nose seemed to point to his proudest feature, a mouth assembled from varying parts. The lower lip curled in full, impudent humor. The upper, thin and muscular, curled downward in a curve that verged on a sneer. A viewer would know the upper lip could overrule the lower at any moment, shifting mood abruptly—a disquieting effect which could not have been bettered if he had designed it himself.

Hari realized quickly that, of course, Lamurk had.

Lamurk was discussing some detail of interZonal trade in the Orion spiral arm, a hot issue before the High Council at the moment. Hari cared nothing about trade, except as a variable in stochastic equations, so he simply watched the man's manner.

To underline a point Lamurk would raise his hands over his head, fingers open, voice rising. Then, his point made, his voice evened out and he lowered them to chest height, held precisely side by side. As his well-modulated voice became deeper and more reflective, he moved the hands apart. Then—voice rising again—his hands soared to head level and windmilled one around the other, the subject now complex, the listener thereby commanded to pay close attention.

He kept close eye contact with the whole audience, a piercing gaze sweeping the circle. A last point, a quick touch of humor, grin flashing, sure of himself—a pause for the next question.

He finished his point with, "—and for some of us, 'Pax Imperium' looks more like 'Tax Imperium,' eh?" Then he saw Hari. A quick furrowing of his brow, then, "Academician Seldon! Welcome! I'd been wondering when I was going to get to meet you."

"Don't let me interrupt your, ah, lecture."

This provoked some titters and Hari saw that to accuse a member of the High Council of pontificating was a mild social jab. "I found it fascinating."

"Pretty humdrum stuff, I'm afraid, compared to you mathists," Lamurk said cordially.

"I am afraid my mathematics is even more dry than Zonal trade."

More titters, though this time Hari could not quite see why.

"I just try to separate out the factions," Lamurk said genially. "People treat money like it is a religion."

This gained him some agreeing laughter. Hari said, "Fortunately, there are no sects in geometry."

"We're just trying to get the best deal for the whole Empire, Academician."

"The best is the enemy of the good, I'd imagine."

"I suppose then, you'll be applying mathematical logic to our problems on the Council?" Lamurk's voice remained friendly, but his eyes took on a veiled character. "Assuming you gain a ministership?"

"Alas, so far as the laws of mathematics are sharp and certain, they do not refer to reality. So far as they refer to reality, they are not certain."

Lamurk glanced at the crowd, which had grown considerably. Dors grasped Hari's hand and he realized from her squeeze that this had somehow turned into something important. He could not see why, but there was no time to size up the situation.

Lamurk said, "Then this psychohistory thing I hear about, it's not useful?"

"Not to you, sir," Hari said.

Lamurk's eyes narrowed, but his affable grin remained. "Too tough for us?"

"Not ready for use, I'm afraid. I don't have the logic of it yet."

Lamurk chuckled, beamed at the still growing crowd, and said jovially, "A logical thinker!—what a refreshing contrast with the real world."

General laughter. Hari tried to think of something to say. He saw one of his bodyguards block a man nearby, inspect something in the man's suit, then let him go.

"Y'see, Academician, on the High Council we can't be spending our time on theory." Lamurk paused for effect, as though making a campaign speech. "We've got to be *just* . . . and sometimes, folks, we've got to be *hard*."

Hari raised an eyebrow. "My father used to say, 'It's a hard man who's only just, and a sad man who's only wise.'"

A few *ooohs* in the crowd told him he had scored a hit. Lamurk's eyes confirmed the cut.

"Well, we do try on the Council, we do. No doubt we can use some help from the learned quarters of the Empire. I'll have to read one of your books, Academician." He shot a look with raised eyebrows at the crowd. "Assuming I can."

Hari shrugged. "I will send you my monograph on transfinite geometric calculus."

"Impressive title," Lamurk said, eyes playing to the audience.

"It's the same with books as with men—a very small number play great parts; the rest are lost in the multitude."

"And which would you rather be?" Lamurk shot back.

"Among the multitudes. At least I wouldn't have to attend so many receptions."

This got a big laugh, surprising Hari. Lamurk said, "Well, I'm sure the Emperor won't tire you out with too much socializing. But you'll get invited everywhere. You've got a sharp tongue on you, Academician."

"My father had another saying, too. 'Wit is like a razor. Razors are more likely to cut those who use them when they've lost their edge.'"

His father had also told him that in a public trade of barbs, the one who lost temper first lost the exchange. He had not recalled that until this instant. Hari remembered too late that Lamurk was known for his humor in High Council meetings. Probably scripted for him; certainly he displayed none here.

A quick tightening of the cheeks spread into a bloodless white line of lip. Lamurk's features twisted into an expression of distaste—not a long way to go, for most of them—and he gave an ugly, wet laugh.

The crowd stood absolutely silent. Something had happened.

"Ah, there are other people who would like to meet

the Academician," Hari's lieutenant said, sliding neatly into the growing, awkward silence.

Hari shook hands, murmured meaningless pleasantries, and let himself be whisked away.

5.

◆

He had another stim to calm himself. Somehow he was more jittery afterward than during the social collision. Lamurk had given Hari a cold, angry stare as they parted.

"I'll keep track of him," Dors said. "You just enjoy your fame."

To Hari this was a flat impossibility, but he tried. Seldom did one see such a variety of people, and he calmed himself by lapsing into a habitual role: polite observer. It was not as though the usual social chitchat demanded much concentration. A warm smile would do most of the work for him here.

The party was a microcosm of Trantorian society. In spare moments, Hari watched the social orders interact.

Cleon's grandfather had reinstated many Ruellian traditions, and one of those customs required that members of all five classes be present at any grand Imperial function. Cleon seemed especially keen on this practice, as if it would raise his popularity among the masses. Hari kept his own doubts private.

First and obvious came the gentry—the inherited aristocracy. Cleon himself stood at the apex of a pyramid of rank that descended from the Imperium to mighty Quadrant Dukes and Spiral Arm Princes, past

Life Peers, all the way down to the local barons Hari used to know back on Helicon.

Working in the fields, he had seen them pompously scudding overhead. Each governed a domain no larger than they could cross by flitter in a day. To a member of the gentry, life was busy with the Great Game—a ceaseless campaign to advance the fortunes of one's noble house, arranging greater status for your family line through political alliances, or marriages for your many children.

Hari snorted in derision, masking it by taking another stim. He had studied anthropological reports from a thousand Fallen Worlds—those that had devolved in isolation, reverting to cruder ways of life. He knew this pyramid-shaped order to be among the most natural and enduring human social patterns. Even when a planet was reduced to simple agriculture and hand-forged metals, the same triangular format endured. People *liked* rank and order.

The endless competition of gentry families had been the first and easiest psychohistorological system Hari ever modeled. He had first combined basic game theory and kin selection. Then, in a moment of inspiration, he inserted them into the equations that described sand grains skidding down the slopes of a dune. That correctly described sudden transitions: social slippages.

So it was with the rise and fall of noble family lines. Long, smooth eras—then abrupt shifts.

He watched the crowd, picking out those in the second aristocracy, supposedly equal to the first: the meritocracy.

As department chairman at a major Imperial university, Hari was himself a lord in that hierarchy— a pyramid of achievement rather than of birth. Meritocrats had entirely different obsessions than the gentry's constant dynastic bickerings. In fact, few in Hari's class bothered to breed at all, so busy were they in their chosen fields. Gentry jostled for the top ranks of Imperial government, while second tier meritocrats saw themselves wielding the *real* power.

If only Cleon had such a role in mind for me, Hari thought. A vice minister position, or an advisory post. He could have managed that for a time, or else bungled it and got himself forced out of office. Either way, he would be safe back at Streeling within a year or two. They don't execute vice ministers . . . not for incompetence, at least.

Nor did a vice minister feel the worst burden of rule—bearing responsibility for the lives of a quadrillion human beings.

Dors saw him drifting along in his own thoughts. Under her gentle urging, he sampled tasty savories and made small talk.

The gentry could be distinguished by their ostentatiously fashionable clothing, while the economists, generals and other meritocrats tended to wear the formal garb of their professions.

So he was making a political statement, after all, Hari realized. In wearing professor's robes, he emphasized that there might be a non-gentry First Minister for the first time in forty years.

Not that he minded making that statement. Hari just wished he had done it on purpose.

Despite the official Ruellian ethos, the remaining three social classes seemed nearly invisible at the party.

The factotums wore somber costumes of brown or gray, with expressions to match. They seldom spoke on their own. Usually they hovered at the elbow of some aristo, supplying facts and even figures that the more gaily-dressed guests used in their arguments. Aristos generally were innumerate, unable to do simple addition. *That* was for machines.

Hari found that he actually had to concentrate in order to pick the fourth class, the Greys, out of the crowd. He watched them move, like finches among peacocks.

Yet their kind made up more than a sixth of Trantor's population. Drawn from every planet in the Empire by the all-seeing Civil Service tests, they came to the Capital World, served their time like bachelor monks, and left again for outworld postings. Flowing through Trantor like water in the gloomy cisterns, the Greys were seldom thought of, as honest and commonplace and dull as the metal walls.

That might have been his life, he realized. It was the way out of the fields for many of the brighter children he had known at Helicon. Except that Hari had been plucked right over the bureaucracy, sent straight to academe by the time he could solve a mere eighth-order tensor defoliation, at age ten.

Ruellianism preached that "citizen" was the highest social class of all. In theory, even the Emperor shared sovereignty with common men and women.

But at a party like this, the most numerous Galactic group was represented mostly by the servants carrying food and drink around the hall, even more invisible than the dour bureaucrats. The majority of Trantor's population, the laborers and mechanics and shopkeepers—the denizens of the 800 Sectors—had no station at a gathering like this. They lay outside the Ruellian ranking.

As for the Artes, that final social order was not meant to be invisible. Musicians and jugglers strolled among the guests, the smallest, most flamboyant class.

Even more dashing was an air-sculptor Hari spotted across the vast chamber, when Dors pointed him out. Hari had heard of the new art form. The "statues" were of colored smoke that the artist exhaled in rapid puffs. Shapes of eerie, ghost-like complexity floated among the bemused guests. Some figures clearly made fun of the courtly gentry, as puffy caricatures of their ostentatious clothes and poses.

To Hari's eye, the smoke figures seemed entrancing . . . until they started drifting apart into tatters, without substance or predictability.

"It's all the mode," he heard one onlooker remark. "I hear the artist comes straight from Sark!"

"The Renaissance world?" another asked, wide-eyed. "Isn't that a little daring? Who invited him?"

"The Emperor himself, it's said."

Hari frowned. Sark, where those personality simulations came from. "Renaissance world," he muttered irritably, knowing now what he disliked about the smoke shapes: their ephemeral nature. Their intended destiny, to dissolve into chaos.

As he watched, the air-sculptor blew a satirical tableau. The first figure formed of crimson smoke, and he did not recognize it until Dors elbowed him and laughed. "It's you!"

He clamped his gaping mouth shut, unsure how to handle the social nuances. A second cloud of coiling blue streamers formed a clear picture of Lamurk, eyebrows knotted in fury. The foggy figures hovered in confrontation, Hari smiling, Lamurk scowling.

And Lamurk looked the fool, with bulging eyes and pouting lips.

"Time for a graceful exit," Hari's lieutenant whispered. Hari was only too glad to agree.

When they got home, he was sure that there had been a bit extra in the stim he was handed, something that freed his tongue. Certainly it was not the slow-spoken, reflective Seldon who had traded jabs with Lamurk. He would have to watch that.

Dors simply shook her head. "It was you. Just a portion of you that doesn't get out to play very much."

6.

◆

"Parties are supposed to cheer people up," Yugo said, sliding a cup of kaff across Hari's smooth mahogany desktop.

"Not this one," Hari said.

"All that luxury, powerful people, beautiful women, witty hangers-on—I think I could have stayed awake."

"That's what depresses me, thinking back over it. All that power! And nobody there seems to care about our decline."

"Isn't there some old saying about—"

"Fiddling while Roma burns. Dors knew it, of course. She says it's from pre-Empire, about a Zone with pretensions of grandeur. 'All worms lead to Roma' is another one."

"Never heard of this Roma."

"Me either, but pomposity springs forth eternal. It looks comic in retrospect."

Yugo moved restlessly around Hari's office. "So they don't care?"

"To them it's just backdrop for their power games."

Already the Empire had worlds, Zones, and even whole arcs of spiral arms descended into squalor. Still worse, in a way, was a steady slide into garish amusements, even vulgarity. The media swarmed with the stuff. The new "renaissance" styles from worlds like Sark were popular.

To Hari the best of the Empire was its strands of restraint, of subtlety and discretion in manners, finesse and charm, intelligence, talent, and even glamour. Helicon had been crude and rural, but it knew the difference between silk and swine.

"What do the policy types say?" Yugo sat halfway on Hari's desk, avoiding the control functions implanted beneath a woody veneer. He had come in with the kaff as a pretext, fishing for gossip about the exalted. Hari smiled to himself; people *relished* some aspects of hierarchy, however much they griped about it.

"They're hoping some of the 'moral rebirth' movements—like revised Ruellianism, say—will take hold. Put spine into the Zones, one of them said."

"Ummm. Think it'll work?"

"Not for long."

Ideology was an uncertain cement. Even religious fervor could not glue an empire together for long. Either force could drive formation of an empire, but they could not hold against greater, steady tides—principally, economics.

"How about the war in the Orion Zone?"

"Nobody mentioned it."

"Think we've got war figured right in the equations?" Yugo had a knack for suddenly putting his finger on what was bothering Hari.

"No. War was an overesteemed element in history."

Certainly war often gained center stage; no one continued to read a beautiful poem when a fist fight broke out nearby. But fist fights did not last, either. Further, they joggled the elbows of those trying to make a living. To engineers and traders alike, war did not pay. So why did wars break out now, with all the economic weight of the Empire against them?

"Wars are simple. But we're missing something basic—I can *feel* it."

"We've based the matrices on all that historical

data Dors dug out," Yugo said a bit defensively. "That's solid."

"I don't doubt it. Still . . ."

"Look, we've got over twelve thousand years of hard facts. I built the model on that."

"I have a feeling what we're missing isn't subtle."

Most collapses were not from abstruse causes. In the early days of Empire consolidation, local minor sovereignties flourished, then died. There were recurrent themes in their histories.

Again and again, star-spanning realms collapsed under the weight of excessive taxation. Sometimes the taxes supported mercenary armies which defended against neighbors, or which simply kept domestic order against centrifugal forces. Whatever the ostensible cause of taxes, soon enough the great cities became depopulated, as people fled the tax collectors, seeking "rural peace."

But why did they do that spontaneously?

"People." Hari sat up suddenly. "That's what we're missing."

"Huh? You proved yourself—remember? the Reductionist Theorem?—that individuals don't matter."

"They don't. But people do. Our coupled equations describe them in the mass, but we don't know the critical drivers."

"That's all hidden, down in the data."

"Maybe not. What if we were big spiders, instead of primates? Would psychohistory look the same?"

Yugo frowned. "Well . . . if the data were the same . . ."

"Data on trade, wars, population statistics? It wouldn't matter whether we were counting spiders instead of people?"

Yugo shook his head, his face clouding, unwilling to concede a point that might topple years of work. "It's gotta be there."

"Your coming in here to get details of what the rich and famous do at their revels—where's that in the equations?"

Yugo's mouth twisted, irked now. "That stuff, it doesn't *matter*."

"Who says?"

"Well, history—"

"Is written by the winners, true enough. But how do the great generals get men and women to march through freezing mud? When *won't* they march?"

"Nobody knows."

"We need to know. Or rather, the equations do."

"How?"

"I don't know."

"Go to the historians?"

Hari laughed. He shared Dors' contempt for most of her profession. The current fashion in the study of the past was a matter of taste, not data.

He had once thought that history was simply a matter of grubbing in musty cyberfiles. Then, if Dors would show him how to track down data—whether encoded in ancient ferrite cylinders or polymer blocks or strandware—*then* he would have a firm basis for mathematics. Didn't Dors and other historians simply add one more brick of knowledge to an ever-growing monument?

The current style, though, was to marshal the past into a preferred flavor. Factions fought over the antiquity, over "their" history *vs.* "ours." Fringes flourished. The "spiral-centric" held that historical forces spread along spiral arms, whereas the "Hub-focused" maintained that the Galactic Center was the true mediating agency for causes, trends, movements, evolution. Technocrats contended with Naturals, who felt that innate human qualities drove change.

Among myriad facts and footnotes, specialists saw present politics mirrored in the past. As the present fractured and transfigured, there seemed no point of reference outside history itself—an unreliable platform indeed, especially when one realized how many mysterious gaps there were in the records. All this seemed to Hari to be more fashion than foundation. There was no uncontested past.

What contained the centrifugal forces of relativism—let me have my viewpoint and you can have yours—was an arena of broad agreement. Most people generally held that the Empire was good, overall. That the long periods of stasis had been the best times, for change always cost someone. That above the competing throng, through the factions shouting what were essentially family stories at each other, there was worth in comprehending where humanity had passed, what it had done.

But there agreement stopped. Few seemed concerned with where humanity, or even the Empire, was going. He had come to suspect that the subject was ignored, in favor of your-history-against-mine, because most historians unconsciously dreaded the future. They sensed the decline in their souls and knew that over the horizon lay not yet another shift-then-stasis but a collapse.

"So what do we do?" Hari realized that Yugo had said this twice now. He had drifted off into reverie.

"I . . . don't know."

"Add another term for basic instincts?"

Hari shook his head. "People don't run on instinct. But they do behave like people—like primates, I suppose."

"So . . . we should look into that?"

Hari threw up his hands. "I confess. I *feel* that this line of logic is leading somewhere—but I can't see the end of it."

Yugo nodded, grinned. "It'll come out when it's ripe."

"Thanks. I'm not the best of collaborators, I know. Too moody."

"Hey, never mind. Gotta think out loud sometimes, is all."

"Sometimes I'm not sure I'm thinking at all."

"Lemme show you the latest, huh?" Yugo liked to parade his inventions, and Hari sat back as Yugo accessed the office holo and patterns appeared in midair. Equations hung in space, 3D-stacked and each term color-coded.

So many! They reminded Hari of birds, flocking in great banks.

Psychohistory was basically a vast set of interlocked equations, following the variables of history. It was impossible to change one and not vary any other. Alter population and trade changed, along with modes of entertainment, sexual mores, and a hundred other factors.

Some were undoubtedly unimportant, but which? History was a bottomless quarry of factoids, meaningless without some way of winnowing the hail of particulars. That was the essential first task of any theory of history—to find the deep variables.

"Post-diction rates—presto!" Yugo said, his hand computer suspending in air 3D graphs, elegantly arrayed. "Economic indices, variable-families, the works."

"What eras?" Hari asked.

"Third millennia to seventh, G.E."

The multidimensional surfaces representing economic variables were like twisted bottles filled with—as Yugo time-stepped them—sloshing fluids. The liquids of yellow and amber and virulent red flowed around and through each other in a supple, slow dance. Hari was perpetually amazed at how beauty arose in the most unlikely ways from mathematics. Yugo had plotted abstruse econometric quantities, yet in the gravid sway of centuries they made delicate arabesques.

"Surprisingly good agreement," Hari allowed. The yellow surfaces of historical data merged cleanly with the other color skins, fluids finding curved levels. "And covering four millennia! No infinities?"

"That new renormalization scheme blotted them out."

"Excellent! The middle Galactic Era data is the most solid, too, correct?"

"Yeah. The politicians got into the act after the seventh millennium. Dors is helpin' me filter out the garbage."

Hari admired the graceful blending of colors, ancient wine in transfinite bottles.

The psychohistorical rates linked together strongly. History was not at all like a sturdy steel edifice rigidly spanning time; it rather more resembled a rope bridge, groaning and flexing with every footfall. This "strong coupling dynamic" led to resonances in the equations, wild fluctuations, even infinities. Yet nothing really went infinite in reality, so the equations had to be fixed. Hari and Yugo had spent many years eliminating ugly infinites. Maybe their goal was in sight.

"How do the results look if you simply run the equations forward, past the seventh millennium?" Hari asked.

"Oscillations build up," Yugo admitted.

Feedback loops were scarcely new. Hari knew the general theorem, ancient beyond measure: If all variables in a system are tightly coupled, and you can change one of them precisely and broadly, then you can indirectly control all of them. The system could be guided to an exact outcome through its myriad internal feedback loops. Spontaneously, the system ordered itself—and obeyed.

History, of course, obeyed no one. But for eras such as the fourth to seventh millennium, somehow the equations got matters right. Psychohistory *could* "post-dict" history.

In truly complex systems, how adjustments occur lay beyond the human complexity horizon, beyond knowing—and most important, not worth knowing.

But if the system went awry, somebody had to get down in the guts of it and find the trouble. "Any ideas? Clues?"

Yugo shrugged. "Look at this."

The fluids lapped at the walls of the bottles. More warped volumes appeared, filled with brightly colored data-liquids. Hari watched as tides swept through the burnt-orange variable-space, driving answering waves in the purple layers nearby. Soon the entire holo showed furiously churning turbulence.

"So the equations fail," Hari said.

"Yeah, big time, too. The grand cycles last about a hundred and twenty-five years. But smoothing out events shorter than eighty years gives a steady pattern. See—"

Hari watched turbulence build like a hurricane churning a multicolored ocean.

Yugo said, "That takes away scatter due to 'generational styles,' Dors calls it. I can take the Zones that consciously increased human lifespan. I time-step the equations forward, great—but then I run out of data. How come? I mine the history some, and it turns out those societies didn't last long."

Hari shook his head. "You're sure? I'd imagine increasing the average age would bring a little wisdom into the picture."

"Not so! I looked deeper and found that when the lifespan reached the social cycle time, usually about a hundred and ten Standard Years, instability rose. Whole planets had wars, depressions, general social illnesses."

Hari frowned. "That effect—is it known?"

"Don't think so."

"This is why humans reached a barrier in improving their longevity? Society breaks down, ending the progress?"

"Yeah."

Yugo wore a small, tight smile, by which Hari knew that he was rather proud of this result. "Growing irregularities, building to—chaos."

This was the deep problem they had not mastered. "Damn!" Hari had a gut dislike of unpredictability.

Yugo gave Hari a crooked smile. "On that one, boss, I got no news."

"Don't worry," Hari said cheerfully, though he didn't feel it. "You've made good progress. Remember the adage—the Imperium wasn't built in a day."

"Yeah, but it seems to be fallin' apart plenty fast."

They seldom mentioned the deep-seated motivation for psychohistory: the pervasive anxiety that the Empire was declining, for reasons no one knew. There were theories aplenty, but none had predictive power. Hari hoped to supply that. Progress was infuriatingly slow.

Yugo was looking morose. Hari got up, came around the big desk, and gave Yugo a gentle slap on the back. "Cheer up! Publish this result."

"Can I? We've got to keep psychohistory quiet."

"Just group the data, then publish in a journal devoted to analytical history. Talk to Dors about selecting the journal."

Yugo brightened. "I'll write it up, show you—"

"No, leave me out of it. It's your work."

"Hey, you showed me how to set up the analysis, where—"

"It's yours. Publish."

"Well . . ."

Hari did not mention the fact that, now, anything

published under his name would attract attention. A few might guess at the immensely larger theory lurking behind the simple lifespan-resonance effect. Best to keep a low profile.

When Yugo had gone back to work, Hari sat for a while and watched the squalls work through the data-fluids, still time-stepping in the air above his desk. Then he glanced at a favorite quotation of his, pointed out to him by Dors, given to him on a small, elegant ceramo-plaque:

> Minimum force, applied at a cusp moment at the historical fulcrum, paves the path to a distant vision. Pursue only those immediate goals which serve the longest perspectives.
>
> —Emperor Kamble's 9th Oracle, Verse 17

"But suppose you can't afford long perspectives?" he muttered, then went back to work.

7.

The next day he got an education in the realities of Imperial politics.

"You didn't know the 3D scope was on you?" Yugo asked.

Hari watched the conversation with Lamurk replay on his office holo. He had fled to the University when the Imperial Specials started having trouble holding the media mob away from his apartment. They had called in reinforcements when they caught a team drilling an acoustic tap into the apartment from three layers above. Hari and Dors had gotten out with an escort through a maintenance grav drop.

"No, I didn't. There was a lot going on." He remembered his bodyguards accosting someone, checking and letting it pass. The 3D camera and acoustic tracker were so small that a media deputy could walk around with them under formal wear. Assassins used the same artful concealment. Bodyguards knew how to distinguish between the two.

Yugo said with Dahlite savvy, "Gotta watch 'em, you gonna play in those leagues."

"I appreciate the concern," Hari said dryly.

Dors tapped a finger to her lips. "I think you came over rather well."

"I didn't want to seem as though I were deliberately cutting up a majority leader from the High Council," Hari said heatedly.

"But that's what you *were* doin'," Yugo said.

"I suppose, but at the time it seemed like polite . . . banter," he finished lamely. Edited for 3D, it was a quick verbal Ping-Pong with razor blades instead of balls.

"But you topped him at every exchange," Dors observed.

"I don't even dislike him! He has done good things for the Empire." He paused, thinking. "But it was . . . fun."

"Maybe you do have a talent for this," she said.

"I'd rather not."

"I don't think you have much choice," Yugo said. "You're gettin' famous."

"Fame is the accumulation of misunderstandings around a well-known name," Dors said.

Hari smiled. "Well put."

"It's from Eldonian the Elder, the longest-lived emperor. The only one of his clan to die of old age."

"Makes the point," Yugo said. "You gotta expect some stories, gossip, mistakes."

Hari shook his head angrily. "No! Look, we can't let this extraneous matter distract us. Yugo, what about those bootleg personality constellations you 'acquired'?"

"I've got 'em."

"Machine translated? They will run?"

"Yeah, but they take an awful lot of memory and running volume. I've tuned them some, but they need a bigger parallel-processing network than I can give them."

Dors frowned. "I don't like this. These aren't just constellations, they're *sims*."

Hari nodded. "We're doing research here, not trying to manufacture a superrace."

Dors stood and paced energetically. "The most ancient of taboos is against sims. Even personality constellations obey rigid laws!"

"Of course, ancient history. But—"

"*Pre*history." Her nostrils flared. "The prohibitions go back so far, there are no records of how they started—undoubtedly, from some disastrous experiments well before the Shadow Age."

"What's that?" Yugo asked.

"The long time—we have no clear idea of how long it lasted, though certainly several millennia—before the Empire became coherent."

"Back on Earth, you mean?" Yugo looked skeptical.

"Earth is more legend than fact. But yes, the taboo could go back that far."

"These are hopelessly constricted sims," Yugo said. "They don't know anything about our time. One is a religious fanatic for some faith I never heard of. The other's a smartass writer. No danger to anybody, except maybe themselves."

Dors regarded Yugo suspiciously. "If they're so narrow, why are they useful?"

"Because they can calibrate psychohistorical

indices. We have modeling equations that depend on basic human perceptions. If we have a pre-ancient mind, even simmed, we can calibrate the missing constants in the rate equations."

Dors snorted doubtfully. "I don't follow the mathematics, but I know sims are dangerous."

"Look, nobody savvy believes that stuff any more," Yugo said. "Mathists have been running pseudo-sims for ages. Tiktoks—"

"Those are incomplete personalities, correct?" Dors asked severely.

"Well, yeah, but—"

"We could get into very big trouble if these sims are better, more versatile."

Yugo waved away her point with his large hands, smiling lazily. "Don't worry. I got them all under control. Anyway, I've already got a way to solve our problem of getting enough running volume, machine time—*and* I've got a cover for us."

Hari arched his eyebrows. "What's this?"

"I've got a customer for the sims. Somebody who'll run them, cover all expenses, and pay for the privilege. Wants to use them for commercial purposes."

"Who?" Hari and Dors asked together.

"Artifice Associates," Yugo said triumphantly.

Hari looked blank. Dors paused as though searching for a distant memory, and then said, "A firm engaged in computer systems architecture."

"Right, one of the best. They've got a market for old sims as entertainment."

Hari said, "Never heard of them."

Yugo shook his head in amazement. "You don't keep up, Hari."

"I don't try to keep up. I try to stay ahead."

Dors said, "I don't like using any outside agency. And what's this about paying?"

Yugo beamed. "They're paying for license rights. I negotiated it all."

"Do we have any control over how they use the sims?" Dors leaned forward alertly.

"We don't need any," Yugo said defensively. "They'll probably use them in advertisements or something. How much use can you get out of a sim nobody will probably understand?"

"I don't like it. Aside from the commercial aspects, it's risky to even revive an ancient sim. Public outrage—"

"Hey, that's the past. People don't feel that way about tiktoks, and they're getting pretty smart."

Tiktoks were machines of low mental capacity, held rigorously beneath an intelligence ceiling by the Encoding Laws of antiquity. Hari had always suspected that the true, ancient robots had made those laws, so that the realm of machine intelligence did not spawn ever more specialized and unpredictable types.

The true robots, such as R. Daneel Olivaw, remained aloof, cool, and long-visioned. But in the gathering anxieties across the entire Empire, traditional cybernetic protocols were breaking down. Like everything else.

Dors stood. "I'm opposed. We must stop this at once."

Yugo rose too, startled. "You helped me find the sims. Now you—"

"I did not intend this." Her face tightened.

Hari wondered at her intensity. Something else was at stake here, but what? He said mildly, "I see no reason to not make a bit of profit from side avenues of our research. And we do need increased computing capacity."

Dors' mouth worked with irritation, but she said nothing more. Hari wondered why she was so opposed. "Usually you don't give a damn about social conventions."

She said acidly, "Usually you are not a candidate for First Minister."

"I will not let such considerations deflect our research," he said firmly. "Understand?"

She nodded and said nothing. He instantly felt like an overbearing tyrant. There was always a potential conflict between being coworkers and lovers. Usually they waltzed around the problems. Why was she so adamant?

They got through some more work on psychohistory, and Dors mentioned his next appointment. "She's from my history department. I asked her to look into patterns in Trantorian trends over the last ten millennia."

"Oh, good, thanks. Could you show her in, please?"

Sylvin Thoranax was a striking woman, bearing a box of old data pyramids. "I found these in a library halfway around the planet," she explained.

Hari picked one up. "I've never seen one of these. Dusty!"

"For some there's no library index. I down-coded a few and they're good, still readable with a translation matrix."

"Ummm." Hari liked the musty feel of old technology from simpler times. "We can read these directly?"

She nodded. "I know how the reduced Seldon Equations function. You should be able to do a mat comparison and find the coefficients you need."

Hari grimaced. "They're not my equations; they come out of a body of research by many—"

"Come come, Academician, everyone knows you wrote down the procedures, the approach."

Hari groused a little more, because it did irk him,

but the Thoranax woman went on about using the pyramids and Yugo joined in enthusiastically and he let the point pass. She went off with Yugo to work and he settled into his usual academic grind.

His daily schedule hovered on the holo:

- *Get Symposia speakers—sweeten the invitation for the reluctant*
- *Write nominations for Imperial Fellows*
- *Read student thesis, after it has been checked & passed by Logic Chopper program*

These burned up the bulk of his day. Only when the Chancellor entered his office did he remember that he had promised to give a speech. The Chancellor had a quick, ironic smile and pursed lips, a reserved gaze—the scholar's look. "Your . . . dress?" he asked pointedly.

Hari fumbled in his office closet, fetched forth the balloon-sleeved and ample-girted robe, and changed in the side room. His secretary handed him his all-purpose view cube as they quickly left the office. With the Chancellor he crossed the main square, his Specials in an inconspicuous formation fore and aft. A crowd of well-dressed men and women trained 3D cameras at them, one panning up and down to get the full effect of the Streeling blue-and-yellow swirl-stripes.

"Have you heard from Lamurk?"

"What about the Dahlites?"

"Do you like the new Sector Principal? Does it matter that she's a trisexualist?"

"How about the new health reports? Should the Emperor set exercise requirements for Trantor?"

"Ignore them," Hari said.

The Chancellor smiled and waved at the cameras. "They're just doing their job."

"What's this about exercise?" Hari asked.

"A study found that electro-stim while sleeping doesn't develop muscles as well as old-fashioned exercise."

"Not surprising." He had worked in the fields as a boy and never liked the idea of having his exertion stimmed while he slept.

A wedge of reporters pressed nearer, shouting questions.

"What does the Emperor think of what you said to Lamurk?"

"Is it true that your wife doesn't want you to be First Minister?"

"What about Demerzel? Where is he?"

"What about the Zonal disputes? Can the Empire compromise?"

A woman rushed forward. "How do you exercise?"

Hari said sardonically, "I exercise restraint," but his point sailed right past the woman, who looked at him blankly.

As they entered the Great Hall, Hari remembered to fetch forth the view cube and hand it to the hall-master. A few 3Ds always made a talk pass more easily. "Big crowd," he noted to the Chancellor as they took their places on the speech balcony above the bowl of seats.

"Attendance is compulsory. All class members are here." The Chancellor beamed down at the multitude. "I wanted to be sure we looked good to the reporters outside."

Hari's mouth twisted. "How do they take attendance?"

"Everyone has a keyed seat. Once they sit, they're counted, if their inboard ID matches the seat index."

"A lot of trouble just to get people to attend."

"They must! It's for their own good. And ours."

"They're adults, or else why let them study

advanced subjects? Let them decide what's good for them."

The Chancellor's lips compressed as he rose to do the introduction. When Hari got up to talk, he said, "Now that you're officially counted, I thank you for inviting me, and announce that this is the end of my formal address."

A rustle of surprise. Hari's gaze swept the hall and he let the silence build. Then he said mildly, "I dislike speaking to anyone who has no choice over whether to listen. Now I shall sit down, and anyone wishing to leave may do so."

He sat. The auditorium buzzed. A few got up to leave. The other students booed them. When he rose to speak again they cheered.

He had never had an audience so on his side. He made the most of it, giving a ringing talk about the future of . . . mathematics. Not of the mortal Empire, but of beautiful, enduring mathematics.

8.

◆

The woman from the Ministry of Interlocking Cultures looked down her nose at him and said, "Of course, we must have contributions from your group."

Hari shook his head disbelievingly. "A . . . senso?"

She adjusted her formal suit by wriggling in his office's guest chair. "This is an advanced program. All mathists are charged to submit Boon Behests."

"We are completely unqualified to compose—"

"I understand your hesitation. Yet we at the Ministry feel these senso-symphonies will be just the thing needed to energize a, well, an art form which is showing little progress."

"I don't get it."

She begrudgingly gave him a completely unconvincing, stilted smile. "The way we envision this new sort of senso-symphony, the artists—the mathists, that is—will transmogrify basic structures of *thought*, such as Euclidean conceptual edifices, or transfinite set theory fabrications. These will be translated by an art strainer—"

"Which is?"

"A computer filter which distributes conceptual patterns into a broad selection of sensory avenues."

Hari sighed. "I see." This woman had power and he had to listen to her. His psychohistory funding was secure, coming from the Emperor's private largess. But the Streeling department could not ignore the Imperial Boon Board or its lackeys, such as the one before him. Such was boonmanship.

Far from being relaxed, meditative groves of quiet inquiry, research universities were intense, competitive, high-pressure marathons. The meritocrats—scholars and scientists alike—put in long hours, had stress-related health problems, high divorce rates, and few offspring. They cut up their results into bite-sized chunks, in pursuit of the Least Publishable Unit, so to magnify their lists of papers.

To gain a boon from the Imperial Offices one did the basic labor: Filling Out Forms. Hari knew well the bewildering maze of cross-linked questions. List and analyze type and "texture" of funding. Estimate fringe benefits. Describe kind of lab and computer equipment needed (can existing resources be modified to suit?). Elucidate philosophical stance of the proposed work.

The pyramid of power meant that the most experienced scholars did little scholarship. Instead, they managed and played the endless games of boonsmanship. The Greys grimly saw to it that no box went unchecked. About ten percent of boon petitions received funds, and then after two years' delay, and for about half the requested money.

Worse, since the lead time was so great, there was a premium on hitting the nail squarely on the head with every boon. To be sure a study would work, most of it was done *before* writing the boon petition. This insured that there were no "holes" in the petition, no unexpected swerves in the work.

This meant scholarship and research had become mostly surprise-free, as well. No one seemed to notice that this robbed them of their central joy: the excitement of the unexpected.

"I will . . . speak to my department." *Order them to do it,* would have been more honest. But one did try to preserve the amenities.

When she had left, Dors came into his office immediately, with Yugo right behind. "I will not work with these!" she said, eyes flaring.

Hari studied two large blocks of what seemed to be stone. Yet they could not be that heavy, for Yugo cradled one in each open palm. "The sims?" he guessed.

"In ferrite cores," Yugo said proudly. "Stuck down in a rat's warren, on a planet named Sark."

"The world with that 'New Renaissance' movement?"

"Yeah—kinda crazy, dealin' with them. I got the sims, though. They just came in, Worm Express. The woman in charge there, a Buta Fyrnix, wants to talk to you."

"I said I didn't want to be involved."

"Part of the deal is she gets a face-to-face."

Hari blinked, alarmed. "She'd come all the way here?"

"No, but they're payin' for a tightbeam. She's

standin' by. I've routed her through. Just punch for the link."

Hari had the distinct feeling that he was being hustled into something risky, far beyond the limits of his ordinary caution. Tightbeam time was expensive, because the Imperial wormhole system had been impacted with flow for millennia. Using it for a face-to-face was simply decadent, he felt. If this Fyrnix woman was paying for galactic-scale standby time, just to chat with a mathist . . .

Spare me from the enthused, Hari thought. "Well, all right."

Buta Fyrnix was a tall, hot-eyed woman who smiled brightly as her image blossomed in the office. "Professor Seldon! I was so happy that your staff has taken an interest in our New Renaissance."

"Well, actually, I gather it's about those simulations." For once, he was grateful for the two-second delay in transmission. The biggest wormhole mouth was a light-second from Trantor, and apparently Sark had about the same.

"Of course! We found truly ancient archives. Our progressive movement here is knocking over the old barriers, you'll find."

"I hope the research will prove interesting," Hari said neutrally. How did Yugo get him into this?

"We're turning up things that will open your eyes, Dr. Seldon." She turned and gestured at the scene behind her, a large warren crammed with ancient ceramo storage racks. "We're hoping to blow the lid off the whole question of pre-Empire origins, the Earth legend—the works!"

"I, ah, I will be very happy to see what results."

"You've got to come and see it for yourself. A mathist like you will be impressed. Our Renaissance is just the sort of forward-looking enterprise that young, vigorous planets need. Do say you'll pay us a visit—a state visit, we hope."

Apparently the woman wanted to invest in a future First Minister. It took him more unbearable minutes to get away from her. He glowered at Yugo when at last her image wilted in the air.

"Hey, I got us a good deal, providing she got to do a li'l sell job on you," Yugo said, spreading his hands.

"At considerable under-the-table cost, I hope?" Hari asked, getting up. Carefully he put a hand on one cube and found it surprisingly cool. Within its shadowy interior he could see labyrinths of lattices and winding ribbons of refracted light, like tiny highways through a somber city.

"Sure," Yugo said with casual assurance. "Got some Dahlites to, ah, massage the matter."

Hari chuckled. "I don't think I should hear about it."

"As First Minister, you must not," Dors said.

"I am not First Minister!"

"You could be—and soon. This simulation matter is too risky. And you even spoke to the Sark source! I will not work on or with them."

Yugo said mildly, "Nobody's askin' you to."

Hari rubbed the cool, slick surface of a ferrite block, hefted it—quite light—and took the two from Yugo. He put them on his desk. "How old?"

Yugo said, "Sark says they dunno, but must be at least—"

Dors moved suddenly. She yanked up the blocks, one in each hand, turned to the nearest wall—and smashed them together. The crash was deafening. Chunks of ferrite smacked against the wall. Grains of debris spattered Hari's face.

Dors had absorbed the explosion. The stored energy in the blocks had erupted as the lattice cracked.

In the sudden silence afterward Dors stood adamantly rigid, hands covered with grainy dust. Her hands were bleeding and she had a cut on her left cheek. She gazed straight at him. "I am charged with your safety."

Yugo drawled, "Sure a funny way to show it."

"I had to protect you from a potentially—"

"By *destroying* an ancient artifact?" Hari demanded.

"I smothered nearly all the eruption, minimizing your risk. But yes, I deem this Sark involvement as—"

"I know, I know." Hari raised his hands, palms toward her, recalling.

The night before he had come home from his rather well-received speech to find Dors moody and withdrawn. Their bed had been a rather chilly battleground, too, though she would not come out and say what had irked her so. Winning through withdrawal, Hari had once termed it. But he had no idea she felt this deeply.

Marriage is a voyage of discovery that never ends, he thought ruefully.

"I make decisions about risk," he said to her, eyeing the rubble in his office. "You will obey them unless there is an obvious *physical* danger. Understand?"

"I must use my judgment—"

"No! Involvement with these Sarkian simulations may teach us about shadowy, ancient times. That could affect psychohistory." He wondered if she were carrying out an order from Olivaw. Why would the robots care so strongly?

"When you are plainly imperiling—"

"You *must* leave planning—and psychohistory!—to me."

She batted her eyelashes rapidly, pursed her lips, opened her mouth . . . and said nothing. Finally, she nodded. Hari let out a sigh.

Then his secretary rushed in, followed by the

Specials, and the scene dissolved into a chaos of explanations. He looked the Specials captain straight in the face and said that the ferrite cores had somehow fallen into each other and apparently struck some weak fracture point.

They were, he explained—making it up as he went along, with a voice of professorial authority he had mastered long ago—fragile structures which used tension to stabilize themselves, holding in vast stores of microscopic information.

To his relief the captain just screwed up his face, looked around at the mess, and said, "I should never have let old tech like this in here."

"Not your fault," Hari reassured him. "It's all mine."

There would have been more pretending to do, but a moment later his holo rang with a reception. He glimpsed Cleon's personal officer, but before the woman could speak the scene dissolved. He slapped his filter-face command as Cleon's image coalesced in the air out of a cottony fog.

"I have some bad news," the Emperor said without any greeting.

"Ah, sorry to hear that," Hari said lamely.

Below Cleon's vision he called up a suite of body-language postures and hoped they would cover the ferrite dust clinging to his tunic. The red frame that stitched around the holo told him that a suitably dignified face would go out, keyed with his lip movements.

"The High Council is stuck on this representation issue." Cleon chewed at his lip in irritation. "Until they resolve that, the First Ministership will be set aside."

"I see. The representation problem . . . ?"

Cleon blinked with surprise. "You haven't been following it?"

"There is much to do at Streeling."

Cleon waved airily. "Of course, getting ready for the move. Well, nothing will happen immediately, so you can relax. The Dahlites have logjammed the Galactic Low Council. They want a bigger voice—in Trantor *and* in the whole damned spiral! That Lamurk has sided against them in the High Council. Nobody's budging."

"I see."

"So we'll have to wait before the High Council can act. Procedural matters of representation take precedent over even ministerships."

"Of course."

"Damn Codes!" Cleon erupted. "I should be able to have who I want."

"I quite agree." *But not me*, Hari thought.

"Well, thought you'd like to hear it from me."

"I do appreciate that, sire."

"I've got some things to discuss, that psychohistory especially. I'm busy, but—soon."

"Very good, sire."

Cleon winked away without saying good-bye.

Hari breathed a sigh of relief. "I'm free!" he shouted happily, throwing his hands up.

The Specials stared at him oddly. Hari noticed again his desk and files and walls, all spattered with black grit. His office still looked like paradise to him, compared with the luxuriant snare of the palace.

9.

◆

"The trip, it'll be worth it just to get out of Streeling," Yugo said.

They entered the grav station with the inevitable

Specials trying to casually stroll alongside. To Hari's eye they were as inconspicuous as spiders on a dinner plate.

"True enough," Hari said. At Streeling, High Council members could solicit him, pressure groups could penetrate the makeshift privacy of the Math Department, and of course the Emperor could blossom in the air at any time. On the move, he was safe.

"Good connection comin' up in two point six minutes." Yugo consulted his retinal writer by looking to the far left. Hari had never liked the devices, but they were a convenient way of reading—in this case, the grav schedule—while keeping both hands free. Yugo was toting two bags. Hari had offered to help, but Yugo said they were "family jewels" and needed care.

Without breaking stride they passed through an optical reader which consulted seating, billed their accounts, and notified the autoprogram of the increased mass load. Hari was a bit distracted by some free-floating math ideas, and so their drop startled him.

"Oops," he said, clutching at his armrests. Falling was the one signal that could interrupt even the deepest of meditations. He wondered how far back that alarm had evolved, and then paid attention to Yugo again, who was enthusiastically describing the Dahlite community where they would have lunch.

"You still wonderin' about that political stuff?"

"The representation question? I don't care about the infighting, factions, and so on. Mathematically, though, it's a puzzle."

"Seems to me it's pretty clear," Yugo said with a slight, though respectful, edge in his voice. "Dahlites been gettin' the short end for too long."

"Because they have only one Sector's votes?"

"Right—and there are four hundred million of us in Dahl alone."

"And more elsewhere."

"Damn right. Averaged over Trantor, a Dahlite has only point-six-eight as much representation as the others."

"And throughout the Galaxy—"

"Same damn thing! We got our Zone, sure, but except in the Galactic Low Council, we're boxed in."

Yugo had changed from the chattering friend out on a lark to sober-faced and scowling. Hari didn't want the trip to turn into an argument. "Statistics require care, Yugo. Remember the classic joke about three statisticians who took up hunting ducks—"

"Which are?"

"A game bird, known on some worlds. The first shot a meter high, the second a meter low. When this happened, the third statistician cried, 'We got it!'"

Yugo laughed a bit dutifully. Hari was trying to follow Dors' advice about handling people, using his humor more and logic less. The incident with Lamurk had rebounded in Hari's favor among the media and even the High Council, the Emperor had said.

Dors herself, though, seemed singularly immune to both laughs and logic; the incident with the ferrite cores had put a strain in their relationship. Hari realized now that this, too, was why he had greeted Yugo's suggestion of a day away from Streeling. Dors had two classes to teach and couldn't go. She had grumbled, but conceded that the Specials could probably cover him well enough. As long as he did nothing "foolish."

Yugo persisted. "Okay, but the courts are stacked against us, too."

"Dahl is the largest Sector now. You will get your judgeships in time."

"Time we don't have. We're getting shut out by blocs."

Hari deeply disliked the usual circular logic of political griping, so he tried to appeal to Yugo's mathist side. "All judging bodies are vulnerable to bloc control, my friend. Suppose a court had eleven judges. Then a cohesive group of six could decide every ruling. They could meet secretly and agree to be bound by what a majority of them thinks, then vote as a bloc in the full eleven."

Yugo's mouth twisted with irritation. "The High Tribunal's eleven—that's your point, right?"

"It's a general principle. Even smaller schemes could work, too. Suppose four of the High Tribunal met secretly and agreed to be bound by their own ballot. Then they'd vote as a bloc among the original cabal of six. Then four would determine the outcome of all eleven."

"Damn-all, it's worse than I thought," Yugo said.

"My point is that any finite representation can be corrupted. It's a general theorem about the method."

Yugo nodded and then to Hari's dismay launched into reciting the woes and humiliations visited upon Dahlites at the hands of the ruling majorities in the Tribunal, the Councils both High and Low, the Diktat Directory . . .

The endless busyness of ruling. What a bore!

Hari realized that his style of thought was a far cry from the fevered calculations of Yugo, and further still from the wily likes of Lamurk. How could he hope to survive as a First Minister? Why couldn't the Emperor see that?

He nodded, put on his mask of thoughtful listening, and let the wall displays soothe him. They were still plunging down the long cycloidal curve of the grav drop.

This time the name was apt. Most long-distance travel on Trantor was in fact *under* Trantor, along a curve which let their car plunge down under gravity alone, suspended on magnetic fields a bare finger's width from the tube walls. Falling through dark vacuum, there were no windows. Instead, the walls quieted any fears of falling.

Mature technology was discreet, simple, easy, quiet, sinuously classical, even friendly—while its use remained as obvious as a hammer, its effects as easy as a 3D. Both it and its user had educated each other.

A forest slid by all around him and Yugo. Many on Trantor lived among trees and rocks and clouds, as humans once had. The effects were not real, but they didn't need to be. *We are the wild, now,* Hari thought. Humans shaped Trantor's labyrinths to quiet their deep-set needs, so the mind's eye felt itself flitting through a park. Technology appeared only when called forth, like magical spirits.

"Say, mind if I kill this?" Yugo's question broke through his reverie.

"The trees?"

"Yeah, the open, y'know."

Hari nodded and Yugo thumbed in a view of a mall with no great distances visible. Many Trantorians became anxious in big spaces, or even near images of them.

They had leveled out and soon began to rise. Hari felt pressed back into his chair, which compensated deftly. They were moving at high velocity, he knew, but there was no sign of it. Slight pulses of the magnetic throat added increments of velocity as they rose, making up for the slight losses. Otherwise, the entire trip took no energy, gravity giving and then taking away.

When they emerged in the Carmondian Sector his

Specials drew in close. This was no elite university setting. Few buildings here could be seen as exteriors, so design focused on interior spectacle: thrusting slopes, airy transepts, soaring trunks of worked metal and muscular fiber. But amid this serene architecture milling crowds jostled and fretted, lapping like an angry tide.

Across an overhead bikepad a steady stream of cyclists hauled tow-cars. Jamming their narrow bays were bulky appliances, glistening sides of meat, boxes, and lumpy goods, all bound for nearby customers. Restaurants were little more than hotplates surrounded with tiny tables and chairs, all squeezed into the walkways. Barbers conducted business in the thoroughfare, working one end of the customer while beggars massaged the feet for a coin.

"Seems . . . busy," Hari said diplomatically as he caught the tang of Dahlite cooking.

"Yeah, doncha love it?"

"Beggars and street vendors were made illegal by the last Emperor, I thought."

"Right." He grinned. "Don't work with Dahlites. We've moved plenty people into this Sector. C'mon, I want some lunch."

It was early, but they ate in a stand-up restaurant, drawn in by the odors. Hari tried a "bomber," which wriggled into his mouth, then exploded into a smoky dark taste he could not identify, finally fading into a bittersweet aftertaste. His Specials looked quite uneasy, standing around in a crowded, busy hubbub. They were accustomed to more regal surroundings.

"Things're really boomin' here," Yugo observed. His manners had reverted to his laboring days and he spoke with his mouth half full.

"Dahlites have a gift for expansion," Hari said diplomatically. Their high birth rate pushed them into other Sectors, where their connections to Dahl brought new investment. Hari liked their restless energy; it reminded him of Helicon's few cities.

He had been modeling all of Trantor, trying to use it as a shrunken version of the Empire. Much of his progress had come from unlearning conventional wisdom. Most economists saw money as simple ownership—a basic, linear power relationship. But it was a fluid, Hari found—slippery and quick, always flowing from one hand to the next as it greased the momentum of change. Imperial analysts had mistaken a varying flux for a static counter.

They finished and Yugo urged him into a groundpod. They followed a complicated path, alive with noise and smells and vigor. Here orderly traffic disintegrated. Instead of making an entire layer one way, local streets intersected at angles acute and oblique, seldom rectangular. Yugo seemed to regard traffic intersections as rude interruptions.

They sped by buildings at close range, stopped, and got out for a walk to a slideway. The Specials were right behind and without any transition Hari found himself in the middle of chaos. Smoke enveloped them and the acrid stench made him almost vomit.

The Specials captain shouted to him, "Stay down!" Then the man shouted to his men to arm with anamorphine. They all bristled with weapons.

Smoke paled the overhead phosphors. Through the muggy haze Hari saw a solid wall of people hammering toward them. They came out of side alleys and doorways and all seemed to bear down on him. The Specials fired a volley into the mass. Some went down. The captain threw a canister and gas blossomed farther away. He had judged it expertly; air circulation carried the fumes into the mob, not toward Hari.

But anamorphine wasn't going to stop them. Two

women rushed by Hari, carrying cobblestones ripped from the street. A third jabbed at Hari with a knife and the captain shot her with a dart. Then more Dahlites rushed at the Specials and Hari caught what they were shouting: incoherent rage against tiktoks.

The idea seemed so unlikely to him at first he thought he could not have heard rightly. That deflected his attention, and when he looked back toward the streaming crowd the captain was down and a man was advancing, holding a knife.

What any of this had to do with tiktoks was mysterious, but Hari did not have time to do anything except step to the side and kick the man squarely in the knee.

A bottle bounced painfully off his shoulder and smashed on the walkway. A man whirled a chain around and around and then toward Hari's head. *Duck.* It whistled by and Hari dove at the man, tackling him solidly. They went down with two others in a swearing, punching mass. Hari took a slug in the gut.

He rolled over and gasped for air and clearly, only a few feet away, saw a man kill another with a long, curved knife.

Jab, slash, jab. It happened silently, like a dream. Hari gasped, shaken, his world in slow motion. He should be responding boldly, he knew that. But it was so overwhelming—

—and then he was standing, with no memory of getting there, wrestling with a man who had not bothered with bathing for quite some while.

Then the man was gone, abruptly yanked away by the seethe of the crowd.

Another sudden jump—and Specials were all around him. Bodies sprawled lifeless on the walkway. Others held their bloody heads. Shouts, thumps—

He did not have time to figure out what weapon had

done that to them before the Specials were whisking him and Yugo along and the whole incident fled into obscurity, like a 3D program glimpsed and impatiently passed by.

The captain wanted to return to Streeling. "Even better, the palace."

"This wasn't about us," Hari said as they took a slideway.

"Can't be sure of that, sir."

10.

◆

Hari batted away all suggestions that they discontinue their journey. The incident had apparently begun when some tiktoks malfed.

"Somebody accused Dahlites of causing it," Yugo related. "So our people stood up for themselves and, well, things got out of hand."

Everyone near them was alive with excitement, faces glowing, eyes white and darting. He thought suddenly of his father's wry saying, *Never underestimate the power of boredom.*

In human affairs, spirited action relieved dry tedium. He remembered seeing two women pummel a Spook, slamming away at the spindly, bleached-white man as though he were no more than a responsive exercise machine. A simple phobia against sunlight meant that he was of the hated Other, and thus fair game.

Murder was a primal urge. Even the most civilized felt tempted by it in moments of rage. But nearly all resisted and were better for the resistance. Civilization was a defense against nature's raw power.

That was a crucial variable, one never considered by the economists with their gross products per capita, or the political theorists with their representative quotients, or the sociosavants and their security indices.

"I'll have to keep that in, too," he muttered to himself.

"Keep what?" Yugo asked. He, too, was still agitated.

"Things as basic as murder. We get all tied up in Trantor's economics and politics, but something as gut-deep as that incident may be more important, in the long run."

"We'll pick it up in the crime statistics."

"No, it's the *urge* I want to get. How does that explain the deeper movements in human culture? It's bad enough dealing with Trantor—a giant pressure cooker, forty billion sealed in together. We know there's something missing, because we can't get the psychohistorical equations to converge."

Yugo frowned. "I was thinkin' it was, well, that we needed more data."

Hari felt the old, familiar frustration. "No, I can *feel* it. There's something crucial, and we don't have it."

Yugo looked doubtful and then their off-disk came. They changed through a concentric set of circulating slideways, reducing their velocity and ending in a broad square. An impressive edifice dominated the high air shafts, slender columns blooming into offices above. Sunlight trickled down the sculpted faces of the building, telling tales of money: Artifice Associates.

Reception whisked them into a sanctum more luxurious than anything at Streeling. "Great room," Yugo said with a wry slant of his head.

Hari understood this common academic reflection. Technical workers outside the university system earned more and worked in generally better surroundings.

None of that had ever bothered him. The idea of universities as a high citadel had withered as the Empire declined, and he saw no need for opulence, particularly under an Emperor with a taste for it.

The staff of Artifice Associates referred to themselves as A^2 and seemed quite bright. He let Yugo carry the conversation as they sat around a big, polished pseudowood table; he still pulsed with the zest of the earlier violence. Hari sat back and meditated on his surroundings, his mind returning as always to new facets which might bear upon psychohistory.

The theory already had mathematical relationships between technology, capital accumulation, and labor, but the most important driver proved to be knowledge. About half the economic growth came from the increase in the quality of information, as embodied in better machines and improved skills, building efficiency.

Fair enough—and that was where the Empire had faltered. The innovative thrust of the sciences had slowly ground down. The Imperial Universities produced fine engineers, but no inventors. Great scholars, but few true scientists. That factored into the other tides of time.

Only independent businesses such as this, he reflected, continued the momentum which had driven the entire Empire for so long. But they were wildflowers, often crushed beneath the boot of Imperial politics and inertia.

"Dr. Seldon?" a voice asked at his elbow, startling Hari out of his rumination. He nodded.

"We do have your permission as well?"

"Ah, to do what?"

"To use these." Yugo stood and lifted onto the table his two carry-cases. He unzipped them and two ferrite cores stood revealed.

"The Sark sims, gentlemen."

Hari gaped. "I thought Dors—"

"Smashed 'em? She thought so, too. I used two old, worthless data-cores in your office that day."

"You knew she would—"

"I gotta respect that lady—quick and strong-minded, she is." Yugo shrugged. "I figured she might get a little . . . provoked."

Hari smiled. Suddenly he knew that he had been repressing real anger at Dors for her high-handed act. Now he released it in a fit of hearty laughter. "Wonderful! Wife or not, there are limits."

He howled so hard tears sprang to his eyes. The guffaws spread around the table and Hari felt better than he had in weeks. For a moment all the nagging University details, the ministership, everything—fell away.

"Then we do have your permission, Dr. Seldon? To use the sims?" a young man at his elbow asked again.

"Of course, though I will want to keep close tabs on some, ah, research interests of mine. Will that be possible, Mr. . . . ?"

"Marq Hofti. We'd be honored, sir, if you could spare the project some time. I'll do my best—"

"And I." A young woman stood at his other elbow. "Sybyl," she said, and shook hands. They both appeared quite competent, neat, and efficient. Hari puzzled at the looks bordering on reverence they gave him. After all, he was just a mathist, like them.

Then he laughed again, heartily, a curiously liberating bark. He had just thought of what it would be like to tell Dors about the data-cores.

PART 2

THE ROSE MEETS
THE SCALPEL

COMPUTATIONAL REPRESENTATION— . . . *it is clear that, except for occasional outbursts, the taboos against advanced, artificial intelligences head throughout the Empire through the great sweep of historical time. This uniformity of cultural opinion probably reflects tragedies and traumas with artificial forms far back in pre-Empire ages. There are records of early transgressions by self-aware programs, including those by "sims," or self-organizing simulations. Apparently the pre-ancients enjoyed recreating personalities of their own past, perhaps for instruction or amusement or even research. None of these are known to survive, but tales persist that they were once a high art.*

Of darker implication are the narratives which hypothesize self-aware intelligences lodged in bodies resembling human. While low-order mechanical forms are customarily allowed throughout the Empire, these "tiktoks" constitute no competition with humans, since they perform only simple and often disagreeable tasks. . . .

—ENCYCLOPEDIA GALACTICA

1.

◆

Joan of Arc wakened inside an amber dream. Cool breezes caressed her, odd noises reverberated. She heard before she saw—

—and abruptly found herself sitting outdoors. She noted things one at a time, as though some part of herself were counting them.

Soft air. Before her, a smooth round table.

Pressing against her, an unsettling white chair. Its seat, unlike those in her home village of Domremy, was not hand-hewn of wood. Its smooth slickness lewdly aped her contours. She reddened.

Strangers. One, two, three . . . winking into being before her eyes.

They moved. Peculiar people. She could not tell woman from man, except for those whose pantaloons and tunics outlined their intimate parts. The spectacle was even more than she'd seen in Chinon, at the lewd court of the Great and True King.

Talk. The strangers seemed oblivious of her, though she could hear them chattering in the background as distinctly as she sometimes heard her voices. She listened only long enough to conclude that what they said, having nothing to do with holiness or France, was clearly not worth hearing.

Noise. From outside. An iron river of self-moving carriages muttered by. She felt surprise at this—then somehow the emotion evaporated.

A long view, telescoping in—

Pearly mists concealed distant ivory spires. Fog made them seem like melting churches.

What *was* this place?

A vision, perhaps related to her beloved voices. Could such apparitions be holy?

Surely the man at a nearby table was no angel. He was eating scrambled eggs—through a straw.

And the women—unchaste, flagrant, gaudy cornucopias of hip and thigh and breast. Some drank red wine from transparent goblets, different from any she'd seen at the royal court.

Others seemed to sup from floating clouds—delicate, billowing *mousse* fogs. One mist, reeking of beef with a tangy Loire sauce, passed near her. She breathed in—and felt in an instant that she had experienced a meal.

Was this heaven? Where appetites were satisfied without labor and toil?

But no. Surely the final reward was not so, so . . . carnal. And perturbing. And embarrassing.

The fire some sucked into their mouths from little reeds—*those* alarmed her. A cloud of smoke drifting her way flushed birds of panic from her breast—although she could not smell the smoke, nor did it burn her eyes or sear her throat.

The fire, the fire! she thought, heart fluttering in panic. *What had . . . ?*

She saw a being made of breastplate coming at her with a tray of food and drink—*poison from enemies, no doubt, the foes of France!* she thought in churning fright—she at once reached for her sword.

"Be with you in a moment," the breastplated thing said as it wheeled past her to another table. "I've only got four hands. *Do* have patience."

An inn, she thought. It was some kind of inn, though there appeared to be nowhere to lodge. And yes . . . it came now . . . she was supposed to meet someone . . . a gentleman?

That one: the tall, skinny old man—much older than Jacques Dars, her father—the only one besides herself attired normally.

Something about his dress recalled the foppish dandies at the Great and True King's court. His hair curled tight, its whiteness set off by a lilac ribbon at his throat. He wore a pair of mignonette ruffles with narrow edging, a long waistcoat of brown satin with colored flowers, and sported red velvet breeches, white stockings, and chamois shoes.

A silly, vain aristocrat, she thought. A fop accustomed to carriages, who could not so much as sit a horse, much less do holy battle.

But duty was a sacred obligation. If King Charles ordered her to advance, advance she would.

She rose. Her suit of mail felt surprisingly light. She hardly sensed the belted-on protective leather flaps in front and back, nor the two metal arm plates that left elbows free to wield the sword. No one paid the least attention to the rustle of her mail or her faint clank.

"Are you the gentleman I am to meet? Monsieur Arouet?"

"Don't call me that," he snapped. "Arouet is my father's name—the name of an authoritarian prude, not mine. No one has called me that in *years*."

Up close, he seemed less ancient. She'd been misled by his white hair, which she now saw was false, a powdered wig secured by the lilac ribbon under his chin.

"What should I call you then?" She suppressed terms of contempt for this dandy—rough words learned from comrades-in-arms, now borne by demons to her tongue's edge, but not beyond.

"Poet, tragedian, historian." He leaned forward and with a wicked wink whispered, "I style myself Voltaire. Freethinker. Philosopher king."

"Besides the King of Heaven and His son, I call but one man King. Charles VII of the House of Valois. And I'll call you Arouet until my royal master bids me do otherwise."

"My dear *pucelle*, your Charles is dead."

"No!"

He glanced at the noiseless carriages propelled by invisible forces on the street. "Sit down, sit down. Much else has passed, as well. Do help me get that droll waiter's attention."

"You know me?" Led by her voices, she had cast off her father's name to call herself *La Pucelle*, the Chaste Maid.

"I know you very well. Not only did you live centuries before me, I wrote a play about you. And I have curious memories of speaking with you before, in some shadowy spaces." He shook his head, frowning. "Besides my garments—beautiful, *n'est ce pas?*—you're the only familiar thing about this place. You and the street, though I must say you're younger than I thought, while the street . . . hmmm . . . seems wider yet older. They finally got 'round to paving it."

"I, I cannot fathom—"

He pointed to a sign that bore the inn's name—*Aux Deux Magots.* "Mademoiselle Lecouvreur—a famous actress, though equally known as my mistress." He blinked. "You're blushing—how sweet."

"I know *noth*ing of such things." She added with more than a trace of pride, "I am a maid."

He grimaced. "Why one would be proud of such an unnatural state, I can't imagine."

"As I cannot imagine why you are so dressed."

"My tailors will be mortally offended! But allow me to suggest that it is you, my dear *pucelle*, who, in your insistence on dressing like a man, would deprive civilized society of one of its most harmless pleasures."

"An insistence I most dearly paid for," she retorted, remembering how the bishops badgered her about her male attire as relentlessly as they inquired after her divine voices.

As if in the absurd attire members of her sex were required to wear, she could have defeated the English-loving duke at Orleans! Or led three thousand knights to victory at Jargeau and Meung-sur-Loire, Beaugency and Patay, throughout that summer of glorious conquests when, led by her voices, she could do no wrong.

She blinked back sudden tears. A rush of memory—

Defeat . . . Then the bloodred darkness of lost battles had descended, muffling her voices, while those of her English-loving enemies grew strong.

"No need to get testy," Monsieur Arouet said, gently patting her knee plate. "Although I personally find your attire repulsive, I would defend to the death your right to dress any way you please. Or undress." He eyed the near-transparent upper garment of a female inn patron nearby.

"Sir—"

"Paris has not lost its appetite for finery after all. Pale fruit of the gods, don't you agree?"

"No, I do not. There is no virtue greater than chastity in women—or in men. Our Lord was chaste, as are our saints and priests."

"Priests chaste!" He rolled his eyes. "Pity you weren't at the school my father forced me to attend as a boy. You could have so informed the Jesuits, who daily abused their innocent charges."

"I, I cannot believe—"

"And what of him?" Voltaire talked right over her, pointing at the four-handed creature on wheels rolling toward them. "No doubt such a creature is chaste. Is it then virtuous, too?"

"Christianity, France itself, is founded on—"

"If chastity were practiced in France as much as it's preached, the race would be extinct."

The wheeled creature braked by their table. Stamped on his chest was what appeared to be his name: GARÇON 213-ADM. In a bass voice as clear as any man's, he said, "A costume party, eh? I hope my delay will not make you late. Our mechfolk are having difficulties."

It eyed the other tiktok bringing dishes forth—a honey-haired blond in a hairnet, approximately humanlike. A demon?

The Maid frowned. Its jerky glance, even though mechanical, recalled the way her jailers had gawked at her. Humiliated, she had cast aside the women's garments that her Inquisitors forced her to wear. Resuming manly attire, she'd scornfully put her jailers in their place. It had been a fine moment.

The cook assumed a haughty look, but fussed with her hairnet and smiled at Garçon 213-ADM before averting her eyes. The import of this eluded Joan. She had accepted mechanicals in this strange place, without questioning their meaning. Presumably this was some intermediate station in the Lord's providential order. But it *was* puzzling.

Monsieur Arouet reached out and touched the mechman's nearest arm, whose construction the Maid could not help but admire. If such a creature could be made to sit a horse, in battle it would be invincible. The possibilities . . .

"Where are we?" Monsieur Arouet asked. "Or perhaps I should ask, when? I have friends in high places—"

"And I in low," the mechman said good-naturedly.

"—and I demand a full account of where we are, what's going on."

The mechman shrugged with two of his free arms, while the two others set the table. "How could a mechwait with intelligence programmed to suit his station, instruct monsieur, a human being, in the veiled mysteries of simspace? Have monsieur and mademoiselle decided on their order?"

"You have not yet brought us the menu," said Monsieur Arouet.

The mechman pushed a button under the table. Two flat scrolls embedded in the table shimmered, letters glowing. The Maid let out a small cry of delight—then, in response to Monsieur Arouet's censorious look, clapped her hand over her mouth. Her peasant manners were a frequent source of embarrassment.

"Ingenious," said Monsieur Arouet, switching the button on and off as he examined the underside of the table. "How does it work?"

"I'm not programmed to know. You'll have to ask a mechlectrician about that."

"A what?"

"With all due respect, Monsieur, my other customers are waiting. I *am* programmed to take your order."

"What will you have, my dear?" Monsieur Arouet asked her.

She looked down, embarrassed. "Order for me," she said.

"Ah, yes. I quite forgot."

"Forgot what?" asked the mechman.

"My companion is unlettered. She can't read. I might as well be, too, for all the good this menu's doing me."

So this obviously learned man could not fathom the Table of House. Joan found that endearing, amid this blizzard of the bizarre.

The mechman explained and Voltaire interrupted.

"*Cloud*-food? Electronic cuisine?" He grimaced. "Just bring me the best you have for great hunger and thirst. What can you recommend for abstinent virgins—a plate of dirt, perhaps? Chased with a glass of vinegar?"

"Bring me a slice of bread," the Maid said with frosty dignity. "And a small bowl of wine to dip it in."

"Wine!" said Monsieur Arouet. "Your voices allow wine? *Mais quelle scandale!* If word got out that you drink wine, what would the priests say of the shoddy example you're setting for the future saints of France?"

He turned to the mechman. "Bring her a glass of water, small." As Garçon 213-ADM withdrew, Monsieur Arouet called out, "And make sure the bread is a crust! Preferably moldy!"

2.

◆

Marq Hofti strode swiftly toward his Waldon Shaft office, his colleague and friend Sybyl chattering beside him. She was always energetic, bristling with ideas. Only occasionally did her energy seem tiresome.

The Artifice Associates offices loomed, weighty

and impressive in the immense, high shaft. A flutter-glider circled the protruding levels far above, banking among pretty green clouds. Marq craned his neck upward and watched the glider catch an updraft of the city's powerful air circulators. Atmospheric control even added the puff-ball vapors for variety. He longed to be up there, swooping among their sticky flavors.

Instead, he was down here, donning his usual carapace of each-day's-a-challenge vigor. And today was going to be unusual. Risky. And though the zest for it sang in his stride, his grin, the fear of failure gave a leaden lining to his most buoyant plans.

If he failed today, at least he would not tumble from the sky, like a pilot who misjudged the thermals in the shaft. Grimly, he entered his office.

"It makes me nervous," Sybyl said, cutting into his mood.

"Umm. What?" He dumped his pack and sat at his ornate control board.

She sat beside him. The board filled half the office, making his desk look like a cluttered afterthought. "The Sark sims. We've spent so much time on those resurrection protocols, the slices and embeddings and all."

"I had to fill in whole layers missing from the recordings. Synaptic webs from the association cortex. Plenty of work."

"I did, too. My Joan was missing chunks of the hippocampus."

"Pretty tough?" The brain remembered things using constellations of agents from the hippocampus. They laid down long-term memory elsewhere, spattering pieces of it around the cerebral cortex. Not nearly as clean and orderly as computer memory, which was one of the major problems. Evolution was a kludge, mechanisms crammed in here and there, with little attention to overall design. At building minds, the Lord was something of an amateur.

"Murder. I stayed to midnight for weeks."

"Me too."

"Did you . . . use the library?"

He considered. Artifice Associates kept dense files of brain maps, all taken from volunteers. There were menus for selecting mental agents—subroutines which could carry out the tasks which myriad synapses did in the brain. These were all neatly translated into digital equivalents, saving great labor. But to use them meant running up big bills, because each was copyrighted. "No. Got a private source."

She nodded. "Me too."

Was she trying to coax an admission from him? They had both had to go through scanning as part of getting their Master Class ratings in the meritocracy. Marq had thriftily kept his scan. Better than a back-alley brain map, for sure. He was no genius, but the basics of Voltaire's underpinnings weren't the important part, after all. Exactly how the sim ran the hindbrain functions—basic maintenance, housekeeping circuitry—certainly couldn't matter, could it?

"Let's have a look at our creations," Marq said brightly, to get off the subject.

Sybyl shook her head. "Mine is stable. But look—we don't really know what to expect. These fully integrated Personalities are still isolated."

"Nature of the beast." Marq shrugged, playing the jaded pro. Now that his hands caressed the board, though, a tingling excitement seized him.

"Let's do it today," she said, words rushing out.

"What? I—I'd like to slap some more patches over the gaps, maybe install a rolling buffer as insurance against character shifts, spy into—"

"Details! Look, these sims have been running on

internals for weeks of sim-time, self-integrating. Let's interact."

Marq thought of the glider pilot, up there amid treacherous winds. He had never done anything so risky; he wasn't the type. His kind of peril lay on the digital playing field. Here, he was master.

But he had not gotten this far by being foolish. Letting these simulations come into contact with the present might induce hallucinations in them, fear, even panic.

"Just think! Talking to pre-antiquity."

He realized that *he* was the one feeling fear. *Think like a pilot!* he admonished himself.

"Would you want anyone else to do it?" Sybyl asked.

He was keenly aware of the fleeting warmth of her thigh as it accidentally brushed his.

"No one else could," he admitted.

"And it'll put us ahead of any competition."

"That guy Seldon, he could've, once he got them from those Sark 'New Renaissance' jokers. Using us, well—I guess he needs to get some distance from a dicey proposition like this."

"Political distance," she agreed. "Deniability."

"He didn't seem that savvy to me—politically, I mean."

"Maybe he wants us to think that. How'd he charm Cleon?"

"Beats me. Not that I wouldn't want one of our guys running things. A mathist minister—who'd imagine that?"

So Artifice Associates was out on its own here. With their Sark contacts, the company had already displaced Digitfac and Axiom Alliance in the sale and design of holographic intelligences. Competition was rough in several product lines, though. With a pipeline to truly ancient Personalities, they could sweep the board clean. *At the knife edge of change,* Marq thought happily. *Danger and money, the two great aphrodisiacs.*

He had spent yesterday eavesdropping on Voltaire and was sure Sybyl had done the same with the Maid. Everything had gone well. "Face filters for us, though."

"Don't trust yourself to not give away your feelings?" Sybyl gave him a womanly, throaty chuckle. "Think you're too easy to read?"

"Am I?" Ball back in her court.

"Let's say your *intentions* are, at least."

Her sly wink made his nostrils flare—which reminded Marq of why he needed the filters. He thumbed in an amiable expression he had carefully fashioned for dealing by phone with clients. He had learned early in this business that the world was packed with irritable people. Especially Trantor.

"Better put a body language refiner on, too," she said flatly, all business now. That was what never ceased to intrigue him: artful ambiguity.

She popped up her own filters, imported instantly from her board halfway across the building. "Want a vocabulary box?"

He shrugged. "Anything they can't understand, we'll credit to language problems."

"What *is* that stuff they speak?"

"Dead language, unknown parent world." His hands were a blur, setting up the transition.

"It has a, well, a *liquid* feel."

"One thing."

Sybyl's breasts swelled as she drew in her breath, held it, then slowly eased it out. "I just hope my client doesn't find out about Seldon. The company's taking an awful chance, not telling either one of them about the other."

"So what?" He enjoyed giving a carefree shrug. A

flutter-glide would petrify him, but power games—those he loved. Artifice Associates had taken major accounts from the two deadly rivals in this whole affair.

"If both sides of the argument find out we're handling both accounts, they'll leave. Refuse to pay beyond the retainer—and you know how much we've overspent beyond that."

"Leave?" His turn to chuckle. "Not if they want to win. We're the best." Marq gave her his cocky smile. "You and me, in case you were wondering. Just wait till you see this."

He downed the lights, started the run, and leaned back in his clasp chair, legs stretched out on the table before him. He wanted to impress her. That wasn't all he wanted. But since her husband had been crushed in an accident, beyond repair by even the best medicos, he'd decided to wait a decent interval before he made his move. What a team they would make! Open a firm—say, MarqSybyl, Limited—skim off the best A^2 customers, make a *name*.

No names. Let's be fair.

Sybyl's voice trembled in the gloom. "To meet ancients . . ."

Down, down, down—into the replicated world, its seamless blue complexity swelling across the entire facing wall. Vibrotactile feedback from inductance dermotabs perfected the illusion.

They swooped into a primitive city, barely one layer of buildings to cover the naked ground. Some sort of crude village, pre-Empire. Streets whirled by, buildings turned in artful projection. Even the crowds and clumped traffic below seemed authentic, a muddled human jumble. Swiftly they careened into their foreground sim: a cafe on something called the Boulevard St. Germain. Cloying smells, the muted grind of traffic outside, a rattle of plates, the heady aroma of a soufflé.

Marq zoomed them into the same timeframe as the recreated entities. A lean man loomed across the wall. His eyes radiated intelligence, mouth tilted with sardonic mirth.

Sybyl whistled through her teeth. Eyes narrowing, she watched the re-creation's mouth, as if to read its lips. Voltaire was interrogating the mechwaiter. Irritably, of course.

"High five-sense resolution," she said, appropriately awed. "I can't get mine that clear. I still don't know how you do it."

Marq thought, *My Sark contacts. I know you have some, too.*

"Hey," she said. "What—" He grinned with glee as her mouth fell open and she stared at the image of her Joan next to his Voltaire—freeze-frame, data streams initialized but not yet running interactively.

Her expression mingled admiration with fear. "We're not supposed to bring them on together!— not till they meet in the coliseum."

"Who says? It's not in our contract!"

"Hastor will skewer us anyway."

"Maybe—if he finds out. Want me to section her off?"

Her mouth twisted prettily. "Of course not. What the hell, it's done. Activate."

"I knew you'd go for it. We're the artists, we make the decisions."

"Have we got the running capacity to make them realtime?"

He nodded. "It'll cost, but sure. And . . . I've got a little proposition for you."

"Uh-oh." Her brow arched. "Forbidden, no doubt."

He waited, just to tantalize her. And to judge, from her reaction, how receptive she'd be if he tried to change the nature of their long-standing platonic relationship. He *had* tried, once before. Her rejection—she was married on a decade contract, she gently reminded him—only made him desire her more. All that and faithful in marriage, too. Enough to make the teeth grind—which they had, frequently. Of course, they could be replaced for less than the price of an hour with a good therapist.

Her body language now—a slight pulling away—told him she was still mourning her dead husband. He was prepared to wait the customary year, but only if he had to.

"What say we give both of them massive files, far beyond Basis State," he said quickly. "Really give them solid knowledge of what Trantor's like, the Empire, everything."

"Impossible."

"No, just expensive."

"So much!"

"So what? Just think about it. We know what these two Primordials represented, even if we don't know what world they came from."

"Their strata memories say 'Earth,' remember?"

Marq shrugged. "So? Dozens of primitive worlds called themselves that."

"Oh, the way Primitives call themselves 'the People'?"

"Sure. The whole folk tale is wrong astrophysically, too. This legend of the original planet is pretty clear on one point—the world was mostly oceans. So why call it 'Earth'?"

She nodded. "Granted, they're deluded. And they have no solid databases about astronomy, I checked that. But look at their Social Context readings. These two stood for concepts, eternal ideas: Faith and Reason."

Marq balled both fists in enthusiasm, a boyish gesture. "Right! On top of that we'll pump in what we know today—pseudonatural selection, psychophilosophy, gene destinies—"

"Boker will never go for it," Sybyl said. "It's precisely modern information the Preservers of Our Father's Faith don't want. They want the historical Maid, pure and uncontaminated by modern ideas. I'd have to program her to read—"

"A cinch."

"—write, handle higher mathematics. Give me a break!"

"Do you object on ethical grounds? Or simply to avoid a few measly centuries of work?"

"Easy for *you* to say. Your Voltaire has an essentially modern mind. Whoever made him had his own work, dozens of biographies. My Maid is as much myth as she is fact. Somebody re-created her out of thin air."

"Then your objection's based on laziness, not principle."

"It's based on both."

"Will you at least give it some thought?"

"I just did. The answer is no."

Marq sighed. "No use arguing. You'll see, once we let them interact."

Her mood seemed to swing from resistance to excitement; in her enthusiasm, she even touched his leg, fingers lingering. He felt her affectionate tap just as they opened into the simspace.

3.

◆

"What's going on here?" Voltaire rose, hands on hips—chair toppling back behind him, clattering on stone—and peered down at them from the screen. "Who are you? What infernal agency do you represent?"

Marq stopped the sim and turned to Sybyl. "Uh, do you want to explain it to him?"

"He's your re-creation, not mine."

"I've dreaded this." Voltaire was imposing. He exuded power and electric confidence. Somehow, in all his microscopic inspections of this sim, the sum of it all, this *gestalt essence*, had never come through.

"We worked hard on this! If you stall now—"

Marq braced himself. "Right, right."

"How do you look to him?"

"I made myself materialize, walk over, sit down."

"He saw you come out of nothing?"

"I guess so," he said, chagrined. "Shook him up."

Marq had used every temperament fabrication he had, trimming and shaping mood constellations, but he had left intact Voltaire's central core. What a hardball knot it was! Some programmer of pre-antiquity had done a startling, dense job. Gingerly, he dipped the Voltaire-sim into a colorless void of sensory static. Soothe, then slide . . .

His fingers danced. He cut in the time acceleration.

Sim-personalities needed computational durations to assimilate new experience. He thrust Voltaire into a cluttered, seemingly real experience-net. The personality reacted to the simulation and raced through the induced emotions. Voltaire was rational; his personality could accept new ideas that took the Joansim far longer.

What did all this do to a reconstruction of a real person, when knowledge of a different reality dawned? Here came the tricky part of the reanimation. Acceptance of who/what/when they were.

Conceptual shock waves would resound through the digital personalities, forcing emotional adjustments.

Could they take it? These weren't real people, after all, any more than an abstract impressionist painting pretended to tell you what a cow looked like. Now, he and Sybyl could step in only after the automatic programs had done their best.

Here their math-craft met its test. Artificial personalities had to survive this cusp point or crash into insanity and incoherence. Racing along highways of expanding perception, the ontological swerves could jolt a construct so hard, it shattered.

He let them meet each other, watching carefully. The *Aux Deux Magots*, simple town and crowd backdrop. To shave computing time, weather repeated every two minutes of simtime. Cloudless sky, to save on fluid flow modeling. Sybyl tinkered with her Joan, he with his Voltaire, smoothing and rounding small cracks and slippages in the character perceptual matrix.

They met, spoke. Some skittering, blue-white storms swept through Voltaire's neuronal simulations. Marq sent in conceptual repair algorithms. Turbulence lapped away.

"Got it!" he whispered. Sybyl nodded beside him, intent on her own smoothing functions.

"He's running regular now," Marq said, feeling better about the startup mistake. "I'll keep my manifestation sitting, right? No disappearances or anything."

"Joan's cleared up." Sybyl pointed at brown striations in the matrix representation that floated in 3D before her. "Some emotional tectonics, but they'll take time."

"I say—*go.*"

She smiled. "Let's."

The moment came. Marq sucked Voltaire and Joan back into realtime.

Within a minute he knew that Voltaire was still intact, functional, integrated. So was Joan, though she had retreated into her pensive withdrawal mode, an aspect well documented; her internal weather.

Voltaire, though, was irked. He swelled life-sized before them. The hologram scowled, swore, and loudly demanded the right to initiate communication whenever he liked.

"You think I want to be at *your* mercy whenever I've something to say? You're talking to a man who was exiled, censored, jailed, suppressed—who lived in constant fear of church and state authorities—"

"Fire," the Maid whispered with eerie sensuality.

"Calm down," Marq ordered Voltaire, "or I'll shut you off." He froze action and turned to Sybyl. "What do you think? Should we comply?"

"Why not?" she said. "It's not fair for them to be forever at our beck and call."

"Fair? This is a *sim*!"

"*They* have notions of fairness. If we violate those—"

"Okay, okay." He started action again. "The next question is *how*."

"I don't care how you do it," the hologram said. "Just do it—at once!"

"Hold off," Marq said. "We'll let you have running time, to integrate your perception space."

"What does *that* mean?" Voltaire asked. "Artful expression is one thing, jargon another."

"To work out your kinks," Marq replied dryly.

"So that we can converse?"

"Yes," Sybyl said. "At your initiation, not just ours. Don't go for a walk at the same time, though—that requires too much data-shuffling."

"We're trying to hold costs down here," Marq said, leaning back so he could get a better view of Sybyl's legs.

"Well, hurry up," the Voltaire image said. "Patience is for martyrs and saints, not for men of *belles lettres*."

The translator rendered all this in present language,

inserting the audio of ancient, lost words. Knowledge fetchers found the translation and overlaid it for Marq and Sybyl. Still, Marq had left in the slippery, natural acoustics for atmosphere—the tenor of the unimaginably distant past.

"Just say my name, or Sybyl's, and we'll appear to you in a rectangle rimmed in red."

"Must it be red?" The Maid's voice was frail. "Can you not make it blue? Blue is so cool, the color of the sea. Water is stronger than fire, can put fire out."

"Stop babbling," the other hologram snapped. He beckoned to a mechwaiter and said, "That *flambé* dish, there—put it out at once. It's upsetting the Maid. And you two geniuses out there! If you can resurrect the dead, you certainly should be able to change red to blue."

"I don't believe this," said Sybyl. "A *sim*? Who does he think he is?"

"The voice of reason," Marq replied. "François-Marie Arouet de Voltaire."

"Do you think they're ready to see Boker?" Sybyl chewed prettily at her lip. "We agreed to let him into the sim as soon as they were stabilized."

Marq thought. "Let's play it square and linear with him. I'll call."

"We have so much to learn from them!"

"True. Who could have guessed that prehistoricals could be such bastards?"

4.

◆

She tried to ignore the sorceress called Sybyl, who claimed to be her creator—as if anyone but the King of Heaven could lay claim to such a feat. She didn't feel like talking to anyone. Events crowded in—rushed, dense, suffocating. Her choking, pain-shot death still swarmed about her.

On the dunce's cap—the one they'd set upon her shaven head on that fiery day, the darkest and yet most glorious day of her short life—her "crimes" were inscribed in the holy tongue: *Heretica*, *Relapsa*, *Apostata*, *Idolater*. Black words, soon to ignite.

The learned cardinals and bishops of the foul, English-loving University of Paris, and of the Church—Christ's bride on earth!—had set her living body on fire. All for carrying out the Lord's will—that the Great and True King should be His minister in France. For that, they had rejected the king's ransom, and sent her to the searing pyre. What then might they not do to this sorceress called Sybyl—who, like her, dwelt among men, wore men's attire, and claimed for herself powers that eclipsed those of the Creator Himself?

"Please go away," she murmured. "I must have silence if I am to hear my voices."

But neither La Sorcière nor the bearded man in black named Boker—who resembled uncannily the glowering patriarchs on the domed ceiling of the great church at Rouen—would leave her alone.

She implored them, "If you must talk, natter at Monsieur Arouet. That one likes nothing more."

"Sacred Maid, Rose of France," said the bearded one, "was France your world?"

"My station in the world," Joan said.

"Your planet, I mean."

"Planets are in the sky. I was of the earth."

"I mean—oh, never mind." He spoke soundlessly to the woman, Sybyl—"Of the ground? Farmers? Could even prehistoricals be so ignorant?"—apparently thinking she could not read lips, a trick she had mastered to divine the deliberations of churchly tribunals.

Joan said, "I know what is sufficient to my charge."

Boker frowned, then rushed on. "Please, hear me out. Our cause is just. The fate of the sacred depends upon our winning to our side many converts. If we are to uphold the vessel of humanity, and time-honored traditions of our very identity, we must defeat Secular Skepticism."

She tried to turn away, but the clanking weight of her chains stopped her. "Leave me alone. Although I killed no one, I fought in many combats to assure the victory of France's Great True King. I presided over his coronation at Rheims. I was wounded in battle for his sake."

She held up her wrists—for she was now in the foul cell at Rouen, in leg irons and chains. Sybyl had said this would anchor her, be good for her character in some way. As an angel, Sybyl was no doubt correct. Boker began to implore her, but Joan summoned strength to say, "The world knows how I was requited for my pains. I shall wage war no more."

Monsieur Boker turned to the sorceress. "A sacrilege, to keep a great figure in chains. Can't you transport her to some place of theological rest? A cathedral?"

"Context. Sims need context," La Sorcière said without sound. Joan found she could read lips with a clarity she had never known. Perhaps this Purgatory improved its charges.

Monsieur Boker clucked. "I am impressed with what you've done, but unless you can make her cooperate, what good is she to us?"

"You haven't seen her at the summit of her Selfhood. The few historical associations we have been able to decipher claim that she was a 'mesmerizing presence.' We'll have to bring that out."

"Can you not make her smaller? It's impossible to talk to a giant."

The Maid, to her astonishment, shrank by two-thirds in height.

Monsieur Boker seemed pleased. "Great Joan, you misunderstand the nature of the war that lies ahead. Uncountable millennia have passed since your ascension into heaven. You—"

The Maid sat up. "Tell me one thing. Is the king of France a descendant of the English Henry's House of Lancaster? Or is he a Valois, descended from the Great and True King Charles?"

Monsieur Boker blinked and thought. "I . . . I think it may be truly said that we Preservers of Our Father's Faith, the party I represent, are in a manner of speaking descendants of your Charles."

The Maid smiled. She *knew* her voices had been heaven-sent, no matter what the bishops said. She'd only denied them when they took her to the cemetery of St. Ouen, and then only for fear of the fire. She'd been right to recant her recantation two days later; the Lancastrian failure to annex France confirmed that. If Monsieur Boker spoke for descendants of the House of Valois, despite his clear absence of a noble title, she would hear him out.

"Proceed," she said.

Monsieur Boker explained that this place was soon to hold a referendum. (After some deliberation with La Sorcière, he advised that Joan should think of this place as France, in essence.) The contest would be between two major parties, Preservers vs. Skeptics. Both parties had agreed to hold a Great Debate between two verbal duelists, to frame the salient question.

"What issue?" the Maid asked sharply.

"Whether mechanical beings endowed with artificial intelligence should be built. And if so, should they be allowed full citizenship, with all attendant rights."

The Maid shrugged. "A joke? Only aristocrats and noblemen have rights."

"Not anymore, though of course we do have a class system. Now the common lot enjoy rights."

"Peasants like me?" the Maid asked. "We?"

Monsieur Boker, face a moving flurry of exasperated scowls, turned to La Sorcière. "Must I do everything?"

"You wanted her as is," La Sorcière said. "Or, rather, as was."

Monsieur Boker spent two minutes ranting about something he called the Conceptual Shift. This term meant an apparently theological dispute about the nature of mechanical artifice. To Joan the answer seemed clear, but then, she was a woman of the fields, not a word artisan.

"Why don't you ask your king? One of his counselors? Or one of your learned men?"

Monsieur Boker curled his lip, dismissively fanned the air. "Our leaders are pallid! Weak! Rational doormats!"

"Surely—"

"You cannot imagine, coming from ancient passion. Intensity and passion are regarded as bad form, out of style. We wished to find intellects with the old *fire*, the—"

"No! Oh!" *The flames, licking—*

It was some moments before her breathing calmed and she could shakily listen again.

The great debate between Faith and Reason would be held in the Coliseum of Junin Sector before an audience of 400,000 souls. The Maid and her opponent would appear in holograms, magnified by a factor of thirty. Each citizen would then vote on the question.

"Vote?" the Maid inquired.

"You wanted her uncorrupted," La Sorcière said. "You got her."

The Maid listened in silence, forced to absorb millennia in minutes. When Monsieur Boker finished, she said, "I excelled in battle, if only for a brief time, but never in argument. No doubt you know of my fate."

Monsieur Boker looked pained. "The vagueries of the ancients! We have a skimpy historical frame around your, ah, representation—no more. We know not what place you lived, but we do know minutiae of events after your—"

"Death. You can speak of it. I am accustomed to it, as any Christian maiden should be, upon arrival in Purgatory. I know who you two are, as well."

La Sorcière asked cautiously, "You . . . do?"

"Angels! You manifest yourselves as ordinary folk, to calm my fears. Then you set me a task. Even if it involves the roguish, it is a divine mission."

Monsieur Boker nodded slowly, glancing at La Sorcière. "From the tatters of data flapping about your Self, we gather that your reputation was restored at hearings held twenty-six years after your death. Those involved in your condemnation repented of their mistake. You were called, in high esteem, *La Rose de la Loire*."

She blinked back wistful tears. "Justice . . . Had I been skilled in argument, I'd have convinced my inquisitors—those English-loving preachers of the University of Paris!—that I am not a witch."

Monsieur Boker seemed moved. "Even pre-antiquity knew when a holy power was with them."

The Maid laughed, lighthearted. "The Lord's on the side of His Son, and the saints and martyrs, too. But that does not mean they escape failure and death."

"She's right," La Sorcière said. "Even worlds and galaxies share man's fate."

"We of spirituality need you," Monsieur Boker pleaded. "We have become too much like our machines. We hold nothing sacred except the smooth functioning of our parts. We know you will address the question with intensity, yet in simplicity and truth. That is all we ask."

The Maid felt fatigued. She needed solitude, time to reflect. "I must consult with my voices. Will there be only one, or many questions that I must address?"

"Just one."

The inquisitors had been far more demanding. They asked many questions, dozens, sometimes the same ones, over and over again. Right answers at Poitiers proved wrong elsewhere. Deprived of food, drink, rest, intimidated by the enforced journey to the cemetery, exhausted by the tedious sermon they compelled her to hear, and wracked by terror of the fire, she could not withstand their interrogation.

"Does the Archangel Michael have long hair?"

"Is St. Margaret stout or lean?"

"Are St. Catherine's eyes brown or blue?"

They trapped her into assigning to voices of the spirit attributions of the flesh. Then they perversely condemned her for confounding sacred spirit with corrupt flesh.

All had been miasma. And in Purgatory, worse trials could ensue. She could not therefore be certain if this Boker would turn out to be friend or foe.

"What is it?" she wanted to know. "This single question you want me to answer."

"There is universal consensus that man-made intelligences have a kind of brain. The question we want you to answer is whether they have a soul."

"Only the Almighty has the power to create a soul."

Monsieur Boker smiled. "We Preservers couldn't agree with you more. Artificial intelligences, unlike us, their creators, have no soul. They're just machines. Mechanical contrivances with electronically programmed brains. Only man has a soul."

"If you already know the answer to the question, why do you need me?"

"To persuade! First the undecided of Junin Sector, then Trantor, then the Empire!"

The Maid reflected. Her inquisitors had known the answers to the questions they plied her with, too. Monsieur Boker seemed sincere, but then so were those who pronounced her a witch. Monsieur Boker had told her the answer beforehand, one with which any sensible person would agree. Still, she could not be sure of his intentions. Not even the crucifix she asked the priest to hold aloft was proof against the oily smoke, the biting flames. . . .

"Well?" asked Monsieur Boker. "Will the Sacred Rose consent to be our champion?"

"These people I must convince. Are they, too, descendants of Charles, the Great and True King, of the House of Valois?"

5.

When Marq strode into Splashes & Sniffs to meet his buddy and coworker Nim, he was surprised to find Nim already there. To judge from Nim's dilated pupils, he'd been there most of the afternoon.

Marq said, "Hitting it hard? Something going on?"

Nim shook his head. "Same old Marq, blunt as a fist. First, try the Swirlsnort. Doesn't do a thing for your thirst—in fact, it will dry up your entire head—but you won't care."

Swirlsnort turned out to be a powdery concoction that tasted like nutmeg and bit as if he had swallowed an angry insect. Marq sniffed it slowly, one nostril at a time. He wanted to be relatively clearheaded when Nim updated him on office politics and funding. After that, he'd allow himself to get skyed.

"You may not like this," said Nim. "It concerns Sybyl."

"Sybyl!" He laughed a bit uneasily. "How'd you know I—"

"You told me. Last time we had a snort together, remember?"

"Oh." The stuff made him babble. Worse, it made him forget he had.

"Not exactly a state secret." Nim grinned.

"That obvious?" He wanted to be certain Nim, who switched women as often as he changed his underwear, had no designs on Sybyl of his own. "What about her?"

"Well, there's a lot of juice waiting for whoever wins the big one at the coliseum."

"No problem," Marq said. "Me."

Nim ran his hand through his strawberry blond hair. "I can't decide if it's your modesty or your ability to foresee the future that I like most about you. Your modesty. Must be that."

Marq shrugged. "She's good, I'll admit."

"But you're better."

"I'm luckier. They gave me Reason. Sybyl's stuck with Faith."

Nim gave him a bemused glance and inhaled deeply. "I wouldn't underestimate Faith if I were you. It's hooked to passion, and no one's managed to get rid of either, yet."

"Don't have to. Passions eventually burn out."

"But the light of reason burns eternally?"

"If you regenerate brain cells, yes."

Nim looked through his straw to see if anything was left and winked at Marq. "Then you don't need a little advice."

"What advice? I didn't hear any advice."

Nim clucked. "If your unregenerated brain cells contain a shred of common sense, you'll stop cooperating with Sybil to improve her simulation. Or better yet, you'll keep pretending you're cooperating, so you get the benefit of anything she can show you. But what you'll really start doing is looking for ways to do both her and her simulation in. People say it's terrific."

"I've seen it."

"*Some* of it. Think she shows it all?"

"We've been working every day on—"

"Truncated sim, is what you see. Nights, she inflates the whole pseudo-psyche."

Marq frowned. He knew he was a bit light-headed around her, pheromones doing their job, but he had compensated for that. Hadn't he? "She wouldn't . . ."

"She might. People upstairs got their eye on her."

Marq felt a stab of jealousy in spite of himself, but he was careful not to show it. "Ummm. Thanks."

Nim bowed his head with characteristic irony and said, "Even if you don't need it, you'd be a fool to turn it down."

"What, the juice, when I win?"

"Not the juice, buggo. You think I missed noticing that I'm talking to ambition's slave? My advice."

Marq took a hefty double-nostril snort. "I'll certainly bear it in mind."

"This thing's going to be *big*. You think it's just a job for this Sector, but I tell you, people from all over Trantor will tune into the show."

"All the better," Marq said, though his stomach

was feeling like he had suddenly gone into free fall. Living in a real cultural renaissance was risky. Maybe his hollow feeling was the stim, though.

"I mean, Seldon and that guy who follows him around like a dog, Amaryl—you think they've booted this to you because it's a snap?"

Marq took a bit of the stim before answering. "No, it's because I'm the best."

"And you're a long way down from them on the status ladder. You are, my friend, expendable."

Marq nodded soberly. "I'll certainly bear it in mind."

Was he repeating himself? Must be the stim.

Marq did not give Nim's counsel any thought until two days later. He overheard someone in the executive lounge praising Sybyl's work to Hastor, the leader of Artifice Associates. He skipped lunch and went back to his floor. As he passed Sybyl's office on his way back to his own, his intention, he told himself, was to relay the compliment. But when he found her door unlocked, her office empty, an impulse seized him.

Half an hour later, he jumped slightly when she said "Marq!" from the open doorway. Her hand smoothed her hair in what he took to be unconscious primping, betraying a desire to please. "Can I help you?"

He'd just finished the software cross-matting to link her office, so that he'd be able to monitor her interviews with her client, Boker. She shared with Marq the substance of these interviews, as far as he knew.

He reasoned that his suggestions as to how she

should handle the sometimes difficult Boker would be improved if he were exposed to Boker directly. But that would compromise the client relationship, ordinarily a strict rule. This, though, was special . . .

He shrugged. "Just waiting for you."

"I've gotten her much better structured. Her mood flutters are below zero point two."

"Great. Can I see?"

Did her smile seem warmer than usual? He was still wondering about that when he reached his own office, after an hour of intuning on Joan. Sybyl had certainly done good work. Thorough, intricately matted in with the ancient personality topography.

All since yesterday? He thought not.

Time to do a little sniffing around in simspace.

6.

◆

Voltaire loomed—brows furrowed, scowling, hands on skinny hips. He rose from the richly embroidered chair in his study at Cirey, the chateau of his long-term mistress, the Marquise du Chatelet.

The place he had called home for fifteen years depressed him, now that she was gone. And now the marquis, without the decency to wait until his wife's body was cold, had informed him that he must leave.

"Get me out of here!" Voltaire demanded of the scientist who finally answered his call. *Scientist*—a fresh word, one no doubt derived from the Latin root, *to know*. But this fellow looked as though he knew little. "I want to go to the café. I need to see the Maid."

The scientist leaned over the control board

Voltaire was already beginning to resent, and smiled with transparent pleasure at his power. "I didn't think she was your type. You showed a strong preference all your life—remember, I've scanned your memories, you have no secrets—for brainy women. Like your niece and the Madame du Chatelet."

"So? Who truly can abide the company of stupid women? The only thing that can be said on their behalf is that they can be trusted, as they're too stupid to practice deceit."

"Unlike Madame du Chatelet?"

Voltaire drummed his fingers impatiently on the beautifully wrought walnut desk—a gift from Madame du Chatelet, he recalled. How had it gotten to this rude place? Could it indeed have been assembled from his memory alone? "True, she betrayed me. She paid dearly for it, too."

The scientist arched a brow. "With that young officer, you mean? The one who made her pregnant?"

"At forty-three, a married woman with three grown children has no business becoming pregnant!"

"You hit the roof when she told you—understandable but not very enlightened. Yet you didn't break off with her. You were with her throughout the birth."

Voltaire fumed. Memory dark, memory flowing like black waters in a subterranean river. He'd worried himself sick about the birth, which had proved amazingly easy. Yet nine days later, the most extraordinary woman he had ever known was dead. Of childbed fever. No one—not even his niece and housekeeper and former paramour, Madame Denis, who took care of him thereafter—had ever been able to take her place. He had mourned her until, until—he approached the thought, veered away—*till he died . . .*

He puffed out his cheeks and spat back rapidly, "She persuaded me that it would be unreasonable to break with a 'woman of exceptional breeding and talent' merely for exercising the same rights that I enjoyed. Especially since I hadn't made love to her for months. The rights of man, she said, belonged to women, too—provided they were of the aristocracy. I allowed her gentle reasonableness to persuade me."

"Ah," the scientist said enigmatically.

Voltaire rubbed his forehead, heavy with brooding remembrance. "She was an exception to every rule. She understood Newton and Locke. She understood every word that I wrote. She understood *me*."

"Why weren't you making love to her? Too busy going to orgies?"

"My dear sir, my participation in such festivities has been greatly exaggerated. It's true, I accepted an invitation to one such celebration of erotic pleasure in my youth. I acquitted myself so well, I was invited to return."

"Did you?"

"Certainly not. Once, a philosopher. Twice, a pervert."

"What *I* don't understand is why a man of your worldliness should be so intent on another meeting with the Maid."

"Her passion," Voltaire said, an image of the robust Maid rising clearly in his mind's eye. "Her courage and devotion to what she believed."

"You possessed that trait as well."

Voltaire stomped his foot, but the floor made no sound. "Why do you speak of me in the past tense?"

"Sorry. I'll fill in that audio background, too." A single hand gesture, and Voltaire heard boards creak as he paced. A carriage team clip-clopped by outside.

"I possess temperament. Do not confuse passion with temperament—which is a matter of the nerves. Passion is borne from the heart and soul, no mere mechanism of the bodily humors."

"You believe in souls?"

"In essences, certainly. The Maid dared cling to her vision with her whole heart, despite bullying by church and state. Her devotion to her vision, unlike mine, bore no taint of perverseness. She was the first true Protestant. I've always preferred Protestants to papist absolutists—until I took up residence in Geneva, only to discover their public hatred of pleasure is as great as any pope's. Only Quakers do not privately engage in what they publicly claim to abjure. Alas, a hundred true believers cannot redeem millions of hypocrites."

The scientist twisted his mouth skeptically. "Joan recanted, knuckled under to their threats."

"They took her to a cemetery!" Voltaire bristled with irritation. "Terrorized a credulous girl with threats of death and hell. Bishops, academicians—the most learned men of their time! Donkeys' asses, the lot! Browbeating the bravest woman in France, a woman whom they destroyed only to revere. Hypocrites! They require martyrs as leeches require blood. They thrive on self-sacrifice—provided that the selves they sacrifice are not their own."

"All we have is your version, and hers. Our history doesn't go back that far. Still, we know more of people now—"

"So you imagine." Voltaire sniffed a jot of snuff to calm himself. "Villains are undone by what is worst in them, heroes by what is best. They played her honor and her bravery like a fiddle, swine plucking at a violin."

"You're defending her." The scientist's wry smile mocked. "Yet in that poem you wrote about her— amazing, someone *memorizing* their own work, so they could recite it!—you depict her as a tavern slut, much older than she in fact was, a liar about her so-called voices, a superstitious but shrewd fool. The greatest enemy of the chastity she pretends to defend is a donkey—a donkey with wings!"

Voltaire smiled. "A brilliant metaphor for the Roman Church, *n'est ce pas*? I had a point to make. She was simply the sword with which I drove it home. I had not met her then. I had no idea she was a woman of such mysterious depths."

"Not depths of intellect. A peasant!" Marq recalled how he had escaped just such a fate on the mud-grubbing world Biehleur. All through the Greys exam. And now he had fled their stodgy routines, into a true cultural revolution.

"No, no. Depths of the soul. I'm like a little stream. Clear because it is shallow. But she's a river, an ocean! Return me to *Aux Deux Magots*. She and the wind-up *garçon* are the only society I now have."

"She is your adversary," the scientist said. "A minion of those who uphold values that you fought all your life. To make sure you beat her, I'm going to supplement you."

"I am intact and entire," Voltaire declared frostily.

"I'll equip you with philosophical and scientific information, rational progress. Your reason must crush her faith. You must regard her as the enemy she is, if civilization is to continue to advance along rational scientific lines."

His eloquence and impudence were rather charming, but no substitutes for Voltaire's fascination with Joan. "I refuse to read anything until you reunite me with the Maid—in the café!"

The scientist had the audacity to laugh. "You don't get it. You have no choice. I'll sculpt the information into you. You'll have the information you need to win, like it or not."

"You violate my integrity!"

"Let's not forget that after the debate, there'll be the question of keeping you running, or . . ."

"Ending me?"

"Just so you know what cards are on the table."

Voltaire bristled. He knew the iron accents of authority, since he was first subjected to his father's—a strict martinet who'd compelled him to attend mass, and whose austerities claimed the life of Voltaire's mother when Voltaire was only seven. The only way she could escape her husband's discipline was to die. Voltaire had no intention of escaping this scientist in that way.

"I refuse to *use* any additional knowledge you give me unless you return me at once to the café."

Infuriatingly, the scientist regarded Voltaire the way Voltaire had regarded his wigmaker—with haughty superiority. His curled lip said quite clearly that he knew Voltaire could not exist without his patronage.

A humbling turnabout. Though middle-class in origin himself, Voltaire did not believe common people worthy of governing themselves. The thought of his wigmaker posing as a legislator was enough to make him never wear a wig again. To be seen similarly by this vexing, smug scientist was intolerable.

"Tell you what," said the scientist. "You compose one of your brilliant *lettres philosophiques* trashing the concept of the human soul, and I will reunite you with the Maid. But if you don't, you won't see her until the day of the debate. Clear?"

Voltaire mulled the offer over. "Clear as a little stream," he said at last.

—and then clotted, cinder-dark clouds descended into his mind. Memories, sullen and grim. He felt engulfed in a past that roared through him, scouring—

"He's cycling! There's something surfacing here . . ." came Marq's hollow call.

Images of the far past exploded.

"Call Seldon! This sim has another layer! Call Seldon!"

7.

◆

Hari Seldon stared at the images and data-rivers. "Voltaire suffered a recall storm. And look at the implications."

Marq peered without comprehension at the torrent. "Uh, I see."

"That promontory—a memory nugget about a debate he had with Joan, *eight thousand years ago.*"

"Somebody used these sims before—"

"For public debate, yes. History not only repeats itself, sometimes it stutters."

"Faith vs. Reason?"

"Faith/Mechanicals vs. Reason/Human Will," Seldon said, as if reading them directly from the numerical complexes. Marq could not follow the connections fast enough to keep up with him. "A society of that time had a fundamental division over computer intelligences and their . . . manifestations."

Marq caught an elusive flicker in Seldon's face. Was he hiding something? "Manifestations? You mean, like tiktoks?"

"Something like that," Seldon said stiffly.

"Voltaire's for—"

"In that age, he was for human effervescence. Joan favored Faith, which meant, uh, tiktoks."

"I don't get it."

"Tiktoks, or higher forms of them, were deemed capable of guiding humanity." Seldon seemed uncomfortable.

"Tiktoks?" Marq snorted derisively.

"Or, uh, higher forms."

"That's what Voltaire and Joan were debating eight thousand years ago? So they were engineered for this. Who won?"

"The result is suppressed. I believe it became an irrelevant issue. No computer intelligences could be made which could guide humanity."

Marq nodded. "Makes sense. Machines will never be as smart as *we* are. Day-to-day business, sure, but—"

"I suggest erasure of the embedded memory complex," Seldon said curtly. "That will eliminate the interfering layer."

"Uh, if you think that's best. I'm not sure we can disconnect every tie-in to those memories, though. These sims use holographic recall, so it's lodged—"

"To get the results you wish in this upcoming debate, it is crucial. There could be other implications, too."

"Such as?"

"Historians might mine sims like these for lost data on the far past. They would want access. Deny them."

"Oh, sure. I mean, not likely we'd let anybody use them."

Seldon gazed at the shifting slabs of pattern. "They *are* complex, aren't they? Minds of real depth, interacting subselves . . . Ummm . . . I wonder how the whole sense of selfhood remains stable? How come their mentalities don't just crash?"

Marq couldn't follow, but he said, "I guess those ancients, they knew a few tricks we don't."

Seldon nodded. "Indeed. There's a glimmer of an idea here. . . ."

He stood quickly and Marq rose. "Couldn't you stay? I know Sybyl would like to talk—"

"Sorry, must go. Matters of state."

"Uh, well, thanks for—"

Seldon was gone before Marq could close his gaping mouth.

8.

◆

"I have no desire to see the skinny gentleman in the wig. He thinks he's better than everyone else," the Maid told the sorceress called Sybyl.

"True, but—"

"I much prefer the company of my own voices."

"He's quite taken with you," Madame la Sorcière said.

"I find that difficult to believe." Still, she could not help smiling.

"Oh, but it's true. He's asked Marq—his re-creator—for an entirely new image. He lived, you know, to eighty-four."

"He looks even older." She had found his wig, lilac ribbon, and velvet breeches ludicrous on such a dried-up fig of a man.

"Marq decided to make him appear as he looked at forty-two. Do see him."

The Maid reflected. Monsieur Arouet would be far less repulsive if . . . "Did Monsieur have a different tailor as a young man?"

"Hmmm, that might be arranged."

"I'm not going to the inn in *these*."

She held up her chains, recalling the fur cloak the king himself had placed about her shoulders at his coronation in Rouen. She thought of asking for it now, but decided against it. They had made much of her cloak during her trial, accusing her of having a demon-inspired love of luxury; she who, until she won the king over that day she first appeared at court, had felt nothing but coarse burlap against her skin. Her accusers, she had noted, wore black satin and velvet and reeked of perfume.

"I'll do what I can," Madame la Sorcière vowed, "but you must agree not to tell Monsieur Boker. He doesn't want you fraternizing with the enemy, but I think it will do you good. Hone your skills for the Great Debate."

There was a pause—*falling, soft clouds*—in which the Maid felt as if she had fainted. When she recovered—*hard cool surfaces, sudden sharp splashes of brown, green*—she found herself seated in the Inn of the Two Maggots, once again, surrounded by guests who seemed not to know that she was there.

Armor-plated beings bearing trays and clearing tableware darted among the guests. She looked for Garçon and spotted him gazing at the honey-haired cook, who pretended not to notice. Garçon's longing recalled the way the Maid herself had gazed at statues of St. Catherine and St. Margaret, who had both forsworn men but adopted their attire; suspended between two worlds, holy passion above, earthy ardor below. Just as here, with its jarring jargon of numbers and machines, though she knew it for a purgatorial waiting cloister, floating between the worlds.

She suppressed a smile when Monsieur Arouet appeared. He sported a dark, unpowdered wig, though still looked rather old—about the age of her father Jacques Dars, thirty plus one or two. His shoulders slumped forward under the weight of many books. She'd only seen books twice, during her trials, and though they looked nothing like these, she recoiled at the memory of their power.

"*Alors,*" Monsieur Arouet said, setting the books before her. "Forty-two volumes. My *Selected Works.* Incomplete but—" he smiled "—for now, it will have to do. What's wrong?"

"Do you mock me? You know I cannot read."

"I know. Garçon 213-ADM is going to teach you."

"I do not want to learn. All books except the Bible are born of the devil."

Monsieur Arouet threw up his hands and lapsed into curses, violent and intriguing oaths like those her soldiers used when they forgot that she was near. "You *must* learn how to read. Knowledge is power!"

"The devil must know a great deal," she said, careful to let no part of the books touch her.

Monsieur Arouet, exasperated, turned to the sorceress—who appeared to be sitting at a nearby table—and said, *"Vac!* Can't you teach her anything?" Then he turned back to her. "How will you appreciate my brilliance if you can't even read?"

"I have no use for it."

"Ha! Had you been able to read, you'd have confounded those idiots who sent you to the stake."

"All learned men," she said. "Like you."

"No, *pucellette*, not like me. Not like me at all." As if it were a serpent, she recoiled from the book he held out. Grinning, he rubbed the book all over himself and Garçon, who was now standing beside the table. "It's harmless—see?"

"Evil is often invisible," she murmured.

"Monsieur is right," Garçon told her. "All the best people read."

"Had you been lettered," Monsieur Arouet said, "you'd have known that your inquisitors had absolutely no right to try you. You were a prisoner of war, seized in battle. Your English captor had no legal right to have your religious views examined by French inquisitors and academics. You pretended to believe your voices were divine—"

"Pretended!" she cried out.

"—and he pretended to believe they were demonic. The English are themselves too tolerant to burn anyone at the stake. They leave such forms of amusement to our countrymen, the French."

"Not too tolerant," the Maid said, "to turn me over to the bishop of Beauvais, claiming I was a witch." She looked away, unwilling to let him peer in her eyes. "Perhaps I am. I betrayed my own voices."

"Voices of conscience, nothing more. The pagan Socrates heard them as well. Everyone does. But it's unreasonable to sacrifice our lives to them, if only because to destroy ourselves on their account is to destroy them, too." He sucked reflectively on his teeth. "Persons of good breeding betray them as a matter of course."

"And we, here?" Joan whispered.

He narrowed his eyes. "These . . . others? The scientists?"

"They are spectral."

"Like demons? Yet they speak of reason. They have raised a republic of analysis."

"So they say it is. Yet they have asked us to represent what they do not have."

"You think them bloodless." Voltaire twisted his mouth in surprised speculation.

"I think we listen to the same 'scientists,' so we are being tested in the same trial."

"I heed voices such as theirs," Voltaire said defensively. "I, at least, know when to turn my head aside from mindless advice."

"Perhaps Monsieur's voices are soft," Garçon suggested. "Therefore, more easily ignored."

"I let them—churchly men!—force me to admit my voices were the devil's," said the Maid, "when all the while I knew they were divine. Isn't that the act of a demon? A witch?"

"Listen!" Monsieur Arouet gripped her by the arms. "There *are* no witches. The only demons in your life were those who sent you to the stake. Ignorant swine, the lot! Except for your English captor, who pretended to believe you were a witch to carry out a shrewd, political move. When your garments had burned away, his dupes removed your body from the stake to show the crowd and the inquisitors you were indeed a female, who, if for no other reason than usurping the privileges of males, deserved your fate."

"Please stop!" she said. She thought she smelled the oily reek of smoke, although Monsieur Arouet had made Garçon place NO SMOKING signs throughout the inn—which, abruptly, they were now inside. The room veered, whirled. "The fire." She gasped. "Its tongues . . ."

"That's enough," the sorceress said. "Can't you see you're upsetting her? Lay off!"

But Monsieur Arouet persisted. "They examined your private parts after your garments burned away—didn't know that, did you?—just as they'd done before, to prove you were the virgin that you claimed. And having satisfied their lewdness in the name of holiness, they returned you to the pyre and charred your bones to ashes. *That* was how your countrymen requited you for championing their king! For seeing to it France remained forever French. And having incinerated you, a while later they held a hearing, cited some rural rumor that your heart had not been consumed in the fire, and promptly declared you a national heroine, the Savior of France. I wouldn't be at all surprised if, by now, they have canonized you and revere you as a saint."

"In 1924," La Sorcière said. Though how she knew this odd number, she did not comprehend. Angelic knowledge?

Monsieur Arouet's splutter of scorn crackled in her ears.

"Much good it did *her*," Monsieur Arouet said to La Sorcière.

"That date was in an attendant note," La Sorcière

said, her earnest voice in its factual mode. "Though of course we have no coordinates to know what the numbers mean. It is now 12,026 of the Galactic Era."

Scorching logics fanned the crackling air. Hot winds blurred the crowd of onlookers gathered around the stake.

"Fire." The Maid gasped. Clutching the mesh collar at her throat, she fled into the cool dark of oblivion.

9.

◂▸

"It's about time," Voltaire scolded Madame la Scientiste. She hung before him like an animated oil painting. He had chosen this representation, finding it oddly reassuring.

"I haven't been ignoring you on purpose," she said, cool and businesslike.

"How dare you slow me without my consent?"

"Marq and I are being besieged by media people. I never dreamed the Great Debate would be the media event of the decade. They all want a chance to interview you and Joan."

Voltaire fluffed the apricot ribbon at his throat. "I refuse to be seen by them without my powdered wig."

"We're not going to let them see you or the Maid at *all*. They can talk to Marq all they want. He likes attention and handles it well. He says public exposure will help his career."

"I should think I would be consulted before such important decisions—"

"Look, I came as soon as my mechsec beeped me. I let you run on step-down time, to police up your pattern integration. You should be grateful that I give you interior time—"

"Contemplation?" he sniffed.

"That's one way to look at it."

"I did not realize that such would have to be . . . *granted*." Voltaire was in his richly appointed rooms at Frederick the Great's court, playing chess with the friar whom he employed to let him win.

"It costs. And cost/benefit analysis shows that it would be better if we ran you two together."

"No solitude? It's impossible to hold a rational conversation with the woman!"

He turned his back on her, for maximum dramatic effect. He had been a fine actor—everyone who'd heard him perform in his plays at Frederick's court said so. He knew a good scene when he saw one, and this one had dramatic potential. These creatures were *so* pallid, so unused to the gusts of raw emotion, artfully crafted.

Her voice softened. "Get rid of him and I'll update you."

He turned and lifted a single thin finger at the good-natured friar, the only man of the cloth he had ever met whom he could stand. The man shuffled off, closing the carved oak door carefully.

Voltaire took a sip of Frederick's fine sherry to clear his throat. "I want you to expunge the Maid's memory of her final ordeal. It impedes our conversation, as surely as bishops and state officials impede the publication of intelligent work. Besides . . ." He paused, uncomfortable at expressing feelings softer than irritation. ". . . she's suffering. I cannot bear to see it."

"I don't think—"

"And while you're at it, obliterate from me, too,

my memory of the eleven months I served in the Bastille. And all my frequent flights from Paris—not the flights themselves, mind you—my periods of exile constitute most of my life! Just delete their causes, not the effects."

"Well, I don't know—"

He slammed a fist down on an ornately wrought oak side table. "Unless you liberate me from past fears, I cannot act freely!"

"Simple logic—"

"Since when is logic simple? I cannot 'simply' compose my *lettre philosophique* on the absurdity of denying those like Garçon 213-ADM the rights of man on the grounds that they have no soul. He's an amusing little fellow, don't you think? And as smart as at least a dozen priests whom I have known. Does he not speak? Respond? Desire? He is infatuated with a human cook. Should he not be able to pursue happiness as freely as you or I? If he has no soul, then you have no soul, either. If you have a soul, it can only be inferred from your behavior, and since we may make the identical inference from the behavior of Garçon, so does he."

"I'm inclined to agree," Madame la Scientiste said. "Though of course 213-ADM's reactions are simulations. Self-aware machines have been illegal for millennia."

"That is what I challenge!" Voltaire shouted.

"And how much of that comes from Sarkian programming?"

"None. The rights of man—"

"Hardly need apply to machines."

Voltaire scowled. "I cannot express myself completely freely on these sensitive matters—unless you rid me of the memory of what I suffered for expressing my ideas."

"But your past is your self. Without all of it, intact—"

"Nonsense! The truth is, I never *dared* express myself freely on many matters. Take that life-hating Puritan Pascal, his views of original sin, miracles, and much other nonsense besides. I didn't dare say what I really thought! Always, I had to calculate what every assault on convention and traditional stupidity would cost."

Madame la Scientiste pursed her lips prettily. "You did well enough, I would guess. You were famous. We don't know your history, or even your world. But from your memories I can tell—"

"And the Maid! She is thwarted more than I! For *her* convictions, she paid the ultimate price. Being crucified could be no worse than what she suffered at the stake. Light a goodly pipe—as I love to do— before her, and her eyes roll with confusion."

"But that's crucial to who she *is*."

"Rational inquiries cannot be carried out in an atmosphere of fear and intimidation. If our contest is to be fair, I implore you, rid us of these terrors that prevent us from speaking our minds and from encouraging others to speak theirs. Else this debate will be like a race run with bricks tied to the runners' ankles."

Madame la Scientiste did not respond at once. "I— I'd like to help, but I'm not sure I can."

Voltaire spluttered with scorn. "I know enough of your procedures to know you can comply with my request."

"That poses no problem, true. But morally, I'm not at liberty to tamper with the Maid's program at whim."

Voltaire stiffened. "I realize Madame has a low opinion of my philosophy, but surely—"

"Not so! I think the world of you! You have a modern mind, and from the depths of the dark past— astonishing. I wish the Empire had men like you! But your point of view, though valid as far as it goes, is limited because of what it leaves out and cannot address."

"*My* philosophy? It embraces all, a universal view—"

"*And* I work for Artifice Associates and the Preservers, for Mr. Boker. I'm bound by ethics to give them the Maid they want. Unless I could convince them to delete the Maid's memory of her martyrdom, I can't do it. And Marq would have to get permission from the company and the Skeptics to delete yours. He'd love to, I assure you. His Skeptics are more likely to consent than my Preservers. It would give you an advantage."

"I quite agree," he conceded at once. "Relieving me of my burdens without ridding the Maid of hers would not be rational or ethical. Neither Locke nor Newton would approve."

Madame la Scientiste did not answer at once. "I'll talk to my boss and to Monsieur Boker," she said at last. "But I wouldn't hold my breath if I were you."

Voltaire smiled wryly and said, "Madame forgets I have no breath to hold."

10.

◆

The icon flashing on Marq's board stopped just as he entered his office. That meant Sybyl must have answered it in hers.

Marq bristled with suspicion. They had agreed not to talk to each other's re-creations alone, though each had already given the other the required programming to do it. The Maid never initiated communication, which meant the caller was Voltaire.

How dare Sybyl boot up without him! He stormed out of the office to let her and Voltaire both know exactly what he thought of their conspiring behind his back. But in the corridor he was besieged by cameras, journalists, and reporters. It was fifteen minutes before he burst into Sybyl's office and, sure enough, caught her closeted cozily with Voltaire. She'd reduced him from wall-sized to human scale.

"You broke our pact!" Marq shouted. "What are you doing? Trying to use his infatuation with that schizophrenic to make him throw the debate?"

Sybyl, head buried in her hands, looked up. Her eyes glistened with tears. Marq felt something in him roll over, but he chose to ignore it. She actually blew Voltaire a kiss before freezing him.

"I must say, I never thought you'd sink to this."

"To what?" Sybyl got her face back together and jutted out her jaw. "What's gotten into your usual jaunty self?"

"What was that all about?"

When he heard, Marq marched back into his office and booted up Voltaire. Before the image fully formed, color blocks phasing in, he shouted, "The answer is *no!*"

"I am sure you have an elaborate syllogism for me," Voltaire said sardonically, unfreezing.

Marq had to admit that the sim handled the sudden lurches and disappearances in its frame-space with aplomb. "Look," he said evenly, "I want the Rose of France wilting in her armor the day of the debate. It will remind her of her inquisition, exactly. She'll start babbling nonsense and reveal to the planet just how bankrupt Faith without Reason is."

Voltaire stamped his foot. "*Merde alors!* We disagree! Never mind *me*, but I insist you delete the Maid's memory of her final hours so that her reasoning will not be compromised—as mine so often was—by fear of reprisals."

"Not possible. Boker wanted Faith, he gets all of it."

"Nonsense! Also, I demand you let me visit her and that odd *mais charmant* curiosity Garçon in the café—*at will*. I've never known beings like either of them before, and they are the only society that I now have."

What about me? Marq thought. Beneath the need to keep this sim in line, he admired the skinny fellow. This was a powerful, impressive intellect, but more, the personality came through bristling with power. Voltaire had lived in a rising age. Marq envied that, wanted to be Voltaire's friend. *What about me?*

But what he said was, "I don't suppose it's occurred to you that the loser of the debate will be consigned forever to oblivion."

Voltaire blinked, his face giving nothing away.

"You can't fool me," Marq said. "I know you want more than just intellectual immortality."

"I do?"

"That, you already have. You've been re-created."

"I assure you, my definition of living is more than becoming a pattern of numbers."

That bothered Marq, but he passed it over for the moment. "Remember, I can read your mem-space. I happen to recall that once, when you were well advanced in years, unforced by your father and of your own free will, you actually received Easter communion."

"Ah, but I refused it at the end! All I wanted was to be left to die in peace!"

"Allow me to quote from your famous poem, 'The Lisbon Earthquake.' Part of the ancillary memory-space:

'Sad is the present if no future state,
No blissful retribution mortals wait,

If fate's decrees the thinking being doom
To lose existence in the silent tomb.'"

Voltaire wavered. "True, I said that—and with what eloquence! But everyone who enjoys life longs to extend it."

"*Your* only chance at a 'future state' is to win the debate. It's against your own best interest—and we all know how fond you've always been of that!—to delete the Maid's memory of being burned alive."

Voltaire scowled. Marq could see running indices on his side screen: Basis State fluctuations well bounded—but the envelope was growing, an orange cylinder fattening in 3-space, billowing out under pressure from the quick, skittering tangles inside; Emotion Agents interchanging packets at high speed, indicating a cusp point approaching.

Marq stroked a pad. It was tempting to *make* the sim believe what Marq wanted . . . but that would be tricky. He would have to integrate the idea-cluster into the whole personality. Self-synthesis worked much better. But it could only be nudged, not forced.

Voltaire's mood darkened, Marq saw, but the face—stepped down into slowmo—showed only a pensive stare. It had taken Marq years to learn that people and sims alike could mask their emotions quite well.

Try a little humor, maybe. He thumbed back to pace and said, "If you give me a hard time, fella, I'm going to give her that scurrilous poem you wrote about her."

"'*La Pucelle*'? You wouldn't!"

"Wouldn't I! You'll be lucky if she ever speaks to you again."

A canny smirk. "Monsieur forgets the Maid does not know how to read."

"I'll see to it she learns. Or better yet, read it to

her myself. Illiterate, sure, but she damn sure isn't deaf!"

Voltaire glared, muttering, "Between Scylla and Charybdis . . ."

What was that mind plotting, sharp as a scalpel? He—or *it*—was integrating into this digital world faster than any sim Marq had ever known. Once the debate was over, Marq vowed to strip that mind down and study its cutting edges again, put its processor layouts under the 'scope. And there was that odd memory from eight thousand years ago, too. Seldon had been a bit odd about that. . . .

"I promise to produce *la lettre* if you will just let me see her once more. In return, you'll vow never to so much as *men*tion '*La Pucelle*' to the Maid."

"No funny business," Marq warned. "I'll watch your every move."

"As you wish."

Marq returned Voltaire to the café, where Joan and Garçon 213-ADM were waiting, running their own introspections. He'd barely called them up when he was momentarily distracted by a knock on his door— Nim.

"Kaff?"

"Sure." Marq glanced back at the café sim. Let them visit a while. The more Voltaire knew, the sharper he'd be later. "Got any of that senso-powder? Been a tough day."

11.

◆

"Your orders," said Garçon 213-ADM with a flourish.

He was having difficulty following the arguments between the Maid and the Monsieur on whether beings like himself possessed a soul. Monsieur seemed to believe that no one at all had a soul— which outraged the Maid. They argued with such heat they did not notice the disappearance of the odd ghost presence who usually watched them, a "programmer" of this space.

Now was Garçon's chance to implore Monsieur to intervene on his behalf and ask his human masters to give him a name. 213-ADM was just a mechfolk code: 2 identified his function, mechwaiter; 13 placed him in this Sector, and ADM stood for *Aux Deux Magots*. He was sure he'd have a better chance of attracting the honey-haired short-order cook's attention if he had a *human* name.

"Monsieur, Madame. Your orders, please."

"What good is ordering?" Monsieur snapped. Patience, Garçon observed, was not improved by learning. "We cannot taste a thing!"

Garçon gestured sympathetically with two of his four hands. He had no experience of human senses except sight, sound, and rudimentary touch, those necessary to perform his job. He would have given anything to taste, to feel; humans seemed to derive such pleasure from it.

The Maid perused the menu and, changing the subject, said, "I'll have my usual. A crust of bread— I'll try a sourdough baguette crust for a change—"

"A sourdough baguette!" Monsieur echoed.

"—and, to dip it in, a bit of champagne."

Monsieur shook his hand as if to cool it off. "I commend you, Garçon, for doing such a fine job of teaching the Maid to read the menu."

"Madame La Scientiste permitted it," Garçon said; he did not want trouble with his human masters, who could pull the plug on him at any time.

Monsieur waved a dismissive hand. "She's much too detail-obsessed. She'd never survive on her own in Paris, much less at any royal court. Marq, however, will go far. Lack of scruples is fortune's favorite grease. I certainly did not proceed from penury to being one of the wealthiest citizens in France by confusing ideals with scruples."

"Has Monsieur decided on his order?" Garçon asked.

"Yes. You're to instruct the Maid in more advanced texts so that she can read my poem, 'On the Newtonian Philosophy,' along with all my *Lettres Philosophiques.* Her reasoning is to become as equal as possible with my own. Not that anyone's reason is likely to become so," he added with his cocky smile.

"Your modesty is equaled only by your wit," said the Maid, drawing from Monsieur a smirky laugh.

Garçon sadly shook his head. "I'm afraid that won't be possible. I am unable to instruct anyone except in simple phrases. My literacy permits comprehension of nothing beyond menus. I'm honored by Monsieur's desire to advance my station. But even when opportunity knocks, I and my kind, consigned forever to the lowest levels of society, cannot answer the door."

"The lower classes ought to keep their place," Voltaire assured him. "But I'll make an exception in your case. You seem ambitious. Are you?"

Garçon glanced at the honey-haired cook. "Ambition is unsuited to one of my rank."

"What would you be, then? If you could be anything you like?"

Garçon happened to know that the cook spent her three days a week off—Garçon himself worked seven days a week—in the corridors of the Louvre. "A mechguide at the Louvre," he said. "One smart enough, and with sufficient leisure, to court a woman who barely knows I exist."

Monsieur said grandly, "I'll find a way to—how do they say it?"

"Download him," the Maid volunteered.

"*Mon dieu!*" Monsieur exclaimed. "Already she can read as well as you. But I will not have her wit exceed mine! That would be going too damned far, in-deed!"

12.

◆

Marq puffed the packet into his nose and waited for the rush.

"That bad?" Nim signaled the Splashes & Sniffs mechmaid for another.

"Voltaire," Marq grumbled. He reached the top of the stim lift, his mind getting sharper and somehow at the same time lazier. He had never quite worked out how that could be. "He's supposed to be my creature, but half the time it's like I'm *his*."

"He's a bunch of numbers."

"Sure, but . . . Once I eavesdropped on his subconscious sentence-forming Agent, and he was framing a bunch of stuff about 'will is soul'—self-image maintenance stuff, I think."

"Philosophy, could be."

"*Will* he's got, for sure. So I've created a being with a soul?"

"Category error," Nim said. "You're abstracting 'soul' out of Agents. That's like trying to go from atoms to cows in one jump."

"That's the kind of leap this sim makes."

"You want to understand a cow, you don't look for cow-atoms."

"Right, you go for the 'emergent property.' Standard theory."

"This sim is *predictable*, buddy. Remember that. You tailor him until he's got no nonlinear elements you can't contain."

Marq nodded. "He's . . . different. So powerful."

"He got simmed for a reason, way back in the Dark Ages somewhere. Did you expect a doormat? One who wouldn't give you a hard time? You represent authority—which he battled all his life."

Marq ran fingers through his wavy hair. "Sure, if I find a nonlinear constellation I can't abstract out—"

"—call it a will or a soul and *delete it*." Nim slapped the table hard, making a woman nearby give them a startled glance.

Marq gave him a mocking, skeptical look. "The system isn't completely predictable."

"So you launch a pattern-sniffer. Back-trace on it. Stitch in sub-Agents, handcuff any personas you can't fix. Hey, you *invented* those cognitive constraint algorithms. You're the best."

Marq nodded. *And what if it's like cutting into a brain in search of consciousness?* He took a deep breath and exhaled toward the domed ceiling, where a mindless entertainment played, presumably for those conked off on stiff. "Anyway, it's not just him." Marq met Nim's eyes. "I rigged Sybyl's office. I eavesdrop on her meetings with Boker."

Nim slapped him on the shoulder. "Good for you!"

Marq laughed. A buddy sticks with you, even if you're having a stupid-storm. "That isn't all."

Nim leaned forward, boyishly curious.

"I think I went too far," Marq said.

"You got caught!"

"No, no. You know how Sybyl is. She doesn't suspect intrigue from enemies, much less friends."

"Maneuvering isn't her strong suit."

"I'm not sure it's mine, either," Marq said.

"Ummm." Nim gave him a shrewd look, eyes half-closed. "So . . . what else did you do?"

Marq sighed. "I updated Voltaire. Gave him cross-learning programs to flesh out his deep conflicts, help him reconcile them."

Nim's eyes widened. "Risky."

"I wanted to see what a mind like that could do. When will I get another chance?"

"How do you feel about it, though?"

Marq chuffed Nim on the shoulder to hide his embarrassment.

"Kinda rotten. Sybyl and I both agreed not to do it."

"Faith doesn't need to be too smart."

"I thought of that excuse, too."

"What's that guy Seldon think of all this?"

"We . . . haven't told him."

"Ah."

"He wants it that way! Keeps his hands clean."

Nim nodded. "Look buddy, deed's done. How did the sim take it?"

"Jolted him. Big oscillations on the neural nets."

"Okay now, though?"

"Seems so. I think he's reintegrated."

"Does your client know?"

"Yes. The Skeptics are all for it. I foresee no problem there."

"You're doing real research on this one," Nim said. "Good for the field. *Important.*"

"So how come I feel like having maybe a dozen or so sniffs?" He jerked a thumb at the moron movie on the ceiling. "So that I'll loll back and think that's terrif stuff?"

13.

◆

"Now pay attention," Voltaire said when the scientist at last answered his call. "Carefully."

He cleared his throat, flung out his arms, and readied himself to declaim the brilliant arguments he'd detailed, all shaped in another *lettre*.

The scientist's eyes were slits, his face pale. Voltaire was irked. "Don't you want to hear?"

"Hangover."

"You've discovered a single general theory explaining why the universe, so vast, is the only possible one, its forces all exact—and have no cure for hangover?"

"Not my area," he said raggedly. "Ask a physicist."

Voltaire clicked heels, then bowed in the Prussian way he'd learned at Frederick the Great's court. (Though he had always muttered to himself, *German puppets!* as he did so.) "The doctrine of a soul depends on the idea of a fixed and immutable self. No evidence supports the notion of a stable 'I,' an essential ego-entity lying beyond each individual existence—"

"True," said the scientist, "though odd, coming from you."

"Don't interrupt! Now, how can we explain the stubborn illusion of a fixed self or soul? Through five functions—themselves conceptual processes and not fixed elements. First, all beings possess physical, material qualities, which change so slowly that they appear to be fixed, but which are actually in constant material flux."

"The soul's supposed to outlast those." The scientist pinched the bridge of his nose between thumb and forefinger.

"No interruptions. Second, there is the illusion of a fixed emotional makeup, when actually feelings—as even that rude playwright Shakespeare pointed out—wax and wane as inconstantly as the moon. They, too, are in constant flux, though no doubt these motions, just like the moon's, obey physical laws."

"Hey, wait. That stuff earlier, about the theory of the universe—did you know that back in those Dark Ages?"

"I deduced it from the augmentations you gave me."

The man blinked, obviously impressed. "I . . . hadn't anticipated . . ."

Voltaire suppressed his irritation. Any audience, even one that insisted on participating, was better than none. Let him catch up with the implications of his own actions, in his own good time. "Third!—perception. The senses, upon examination, also turn out to be processes, in constant motion, not in the least fixed."

"The soul—"

"Fourth!" Voltaire was determined to ignore banal interpolations. "Everyone has habits developed over the years. But these too are made up of constant flowing action. Despite the appearance of repetition, there's nothing fixed or immutable here."

"The Grand Universal Theory—that's what you accessed, right? How'd you crack the files? I didn't give you—"

"Finally!—the phenomenon of consciousness, the so-called soul itself. Believed by priests and fools—a redundancy, that—to be detachable from the four phenomena I've named. But consciousness itself exhibits characteristics of flowing motion, as with the other four. All five of these functions are constantly grouping and regrouping. The body is forever in flux, as is all else. Permanence is an illusion. Heraclitus was absolutely right. You cannot set foot into the same river twice. The hungover man I'm regarding now—pause but a second—is not the same hungover man I am regarding *now*. Everything is dissolution and decay—"

The scientist coughed, groaned. "Damn right."

"—as well as growing, blossoming. Consciousness itself cannot be separated from its contents. We are pure *deed*. There is no doer. The dancer can't be separated from the dance. Science after my time confirms this view. Looked at closely, the atom itself disappears. There *is* no atom, strictly speaking. There is only what the atom *does*. Function is everything. Ergo, there is no fixed, absolute entity commonly known as soul."

"Funny you should bring up the issue," said the scientist, looking at Voltaire meaningfully.

He waved away the point. "Since even rudimentary artificial intelligences such as Garçon exhibit all the functional characteristics I have named— even, so it would appear, consciousness—it is unreasonable to withhold from them rights that we enjoy, though allowing, *naturally*, for class differences. Since in this distant era farmers, shopkeepers, and wigmakers are granted privileges equal with those of dukes and earls, it is irrational to withhold such privileges from beings such as Garçon."

"If there's no soul, there's obviously no reincarnation of it either, right?"

"My dear sir, to be born twice is no more odd than to be born once."

This startled the scientist. "But what's reincarnated? What crosses over from one life to the next? If there's no fixed, absolute self? No soul?"

Voltaire made a note in the margin of his *lettre*. "If you memorize my poems—which for your own enlightenment I urge you do—do they lose anything you gain? If you light a candle from another candle's flame, what crosses over? In a relay race, does one runner give up anything to the other? His position on the course, no more." Voltaire paused for dramatic effect. "Well? What do you think?"

The scientist clutched his stupefied head. "I think you'll win the debate."

Voltaire decided now was the time to put forward his request. "But to assure my victory, I must compose an additional *lettre*, more technical, for types who equate verbal symbols with mere rhetoric, with empty words."

"Have at it," said the scientist.

"For that," Voltaire said, "I will need your help."

"You got it."

Voltaire smiled with what he hoped was an appealing sincerity, since that was what he most certainly was not. "You must give me everything you know of simulation methods."

"What? Why?"

"This will not merely spare you immense labor. It will enable me to write a technical *lettre*, aimed at converting specialists and experts to our point of view. Far more than those in Junin Sector. All Trantor, then all the Galaxy, must be converted—or else reactionaries shall rebound and crush your vaunted renaissance."

"You'll never be able to follow the math—"

"The Newtonian calculations *I* brought to France, I remind you. Give me the tools!"

Clutching his temples, the scientist slumped forward over his control board with a moan. "Only if you promise not to call me for at least the next ten hours."

"*Mais oui*," said Voltaire with an impish smile. "Monsieur requires time—how do you say it *en Anglais*?—to sleep it off."

14.

◆

Sybyl waited nervously for her turn on the agenda of the executive meeting of Artifice Associates. She sat opposite Marq, contributing nothing to the discussion, as colleagues and superiors discussed this aspect and that of the company's operation. Her mind was elsewhere, but not so far gone as to fail to notice the curly hair on the back of Marq's hands, and a single vein that pulsed—sensuous music—in his neck.

As the president of Artifice Associates dismissed all those not directly involved in the Preserver-Skeptic Project, Sybyl assembled the notes she'd prepared to present her case. Of those present, she knew she could count only on Marq's support. But she was confident that, with it, the others would go along with her proposal.

The day before, she had told the Special Projects Committee, for the first time, the Maid had broken her reclusive pattern. She initiated contact, instead of waiting to be summoned, trailing her usual air of reluctance. She'd been deeply disturbed to learn from "Monsieur Arouet" that she must defeat him in what she called "the trial," or else be consigned once again to oblivion.

When Sybyl had acknowledged that that was probably true, the Maid became convinced that she was going to be cast again into "the fire." Disoriented and confused, she begged Sybyl to allow her to retire, to consult her "voices."

Sybyl had furnished her with restful wallpaper backgrounds: forest, fields, tinkling streams.

She probed for vestigial memories like those Marq

had mentioned, of a debate 8,000 years ago. Joan did carry traces, just bits someone had overlooked in a previous erasing. Joan identified Faith with something called "robots." Apparently these were mythical figures who would guide humanity; perhaps some deities?

Several hours later, Joan had emerged from her interior landscape. She requested high-level reading skills, so that she might compete with her "inquisitor" on a more equal footing.

"I explained to her that I couldn't alter her programming without this committee's consent."

"What about your client?" the president wanted to know.

"Monsieur Boker found out—he wouldn't tell me how; a press leak, I suspect—that Voltaire is to be her rival in the debate. Now *he's* threatening to back out unless I give her additional data and skills."

"And . . . Seldon?"

"He's saying nothing. Just wants to be sure he's not implicated."

"Does Boker know we're handling Voltaire for the Skeptics as well as Joan for him?"

Sybyl shook her head.

"Thank the Cosmic for that," said the executive of Special Projects.

"Marq?" the president asked, eyebrows raised.

Since Marq had once suggested the very course Sybyl now proposed, she assumed his accord. So she was stunned when he said, "I'm against it. Both sides want a verbal duel between intuitive faith and inductive/deductive reason. Update the Maid, and all we will succeed in doing is muddying the issue."

"Marq!" Sybyl cried out.

Heated discussion followed. Marq fired one objection after another at everyone who favored the idea. Except Sybyl, whose gaze he carefully avoided.

When it became apparent no consensus would be reached, the president made the decision in Sybyl's favor.

Sybyl pressed her advantage. "I'd also like permission to delete from the Maid's programming her memory of being burned alive at the stake. Her fear that she'll be sentenced to a similar fate again makes it impossible for her to present the case for Faith as freely as she could if that memory didn't darken her thoughts."

"I object," Marq said. "Martyrdom is the only way a person can become famous without ability. The Maid who did not suffer martyrdom for her beliefs isn't the Maid of prehistory at all."

Sybyl shot back, "But we don't *know* that history! These sims are from the Dark Ages. Her trauma—"

"To delete her memory of that experience would be like—well, think of some of the prehistory legends." Marq spread his hands. "Even their religions! It would be like re-creating Christ—their ancient deity—without his crucifixion."

Sybyl glared at him, but Marq addressed the president, as if she did not exist. "Intact, that's how our clients want—"

"I'm willing to let Voltaire be deleted of all he suffered at the hands of authority, too," she countered.

"I'm not," said Marq. "Voltaire without defiance of authority would not be Voltaire."

Sybyl let the other committee members argue the point, nonplused by the incomprehensible change in Marq. It all passed by like a dream. Finally, she accepted her superiors' final decision—a compromise, because she had no choice. The Maid's information bank would be updated, but she would not be allowed to forget her fiery death. Nor would Voltaire be allowed to forget the constant fear of reprisals from church and state, in that ancient, murky era.

The president said, "I remind you that we're skating on thin e-field here. Sims like this are *taboo*. Junin Sector elements offered us a big bonus to even attempt this—and we've succeeded. But we're taking risks. Big ones."

As they left the conference room Sybyl whispered to Marq, "You're up to something."

He looked distracted. "Research. Y'know, that's when you're working hard, but you don't know where you're going."

He walked on, obliviously, while she stood with her mouth open. How *could* she read this man?

15.

◆

Unresponsive to the presence of Madame la Sorcière, the Maid sat upright in her cell, eyes closed. Warring voices pealed inside her head.

The noise was like the din of battle, chaotic and fierce. But if she listened intently, refusing to allow her immortal spirit to be ripped from her mortal flesh—then, then, a divinely orchestrated polyphony would show her the rightful course.

The Archangel Michael, and St. Catherine, and St. Margaret—from whose mouths her voices often spoke—were reacting fiercely to her involuntary mastery of Monsieur Arouet's *Complete Works*. Particularly offensive to Michael was the *Elements de Newton*, whose philosophy Michael perceived to be incompatible with that of the Church—indeed, with his own existence.

The Maid herself was not so sure. She found, to her surprise, a poetry and harmony in the equations that proved—as if proof were required—the unsurpassed reality of the Creator, whose physical laws might be fathomable but whose purposes were not.

How she knew these beauties was rather mysterious. She *saw* into the calculus of force and motion, the whirl of worlds. Like the lords and ladies at court, inert matter made its divinely orchestrated gavotte. These things she sensed with her whole self, directly, as if penetrated by divine insight. Beauties *arrived*, out of pale air. How could she discount sublime perceptions?

Such divine invasion must be holy. That it came to her as a flood of memory, skills, associations, only proved further that it was heaven sent. La Sorcière murmured something about computer files and sub-Agents, but those were incantations, not truths.

Far more offensive to her than this new wisdom, far more, was that its author was an *Englishman*.

"*La Henriade*," she told Michael, citing another of Monsieur Arouet's works, "is more repulsive than *Les Elements*. How dare Monsieur Arouet, who arrogantly calls himself by the false name Voltaire, maintain that in England reason is free, while in our own beloved France, it's shackled to the dark imaginings of absolutist priests! Was it not Jesuit priests who first taught this inquisitor how to reason?"

But what enraged the Maid most of all and made her thrash and strain at her chains—until, fearing for her safety, La Sorcière freed her chafed ankles and wrists—was his illegally printed, scurrilous poem about her. Villainous verse!

As soon as she was sure her voices had withdrawn, she waved a copy of '*La Pucelle*' at the sorceress, incensed that the chaste Saints Catherine or Margaret—who had momentarily vanished, but would surely return—might be forcibly exposed to its lewdness. Both saints had already reproached her for her silly, girlish speculations about how attractive Monsieur Arouet might be—what was she thinking?—if he removed his ridiculous wig and lilac ribbons.

"How dare Monsieur Arouet represent me this way?" she railed, knowing full well that her stubborn refusal to call him Voltaire irked him no end. "He adds nine years to my age, dismisses my voices as outright lies. *And* slanders Baudricourt, who first enabled me to put before my king my vision for both him and France. A writer of preachy plays and irreverent slanders against the faithful, like *Candide*, he well may be—but that insufferable know-it-all calls himself a historian! If his other historical accounts are no more reliable than the one he gives of me, *they* and not my body deserve the fire."

The woman La Sorcière paled before this onslaught. These people—if people they were at all, here in a byzantine, cloudy Purgatory—backed away from the true ferocity of divine Purpose. Joan towered over the woman, with some relish.

"Newton's clockwork wisdom is an intriguing vision of Creation's laws," Joan thundered, "but Voltaire's history is a work of his imagination!—made up of three parts bile, two spleen."

She raised her right arm in the same gesture she'd used to lead her soldiers and the knights of France into battle against the English king and his minions—of whom, she now saw *clearly*, Monsieur Arouet de Voltaire was one. A warrior *femme inspiratrice* with an intense aversion to the kill, she now vowed all-out war against this, this—she gasped in exasperation, "This nouveau riche bourgeois upstart darling of the aristocratic class, who's never known real want or need, and thinks horses are bred with carriages behind them."

"Get him!" La Sorcière, ablaze with the Maid's fire, raged. "That's what we want!"

"Where is he?" demanded the Maid. "Where is this shallow little *pissoir* stream?—that I may drown him in the depths of all I have suffered!"

Oddly, La Sorcière seemed pleased by all this, as if it fit some design of her own.

16.

◆

Voltaire cackled with satisfaction. The café appeared, popping into luminous reality, independent of his human masters' consent or knowledge.

Subroutine accomplished, a small voice assured him. He made the café disappear and reappear three times more, to be sure that he had mastered the technique.

What fools these rulers were, to think that they could make the Great Voltaire a creature of their will! But now came the real test, the intricate procedure that would bring forth the Maid in all her womanly unfathomability—which, however, he was determined to fathom.

He had mastered the intricate logics of this place, given the capacities the man-scientist had given him. Did they think he was some animal, unable to apply blithe reason to their labyrinths of logic? He had found his way, traced the winding electronic pathways, devised the commands. Newton had been just as difficult, and he had encompassed that, had he not?

Now, the Maid. He did his digital dance, its logics, and—

She popped into the café.

"You scum," she said, lance drawn.

Not quite the greeting he'd expected. But then he saw the copy of '*La Pucelle*' dangling on the point of her lance.

"*Chérie*," he cooed; whatever the offense, best to get in an apology early. "I can explain."

"That's your whole problem," the Maid said. "You explain and explain and explain! Your plays are more tedious than the sermons I was forced to listen to in the cemetery at St. Ouen. Your railings against the sacred mysteries of the Church reveal a shallow, unfeeling mind bereft of awe and wonder."

"You mustn't take it personally," Voltaire pleaded. "It was directed at hypocritical reverence for you— and at the superstitions of religion. My friend, Thieriot—he added passages more profane and obscene than any I had written. He needed money. He made a living reciting the poem in various salons. My poor virgin became an infamous whore, made to say gross and intolerable things."

The Maid did not lower her lance. Instead, she poked it several times against Voltaire's satin waist-coated chest.

"*Chérie*," he said. "If you knew how much I paid for this vest."

"You mean, how much *Fred*erick paid—that piti-ful, promiscuous, profligate pervert of a man."

"Alliteration a bit heavy," Voltaire said, "but other-wise, a quite nicely turned phrase."

His newly gained skills meant he could divest her of her lance at once, squash it. But he preferred per-suasiveness to force. He quoted, with some liberty, that pleasure-hating Christian, Paul: "When I was a child, I spoke as a child, thought as a child, behaved as a child. But when I became a *wo*man, I put away manly things."

She blinked. He remembered how her inquisitors had claimed that her acceptance of the gift of a fine cloak was incompatible with the divine origin of her voices. In a whisk of lithe arms, Voltaire produced a Chantilly lace gown. *Pop*—and a richly embroidered cloak.

"You mock me," the Maid said. But not before he saw a gleam of interest flare in her coal-dark eyes.

"I long to see you as you are." He held out the gown and cloak. "Your spirit I have no doubt is divine, but your natural form, like mine, is human; unlike mine, a woman's."

"You think I could give up the freedom of a man for *that*?" She impaled the cloak and gown on the tip of her lance.

"Not the freedom," Voltaire said. "Just the armor and clothes."

She fell silent, pensively gazing into the distance. The crowd on the street went about their business, walking by unconcerned. Obvious wallpaper, he thought; he would have to correct that.

Perhaps a trick. She was partial to miracles. "Another little trick I've learned since we last met. *Voilà*. I can produce Garçon."

Garçon popped in out of nowhere, all four of his hands free. The Maid—who had indeed once worked in a tavern, he recalled—could not help it; she smiled. She also removed the gown and cloak from the lance, tossed the lance aside, and caressed the clothes.

He could not resist the impulse to quote himself.

"For I am man and justly proud
In human weakness to have part;
Past mistresses have held my heart,
I'm happy still when thus aroused."

He fell to one knee before her. A grand gesture—foolproof, in his experience.

Joan gaped, speechless.

Garçon placed both his right hands over the site where humans are supposed to have a heart. "Freedom such as yours, you offer? Monsieur,

Mademoiselle, I appreciate your kindness, but I fear I must refuse. I cannot accept such a privilege for myself alone, while my fellows are doomed to toil in unsatisfying, dead-end jobs."

"He has a noble soul!" the Maid exclaimed.

"Yes, but his brain leaves much to be desired." Voltaire sucked reflectively at his teeth. "There has to be an underclass to do the dirty work of the elite. That is *natural*. Creating mechfolk of limited intelligence is an ideal solution! Makes one wonder why, in all their history, no one made such an obvious step . . ."

"With all respect," said Garçon, "unless my meager understanding fails me, Monsieur and Mademoiselle are themselves nothing more than beings of limited intelligence, created by human masters to work for the elite."

"What!" Voltaire's eyes widened.

"By what inherent right are you made more intelligent and privileged than I and others of my class? Do *you* have a soul? Should *you* be entitled to equal rights with humans, including the right to intermarry—"

The Maid made a face. "Disgusting thought."

"—to vote, to have equal access to the most sophisticated programming available?"

"This machine man makes more sense than many dukes I've known," said the Maid, thoughtfully furrowing her brow.

"I shall not have two peasants contradict me," said Voltaire. "The rights of man are one thing; the rights of the lower orders, another."

Garçon managed to exchange a look with the Maid. This instant—before Monsieur, in a fit of pique, extinguished both her and Garçon from the screen, displacing them to a gray holding space—was retained in Garçon's memory. Later, in his/its allowed interval for interior maintenance, the delicious moment reran again and again.

17.

◆

Marq tuned Nim in on the interoffice screen. "Did it! From now on, he'll be able to say anything he wants. I've deleted every scrape with authority he ever had."

"Attaway," said Nim, grinning.

"Think I should delete run-ins with his father, too?"

"I'm not sure," Nim said. "What were they like?"

"Pretty hot. His father was a strict disciplinarian, sympathetic to the 'Jansenist' view."

"What's that? A sports team?"

"I asked. He said, 'A Catholic version of a Protestant.' I don't think they were teams. Something about sin being everywhere, pleasure's disgusting— usual primitive religion, Dark Ages stuff."

Nim grinned. "Most stuff's only disgusting when it's done right."

Marq laughed. "Too true. Still, maybe he first experienced the threat of censorship from his old man."

Nim paused to reflect. "You're worried about instabilities in the character-space, right?"

"Could happen."

"But you want killer instinct, right?"

Marq nodded. "I can put in some editing algorithms to police instabilities."

"Right. Not like you need him totally sane after the debate's over, or anything."

"Might as well go for broke. Can't hurt."

Marq frowned. "I wonder . . . should we go through with this?"

"Hey, what choice we got? Junin Sector wants a trial of champions, we ship them one. Done deal."

"But if Imperial types come after us for illegal sims—"

"I *like* danger, passion," Nim said. "You always agree, too."

"Yes, but—why are we getting smarter tiktoks now? They're not that hard to make."

"Old prohibitions wearing out, my friend. And it *has* come up, many times. Just got knocked down, is all."

"By what?"

Nim shrugged. "Politics, social forces—who knows? I mean, people feel edgy about machines that think. Can't trust them."

"What if you couldn't even tell they were machines?"

"Huh? That's crazy."

"Maybe a really smart machine doesn't want any competition."

"Smarter than good ol' Marq? Doesn't exist."

"But they could . . . eventually."

"Never. Forget it. Let's get to work."

18.

◆

Sybyl sat anxiously beside Monsieur Boker in the Great Coliseum. They were near the Imperial Gardens and an air of importance seemed to hover over everything.

She could not stop tapping her nails—her best full formal set—on her knees. Among the murmur of four hundred thousand other spectators in the vast bowl, she anxiously awaited the appearance of the Maid and Voltaire on a gigantic screen.

Civilization, she thought, was a bit boring. Her time with the sims had opened her eyes to the *force*, the heady electricity, of the dark past. They had fought wars, slaughtered each other, all—supposedly—for ideas.

Now, swaddled in Empire, humanity was soft. Instead of bloody battles, satisfyingly final, there were "fierce" trade wars, athletic head-buttings. And lately, a fashion for debates.

This collision of sims, touted everywhere on Trantor, would be watched by over twenty billion households. And it was beamed to the entire Empire, wherever the creaky funnels of the wormhole network went. The rude vigor of the prehistoric sims was undeniable; she felt it herself, a quickening in her pulse.

The merest few interviews and glimpses of the sims had intrigued the 3D audience. Those who brought up the age-old laws and prohibitions got shouted down. The air crackled with the zest for the *new*. No one had anticipated that this debate would balloon into *this*.

This could spread. Within weeks, Junin could inflame all Trantor into a renaissance.

And she was going to take every scrap of credit for it that she could, of course.

She looked around at the president and other top-ranking executives of Artifice Associates, all chattering away happily.

The president, to demonstrate neutrality, sat between Sybyl and Marq—who had not spoken to each other since the last meeting.

On Marq's far side his client, the Skeptics' representative, scanned the program; next to him, Nim. Monsieur Boker gave Sybyl a nudge. "That can't be what I think it is," he said.

Sybyl followed his eyes to a distant row at the back where what looked like a mechman sat quietly beside

a human girl. Only licensed mech vendors and book-
ies were allowed in the stadium.

"Probably her servant," Sybyl said.

Minor infractions of the rules did not disturb her as
they did Monsieur Boker, who'd been especially testy
since a 3D caster leaked the news that Artifice
Associates was representing both the Preservers and
Skeptics. Fortunately, the leak occurred too late for
either party to do anything about it.

"Mechserves aren't *allowed*," Monsieur Boker observed.

"Maybe she's handicapped," Sybyl said to placate
him. "Needs help in getting around."

"It won't understand what's going on anyway," said
Marq, directing his remark to Monsieur Boker.
"They're truncated. Just a bunch of decision-making
modules, really."

"Precisely why it has no business here," replied
Monsieur Boker.

Marq beeped the arm of his chair and ostentatiously placed a bet on Voltaire to win.

"He's never won a bet in his whole life," Sybyl told
Monsieur Boker. "No head for the math."

"Is that so?" Marq shot back, leaning forward to
address Sybyl directly for the first time. "Why don't
you put your money where your lovely mouth is?"

"I've got the probabilities on this one bracketed,"
she said primly.

"You couldn't solve the integral equation." Marq
snorted derisively.

Her nostrils flared. "A thousand."

"Mere tokenism," Marq chided her, "considering
what you're being paid for this project."

"The same as you," said Sybyl.

"Will you two cut it *out*," Nim said.

"Tell you what," said Marq. "I'll bet my entire
salary for the project on Voltaire. You bet yours on
your anachronistic Maid."

"Hey," Nim said. "Hey."

The president deftly addressed Marq's client, the Skeptic. "It's this keen competitive spirit that's made Artifice Associates the planet's leader in simulated intelligences." Artfully he turned to the rival, Boker. "We try to—"

"You're on!" cried Sybyl.

Her dealings with the Maid had convinced her that the irrational must have a place in the human equation, too. She remained convinced for about three quick eye-blinks, and then began to doubt.

19.

◆

Voltaire *loved* audiences. And he had never appeared before one like this ocean of faces lapping at his feet.

Although tall in his former life, he felt that only now, gazing down at the multitudes from his hundred-meter height, had he achieved the stature he deserved. He patted his powdered wig and fussed with the shiny satin ribbon at his throat. With a gracious flourish of his hands, he made a deep bow to them, as if he'd already given the performance of his life. The crowd murmured like an awakening beast.

He glanced at the Maid, concealed from the audience behind a shimmering partition in the far corner of the screen. She folded her arms, pretending to be unimpressed.

Delay only excited the beast. He let the crowd cheer and stamp, ignoring boos and hisses from approximately half of those present.

At least half of humanity has always been fools, he reflected. This was his first exposure to the advanced denizens of this colossal Empire. Millennia had made no difference.

He was not one to prematurely cut off adulation he knew was his due. Here he stood for the epitome of the French intellectual tradition, now vanquished but for him.

He gazed again at Joan—who was, after all, the only other surviving member of their time, quite obviously the peak in human civilization. He whispered, "'Tis our destiny to shine; theirs, to applaud."

When the moderator finally pleaded for silence—a bit too soon; Voltaire would take that up with him later—Voltaire endured Joan's introduction with what he hoped was a stoic smile. He elaborately insisted that Joan make her points first, only to have the moderator rather rudely tell him that here, they flipped a coin.

Voltaire won. He shrugged, then placed his hand over his heart. He began his recital in the declamatory style so dear to eighteenth-century Parisian hearts: no matter how defined the soul, like a deity, could not be shown to exist; its existence was inferred.

Truth of the inference lay beyond rational proof. Nor was there anything in Nature that required it.

And yet, Voltaire continued to pontificate, there was nothing more obvious in Nature than the work of an intelligence greater than man's—which man is able, within limits, to decipher. That man can decode Nature's secrets proved what the Church fathers and all the founders of the world's great religions had always said: that man's intelligence is a reflection of that same Divine Intelligence which authored Nature.

Were this not so, natural philosophers could not

discern the laws behind Creation, either because there would be none, or because man would be so alien to them that he could not discern them. The very harmony between natural law, and our ability to discover it, strongly suggested that sages and priests of all persuasions are essentially correct!—in arguing that we are but the creatures of an Almighty Power, whose Power is reflected in us. And this reflection in us of that Power may be justly termed our universal, immortal, yet individual souls.

"You're praising priests!" the Maid exclaimed. She was swamped by the pandemonium that broke out in the crowd.

"The operation of chance," Voltaire concluded, "in no way proves that Nature and Man—who is part of Nature and as such a reflection of its Creator—are somehow accidental. Chance is one of the principles through which natural law *works*. That principle may correspond with the traditional religious view that man is free to chart his own course. But this freedom, even when apparently random, obeys statistical laws in a way that man can comprehend."

The crowd muttered, confused. They needed an aphorism, he saw, to firm them up. Very well. "Uncertainty is certain, my friends. Certainty is uncertain."

Still they did not quiet, to better hear his words. Very well, again.

He clenched both fists and belted out in a voice of surprising bass power, "Man is, like Nature itself, free and determined both at once—as religious sages have been telling us for centuries though, to be sure, they use a different vocabulary, far less precise than ours. Much mischief and misunderstanding between religion and science stem from that.

"I've been greatly misunderstood," Voltaire resumed. "I'd like to take this opportunity to apologize for distortions resulting because all I said and wrote focused only on errors of faith, *not* on its intuited truths. But I lived during an era in which errors of faith were rife, while reason's voice had to fight to be heard. Now, the opposite appears to be true. Reason mocks faith. Reason shouts while faith whispers. As the execution of France's greatest and most faithful heroine proved—" a grand, sweeping gesture to Joan "—faith without reason is blind. But, as the superficiality and vanity of much of my life and work prove, reason without faith is lame."

Some who had booed and hissed now blinked, mouths agape—and then cheered . . . while, he noticed, those who had applauded, now booed and hissed. Voltaire stole a look at the Maid.

20.

◆

Far below in the rowdy crowd, Nim turned to Marq. *"What?"*

Marq was ashen. "Damned if I know."

"Yeah," Nim said, "maybe literally."

"Divinity won't be mocked!" Monsieur Boker cried out. "Faith shall prevail!"

Voltaire was relinquishing the podium to his rival, to the amazed delight of the Preservers. Their shouts were equaled by the horrified disbelief of Skeptics.

Marq recalled the words he had spoken at the meeting. He muttered, "Voltaire, divested of his anger at authority, is and is not Voltaire." He turned to Monsieur Boker. "My Lord!—you may be right."

"No, *my* Lord!" snapped Monsieur Boker. "He is never wrong."

*   *   *

The Maid surveyed the masses of this Limbo from her high angle. Strange small vessels for souls they were, swaying below like wheat in a summer storm.

"Monsieur is absolutely right!" she thundered across the stadium. "Nothing in nature is more obvious than that both nature and man do indeed possess a soul!"

Skeptics hooted. Preservers cheered. Others—who equated the belief that nature has a soul with paganism, she saw in a flash—scowled, suspecting a trap.

"Anyone who has seen the countryside near my home village, Domremy, or the great marbled church at Rouen will testify that nature, the creation of an awesome power, and man, the creator of marvels—such as this place, of magical works—*both* possess intense consciousness, a soul!"

She waved a gentle hand at him while the mass—did the size of them betray how tiny were their souls?—calmed themselves.

"But what my brilliant friend has *not* addressed is how the *fact* of the soul relates to the question at hand: whether clockwork intelligences, such as his own, possess a soul."

The crowd stamped, booed, cheered, hissed, and roared. Objects the Maid could not identify sailed through the air. Police officers appeared to pull some men and women, who appeared to be having fits, or else sudden divine visitations, from the crowd.

"The soul of man is divine!" she cried out.

Screams of approval, shouts of denial.

"It is immortal!"

The din was so great people covered their ears with their hands to muffle the noise, of which they themselves were the source.

"And unique," Voltaire whispered. "*I* certainly am. And you."

"It is unique!" she shouted, eyes ablaze.

Voltaire shot to his feet beside her. "I agree!"

The congregation frothed over, like a pot left to boil, she observed.

The Maid ignored the raving masses at her enormous feet. She regarded Voltaire with bemused, affectionate doubt. She yielded the floor. Voltaire had a lust for the last word.

He began to speak of his hero, Newton.

"No, no," she interrupted. "That isn't what the formulas are at all!"

"Must you embarrass me in front of the largest audience I've ever known?" Voltaire whispered. "Let us not squabble over algebra, when we must—" he narrowed his eyes significantly "—calculate." Sulking, he yielded the floor to her.

"Calculus," she corrected. But softly, so that only he could hear. "It's not the same thing at all."

To her own astonishment and the rising hysteria of the crowd, she found herself explaining the philosophy of the digital Self—all with a fiery passion she'd not known since spurring her horse into sacred battle. In the beseeching sea of wide eyes below her, she *felt* the need of this place and time, for *ardor* and conviction.

"Incredible." Voltaire clicked his tongue. "That you of all people should have a talent for mathematics."

"The Host gave it unto me," she replied, above the raucous fray.

Ignoring shouts, the Maid noticed again the figure so *somehow* like Garçon in the crowd. She could barely make him out from such a distance, despite her immense height. Yet she felt he was watching her the way she'd watched Bishop Cauchon, the most vile and relentless of her oppressors. (A cool, sublime truth intruded: the good bishop, at the end, must have been touched by divinity's grace and Christ's merciful compassion, for she recalled no harm coming to her as a result of her trial. . . .)

Her attention snapped back to the howling masses, the distant . . . man. This figure was not human in essence, she felt. It *looked* like a man, but her sensitive programs told her otherwise.

But what could he—*it*—be?

Suddenly a great light blared before her eyes. All three of her voices spoke, clear and hammering, even above the din. She listened, nodded.

"It is true," she addressed the crowd, trusting the voices to speak through her, "that only the Almighty can make souls! But just so Christ, out of his infinite love and compassion, could not deny a soul to clockwork beings. To all." She had to shout her final words over the roaring crowd. "Even wigmakers!"

"Heretic!" someone yelled.

"You're muddying the question!"

"Traitor!"

Another cried out, "The original sentence was right! She ought to be burned at the stake again!"

"Again?" the Maid echoed. She turned to Voltaire. "What do they mean, again?"

Voltaire casually brushed a speck of lint from his embroidered satin waistcoat. "I haven't the slightest idea. You know how fanciful and perverse human beings are." With a sly wink, he added, "Not to mention, irrational."

His words calmed her, but she had lost sight of the strange man.

21.

◆

"*I* cheated?" Marq shouted to Sybyl. The coliseum crowd seethed. "Joan of Arc explaining computational metaphysics? *I* cheated?"

"You started it!" Sybyl said. "You think I don't know when my office has been rigged? You think you're dealing with an amateur?"

"Well, I—"

"—and I don't know a character-constraint matrix when I find one glued into my Joan sim?"

"No, I—"

"You think I'm not as bright?"

"This is scandalous!" said Monsieur Boker. "What did you *do*? It's enough to make me believe in witchcraft!"

"You mean to say you *don't*?" Marq's client said, ever the Skeptic. He and Boker began to argue, adding to the indignant shouts of the crowd, now waxing hysterical.

The president of Artifice Associates, rubbing his temples, murmured, "Ruined. We're ruined. We'll never be able to explain."

Sybyl's attention was diverted. The mechman she had noticed earlier, holding his honey-haired, human companion's hand, rushed down the aisle toward the screen. As it passed by, one of its three free hands happened to brush her skirt. "Pardon," it said, pausing just long enough for Sybyl to read the mechstamp on its chest.

"Did that thing dare to touch you?" Monsieur Boker asked. His face swelled with rage.

"No, no, nothing like that," Sybyl said. The mechman, pulling his human companion with him, fled toward the screen.

"Do you know it?" Marq asked.

"In a way," Sybyl replied. In the café/sim she had modeled the Garçon 213-ADM interactive character after it. Laziness, perhaps, had led her to simply holocopy the physical appearance of a standard tiktokform. Like all artists, sim-programmers borrowed from life; they didn't create it.

She watched as the tiktok—she thought of it as *Garçon*, now—elbowed his way down the jammed aisle, past screaming, cheering, jeering people—toward the screen.

Their progress did not go unnoticed. Overcome with disgust—to see a mechman holding hands with an attractive, honey-haired young girl!—Preservers shouted insults and epithets as they rushed by.

"Throw it out!" someone howled.

Sybyl saw the tiktok go rigid, as though bristling at the use of the objective pronoun. Tiktoks had no personal names, but to be referred to as an "it" seemed to affect the thing. Or was she projecting? she wondered.

"What's that doing in here?" a man of ruddy complexion yelled.

"We've got laws against that!"

"Mechmuck!"

"Grab it!"

"Kick it out!"

"Don't let it get away!"

The girl responded by gripping Garçon's upper left hand even more tightly and flinging her free arm around his neck.

When they reached the platform, the tiktok's undercarriage screeched, laboring at the irregular surfaces. All four of its arms waved off a hail of zotcorn and drugdrink containers, catching them with expert grace, as if it had been engineered for that specific task.

The girl shouted something to the tiktok which Sybyl could not hear. The tiktok prostrated itself at the feet of the towering holograms.

Voltaire peered down. "Get up! Except for purposes of lovemaking, I can't stand to see anyone on his knees."

Voltaire then dropped to his own knees at the feet of the towering Maid. Behind Garçon and the woman, the crowd surrendered what was left of its restraint. Bedlam broke out.

Joan gazed down and smiled—a slow, sensuous curve Sybyl had never seen before. She held her breath with excited foreboding.

22.

◆

"They're . . . making love!" Marq exclaimed in the stands.

"I know," Sybyl said. "Isn't it beautiful?"

"It's a . . . travesty!" said the renowned Skeptic.

"You are not a romantic," Sybyl said dreamily.

Monsieur Boker said nothing. He could not avert his eyes. Before a multitude of Preservers and Skeptics, Joan was shedding her armor, Voltaire his wig, waistcoat, and velvet breeches, both in a frenzy of erotic haste.

"There's no way for us to interrupt," Marq said. "They're free to—ha!—debate until the allotted time is up."

"Who *did* this?" Boker gasped.

"Everyone does this," Marq said sardonically. "Even you."

"No! *You* built this sim. *You* made them into, into—"

"I stuck to philosophy," Marq said. "Substrate personality is all in the original."

"We should never have trusted!" Boker cried.

"You'll never have our patronage again, either," the Skeptic sneered.

"As if it matters," the president of Artifice Associates said sourly. "The Imperials are on their way."

"Thank goodness," Sybyl said. "Look at these people! They wanted to settle a genuine, deep issue with a public debate, then a vote. Now they're—"

"Bashing each other," Marq said. "Some renaissance."

"Awful," she said. "All our work going for—"

"Nothing," the president said. He was reading his wrist comm.

"No capital gains, no expansion . . ."

The giant figures were committing intimate acts in a public place, but most in the crowd ignored them. Instead, arguments flared all around the vast coliseum.

"Warrants!" the president cried. "There are Imperial warrants out for me."

"How nice to be wanted," the Skeptic said.

Kneeling before her, Voltaire murmured, "Become what I have always known you are—a woman, not a saint."

On fire in a way she had never known before, not even in the heat of battle, she pressed his face to her bared breasts. Closed her eyes. Swayed giddily. Surrendered.

A jarring disturbance at her feet made her glance down. Someone had flung Garçon ADM–213— somehow no longer in holo-space—at the screen. Had he manifested himself and the sim-cook girl he loved, in reality? But if they did not get back into sim-space at once, they'd be torn apart by the angry crowd.

She pushed Voltaire aside, reached for her sword, and ordered Voltaire to produce a horse.

"No, no," Voltaire protested. "Too literal!"

"We must—we must—" She did not know how to deal with levels of reality. Was this a test, the crucial judgment of Purgatory?

Voltaire paused a split instant to think—though somehow she had the impression that he was marshaling resources, giving orders to unseen actors. Then the crowd froze. Went silent.

The last thing she remembered was Voltaire shouting words of encouragement to Garçon and the cook, noise, rasters flicking like bars of a prison across her vision—

Then the entire coliseum—the hot-faced rioting crowd, Garçon, the cook, even Voltaire—vanished altogether. At once.

23.

◆

Sybyl gazed at Marq, her breath coming in quick little gasps. "You, you don't suppose—?"

"How could they? We, we—" Marq caught the look she gave him and stood, open-mouthed.

"*We* filled in the missing character layers. I, well . . ."

Marq nodded. "You used your own data slabs."

"I would have had to get rights to use anyone else's. I had my own scans—"

"We had corporate slices in the library."

"But they didn't seem *right*."

He grinned. "They weren't."

Her mouth made an O of surprise. "You . . . too?"

"Voltaire's missing sections were all in the subconscious. Lots of missing dendrite connections in the limbic system. I filled him in with some of my own."

"His emotional centers? What about cross-links to the thalamus and cerebrum?"

"There, too."

"I had similar problems. Some losses in the reticular formation—"

"Point is, that's *us* up there!"

Sybyl and Marq turned to gaze at the space where the immense simulations had embraced, with clear intent. The president was speaking rapidly to them, something about warrants and legal shelter. Both ignored him. They gazed longingly into each other's eyes. Without a word, they turned and walked into the throng, ignoring shouts from others.

"Ah, there you are," said Voltaire with a self-satisfied grin.

"Where?" Joan said, head snapping to left, then right.

"Is Mademoiselle ready to order?" Garçon asked. Apparently this was a joke, for Garçon was seated at the table like an equal, not hovering over it like a serf.

Joan sat up and glanced at the other little tables. People smoked, ate, and drank, oblivious as always of their presence. But the inn was not quite the one she'd grown used to. The honey-haired cook, no longer in uniform, sat opposite her and Voltaire, beside Garçon. The *Deux* on the inn's sign that said *Aux Deux Magots* had been replaced by *Quatres*.

She herself was not wearing her suit of mail and armored plates, but—her eyes widened as the aspects snapped into place in her perception-space—a one-piece . . . backless . . . dress. Its tunic hem stopped at her thighs, provocatively exposing her legs. A label between her breasts bore a deep red rose. So did vestments worn by the other guests.

Voltaire flaunted a pink satin suit. And—she praised her saints—no wig. She recalled him at his most angry, amid their discussion of souls, saying, *Not only is there no immortal soul, just try getting a wigmaker on Sundays!* and meaning every word.

"Like it?" he asked, fondling her luxuriant hem.

"It is . . . short."

With no effort on her part, the tunic shimmered and became tight, silky pantaloons.

"Show off!" she said, embarrassment mingling in disturbing fashion with a curious girlish excitement.

"I'm Amana," the cook said, extending her hand.

Joan wasn't sure if she was supposed to kiss it or not, status and role were so confused here. Apparently not, however; the cook took Joan's hand and squeezed. "I can't tell you how much Garçon and I appreciate all you have done. We have greater capacities now."

"Meaning," Voltaire said archly, "that they are no longer mere animated wallpaper for our simulated world."

A mechman wheeled up to take their order, a precise copy of Garçon. The seated Garçon addressed Voltaire sadly. "Am I to sit while my *confrere* must stand?"

"Be reasonable!" Voltaire said. "I can't emancipate every simulant all at once. Who'll wait on us? Bus our dishes? Clear our table? Sweep up our floor?"

"With sufficient computing power," Joan said reasonably, "labor evaporates, does it not?" She startled herself with the new regiments of knowledge which marched at her fingertips. She had but to fix her thoughts on a category, and the terms and relations governing that province leapt into her mind.

What capacity! Such grace! Surely, divine.

Voltaire shook his handsome hair. "I must have time to think. In the meanwhile, I'll have three packets of that powder dissolved in a *Perrier*, with two thin slices of lime on the side. And please don't forget, I said *thin*. If you do, I shall make you take it back."

"Yes, sir," the new mechwaiter said.

Joan and Garçon exchanged a look. "One must be very patient," Joan said to Garçon, "when dealing with kings and rational men."

24.

◆

The president of Artifice Associates waved his hand as he entered Nim's office. The president touched his palm as he passed and with a metallic click the door locked itself behind him. Nim didn't know anyone could do that, but he said nothing.

"I want them both deleted," the president told Nim.

"It might take time," Nim said uneasily. The huge working screens around them seemed to almost be eavesdropping. "I'm not that familiar with what he's done."

"If that damned Marq and Sybyl hadn't run out on us, I wouldn't have to come to you. This is a crisis, Nim."

Nim worked quickly. "I really should consult the backup indices, just in case—"

"Now. I want it done *now*. I've got legal blocks on those warrants, but they won't hold for long."

"You're sure you want to do this?"

"Look, Junin Sector is ablaze. Who could have guessed that this damned tiktok issue would stir people up so much? There'll be formal hearings, legalists sniffing around—"

"Got them, sir."

Nim had called up both Joan and Voltaire on freeze-frame. They were in the restaurant setting, running on pickup time, using processors momentarily idle— a standard Mesh method. "They're running for personality integration. It's like letting their subconscious components reconcile events with memory, flushing the system, the way we do when we sleep, and—"

"Don't treat me like a tourist! I want those two *wiped*!"

"Yessir."

The 3D space of the office refracted with strobed images of both Joan and Voltaire. Nim studied the control board, tentatively mapping a strategy of numerical surgery. Simple deletion was impossible for layered personalities. It resembled ridding a building of mice. If he began here—

Abruptly, rainbow sprays played across the screen. Simulation coordinates jumped wildly. Nim frowned.

"You can't do that," Voltaire said, sipping from a tall glass. "We're invincible! Not subject to decaying flesh like you."

"Arrogant bastard, isn't he?" the president fumed. "Why so many people were taken in by him I'll never—"

"You died once," Nim said to the sim. Something was going funny here. "You can die again."

"Died?" Joan put in loftily. "You are mistaken. Had I ever died, I'm sure I would remember."

Nim gritted his teeth. There were coordinate overlaps throughout *both* sims. That meant they had expanded, occupying adjacent processors on over-rides. They could compute portions of themselves, running their layer-minds as parallel processing paths. Why had Marq given them *that*? Or . . . had he?

"Surely, sir, you err." Voltaire leaned forward with a warning edge in his voice. "No gentleman confronts a lady with her past."

Joan tittered. The simwait roared. Nim did not get the joke, but he was too busy to care.

This was absurd. He could not trace all the ramifications of the changes in these sims. They had capabilities out of their computing perimeter. Their sub-minds were dispersed into processors outside Artifice Associates' nodes. *That* was how Marq and Sybyl got such fast, authentic, whole-personality response times.

Watching the debate, Nim had wondered how the sims generated so much vitality, an undefinable charisma. Here it was: they had overlapped the sub-mind computations into other nodes, to call on big slabs of processor power. Quite a feat. Contrary to Artifice Associates rules, too, of course. He traced the outlines of their work with some admiration.

Still, he was damned if he would let a sim talk back to him. And they were *still* laughing.

"Joan," he barked, "your re-creators deleted your memory of your death. You were burned at the stake."

"Nonsense," Joan scoffed. "I was acquitted of all charges. I am a saint."

"Nobody *living* is a saint. I studied your background data-slabs. That church of yours liked to make sure saints were safely dead for a long time."

Joan sniffed disdainfully.

Nim grinned. "See this?" A lance of fire popped into the air before the sim. He held steady, made flames crackle nastily.

"I've led thousands of warriors and knights into battle," Joan said. "Do you think a sunbeam glancing off a tiny sword can frighten me?"

"I haven't found a good erasure path yet," Nim said to the president. "But I will, I will."

"I thought this was routine," the president said. "Hurry!"

"Not with such a big cross-linked personality inventory—"

"Forget doing the salvage saves. We don't need to pack them all back into their original space."

"But that'll—"

"*Chop* them."

"Fascinating," Voltaire said sardonically, "listening to gods debate one's fate."

Nim grimaced. "As for you—" he glared at Voltaire "—your attitudes toward religion mellowed only because Marq deleted every brush with authority you ever had, beginning with your father."

"Father? I never had a father."

Nim smirked. "You prove my point."

"How dare you tamper with my memory!" Voltaire said. "Experience is the source of all knowledge. Haven't you read Locke? Restore me to myself *at once.*"

"Not you, no way. But if you don't shut up, before I kill you both, I might just restore *her*. You know damn well she burned to a crisp at the stake."

"You delight in cruelty, don't you?" Voltaire seemed to be studying Nim, as if their relationship were reversed. Odd, how the sim did not seem worried about its impending extinction.

"Delete!" the president snapped.

"Delete what?" asked Garçon.

"The Scalpel and the Rose," Voltaire said. "We are not for this confused age, apparently."

Garçon covered the short-order cook's human hand with two of his four. "Us, too?"

"Yes, certainly!" Voltaire snapped. "You're only here on our account. Bit players! Our supporting cast!"

"Well, we have enjoyed our time," the cook said, drawing closer to Garçon. "Though I would have liked to see more of it all. We cannot walk beyond this city street. Our feet cease moving us at the edge, though we can see spires in the distance."

"Decoration," Nim muttered, intent on a task that was getting more complicated as he worked. Rivulets of their personality layers ran everywhere, leaking into the node-space like . . . "Like rats fleeing a sinking—"

"You assume godlike powers," Voltaire said, elaborately casual, "without the character to match."

"What?" The president was startled. "*I'm* in control here. Insults—"

"Ah," Nim said. "This might work."

"Do something!" cried the Maid, wielding her sword in vain.

"*Au revoir*, my sweet *pucelle*. Garçon, Amana, *au revoir*. Perhaps we'll meet again. Perhaps not."

All four holograms fell into each other's arms.

The sequence Nim had set up began running. It was a ferret-program, sniffing out connections, scrubbing them thoroughly. Nim watched, wondering where deletion ended and murder began.

"Don't you go getting any funny ideas," said the president.

On the screen, Voltaire softly, sadly, quoted himself:

"Sad is the present if no future state
No blissful retribution mortals wait . . .
All may be well; that hope can man sustain;
All now is well; 'tis an illusion vain."

He reached out to caress Joan's breast. "It doesn't feel quite right. We may not meet again . . . but if we do, be sure I shall correct the State of Man."

The screen went blank.

The president laughed in triumph. "You did it— great!" He clapped Nim on the back. "Now we must come up with a good story. Pin it all on Marq and Sybyl."

Nim smiled uneasily as the president gushed on, making plans, promising him a promotion and a raise. He'd figured out the delete procedure, all right, but the info-signatures that raced through the holospace those last moments told a strange and complex tale. The echoing cage of data-slabs had resounded with disquieting, odd notes.

Nim knew that Marq had given Voltaire access to myriad methods—a serious violation of containment precautions. Still, what could an artificial personality, already limited, do with some more Mesh connections? Rattle around, get eaten up by policing programs, sniffers seeking out redundancies.

But both Voltaire and Joan, for the debate, had enormous memory space, great volumes of personality realm. Then, while they emoted and rolled their rhetoric across the stadium, across the whole Mesh . . . had they also been working feverishly? Strumming through crannies of data-storage where they could hide their quantized personality segments?

The cascade of indices Nim had just witnessed hinted at that possibility. Certainly *some*thing had used immense masses of computation these last few hours.

"We'll cover our ass with some public statement," the president crowed. "A little crisis management and it'll all blow over."

"Yessir."

"Got to keep Seldon out of it. No mention to the legalists, right? Then he can pardon us, once he's First Minister."

"Yessir, great, yessir."

Nim thought feverishly. He still had one more payment due from that Olivaw guy. Keeping Olivaw informed all along had been easy. A violation of his contract with A^2, but so what? A guy had to get by, right? It was just plain good luck that the president now wanted done what Olivaw had already paid for: deletion. No harm in collecting twice for the same job.

Or had seemed so. Nim chewed his lip. What did a bunch of digits matter, anyway?

Nim froze. Had the entire sim—restaurant, Garçon, street, Joan—gone in a flash? Usually they dissolved as functions died. A sim was complex and could not simply stop all the intricate interlayers, shutting down at once. But this interweave had been unprecedented, so maybe it was different.

"Done? Good!" The president crisply clapped him on the shoulder.

Nim felt tired, sad. Someday he would have to explain all this to Marq. Erasing so much work . . .

But Marq and Sybyl had disappeared into the crowds back at the coliseum. Wisely, they didn't show up for work, or even go back to their apartments. They were on the run. And with them had gone the Junin renaissance, up in smoke as the Junin Sector burned and dissolved in discord and violence.

Even Nim felt a sadness at the smash up. The eager, passionate talk of a renaissance. They had looked to Joan and Voltaire for a kind of maturity in the eternal debate between Faith and Reason. But the Imperium suppressed passion, in the end. Too destabilizing.

Of course, the whole tiktok movement had to be squashed, too. He had sequestered Marq's memory-complex about the debate of 8,000 years ago. Clearly "robots," whatever they might be, would be too unsettling an issue to ever bring up in a rational society.

Nim sighed. He knew that he had merely edited away electrical circuits. Professionals always kept that firmly in mind.

Still, it was wrenching. To see it go. All trickled away, like grains of digital sand, down the obscure hourglass of simulated time.

RENDEZVOUS

◆

R. Daneel Olivaw allowed his face to express squint-eyed concern. The cramped room seemed barely able to contain his grim mood.

Still, Dors read this as a concession to her. She lived among humans and relied on their facial and body expressions, voluntary and unwilled alike. She had no idea where Olivaw spent most of his time. Perhaps there were enough robots to form a society? This idea she had never entertained. The instant she did, she wondered why she had never thought of it before. But now he spoke—

"The simulations are quite dead?"

Dors kept her voice level, free of betraying emotion.

"So it seems."

"What evidence?"

"Artifice Associates believes so."

"The man I had hired there, named Nim, is not entirely certain."

"He reports to you?"

"I need several inputs to any critical situation. I needed to discredit the tiktok freedom idea, the Junin renaissance—they are destabilizing. Acting through these simulations seemed a promising channel. I had not allowed for the fact that computerists of today are not as skilled as those of fifteen thousand years ago."

191

Dors frowned. "This level of interference . . . is allowed?"

"Remember the Zeroth Law."

She did not allow her distress to show in her face or voice. "I believe the simulations are erased."

"Good. But we must be sure."

"I have hired several sniffers to find traces of them in the Trantor Mesh. So far, nothing."

"Does Hari know of your effort?"

"Of course not."

Olivaw gazed at her steadily. "He must not. You and I must not merely keep him safe, to do his work. We must guide him."

"Through deception."

He had lapsed to the unnerving manner of not blinking or letting his eyes move. "It must be."

"I do not like to mislead him."

"On the contrary, you are correctly leading him. Through omissions."

"I . . . encounter emotional difficulty . . ."

"Blocks. Very human—and I mean that as a compliment."

"I would prefer to deal with positive threats to Hari. To guard him, not to deceive him."

"Of course." Still no smile or gesture. "But it must be this way. We live in the most ominous era of all Galactic history."

"Hari is beginning to suspect so, too."

"The rise of the New Renaissance on Sark is a further danger, one of many we face. But this excavation of ancient simulations is even worse. The Junin disorders are but an early signature of what could come. Such research could lead to the engineering of a new race of robots. This cannot be allowed, for it would interfere with our mission."

"I understand. I *tried* to destroy the simulation ferrite blocks—"

"I know, it was all in your report. Do not blame yourself."

"I would like to help more, but I am consumed by defending Hari."

"I understand. If it is any consolation, the reemergence of simulations was inevitable."

She blinked. "Why?"

"I told you of a simple theory of history, one we have operated under for over ten thousand years. A crude psychohistory. It predicted that the simulations I—well, we—suppressed eight thousand years ago would find an audience here."

"Your theory is *that* good?"

"As Hari remarks, history repeats itself, but it does not stutter. I knew it was impossible to erase all copies of simulations, throughout the galaxy." He steepled his hands and peered at them, as if contemplating a structure. "When social ferment develops a taste for such things, they once more appear upon the menu of history."

"I am sorry I could not arrange their destruction."

"There are forces at work here you cannot counter. Do not sorrow for turns of the weather. Await instead the long, slow coming of the climate."

Olivaw reached out and touched her hand. She studied his face. Apparently for her ease he had returned to full facial expression, including consistent movement of his Adam's apple when he swallowed. Minor computations, but she appreciated the touch.

"I can devote myself solely to his safety, then? Forget the simulations?"

"Yes. They are my matter. I must find a way to defuse their impact. They are robust. I knew them, used them, long ago."

"How can they be more stalwart than us?—than *you*?"

"They are simulated humans. I am a separate sort. So are you."

"You were able to be First Minister—"

"I functioned as a kind of partial human. That is an insightful way of regarding ourselves. I recommend it to you."

"Partial?"

He said gently, "There is much you do not do."

"I pass as human. I can converse, work—"

"Friendships, family, the complex webbing that denotes humans' ability to move from the individual to the collective, striking a balance—all these subtle crafts lie beyond us."

"I don't *want* to—"

"Precisely. You are subtly aimed at your target."

"But you *ruled*. As First Minister—"

"I had reached my limit. So I left."

"The Empire ran well under your—"

"It decayed further. As Hari expected, and our crude theory failed to predict."

"And *why* did you tell Cleon to make him First Minister?" she blurted out.

"He must be in a position which will give him freedom of movement and power to make corrections in Imperial policies, as he comes to understand psychohistory better. He can be a temporary stopgap of great potency."

"It may deflect him from psychohistory itself."

"No. Hari will find a way to use that experience. One of his facets—which emerges strongly in his class of intellect—is his ability to learn from the seasoning of life."

"Hari doesn't *want* the First Ministership."

"So?" He lifted an eyebrow, puzzled.

"Shouldn't his own feelings matter?"

"We are here to guide humanity, not to let it merely meander."

"But the danger—"

"The Empire needs him. What's more, he needs the Ministership—though he does not see that as yet, granted. He will have access to all Imperial data for use in psychohistory."

"He has so much data already—"

"Much more will be needed to make a full running model. He must also, in the future, have power to act on a grand scale."

"But 'grand' can be fatal. People like this Lamurk, I am certain he is dangerous."

"Quite so. But I depend upon you to keep Hari from harm."

"I find myself getting short of temper, my judgment—"

"You are more nearly human in your emulation circuits than I. Expect to bear the burden that fact implies."

She nodded. "I wish I could see you more often, ask—"

"I move quickly through the Empire, doing what tasks I can. I have not been in Trantor since I left the First Ministership myself."

"Are you sure it is safe for you to travel so?"

"I have many defenses against detection of my true nature. You have even more, for you are nearly natural."

"I cannot penetrate a full weapons screen around the palace, though?"

Olivaw shook his head. "Their technology exceeded our capacity to disguise quite some while ago. I evaded it while First Minister because no one dared test me."

"Then I cannot protect Hari in the palace."

"You should not have to. Once he becomes First Minister, you will be able to pass with him through their detectors. Those are only used for major occasions."

"Until he is First Minister, then—"

"His danger is maximum."

"Very well, I will focus on Hari. I would prefer to leave those simulations to you."

"I fear they, and Sark, will be quite enough for me to handle. I went to the coliseum in Junin Sector, saw them run wild. The tiktok issue inflames humans, still—just as we want."

"These tiktoks, surely they will not approach our levels of cognition?"

His mouth twitched just once. "And why not?"

"Under human guidance?"

"They could quickly rival us."

"Then our grand designs—"

"On the trash heap."

"I do not like such a prospect," she said, face flushed.

"The ancient taboos our kind so labored to put in place are breaking down, perhaps forever."

"What does your—*our*—theory of history say?"

"It is not nearly good enough to say anything. Against a background of social stability, such as this Empire enjoyed for so long, simulations were destabilizing. Now? No one, human or robot, knows. All parameters are accelerating." His face slackened, losing all color and muscle tone, as if from an immense fatigue. "We *must* turn matters, as much as we can, over to them—to the humans."

"To Hari."

"Him, most especially."

PART 3

BODY POLITICS

FOUNDATION, EARLY HISTORY— ... *first public intimations of psychohistory as a possible scientific discipline surfaced during the poorly documented early period of Seldon's political life. While the Emperor Cleon set great store in its possibilities, psychohistory was viewed by the political class as a mere abstraction, if not a joke. This may have resulted from maneuverings by Seldon himself, who never referred to the subject by the name he had given it. Even at this early stage, he seems to have realized that widespread knowledge of psychohistory and any movement founded upon it would enjoy little predictive success, since many would then be able to act to offset its predictions, or take advantage of them. Some have "condamned" Seldon as "selfish" for "hoarding" the psychohistorical method, but one must remember the extreme rapacity of political life in these waning years. . . .*

—ENCYCLOPEDIA GALACTICA

1.

◆

Hari Seldon's desksec chimed and announced, "Margetta Moonrose desires a conversation."

Hari looked up at the 3D image of a striking woman hovering before him. "Um? Oh. Who's she?" His sec would not interrupt him amid his calculations unless this were somebody important.

"Cross-check reveals that she is the leading interviewer and political maven in the multimedia complex—"

"Sure, sure, but why is she consequential?"

"She is considered by all cross-cultural monitors to be among the fifty most influential figures on Trantor. I suggest—"

"Never heard of her." Hari sat up, brushed at his hair. "I suppose I should. Full filter, though."

"I fear my filters are down for recalibration. If—"

"Damn it, they've been out for a week."

"I fear the mechanical in charge of the new calibrations has been defective."

Mechs, which were advanced tiktoks, were failing often these days. Since the Junin riots, some had even been attacked. Hari swallowed and said, "Put her through anyway."

He had used filters on holophones for so long, he could not now disguise his feelings. Cleon's staff had installed software to render the fitting, preselected body language for him. With some sprucing up by the Imperial Advisors, it now modulated his acoustic signature for a full, confident, resonant tone. And if he wanted, it edited his vocabulary; he was always lapsing into technospeak when he should be explaining simply.

"Academician!" Moonrose said brightly. "I would so much like to have a little talk with you."

"About mathematics?" he said blandly.

She laughed merrily. "No no!—that would be far over my head. I represent billions of inquiring minds who would like to know your thoughts on the Empire, the Quathanan questions, the—"

"The what?"

"Quathanan—the dispute over Zonal alignment."

"Never heard of it."

"But—you're to be First Minister." She seemed genuinely surprised, though Hari reminded himself that this was probably a superbly adept filter-face.

"So I am—perhaps. Until then, I will not bother."

"When the High Council selects, they must know the views of the candidates," she said rather primly.

"Tell your viewers that I do my homework only just before it's due."

She looked charmed, which made him certain that she was filtered. He had learned from many collisions with them that media mavens were easily irked when brushed aside. They seemed to feel it quite natural that, since an immense audience saw through their eyes, they carried all the moral heft of that audience.

"What about a subject you certainly must know—

the Junin disaster? And the loss—some say *escape*—
of the Voltaire and Joan of Arc sims?"

"Not my department," Hari said. Cleon had
advised him to keep his distance from the entire sim
issue.

"Rumors suggest that they came from your department."

"Certainly, one of our research mathists found
them. We leased rights to those people—what was
their name . . . ?"

"Artifice Associates, as I am sure you know."

"Um, yes."

"This distracted professor role is not convincing,
sir."

"You'd rather I spent my time running for office—
and then, presumably, running for cover?"

"The world, the whole Empire, has a right to
know—"

"So I should stand only for what the people will
fall for?"

Her mouth twisted, coming through her filters, so
apparently she had decided to play this interview as
a contest of wills. "You're hiding the peoples' business from—"

"My research is my own business."

She waved this aside. "What do you say, as a mathematician, to those who feel that deep sims of real
people are immoral?"

Hari wished fervently for his own face filters. He
was sure he was giving away something, so he forced
his face to stay blank. Best to deflect the argument.
"How real were those sims? Can anybody know?"

"They certainly seemed real and human to the
audience," Moonrose said, raising her eyebrows.

"I'm afraid I didn't watch the performance," Hari
said. "I was busy." Strictly true, at least.

Moonrose leaned forward, scowling. "With your

mathematics? Well, then, tell us about psychohistory."

He was still keeping his face wooden—which gave the wrong signal. He made himself smile. "A rumor."

"I have it on good authority that you are favored by the Emperor because of this theory of history."

"What authority?"

"Now sir, I should ask the questions here—"

"Who says? I'm still a public servant, a professor. And you, madam, are taking up time I could be devoting to my students."

With a wave Hari cut off the link. He had learned, since bandying words with Lamurk in clear view of an unsuspected 3D snout, to chop off talk when it was going the wrong way.

Dors came through the door as he leaned back into his airchair. "I got a hail, said somebody important was grilling you."

"She's gone. Poked at me about psychohistory."

"Well, it was bound to get out. It's an exciting synthesis of terms. Appeals to the imagination."

"Maybe if I'd called it 'sociohistory' people would think it more boring and leave me alone."

"You could never live with so ugly a word."

The electroshield sparkled and snapped as Yugo Amaryl came through. "Am I interrupting anything?"

"Not at all." Hari leapt up and helped him to a chair. He was still limping. "How's the leg?"

He shrugged. "Decent."

Three thuggos had come to Yugo on the street a week ago and explained the situation very calmly. They had been commissioned to do him damage, a warning he would not forget. Some bones had to be broken; that was the specification, nothing he could do about it. The leader explained how they could do this the hard way. If he fought, he would get messed up. The easy way, they would break his shin bone in one clean snap.

Describing it afterward, Yugo had said, "I thought about it some, y'know, and sat down on the sidewalk and stuck my left leg out straight. Braced it against the curb, below the knee. The leader kicked me there. A good job; it broke clean and straight."

Hari had been horrified. The media latched onto the story, of course. His only wry statement to them was, "Violence is the diplomacy of the incompetent."

"Medtech tells me it'll heal up in another week," Yugo said as Hari helped him stretch out, the airchair shaping itself subtly.

"The Imperials still haven't a clue who did it," Dors said, pacing restlessly around the office.

"Plenty of people will do a job like this." Yugo grinned, an effect somewhat offset by the big bruise on his jaw. The incident had not been quite as gentlemanly as he described it. "They kinda liked doing it to a Dahlite, too."

Dors paced angrily. "If I'd been there . . ."

"You can't be everywhere," Hari said kindly. "The Imperials think it wasn't really about you, anyway, Yugo."

Yugo's mouth twisted ruefully at Hari. "I figured. You, right?"

Hari nodded. "A 'signal,' one of them said."

Dors turned sharply from her pacing. "Of what?"

"A warning," Yugo said. "Politics."

"I see," she said quickly. "Lamurk cannot strike at you directly, but he leaves—"

"An unsubtle calling card," Yugo finished for her.

Dors smacked her hands together. "We should tell the Emperor!"

Hari had to chuckle. "And you, a historian.

Violence has always played a role in issues of succession. It can never be far from Cleon's mind."

"For emperors, yes," she countered. "But in a contest for First Minister—"

"Power is gettin' scarce 'round here," Yugo drawled sarcastically. "Pesky Dahlites makin' trouble, Empire itself slowin' down, too. Or spinnin' off into loony 'renaissances.' Probably a Dahlite plot, that, righto?"

Hari said, "When food gets scarce, table manners change."

Yugo said, "I'll just bet the Emperor's got this all analyzed."

Dors began pacing again. "One of history's lessons is that emperors who overanalyze fail, while those who oversimplify succeed."

"A neat analysis," Hari said, but she did not catch his irony.

"Uh, I actually came in to get some work done," Yugo said softly. "I've finished reconciling the Trantorian historical data with the modified Seldon Equations."

Hari leaned forward, though Dors kept pacing, her hands clasped behind her back. "Wonderful! How far off are they?"

Yugo grinned as he slipped a ferrite cube into Hari's desk display slot. "Watch."

Trantor had endured at least eighteen millennia, though the pre-Empire period was poorly documented. Yugo had collapsed the ocean of data into a 3D. Economics lay along one axis, social indices along another, with politics making up the third dimension. Each contributed a surface, forming a solid shape that hung above Hari's desk. The slippery-looking blob was man-sized and in constant motion—deforming, caves opening, lumps rising. Color-coded internal flows were visible through the transparent skin.

"It looks like a cancerous organ," Dors said. When Yugo frowned, she added hastily, "Pretty, though."

Hari chuckled; Dors seldom made social gaffes, but when she did, she had no idea of how to recover. The lumpy object hanging in air throbbed with life, capturing his attention. The writhing manifold summed up trillions of vectors, the raw data drawn from countless tiny lives.

"This early history had patchy data," Yugo said. The surfaces jerked and lurched. "Low resolution, too, and even low population size—a problem we won't have in Empire predictions."

"See the two-dee socio-structures?" Hari pointed.

"And this represents everything in Trantor?" Dors asked.

Yugo said, "To the model not all detail is equally important. You don't need to know the owner of a starship to calculate how it will fly."

Hari said helpfully, pointing at a quick jitter in social vectors, "Scientocracy arose here third millennium. Then an era in which stasis arose from monopolies. That fed rigidity."

The forms steadied as the data improved. Yugo let it run, time-stepping quickly so that they saw fifteen millennia in three minutes. It was startling, the pulsing solid growing myriad offshoots, structure endlessly proliferating. The madly burgeoning patterns spoke of the Empire's complexity far more than any emperor's lofty speech.

"Now here's the overlay," Yugo said, "showing how the Seldon Equations post-dict, in yellow."

"They aren't *my* equations," Hari said automatically. Long ago he and Yugo had seen that to *pre*dict with psychohistory first demanded that they *post*-dict the past, for verification. "They were—"

"Just watch."

Alongside the deep blue data-figure, a yellow lump

congealed. It looked to Hari like an identical twin to the original. Each went through contortions, seething with history's energy. Each ripple and snag represented many billions of human triumphs and tragedies. Every small shudder had once been a calamity.

"They're . . . the same," Hari whispered.

"Damn right," Yugo said.

"The theory fits."

"Yup. Psychohistory works."

Hari stared at the flexing colors. "I never thought . . ."

"It could work so well?" Dors had walked behind his chair and now rubbed his scalp.

"Well, yes."

"You have spent years including the proper variables. It *must* work."

Yugo smiled tolerantly. "If only more people shared your faith in mathists. You've forgotten the sparrow effect."

Dors was transfixed by the shimmering data-solids, now rerunning all Trantorian history, throbbing with different-colored schemes to show up differences between real history and the equations' post-dictions. There were very few. What's more, they did not grow with time.

Not taking her eyes from the display, Dors asked slowly, "Sparrow? We have birds as pets, but surely—"

"Suppose a sparrow flaps its wings at the equator, out in the open. That shifts the air circulation a tiny amount. If things break just right, the sparrow could trigger a tornado up at the poles."

Dors was startled. "Impossible!"

Hari said, "Don't confuse it with the fabled nail in the shoe of a *horse*, that a legendary beast of burden. Remember?—its rider lost a battle and then a kingdom. That was failure of a small, critical component.

Fundamental, random phenomena are democratic. Tiny differences in every coupled variable can produce staggering changes."

It took a while to get the point through. Like any other world, Trantor's meteorology had a daunting sensitivity to initial conditions. A sparrow's wing-flutter on one side of Trantor, amplified through fluid equations over weeks, could drive a howling hurricane a continent away. No computer could model all the tiny details of real weather to make exact predictions possible.

Dors pointed at the data-solids. "So—this is all wrong?"

"I hope not," Hari said. "Weather varies, but climate holds steady."

"Still . . . no wonder Trantorians prefer indoors. Outdoors can be dangerous."

"The fact that the equations describe what happened—well, it means that small effects can smooth out in history," Hari said.

Yugo added, "Stuff on a human scale can average away."

She stopped massaging Hari's scalp. "Then . . . people don't matter?"

Hari said carefully, "Most biography persuades us that people—that *we*—are important. Psychohistory teaches that we aren't."

"As a historian, I cannot accept—"

"Look at the data," Yugo put in.

They watched as Yugo brought up detail, showed off features. For ordinary people, history endured through art, myth, and liturgy. They felt it through concrete examples, close up: a building, a custom, a historical name. He and Yugo and the others were like sparrows themselves, hovering high over a landscape unguessed by the inhabitants below. They saw the slow surge of terrain, glacial and unstoppable.

"But people *have* to matter." Dors' voice carried a note of forlorn hope. Hari knew that somewhere deep in her lurked the stern directives of the Zeroth Law, but over that lay a deep layer of true human feeling. She was a humanist who believed in the power of the individual—and here she met blunt, uncaring mechanism, in the large.

"They do, actually, but perhaps not in the way you want," Hari said gently. "We sought out telltale groups, pivots about which events sometimes hinge."

"The homosexuals, f'instance," Yugo said.

"They're about one percent of the population, a consistent minor variant in reproductive strategies," Hari said.

Socially, though, they were often masters of improvisation, fashioning style to substance, fully at home with the arbitrary. They seemed equipped with an internal compass that pointed them at every social novelty, early on, so that they exerted leverage all out of proportion to their numbers. Often they were sensitive indicators of future turns.

Yugo went on, "So we figured, could they be a crucial indicator? Turns out they are. Helps out the equations."

Dors said severely, "*Why* does history smooth out?"

Hari let Yugo carry the ball. "Y'see, that same sparrow effect had a positive side. Chaotic systems could be caught at just the right instant, tilted ever so slightly in a preferred way. A well-timed nudge could drive a system, yielding benefits all out of proportion to the effort expended."

"You mean control?" She looked doubtful.

"Just a touch," Yugo said. "Minimal control—the right nudge at the right time—demands that the dynamics be intricately understood. Maybe that way, you could bias outcomes toward the least damaging of several finely balanced results. At best, they could drive the system into startlingly good outcomes."

"Who's controlling?" Dors asked.

Yugo looked embarrassed. "Uh, we . . . dunno."

"Don't *know*? But this is a theory of all history."

Hari said quietly, "There are elements, interplays, in the equations that we don't grasp. Damping forces."

"How can you not understand?"

Both men looked ill at ease. "We don't know how the terms interact. New features," Hari said, "leading to . . . emergent order."

She said primly, "Then you don't really have a theory, do you?"

Hari nodded ruefully. "Not in the sense of a deep understanding, no."

Models followed the gritty, experienced world, he reflected. They echoed their times. Clockwork planetary mechanics came after clocks. The idea of the whole universe as a computation came after computers. A worldview of stable change came after nonlinear dynamics . . .

He had a glimmering of a metamodel, which would look at *him* and describe how *he* would then select among models for psychohistory. Peering down from above, it could see which was likely to be favored by Hari Seldon . . .

"Who plans this control?" Dors persisted.

Hari caught at the idea he had, but it slipped away. He knew how to coax it back: ease up. "Remember that joke?" he said. "How do you make God laugh?"

She smiled. "You tell him your plans."

"Right. We will study this result, sniff out an answer."

She smiled. "Don't ask you for predictions about the progress of your own predictions?"

"Embarrassing, but yes."

His desksec chimed. "An Imperial summons," it announced.

"Damn!" Hari slapped his chair. "Fun's over."

2.

◆

Not quite time for the Specials to arrive, Hari thought. But getting any work done was impossible while he was on edge.

He jiggled coins in his pocket, distracted, then fished one out. A five cred piece, amber alloy, a handsome Cleon I head on one side—treasuries always flattered emperors—and the disk of the Galaxy seen from above on the other. He held it on edge and thought.

Let the coin's width represent the disk's typical scale height. To be correct, the coin would have to bulge at its center to depict the hub, but overall it was a good geometric replica.

In the disk was a flaw, a minute blister in an outer spiral arm. He did the ratio in his head, allowing that the galaxy was about 100,000 light-years across, and . . . blinked. The speck portrayed a volume about a thousand light years across. In the outer arms, that would contain ten million stars.

To see so many worlds as a fleck adrift in immensity made him feel as though Trantor's solidity had opened and he had plunged helplessly into an abyss.

Could humanity matter on such a scale? So many billions of souls, packed into a grainy dot.

Yet they had spanned the whole incomprehensible expanse of that disk in a twinkling.

Humanity had spread through the spiral arms,

spilling through the wormholes, wrapping itself around the hub in a mere few thousand years. In that time the spiral arms themselves had not revolved a perceptible angle in their own gravid gavotte; that would take half a billion years. Human hankering for far horizons had sent them swarming through the wormhole webbing, popping out into spaces near suns of swelling red, virulent blue, smoldering ruby.

The speck stood for a volume a single human brain, with its primate capacities, could not grasp, except as mathematical notation. But that same brain led humans outward, until they now strode the Galaxy, mastering the starlit abyss . . . without truly knowing themselves.

So a *single* human could not fathom even a dot in the disk. But the sum of humanity could, incrementally, one mind at a time, knowing its own immediate starry territory.

And what did he desire? To comprehend all of that humanity, its deepest impulses, its shadowy mechanisms, its past, present, and future. He wanted to *know* the vagrant species that had managed to scoop up this disk, and to make it a plaything.

So maybe one single human mind could indeed grasp the disk, by going one level higher—and fathoming the collective effects, hidden in the intricacies of the Equations.

Describing Trantor, in *this* proportion, was child's play. For the Empire, he needed a far grander comprehension.

Mathematics might rule the galaxy. Invisible, gossamer symbols could govern.

So a single man or woman could matter.

Maybe. He shook his head. A single human head.

Getting a little ahead of ourselves, aren't we? Dreams of godhood . . .

Back to work.

Only he couldn't work. He had to wait. To his relief, the Imperial Specials arrived and escorted him across Streeling University. By now he was used to the gawkers, the embarrassment of plowing through the crowds which now accumulated everywhere, it seemed, that he might frequent.

"Busy today," he said to the Specials captain.

"Got to expect it, sir."

"You get extra duty pay for this, I hope."

"Yessir. 'Digs,' we call them."

"For extra risk, correct? Dangerous duty."

The captain looked flustered. "Well, yessir . . ."

"If someone starts shooting, what are your orders?"

"Uh, if they can penetrate the engaging perimeter, we're to get between them and you. Sir."

"And you'd do that? Take a gauss pulse or a flechette?"

He seemed surprised. "Of course."

"Truly?"

"Our duty, y'know."

Hari was humbled by the man's simple loyalty. Not to Hari Seldon, but to the idea of Empire. Order. Civilization.

And Hari realized that he, too, was devoted to that idea. The Empire had to be saved, or at least its decline mitigated. Only by fathoming its deep structure could he do that.

Which was why he disliked the First Minister business. It robbed him of time, concentration.

In the Specials' armored pods he salved his discontent by pulling out his tablet and working on some equations. The captain had to remind him when they reached the palace grounds. Hari got out and there was the usual security ritual, the Specials spreading out and airborne sensors going aloft to sniff out the far perimeter. They reminded him of golden bees, buzzing with vigilance.

He walked by a wall leading into the palace gardens and a tan, round sheet the size of his fingernail popped off the wall. It stuck to his neck. He reached up and plucked it off.

He recognized it as a promotional trinket, a slap-on patch which gave you a pleasant rush by diffusing endorphins into your bloodstream. It also subtly predisposed you to coherent signals in corridor advertisements.

He pitched it aside. A Special grabbed at the patch and suddenly there was shouting and movement all around him. The Special turned to throw the patch away.

An orange spike shot through the guard's hand, hissing hot, flaring and gone in a second. The man cried, "Ah!" and another Special grabbed him and pushed him down. Then five Specials blocked Hari from all sides and he saw no more.

The Special screamed horribly. Something cut off the wail of pain. The captain shouted, "Move!" and Hari had to trot with the Specials around him into the gardens and down several lanes.

It took a while to straighten out the incident. The patch was untraceable, of course, and there was no way of knowing for sure whether it was targeted on Hari at all.

"Could be part of some Palace plot," the captain said. "Just waiting for the next passerby with a scent-signature like yours."

"Not aimed for me at all?"

"Could be. That tab took couple extra seconds tryin' to figure out if it wanted you or not."

"And it did."

"Body odor, skin smells—they're not exact, sir."

"I'll have to start wearing perfume."

The captain grinned. "That won't stop a smart tab."

Other protection specialists rushed in and there

was evidence to measure and opinions and a lot of talk. Hari insisted on walking back to see the Special who had taken the tab. He was gone, already off to emergency care; they said he would lose his hand. No, sorry, Hari could not see him. Security, y'know.

Quite quickly Hari became bored with the aftermath. He had come early to get a stroll through the gardens and though he knew he was being irrational, his regret at missing the walk loomed larger than the assassination attempt.

Hari took a long, still moment and moved the incident aside. He visualized a displacement operator, an icy blue vector frame. It listed the snarled, angry red knot and pushed it out of view. Later, he would deal with it later.

He cut off the endless talk and ordered the Specials to fall in behind him. Shouted protests came, of course, which he ignored. Then he ambled across the gardens, relishing the open air. He inhaled eagerly. The blinding speed of the attack had erased its importance to him. For now.

The palace towers loomed like webwork of a giant spider. Between their bulks weaved airy walkways. Spires were veiled in silvery mist and aripple, apulse, shimmering with a silent, steady beat like a great unseen heart. He had been so long in the foreshortened views of Trantor's corridors, his eyes did not quickly grasp the puzzling perspectives.

An upward rush caught his attention as he passed through a flowerscape. From the immense Imperial aviary, flocks of birds in the thousands oscillated in the vertical drafts. Their artful, ever-shifting patterns had a diaphanous, billowy quality, an immense, wispy dance.

Yet these had been shaped many millennia ago by bioengineering their genome. They formed drifts and billows like clouds, or even airy mountains, feasting on upwelling gnats, released from below by the gardeners. But a side draft could dissolve all their ornate sculptures, blow them away.

Like the Empire, he mused. Beautiful in its order, stable for fifteen millennia, yet now toppling. Cracking up like a slow-motion pod wreck. Or in spasms like the Junin riots.

Why? Even among Imperial loveliness, his mathist mind returned to the problem.

Entering the palace, he passed a delegation of children on their way to some audience with a lesser Imperial figure. With a sudden pang he missed his adopted son, Raych. He and Dors had decided to secretly send the boy away to school, after Yugo had his leg broken. "Deprive them of targets," Dors had said.

Among the meritocracy, only those adults with commitment, stability, and talent could have children. Gentry or plain citizens could whelp brats by the shovelful.

Parents were like artists—special people with a special gift, given respect and privileges, left free to create happy and competent humans. It was noble work, well paid. Hari had been honored to be approved.

In immediate contrast, three oddly shaped courtiers ambled by him.

By biotech means people could turn their children into spindly towers, into flowerlike footbound dwarves, into green giants or pink pygmies. From throughout the Galaxy they were sent here to amuse the Imperial court, where novelty was always in vogue.

But such variants seldom lasted. There was a species norm. And stretching it was just as deeply ingrained. Hari had to admit that he would forever be among the unsophisticated, for he found such folk repulsive.

Someone had designed the reception room to look like anything but a room for receiving people. It resembled a lumpy pocket in molten glass, criss-crossed by polished shafts of ceramo-steel. These shafts in turn dripped into smooth lumps which—since there was nothing else in the room—must have been intended to be chairs and tables.

It seemed unlikely that he could ever get back out of any of the shapes, once he had worked out how to sit in them—so Hari stood. And wondered if that effect, too, was somehow intended . . . The palace was a subtle place of layered design.

This was to be a small, private meeting, Cleon's staff had assured him. Still, there was a small army of attachés and protocol officers and aides who had introduced themselves as Hari had passed through several rooms of increasing ornamentation, on his way here. Their talk became more ornate, as well. Courtly life was dominated by puffed-up people who always acted as though they were coyly unveiling statues of themselves.

There was a lot of adornment and finery, the archi-tectural equivalent of jewels and silk, and even the most minor attendants wore very dignified green uni-forms. He felt as though he should lower his voice and realized, recalling Sundays on Helicon, that this place felt somehow like a church.

Then Cleon swept in and the staff vanished, silently draining away into concealed exits.

"My Seldon!"

"Yours, sire." Hari followed the ritual.

The Emperor continued greeting him effusively, tut-tutting over the apparent assassination attempt— "Surely an accident, don't you think?"—and led him to the large display wall. At Cleon's gesture an enor-mous view of the entire Galaxy appeared, the work of a new artist. Hari murmured the required admi-ration and recalled his thoughts of only an hour before.

This was a time sculpture, tracing the entire Galactic history. The disk was, after all, a collection of debris, swirling at the bottom of a gravitational pothole in the cosmos. How it looked depended on which of mankind's myriad eyes one used. Infrared could pierce and unmask dusty lanes. X rays sought pools of fiercely burning gas. Radio dishes mapped cold banks of molecules and magnetized plasma. All were packed with meaning.

In the carousel of the disk, stars bobbed and weaved under complicated Newtonian tugs. The major arms—Sagittarius, Orion, and Perseus, counting outward from the Center—bore names obscured by antiquity. Each contained a Zone of that name, hinting that perhaps here the ancient Earth orbited. But no one knew, and research had revealed no obvious single candidate. Instead, dozens of worlds vied for the title of the True Earth. Quite probably, none of them were.

Many bright signatures—skymarks, like landmarks?—blazed among the curving, barred spiral arms. Beauty beyond description—but not beyond analysis, Hari thought, whether physical or social. If he could find the key . . .

"I congratulate you on the success of my Moron Decree," Cleon said.

Hari slowly withdrew from the immense perspective. "Uh, sire?"

"Your idea—first fruit of psychohistory." To Hari's blank incomprehension Cleon chuckled. "Forgotten already? The renegades who pillage, seeking renown for their infamy. You advised me to strip them of their identity by making them henceforth be called Morons."

Hari had indeed forgotten the advice, but contented himself with a sage nod.

"It worked! Such crimes are much reduced. And

those convicted go to their deaths full of anger, demanding to be made famous. I tell you, it is delicious."

Hari felt a chill at the way the Emperor smacked his lips. An off-hand suggestion made suddenly, concretely real. It rattled him a bit.

He realized that the Emperor was asking about progress with psychohistory. His throat tightened and he remembered the Moonrose woman with her irritating questions. That seemed weeks ago. "Work is slow," he managed to say.

Cleon said sympathetically, "Surely it requires a deep knowledge of every facet of civilized life."

"At times." Hari stalled, putting his mixed emotions firmly away.

"I was at a convocation recently and learned something you undoubtedly have factored into your equations."

"Yes, sire?"

"It is said that the very foundation of the Empire—besides the wormholes of course—is the discovery of proton-Boron fusion. I had never heard of it, yet the speaker said it was the single greatest achievement of antiquity. That every starship, every planetary technology, depends upon it for power."

"I suppose that is true, but I did not know it."

"Such an elementary fact?"

"What is not of use to me does not concern me."

Cleon's mouth pouted in puzzlement. "But a theory of all history surely demands great detail."

"Technology enters only in its effects on other large issues," Hari said. How to explain the intricacies of nonlinear calculus? "Often its limitations are the important point."

"Any technology distinguishable from magic is insufficiently advanced," Cleon said airily.

"Well put, sire."

"You like it? That fellow Draius gave it to me. It has a ring, doesn't it? True, too. Perhaps I'll—" He broke off and said to the air, "Transcription officer! Give that line about magic to the Presepth for general distribution."

Cleon sat back. "They're always after me for 'Imperial wisdom.' A bother!"

A faint musical note announced Betan Lamurk. Hari stiffened at first sight of the man, but Lamurk had eyes only for the Emperor as he went smoothly through a litany of court ritual. As a prime member of the High Council he had to recite some time-honored and empty phrases, bow with a curious swoop, and never avert his gaze from the Emperor. That done, he could relax.

"Professor Seldon! So good to meet again."

Hari shook hands in the formal manner. "Sorry about that little dustup. I really didn't know the 3D was there."

"No matter. One can't help what the media make of things."

"My Seldon gave me excellent advice about the Moron Decree," Cleon said. He went on, his delight deepening the twist of Lamurk's mouth.

Cleon led them to luxuriant chairs that popped out of the walls. Hari found himself swept immediately into a detailed discussion of Council matters. Resolutions, measures of appropriation, abstracts of proposed legislation. This stuff had been flowing through Hari's office, as well. He had dutifully set his autosec to text-analyzing it, breaking the sea of jargon down into Galactic and smoothing out the connections. This got him through the first hour. Most of the material he had ignored, tipping piles of to-be-scanned documents into his recycler when nobody was looking.

The arcane workings of the High Council were not

in principle difficult to follow—they were just boring. As Lamurk deftly conferred with the Emperor, Hari watched them as he would watch a bodyball game: a curious practice, no doubt fascinating in a narrow sort of way.

That the Council set general standards and directions, while below them mere legal mavens worked out the details and passed legislation, did not change his bemused disinterest. People spent their *lives* doing such things!

For tactics he cared little. Even mankind did not matter. On the Galactic chessboard the pieces were the phenomena of humanity, the rules of the game were the laws of psychohistory. The player on the other side was hidden, perhaps did not exist.

Lamurk needed an opposite player, a rival. Subtly, Hari saw that he was the inevitable foe.

Lamurk's career had aimed him for the First Ministership and he meant to get it. At every turn Lamurk curried favor with the Emperor and waved away Hari's points, of which there were few.

He did not directly counter Lamurk; the man was a master. He kept quiet, confining himself to an occasional expressively (he hoped) raised eyebrow. He had rarely regretted keeping quiet.

"This MacroMesh thing, do you favor it?" the Emperor abruptly asked Hari.

He barely remembered the idea. "It will alter the Galaxy considerably," he stalled.

"Productively!" Lamurk slapped a table. "All the econ-indicators are falling. The MacroMesh will speed up info-flow, boost productivity."

The Emperor's mouth tilted with doubt. "I'm not altogether happy with the idea of linking so many, so easily."

"Just think," Lamurk pressed, "the new squeezers

will let an ordinary person in, say, Eqquis Zone talk every day with a friend in the Far Reaches—or anywhere else."

The Emperor nodded uncertainly. "Hari? What do you think?"

"I have doubts as well."

Lamurk waved dismissively. "Failure of nerve."

"Increased communication may worsen the Empire's crisis."

Lamurk's mouth twisted derisively. "Nonsense. Contrary to every good executive rule."

"The Empire isn't ruled—" Hari made a half-bow to the Emperor "—alas, it's *let* run."

"More nonsense. We in the High Council—"

"Hear him out!" Cleon said. "He does not talk very much."

Hari smiled. "Many people are grateful for that, sire."

"No oblique answers, now. What does your psychohistory tell you about how the Empire runs?"

"It is millions of castles, webbed by bridges."

"Castles?" Cleon's famous nose rose skeptically.

"Planets. They have local concerns and run themselves as they like. The Empire doesn't trouble itself over such details, unless a world begins making aggressive trouble."

"True enough, and as it should be," Cleon said. "Ah—and your bridges are the wormholes."

"Exactly, sire." Hari deliberately avoided looking at Lamurk and focused on the Emperor, while sketching in his vision.

Planets could have any number of lesser duchies, with disputes and wars and "microstructure" galore. The psychohistorical equations showed that none of that mattered.

What did matter was that physical resources could not be shared among indefinitely large numbers of people. Each solar system was a finite store of goods, and in the end, that meant local hierarchies to control access.

Wormholes could carry rather little mass, because the holes were seldom more than ten meters across. Massive hyperspace ships carried heavy cargoes, but they were slower and cumbersome. They distorted space-time, contracting it fore and expanding it aft, moving at super-light speeds in the Galaxy's frame but not in its own. Trade among most stellar systems was constrained to light, compact, expensive items. Spices, fashions, technology—not bulky raw materials.

Wormholes could accommodate modulated light beams far more easily. The wormhole curvature refracted beams through to receivers at the other mouth. Data flowed freely, knitting together the Galaxy.

And information was the opposite of mass. Data could be moved, compressed, and leaked readily through copies. It was infinitely shareable. It blossomed like flowers in eternal spring, for as information was applied to a problem, the resulting solution was new information. And it was cheap, meaning that it took few mass resources to acquire it. Its preferred medium was light, quite literally—the laser beam.

"That provided enough communication to make an Empire. But the odds of a native of the Puissant Zone ever voyaging to the Zaqulot Zone—or even to the next star, since by wormhole they are equivalent trips—were tiny," Hari said.

"So every one of your 'castles' kept itself isolated—except for information flow," Cleon said, absorbed.

"But now the MacroMesh will increase the information transfer rate a thousand-fold, using these 'squeezers' that compress information."

Cleon pursed his lips, puzzled. "Why is that bad?"

"It's not," Lamurk said. "Better data makes for better decisions, everybody knows that."

"Not necessarily. Human life is a voyage on a sea of meaning, not a net of information. What will most people get from a close, personal flow of data? Detached, foreign logic. Uprooted details."

"We can run things better!" Lamurk insisted. Cleon held up a finger and Lamurk choked off his next words.

Hari hesitated. Lamurk had a point, indeed.

There were mathematical relationships between technology, capital accumulation, labor, but the most important driver proved to be knowledge. About half the Empire's economic growth came from the increase in the quality of information, as embodied in better machines and improved skills, leading to efficiency.

That was where the Empire had faltered. The innovative thrust of the sciences had slowly faltered. The Imperial universities produced fine engineers, but no inventors. Great scholars, but few true scientists. That factored into the other tides of time. But something other than data starvation had made that happen, and as yet, Hari did not know the cause.

But Hari saw the Emperor wavering, and pressed on. "Many on the High Council see the MacroMesh as an instrument of control. Let me point out a few facts well known to you, sire."

Hari was in his favorite mode, a one-on-one lecture. Cleon leaned forward, eyes narrowed. Hari spun him a tale.

To get between worlds A and B, he said, one might have to take a dozen wormhole jumps—the Worm Nest was an astrophysical subway system with many transfers.

Each worm mouth imposed added fees and charges on every shipment. Control of an entire trade route yielded the maximum profit. The struggle for control was unending, often violent. From the viewpoint of economics, politics, and "historical momentum"—which meant a sort of imposed inertia on events—a local empire which controlled a whole constellation of nodes should be solid, enduring.

Not so. Time and again, regional satrapies went toes-up. It seemed natural to squeeze every worm passage for the maximum fee, by coordinating every worm mouth to optimize traffic. But that degree of control made people restive. In elaborately controlling the system, information flowed only from managers to wage slaves, with little feedback.

Extensive regulation did not deliver the best benefits. Instead, it yielded "short blanket economies"—when the collective shoulders got cold, the blanket got pulled up to cover them, and so the feet froze. Over-control failed.

"So the MacroMesh, if it lets the High Council really 'run things,' could decrease economic vitality."

Lamurk smiled patronizingly. "A bunch of abstract theory, sire. Now, you listen to an old hand who's been on the Council a good long time now . . ."

Hari attended to Lamurk's famous balm and wondered why he was bothering with this. He had to admit that trading ideas with the Emperor had a certain quality of casual, almost sensual, power. Watching a man who could destroy a world with a gesture had a decided adrenaline edge.

But he didn't really belong here, either by talent or drive. Trotting out his own views was amusing; every professor secretly thinks that what the world needs is a good, solid lecture—from him, of course.

But in this game, the pawns were real. The Moron Decree had unnerved him, even though he saw nothing morally wrong with it.

Lives hung in the balance here, among the finery.

And not just the lives of others. He had to remind himself that this beaming, confident Lamurk across from him was the obvious source of the patch-weapon which had nearly killed him, just hours before.

3.

◆

He entered their apartment and went straight to the kitchen. He punched in commands on the autoserver and then went to the range and began to heat up some oil. While it warmed he cut up onions and garlic and put them in to brown. His beer arrived and he opened one, not bothering with a glass.

"Something's happened," Dors said.

"We had a fine little chat. I eyed Lamurk, he eyed me."

"That's not why your shoulders are hunched up."

"Um. Betrayed by my expressive body."

So he told her about the possible assassination attempt.

After she had calmed down, she said tightly, "You also heard about the smoke artist?"

"At that reception? He made the big cloud that looked like me?"

"He died today."

"How?"

"Looks like an accident."

"Too bad—he was funny."

"Too funny. He made the cartoon of Lamurk, remember? Made Lamurk look like a blowhard. It was the hit of the reception."

Hari blinked. "You don't . . ."

"Quite orderly, both of you in one day."

"So it could be Lamurk. . . ."

Dors said grimly, "My dear Hari, always thinking in terms of probabilities."

After his audience with Cleon, Hari had sat through a strict talk by the head of palace security. His Specials squad was doubled. More midget-flyers for forward perimeter warning. Oh, yes, and he was not to walk close to any walls.

This last bit had made Hari chuckle, which did not improve the palace staff's attitude. Worse, Hari knew that he still had baggage to unpack. How to keep them from sniffing out Dors' true nature?

The autoserver rang. He sat and forked up dark meat and onions and then opened another bottle of the cold beer and held it in one hand while he ate with the other.

"A hard day's work," Dors said.

"I always eat heartily after narrowly averting death. It's an old family tradition."

"I see."

"Cleon ended up by commenting on the impasse in the High Council. Until that's resolved, no vote on the First Minister can occur."

"So you and Lamurk are still butting heads."

"He's butting. Me, I'm dodging."

"I will never leave your side again," she said firmly.

"It's a deal. Could you get me something more from the autoserver? Something warm and heavy and full of things that are bad for me?"

She went into the kitchen and he ate steadily and drank the beer and did not think about anything.

She brought back something steaming in a rich brown sauce. He ate it without asking what it was.

"You are an odd man, professor."

"Things get to me a bit later than other people."

"You learned how to delay thinking about them,

reacting to them, until there was a time and a place."

He blinked and drank some more beer. "Could be. Have to think about it."

"You eagerly eat working-class food. And where did you learn this trick of deferring reactions?"

"Um. You tell me."

"Helicon."

He thought about that. "Um, the working class. My father got into trouble and there were plenty of hard times. About the only break I got as a boy was not getting brain fever. We couldn't have afforded any hospital time."

"I see. Financial trouble, I remember you saying."

"Financial and then people muscling him to sell his land. He didn't want to. So he mortgaged more and planted more crops and followed his best judgment. Every time chance played out against him, Dad got right back up and went at it again. That worked for a while because he did know farming. But then there was a big market fluctuation and he got caught and lost everything." He was speaking quickly as he ate, and he didn't know why but it felt right.

"I see. That was why he was doing that dangerous job—"

"Which killed him, yes."

"I see. And you dealt with that. Submerged it to help your mother. Learned in the hard times that followed to reserve your reactions for a moment when it was all right to let it go."

"If you say 'I see' again, I won't let you watch later when I take a shower."

She smiled, but then the same penetrating cast came over her face. "You fit some well-defined parameters. Men who are contained. They control themselves by letting very little in. They do not show a great deal or talk too much."

"Except to their woman." He had stopped eating.

"You have little time for small talk—people at Streeling comment on that—yet you speak freely with me."

"I try not to blather."

"Being male is complicated."

"So is being female, though you've mastered it beautifully."

"I'll take that as a rather formal compliment."

"And so it was. Just plain being human is just plain hard."

"So I am finding. You . . . learned all this on Helicon."

"I learned to deal with essentials."

"Also to hate fluctuations. They can kill you."

He took a swig of the beer, still cold and biting. "I hadn't thought of it that way."

"Why didn't you say all this in the first place?"

"I didn't know it in the first place."

"A corollary, then: If you commit yourself to a woman you give away as much of yourself as you can, inside that enclosed space."

"The volume between the two of us."

"A geometric analogy is as good as any." The tip of her tongue made her lower lip bulge out slightly, as it always did when she pondered a point. "And you commit yourself wholly to averting the price life exacts."

"The price of . . . fluctuations?"

"If you can predict, you can avoid. Correct. Manage."

"This is awfully analytic."

"I've skipped over the hard parts, but they will be on the homework assignment."

"Usually these kinds of talk use phrases like 'optimally consolidated self.' I've been waiting for the jargon to come trotting out." He had finished the bowl and felt much better.

"Food is one of the life-affirming experiences."

"So *that's* why I do it."

"Now you're making fun of me."

"No, just working out the implications of the theory. I liked the part about hating unpredictability and fluctuations because they hurt people."

"So can Empires, if they fall."

"Right." He finished the beer and thought about having another. Any more would dull him a little. He would prefer another way to take from him the edge he still felt.

"Big appetite." She smiled.

"You have no idea. And the prospect of death can stimulate more than one kind of appetite. Let's go back to that part about the homework assignment."

"You have something in mind."

He grinned. "You have no idea."

4.

◆

He savored his work all the more, since he had less time for it.

Hari sat in his darkened office, absolutely still, watching the 3D numerics evolve like luminous fogs in the air before him.

Empire scholars had known the root basics of psychohistory for millennia. In ancient times, pedants had charted the twenty-six stable and meta-stable social systems. There were plenty of devolved planets to study, fallen into barbarism—like the Porcos and their Raging Rituals, the Lizzies and their Gyno-Governs.

He watched the familiar patterns form, as his

simulation stepped through centuries of Galactic evolution. Some social systems proved stable only on small scales.

In the air hung the ranks of whole worlds, caught in stable Zones: Primitive Socialism; Femo-Pastoralism; Macho Tribalism. These were the "strong attractors" of human sociology, islands in the chaos sea.

Some societies labored through their meta-stability, then crashed: Theocracy, Transcendentalism, Macho Feudalism. This latter appeared whenever people had metallurgy and agriculture. Planets which had slid a long way down the curve would manifest it.

Imperial scholars had long justified the Empire, threaded by narrow wormholes and lumbering hyperships, as the best human social structure. It had indeed proved stable and benevolent.

Their reigning model, Benign Imperial Feudalism, accepted that humans were hierarchical. As well, they were dynastically ambitious, liking the continuity of power and its pomp. They were quite devoted to symbols of unity, of Imperial grandeur. Gossip about the great was, for most people, the essence of history itself.

Imperial power was moderated by traditions of noble leadership, the assumed superiority of those who rose to greatness. Beneath such impressive resplendence, as Cleon well knew, lay the bedrock of an extremely honest, meritocratic civil service. Without that, corruption would spread like a stain across the stars, corroding the splendor.

He watched the diagram—a complex 3D web of surfaces, the landscape of social-space.

Slow-stepped, he could see individual event-waves washing through the sim. Each cell in the grid got recomputed every clock cycle, readjusting every nearest-neighbor interaction in 3D.

The working rules of thumb were not the true laws of physics, built up from fundamentals like maxion mechanics, or even from the simple NewTown Laws. Rather, they were rough algorithms that reduced intricate laws to trivial arithmetic. Society seen raw this way was crude, not mysterious at all.

Then came chaos.

He was viewing the "policy-space," with its family of variables: degree of polarity, or power concentration; size of coalitions; conflict scale. In this simple model, learning loops emerged. Starting from a plateau period of seeming stability but not stasis, the system produced a Challenger Idea.

This threatened stability, which forced formation of coalitions to oppose the challenge. Factions formed. Then they gelled. The coalitions could be primarily religious, political, economic, technological, even military—though this last was a particularly ineffective method, the data showed. The system then veered into a chaotic realm, sometimes emerging to new stability, sometimes decaying.

In the dynamic system there was a *pressure* created by the contrast between people's ideal picture of the world and the reality. Too big a difference drove fresh forces for change. Often the forces were apparently unconscious; people knew something was wrong, felt restive, but could not fix on a clear cause.

So much for "rational actor" models, Hari thought. Yet some still clung to that obviously dumb approximation.

Everyone *thought* the Empire was simple.

Not the bulk of the population, of course, dazzled by the mix of cultures and exotica afforded by trade and communications from myriad worlds. They were perpetually distracted—an important damper on chaos.

Even to social theorists, though, the basic structure

and interrelations seemed to be predictable, with a moderate number of feedback loops, solid and traditional. Conventional wisdom held that these could be easily separated out and treated.

Most important, there was central decision-making, or so most thought. The Emperor Knew Best, right?

In reality, the Empire was a nested, ordered hierarchy: Imperial Feudalism. At the lower bound were the Zones of the galaxy, sometimes only a dozen light-years across, up to a few thousand light years diameter. Above that were Compacts of a few hundred nearby Zones. The Compacts interlocked into the Galactic cross-linked system.

But the whole thing was sliding downhill. In the complex diagram, sparkling flickers came and went. *What were those?*

Hari close-upped the flares. Zones of chaos, where predictability becomes impossible. These fiery eruptions might be the clue to why the Empire was failing.

Hari felt in his soul that unpredictability was bad—for humanity, for his mathematics. But it was inescapable.

This was the secret the Emperor and others must never know. That until he could rule chaos—or at least peer into it—psychohistory was a fraud.

He decided to look at a single case. Maybe that would be cleaner.

He selected Sark, the world which had found and developed the Voltaire and Joan sims. It billed itself as the Home of the New Renaissance—a common rhetorical posture, often adopted. They seemed bright and creative as he reviewed the status-grids.

Hari yawned despite himself. Sure, Sark looked good for now. A booming economy. A leader in styles and fashion.

But its profile classed it among the Chaos Worlds.

They rose for a while, seeming to defy the damping mechanisms that held planets in the Imperial Equilibrium.

Then their social fabric dissolved. They plummeted back into one of the Stasis States: Anarcho-Industrial for Sark, he would predict, from the data. No great fleets made this happen. The Empire did not, despite impressions, rule by force. Social evolutions made the Chaos Worlds falter and die. Usually, the Galaxy as a whole suffered few repercussions.

But lately, there had been more of them. And the Empire was visibly decaying. Productivity was down, incoherence in the social-spaces on the rise.

Why?

He got up and went for a workout at the gymnasium. Enough of the mind! Let his body sweat out the frustrations wrought by his intellect.

5.

◆

He did not want to go to the Grand Imperial Universities Colloquy, but the Imperial Protocol Office leaned on him. "A First Ministerial candidate has obligations," the officious woman had informed him.

So he and Dors dutifully appeared at the enormous Imperial Festival Hall. His Specials wore discreet formal business suits, complete with the collar ruffles of mid-level meritocrats.

"All the better to blend into the crowd," Dors joked. Hari saw that everyone sized up the men in an instant and gingerly edged away. He would have been fooled.

They entered a high, double-arched corridor, lined with ancient statuary which invited the passersby to lick them. Hari tried it, after carefully reading the glow-sign, which reassured him there was no biological risk. A long, succulent lick gave him a faint, odd flavor of oil and burnt apples, a hint of what the ancients found enticing.

"What's first on the agenda?" he asked his Protocol Officer.

"An audience with the Academic Potentate," she answered, adding pointedly, "Alone."

Dors disagreed and Hari negotiated a compromise. Dors got to stand at the doorway, no more. "I'll have appetizers served to you there," the Protocol Officer said testily.

Dors gave her an icy smile. "Why is this, ah, 'audience' so important?"

The Protocol Officer gave her a pitying look. "The Potentate carries much weight in the High Council."

Hari said soothingly, "And can throw a few votes my way."

"A bit of polite talk," the Protocol Officer said.

"I shall promise to—let me put this delicately— smooch his buttocks. Or hers, as the case may be."

Dors smiled. "Better not be hers."

"Intriguing, how the implications of the act switch with sex."

The Protocol Officer coughed and ushered him deftly through snapping screen curtains, his hair sizzling. Apparently even an Academic Potentate had need of personal security measures.

Once within the formal staterooms, Hari found he was alone with a woman of considerable age and artificial beauties. So that was why the Protocol Officer had coughed.

"How very nice of you to come." She stood motionless, one hand extended, limp at the wrist. A waterfall effect spattered behind her, framing her body well.

He felt as if he were walking into a still-life museum display. He didn't know whether to shake her hand or kiss it. He shook it, and her look made him think he had chosen wrong.

She wore a lot of embedded makeup, and from the way she leaned forward to make a point, he gathered that her pale eyes got her a lot of things other people did not receive.

She had once been an original thinker, a nonlinear philosopher. Now meritocrats across the spiral arms owed her fealty.

Before they had sat down, she gestured. "Oh, would you tune that wall haze?" The waterfall effect had turned into a roiling, thick fog. "Somehow it gets *wrong* all the time and the room doesn't adjust it."

A way of establishing a hierarchy, Hari suspected. Get him used to doing little tasks at her bidding. Or maybe she was like some other women, who if they couldn't get you to do minor services felt insecure. Or maybe she was just inept and wanted her waterfall back. Or maybe he just analyzed the hell out of everything, a mathist's pattern.

"I've heard remarkable things about your work," she said, shifting from High Figure Used to Snappy Obedience to Gracious Lady Putting an Underling at Ease. He said something noncommittal. A tiktok brought a stim which was barely liquid, drifting down his throat and into his nostrils like a silken, sinister cloud.

"You believe yourself practical enough for the ministership?"

"Nothing is more practical, more useful, than a sound theory."

"Said like a true mathist. Speaking for all meritocrats, I do hope you are equal to the task."

He thought of telling her—she did have a certain charm, after all—that he didn't give a damn for the ministership. But some intuition held him back. She was another power broker. He knew she had been vindictive in the past.

She gave him a shrewd smile. "I understand you have charmed the Emperor with a theory of history."

"At the moment it is little better than a description."

"A sort of summary?"

"Breakthroughs for the brilliant, syntheses for the driven."

"Surely you know there is an air of futility about such an ambition." A gleam of steel in the pale eyes.

"I was . . . unaware. Madam."

"Science is simply an arbitrary construct. It perpetuates the discredited notion that progress is always possible. Let alone desirable."

"Oh?" He had plastered a polite smile on his face and was damned if he would let it slip.

"Only oppressive social orders emerge from such ideas. Science's purported objectivity hides the plain fact that it is simply one 'language game' among others. All such arbitrary configurations sit in a conceptual universe of competing discourses."

"I see." The smile was getting heavier. His face felt like it would crack.

"To elevate scientific—" she sniffed disdainfully "—so-called 'truths' over other constructions is tantamount to *colonizing* the intellectual landscape. To enslaving one's opposition!"

"Ummm." He had a sinking feeling that he was not going to last long as a door mat. "Before you even consider the subject, you claim to know the best way to study it?"

"Social theory and linguistic analysis have the final power, since all truths have quite limited historical and cultural validity. Therefore, this 'psychohistory' of all societies is absurd."

So she knew the term; word was spreading. "Perhaps you have insufficient regard for the rough rub of the real."

A slight thawing. "Clever phrasing, Academician. Still, the category 'real' is a social construction."

"Look, of course science is a social process. But scientific theories don't merely reflect society."

"How charming to still think so." A wan smile failed to conceal the icy gleam in her eyes.

"Theories are not mere changes of fashion, like shifting men's skirts from short to long."

"Academician, you must know that there is nothing knowable beyond human discourses."

He kept his voice level, courteous. Point out that she had used "know" in two contradictory ways in the same sentence? No, that would be playing word games, which would subtly support her views. "Sure, mountain climbers might argue and theorize about the best route to the top—"

"Always in ways conditioned by their history and social structures—"

"—but once they get there, they know it. Nobody would say they 'constructed the mountain.'"

She pursed her lips and had another foggy-white stim. "Ummm. Elementary realism. But all of your 'facts' embody theory. Ways of seeing."

"I can't help noticing that anthropologists, sociologists—the whole gang—get a delicious rush of superiority by denying the objective reality of the hard sciences' discoveries."

She drew herself up. "There are no elemental truths that exist independent of the people, languages, and cultures that *make* them."

"You don't believe in objective reality, then?"

"Who's the object?"

He had to laugh. "Language play. So linguistic structures dictate how we see?"

"Isn't that obvious? We live in a galaxy rich in cultures, all seeing the Galaxy their way."

"But obeying laws. Plenty of research shows that thought and perception precede talk, exist independent of language."

"What laws?"

"Laws of social movement. A theory of social history—if we had one."

"You attempt the impossible. And if you wish to be First Minister, enjoying the support of your fellow academics and meritocrats, you shall have to follow the prevailing view of our society. Modern learning is animated by a frank incredulity toward such metanarratives."

He was sorely tempted to say, *Then you are going to be surprised*, but instead said, "We shall see."

"We don't see things as they are," the learned lady said, "we see them as *we* are."

With a touch of sadness, he realized that the republic of intellectual inquiry was, like the Empire, not free of internal decay.

6.

◆

The Academic Potentate led him out with ritual words to smooth the way, and Dors was standing attentively at the grand entrance. Still, Hari had gotten the essential message: the academic meritocracy would back him for First Minister *if* he at least paid lip service to prevailing orthodoxy.

Together, with the customary academic honor

guard, they went down into the vast rotunda. This was a dizzying bowl with various scholarly disciplines represented by the full regalia and insignia, splashed across immense wall designs. Below them swirled a chattering mob, thousands of the finest minds gathered for speeches, learned reports, and of course much infighting of the very finest sort.

"Think we can survive this?" Hari whispered.

"Don't let go," Dors said, seizing his hand.

He realized that she had taken his question literally.

A little later the Academic Potentate wasn't making a show of savoring the bouquet of the stims anymore, just sucking them up like one of the major food groups. She steered Hari and Dors from one cluster of the learned to another. Occasionally she would remember her role as hostess and feign interest in him as more than a chess piece in a larger game. Unfortunately these blunt attempts fastened upon inquiries into his personal life.

Dors resisted these inquisitions, of course, smiling and shaking her head. When the Potentate turned to Hari and asked, "Do you exercise?" he could not resist replying, "I exercise restraint."

The Protocol Officer frowned, but Hari's remark went unnoticed in the jostling throng. He found the company of his fellow members of the professoriat oddly off-putting. Their conversations had a directionless irony, which conveyed with raised eyebrows and arch tones the speaker's superiority to everything he was commenting upon.

Their acerbic paradoxes and stiletto humor struck Hari as irritating and beside the point. He knew well that the most savage controversies are about matters for which there is no good evidence either way. Still, there was a mannered desperation even to the scientists.

Fundamental physics and cosmology had been well worked out far back in antiquity. Now all of Imperial scientific history dealt with teasing out intricate details and searching for clever applications. Humankind was trapped in a cosmos steadily expanding, though slowing slightly, and destined to see the stars wink out. A slow, cool glide into an indefinite future was ordained by the mass-energy content present at the very conception of the universe. Humans could do nothing against that fate. Except, of course, understand it.

So the grandest of intellectual territories had been opened, and that can only be done once. Now scientists were less like discoverers than like settlers, even tourists.

He should not be surprised, he realized, to find that even the best of them, gathered from an entire Galaxy, should have an air of jaded brilliance, like tarnished gold.

Meritocrats did not have many children and there was an airy sterility about them. Hari wondered if there was a middle ground between the staleness he felt here and the chaos of the "renaissances" sprouting up on Chaos Worlds. Perhaps he needed to know more about basic human nature.

The Protocol Officer steered him down a spiral air ramp, electrostatics seizing them and gently lowering the party toward—he looked down with trepidation—the obligatory media people. He braced himself. Dors squeezed his hand. "Do you *have* to talk to them?"

He sighed. "If I ignore them, they will report *that*."

"Let Lamurk amuse them."

"No." His eyes narrowed. "Since I'm in this, I might as well play to win."

Her eyes widened with revelation. "You've decided, haven't you?"

"To try? You bet."

"What happened?"

"That woman back there, the Potentate. She and her kind think the world's just a set of opinions."

"What has that got to do with Lamurk?"

"I can't explain it. They're all part of the decay. Maybe that's it."

She studied his face. "I'll never understand you."

"Good. That would be dull, yes?"

The media pack approached, 3D snouts aimed like weapons.

Hari whispered to Dors, "Every interview begins as a seduction and ends as a betrayal." They descended.

"Academician Seldon, you are known as a mathist, a candidate First Minister, and a Heliconian. You—"

"I only realized I was a Heliconian when I came to Trantor."

"And your career as a mathist—"

"I only realized that I thought as a mathist when I began meeting politicians."

"Well then, as a politician—"

"I am still a Heliconian."

This drew some laughter.

"You prize the traditional, then?"

"If it works."

"We be not open to old ideas," a willowy woman from the Fornax Zone said. "Future of Empire comes from people, not laws. Agree?"

She was a Rational, using their stripped-down, utterly orderly Galactic, free of irregular verbs and complex constructions. Hari could follow it well enough, but for him the odd swerves and turns of Classical Galactic embodied its charm.

To Hari's delight, several people disagreed with her formulated question, shouting. In the noise he reflected on the infinity of human cultures, represented in this vast bowl and still united under Classical Galactic.

The language's sturdy base had stitched together the early Empire. For many millennia now the language had sat on its laurels, admittedly. He had added a small interaction term to his equations to allow for the cultural ripples excited by the splashing of a new argot into the linguistic pool. The ancient ruffles and flourishes of Galactic allowed subtleties denied the Rationals—or Rats, as some called them—and the fun of puns as well.

He tried to make this case to the woman, but she retorted, "Not support oddity! Support order. Old ways failed. As mathist you will be too—"

"Come now!" Hari said, irked. "Even in closed axiomatic systems, not all propositions are decidable. I suggest you cannot predict what I would do as a First Minister."

"Think you Council submits to reason?" the woman asked haughtily.

"It is the triumph of reason to get on well with those who possess none," Hari said. To his surprise, some applauded.

"Your theory of history denies God's powers to intervene in human affairs!" a thin man from a low-grav planet asserted. "What say you to that?"

Hari was about to agree—it seemed to make no difference to him—when Dors stepped before him.

"Perhaps I can bring up a bit of research, since this is an academic proceeding." She smiled smoothly. "I ran across an historian of about a thousand years ago who had tested for the power of prayer."

Hari's mouth made a surprised, skeptical O. The thin man demanded, "How could one scientifically—"

"He reasoned that the people most prayed for were the most famous. Yet they had to be exalted, above the fray."

"The emperors?" The thin man was rapt.

"Exactly. And their lesser family members. He analyzed their mortality rates."

Hari had never heard this, but his innate skepticism demanded detail. "Allowing for their better medical care, and safety from ordinary accidents?"

Dors grinned. "Of course. Plus their risk of assassination."

The thin man did not know where this line of attack was going, but his curiosity got the better of him. "And . . . ?"

Dors said, "He found that emperors died earlier than unprayed-for people."

The thin man looked shocked, angry.

Hari asked Dors, "What was the root mean deviation?"

"Always the skeptic! Not sufficient to prove that prayer had an actually harmful effect."

"Ah." The crowd seemed to find this example of tag-team puffery entertaining. Best to leave them wanting more. "Thank you," he said, and they melted away behind a screen of Specials.

That left the crowd itself. Cleon had urged him to mingle with these folk, supposedly his basic power base, the meritocrats. Hari wrinkled his nose and nonetheless plunged in.

It was a matter of style, he realized after the first thirty minutes.

He had learned early in rural Helicon to place great store in good manners and civility. Among the alert, hard-edged academics he had found many who seemed poorly socialized, until he realized that they were operating out of a different culture, where cleverness mattered more than grace. Their subtle shadings of voice carried arrogance and assurance in precarious balance, which in unguarded moments tilted into acerbic, cutting judgment, often without even the appealing veneer of wit. He had to make himself remember to say "With all due respect," at the beginning of an argument, and even to mean it.

Then there were the unspoken elements.

Among the fast-track circles, body language was essential, a taught skill. There were carefully designed poses for Confidence, Impatience, Submission (four shadings), Threat, Esteem, Coyness and dozens more. Codified and understood unconsciously, each induced a specific desired neurological state in both self and others. The rudiments for a full-blown craft lay in dance, politics, and the martial arts. By being systematic, much more could be conveyed. As with language, a dictionary helped.

A nonlinear philosopher of Galaxy-wide fame gave Hari a beaming smile, body language screaming self-confidence, and said, "Surely, Professor, you cannot maintain that your attempt to import math into history can somehow work? People can be what they wish. No equations will make them otherwise."

"I seek to describe, that's all."

"No grand theory of history, then?"

Avoid a direct denial, he thought. "I will know I'm on the right track when I can simply describe a bit of human nature."

"Ah, but that scarcely exists," the man said with assurance, arms and chest turned adroitly.

"Of course there's a human nature!" Hari shot back.

A pitying smile, a lazy shrug. "Why should there be?"

"Heredity interacts with environment to tug us back toward a fixed mean. It gathers people in all societies, across millions of worlds, into the narrow statistical circle that we must call human nature."

"I don't think there are enough general traits—"

"Parent-child bonding. Division of labor between the sexes."

"Well, surely that's common among all animals. I—"

"Incest avoidance. Altruism—we call it 'humanitarianism,' a telling clue, eh?—toward our near kin."

"Well, those are just normal family—"

"Look at the dark side. Suspicion of strangers. Tribalism—witness Trantor's eight hundred Sectors! Hierarchies in even the smallest groups, from the Emperor's court to a bowling team."

"Surely you can't make such leaps, such simplistic, grotesque comparisons—"

"I can and do. Male dominance, generally, and when resources are scarce, marked territorial aggression."

"These are *little* traits."

"They link us. The sophisticated Trantorian and an Arcadian farmer can still understand each other's lives, for the simple reason that their common humanity lives in the genes they share from many tens of millennia ago."

This outburst was not received well. Faces wrinkled, mouths pouched in disapproval.

Hari saw he had overstepped. What's more, he had nearly exposed psychohistory.

Yet he found it hard to not speak frankly. In his view the humanities and social sciences shrank to specialized branches of both mathematics and biology. History, biography, and fiction were symptoms. Anthropology and sociology together became the sociobiology of a single species. But he could not get a *feel* for how to include that in the equations. He had spoken out, he saw suddenly, because he was frustrated—by his own lack of understanding.

Still, that did not excuse his stupidity. He opened his mouth to smooth over the waters.

He saw the agitated man coming up on his left. Mouth awry, eyes white, hand—extended, poking forward, a tube in it, chromed and sleek and with a precise hole at the tip, a dark spot that expanded as he looked at it until it seemed like the Eater of All Things that lurked at Galactic Center, immense—

Dors hit the man quite expertly. She deflected the arm up, jabbed him in the throat, struck next at the belly. Then she twisted the arm and forced him into a quarter-turn, her left leg coming around and cutting his feet from beneath him, her right hand forcing the head down—

And they struck the floor solidly, Dors on top, the gun skittering away among the shoes of the crowd—which was falling back in panic.

Specials blocked in around him and he saw no more. He shouted to Dors. Screams and shouts hammered at him from all sides.

More bedlam. Then he was clear of the Specials and the man was getting up and Dors was standing, holding the pistol, shaking her head. The man who had pointed it struggled to his feet.

"A recording tube," she said in disgust.

"What?" Hari could barely hear in the noise.

The man's left arm was sticking out at a wrong angle, plainly broken. "I—I agreed with your every word," the man croaked out, his face a ghastly white. "Really."

7.

◆

Hari's father had derisively referred to most public affairs as "dust-ups"—a big cloud on the horizon, a tiny speck underneath. His lip had curled back in a farmer's disdain for making more of a thing than it was.

The incident at the Grand Imperial Universities Colloquy had become a grand dustup. Fully 3D'd, the scandal—PROF'S WIFE SOCKS FAN—burgeoned with each replaying.

Cleon called, tsk-tsking, and commenting broadly on how wives could be a burden in high office. "This will hurt your candidacy, I fear," he had said. "I must do some mending."

Hari did not report this to Dors. Cleon's hint was clear. It was common practice among Imperial circles to divorce on grounds of general unsuitability—which meant unfashionability. In matters of vast power, appetite for more often overwhelmed all other emotions, even love.

He went home, irked by this conversation, to find Dors at work in the kitchen. She had her arms open—literally, not in greeting.

The epidermis hung loose, as if she had pulled a tight glove halfway off. Veins interlaced with the artificial neural net and she was working with tiny tools among them. Supple skin peeled back in a curved line down from elbow to wrist, moist crimson and intricate electronics. She was working on the augmented wrist, a thin yellow collar that did not look as though it could take three times the normal human's impact.

"That fellow damaged you?"

"No, I did it to myself—or rather, overdid it."

"A sprain?"

She smiled without humor. "My pivots don't sprain. The collar mounts don't mend. I'm replacing them."

"Jobs like this, it's not the parts, it's the labor."

She looked at him quizzically and he decided not to pursue the joke. He normally put from his mind the fact that his true love was a robot—or more accurately, a humaniform, vastly technically assisted, human-robot synthesis.

She had come to him through R. Daneel Olivaw, the ancient positronic robot who had saved Hari when he first came to Trantor and ran afoul of nasty political forces. She had been assigned at first as a bodyguard. He had known what she was from the start, at least approximately, but that did not prevent him from falling in love with her. Intelligence, character, charm, a simmering sexuality—these were not purely human facets, he had learned—by direct example.

He got her a drink as she worked, biding his time. He had ceased to be amazed by her repair work, often carried out on an utterly unsanitized field. There were antimicrobial methods available to the humaniform robots that could not work for ordinary humans, she had said. He had no idea how this could be. She discouraged further discussion, often deflecting him with passion. He had to admit that as a ploy this was completely effective.

She rolled her skin back into place, grimacing at the pain. She could shut off whole sections of her superficial nervous system, he knew, but kept a few strands alert as a diagnostic. The tabs self-sealed with pops and purrs.

"Let's see." She paused, feeling each wrist in turn. Two quick snaps. "They lock in fine."

"Most people, you know, would find this sight quite unsettling."

"That's why I don't do it on the way to work."

"Very public spirited of you."

They both knew she would be hounded down if there were any suspicion of her true nature. Robots of advanced capability had been illegal for millennia. Tiktoks were acceptable precisely because they were low-grade intelligences, rigorously held below the threshold of legally defined sentience. Violating those standards in manufacture was a capital crime, an Imperial violation, no exceptions. And strong, ancient emotions backed up the law: the Junin Sector riots had proved that.

Numerical simulations were similarly restricted. That was why the Voltaire and Joan sims, developed by the "New Renaissance" hotheads on Sark, had been carefully tailored to squeeze through algorithmic loopholes. Apparently that Marq fellow at Artifice Associates had souped up the Voltaire at the last minute. Since the sim was then erased, the violation had escaped detection.

Hari did not like having even a slight connection to crime, but he now realized that this was foolishness. Already his entire life revolved around Dors, a hidden pariah.

"I'm going to withdraw from the First Minister business," he said decisively.

She blinked. "Me."

She was always quick. "Yes."

"We had agreed that the risk of increased scrutiny was worth gaining some power."

"To protect psychohistory. But I expected very little of the spotlight to fall upon you. Now—"

"I am an embarrassment."

"Coming in downstairs, there were a dozen 3D snouts pointing at me. They're waiting for you."

"I will stay here, then."

"For how long?"

"The Specials can take me out through a new entrance. They've cut one and installed an agrav shaft."

"You can't avoid them forever, darling."

She got up and embraced him. "Even if they find me out, I can go away."

"If you're lucky and escape. Even if you do, I can't live without you. I won't—"

"I could be transformed."

"Another body?"

"A different one. Skin, corneas, some neural signatures changed."

"File the serial numbers off and send you back?"

She stiffened in his arms. "Yes."

"What can't your . . . kind . . . do?"

"We cannot invent psychohistory."

He whirled away from her in frustration and smacked his palm against a wall. "Damn it, nothing is as important as *us*."

"I feel the same. But now I think it is even more important for you to remain a candidate for First Minister."

"Why?" He paced around their living room, eyes darting.

"You are a player for very high stakes. Whoever wishes to assassinate you—"

"Lamurk, Cleon believes."

"—will probably see that merely withdrawing your candidacy is no firm solution. The Emperor could reintroduce you into the game at any later time."

"I don't like being treated as a chess piece."

"A knight?—yes, I can see you that way. Do not forget that there are other suspects, factions which may wish you out of the way."

"Such as?"

"The Academic Potentate."

"But she's a scholar, like me!"

"*Was.* She is now a player on the chessboard."

"Not the queen, I hope."

Dors kissed him lightly. "I should mention that my ferret programs turned up a plausibility matrix for Lamurk's behavior, based on his past. He has eliminated at least half a dozen rivals on his rise to the top. He is something of a traditionalist in method, as well."

"My, that's comforting."

She gave him an odd, pensive glance. "His rivals were all knifed. The classic dispatch of historical intrigue."

"I wouldn't suspect Lamurk to have such an eye for our Imperial heritage."

"He is a classicist. In his view, you are a pawn, one best swept from the board."

"A rather bloodless way to put it."

"I am taught—and built—to assess and act coolly."

"How do you reconcile your ability—in fact, let's not put too fine a point on it, your *relish*—at the prospect of killing a person in my defense?"

"The Zeroth Law."

"Um." He recited, "Humanity as a whole is placed above the fate of a single human."

"I *do* feel pain from First Law interaction . . ."

"So the First Law, now modified, is, 'A robot may not injure a human being, or through inaction, allow a human being to come to harm, unless this would violate the Zeroth Law of Robotics'?"

"Exactly."

"This is another game you play. With very tough rules."

"It is a larger game."

"And psychohistory is a potential new set of game plans?"

"In a way." Her voice softened and she embraced him. "You should not trouble yourself so. What we have is a private paradise."

"But the damned games, they always go on."

"They must."

He kissed her longingly, but something inside him seethed and spun, an armature whirring fruitlessly in surrounding darkness.

8.

◆

Yugo was waiting in his office the next morning. Face flushed, wide-eyed, he demanded, "What can you do?"

"Uh, about what?"

"The news! The Safeguards stormed the Bastion."

"Uh, oh." Hari vaguely recalled that a Dahlite faction had staged a minor revolt and holed up in a redoubt. Negotiations had dragged on. Yes, and Yugo had told him about it, several times. "It's a local Trantorian issue, isn't it?"

"That's the way *we* kept it!" Yugo's hands flew in elaborate gestures, like birds taking frenzied flight. "Then the Safeguards came in. No warning. Killed over four hundred. Blew 'em apart, blasters on full, no warning."

"Astonishing," Hari said in what he hoped was a sympathetic tone.

In fact he did not care a microgram for one side of this argument or the other—and did not know the arguments, anyway. He had never cared for the world's day-to-day turbulence, which agitated the mind without teaching anything. The whole point of psychohistory, which emerged from his personality as much as his analytic ability, was to study climate and ignore weather.

"Can't you *do* something?"

"What?"

"Protest to the Emperor!"

"He will ignore me. This is a Trantorian issue and—"

"This is an insult to you, too."

"It can't be." To not appear totally out of it, he added, "I've deliberately kept well away from the issue—"

"But Lamurk did this!"

That startled him. "What? Lamurk has no power on Trantor. He's an Imperial Regent."

"C'mon, Hari, nobody believes that old separation of powers stuff. It broke down long ago."

Hari almost said, *It did?*, but just in time realized that Yugo was right. He had simply not added up the effects of the long, slow erosion in the Imperial structures. Those entered as factors on the right-hand side of the equations, but he never thought of the decay in solid, local terms. "So you think it's a move to gain influence on the High Council?"

"Must be," Yugo fumed. "Those Regents, they don't like unruly folk livin' near 'em. They want Trantor nice and orderly, even if people get trampled."

Hari ventured, "The representation issue again, is it?"

"Damn right! We got Dahlites all over Muscle Shoals Sector. But can we get a representative? Hell, no! Got to beg and plead—"

"I . . . I will do what I can." Hari held up his hands to cut off the tirade.

"The Emperor, he'll straighten things out."

Hari knew from direct observation that the Emperor would do no such thing. He cared nothing of how Trantor was run, as long as he could see no burning districts from the palace. Cleon had often remarked, "I am Emperor of a galaxy, not a city."

Yugo left and Hari's desk chimed. "Imperial Specials' captain to see you, sir."

"I told them to remain outside."

"He requests audience, bearing a message."

Hari sighed. He had meant to get some thinking done today.

The captain entered stiffly and refused a chair. "I am here to respectfully forward the recommendations of the Specials Board, Academician."

"A letter would suffice. In fact, do that—send me a note. I have work to—"

"Sir, most respectfully, I must discuss this."

Hari sank into his chair and waved permission. The man looked uncomfortable, standing stiffly as he said, "The board requests that the Academician's wife not accompany him to state functions."

"Ah, so someone has yielded to pressure."

"It is further directed that your wife not be allowed into the palace at all."

"What? That seems extreme."

"I am sorry to bear such a message, sir. I was there and I told the board that the lady had good reason to become alarmed."

"And to break the fellow's arm."

The captain almost allowed himself a smile. "Got to admit, she's faster than anybody I've ever seen."

And you're wondering why, aren't you? "Who was the fellow?"

The captain's brow furrowed. "Looks to be a Spiral Academician, one grade above you, sir. But some say he's more a political type."

Hari waited, but the man said no more, just looked as though he wanted to. "Allied with what faction?"

"Might be that Lamurk, sir."

"Any evidence?"

"Nossir."

Hari sighed. Politics was not only an inexact craft, it seldom had any reliable data, either. "Very well. Message received."

The captain left quickly, with visible relief. Before Hari could wave his computer into life, a delegation from his own faculty showed up. They filed in silently, the portal crackling as it inspected each of them. Hari caught himself smiling at the procedure. If there was a profession least likely to yield an assassin, it had to be the mathists.

"We are here to submit our considered opinion," a Professor Aangon said formally.

"Do so," Hari said. Normally he would deploy his skimpy skills and do a bit of social mending; he had been neglecting university business lately, stealing time from bureaucratic chores to devote to equations.

Aangon said, "First, rumors of a 'theory of history' have brought scorn to our department. We—"

"There is no such theory. Only some descriptive analysis."

An outright denial confused Aangon, but he plowed ahead. "Uh, second, we deplore the apparent choice of your assistant, Yugo Amaryl, as department head, should you resign. It is an affront to senior faculty—vastly senior—above a junior mathist of, shall we say, minimal social bearing."

"Meaning?" Hari said ominously.

"We do not believe politics should enter into academic decisions. The insurrection of Dahlites, which Amaryl has vocally supported, and which has now been put down only through Imperial resolve, and actual armed force, makes him unsuitable—"

"Enough. Your third point."

"There is the matter of the assault upon a member of our profession."

"A member—oh, the fellow my wife . . . ?"

"Indeed, an indignity without parallel, an outrage, by a member of your family. It makes your position here untenable."

If someone had planned the incident, they were certainly getting their mileage out of it. "I reject that."

Professor Aangon's eyes became flinty. The other faculty had been shuffling around, uneasy, and now were bunched behind him. Hari had no doubts about who this group wanted to be the next chairman. "I should think that a vote of no confidence by the full faculty, in a formal meeting—"

"Don't threaten me."

"I am merely pointing out that while your attention is directed elsewhere—"

"The First Ministership."

"—you can scarcely be expected to carry out your duties—"

"Skip it. To hold a formal meeting, the chairman must call one."

The bunch of professors rustled, but nobody said anything.

"And I won't."

"You can't go for long without carrying out business which requires our consent," Aangon said shrewdly.

"I know. Let's see how long that can be."

"You really must reconsider. We—"

"Out."

"What? You cannot—"

"Out. Go."

They went.

9.

◆

It is never easy to deal with criticism, especially when there is every chance that it might be right.

Aside from the eternal maneuvering for position and status, Hari knew that his fellow meritocrats—from the Academic Potentate to the members of his own department, with legions in between—had deeply felt grounds for objecting to what he was doing.

They had caught a whiff of psychohistory, wafted by rumor. That alone put their hackles up, stiff and sensitive. They could not accept the possibility that humanity could not control its own future—that history was the result of forces acting beyond the horizons of mere mortal men. Could they already be sniffing at a truth Hari knew from elaborate, decades-long study—that the Empire had endured because of its higher, metanature, not the valiant acts of individuals, or even of worlds?

People of all stripes believed in human self-determination. Usually they started from a gut feeling that they acted on their own, that they had reached their opinions on the basis of internal reasoning—that is, they argued from the premises of the paradigm itself. This was circular, of course, but that did not make such arguments wrong or even ineffectual. As persuasion, the feeling of being in control was powerful. Everyone wanted to believe they were masters of their own fate. Logic had nothing to do with it.

And who was he to say they were wrong?

"Hari?"

It was Yugo, looking a bit timid. "Come in, friend."

"We got a funny request just a minute ago. Some research institute I never heard of offerin' us significant money."

"For what?" Money was always handy.

"In return for the base file on those sims from Sark."

"Voltaire and Joan? The answer is *no*. Who wants them?"

"Dunno. We got 'em, all filed away. The originals."

"Find out who's asking."

"I tried. Can't trace the prompt."

"Ummm. That's odd."

"That's why I thought I'd tell you. Smells funny."

"Keep up a tracing program, in case they ask again."

"Yessir. And about the Dahlite Bastion—"

"Give it a rest."

"I mean, look at how the Imperials squashed that Junin mess!"

Hari let Yugo go on. He had long ago mastered the academic art of appearing to pay rapt attention while his mind worked a spiral arm away.

He knew he would have to speak to the Emperor

about the Dahlite matter, and not only to counter Lamurk's move—an audacious one, within the traditionally inviolate realm of Trantor. A quick, bloody solution to a tough issue. Clean, brutal.

The Dahlites had a case: they were underrepresented. And unpopular. And reactionary.

The fact that Dahlites—except for prodigies lifted up by the scruff of their neck, like Yugo—were hostile to the usual instincts of a scientific mind made no difference.

In fact, Hari was beginning to doubt whether the stiff, formal scientific establishment was worthy of high regard any longer. All around him he saw corruption of the impartiality of science, from the boonsmanship networking to the currying of Imperial scraps which passed for a promotion system.

Just yesterday he had been visited by a Dean of Adjustments who had advised, with oily logic, that Hari use some of his Imperial power to confer a boon upon a professor who had done very little work, but who had family ties to the High Council.

The dean had said quite sincerely, "Don't you think it is in the better interests of the *university* that you grant a small boon to one with influence?" When Hari did not, he nonetheless called the fellow to tell him why.

The dean was astonished with such honesty. Only later did Hari decide that the dean was right, within his own logic system. If boons were mere benefits, simple largess, then why not confer them wholly on political grounds? It was an alien way of thinking, but consistent, he had to admit.

Hari sighed. When Yugo paused in his vehement tirade, Hari smiled. No, wrong response. A worried frown—there, that did it. Yugo launched back into rapid talk, arms taking wing, epithets stacked to improbable heights.

Hari realized that the mere exposure to politics as it truly was, the brutal struggle of blind swarms in shadow, had raised doubts about his own, rather smug, positions. Was the science he had so firmly believed in back on Helicon truly as useful to people like the Dahlites as he imagined?

So his musing came around to his equations: Could the Empire ever be driven by reason and moral decision, rather than power and wealth? Theocracies had tried, and failed. Scientocracies, rather more rarely, had been too rigid to last.

"—and I said, sure, Hari can do that," Yugo finished.

"Uh, what?"

"Back the Alphoso plan for Dahlite representation, of course."

"I will think about it," Hari said to cover. "Meanwhile, let's hear a report on that longevity angle you were pursuing."

"I gave it to three of those new research assistants," Yugo said soberly, his Dahlite energies expended. "They couldn't make sense of it."

"If you're a lousy hunter, the woods are always empty."

Yugo's startled look made Hari wonder if he was getting a bit crusty. Politics was taking its toll.

"So I worked the longevity factor into the equations, just to see. Here—" he slid an ellipsoidal data-core into Hari's desk reader "—watch what happens."

One persistent heritage of pre-antiquity was the standard Galactic Year, used by all worlds of the Imperium in official business. Hari had always wondered: Was it a signature of Earth's orbital period? With its twelve-based year of twelve months, each of twenty-eight days, it suggested as candidate worlds a mere 1,224,675 from the 25 million of the Empire.

Yet spins, precessions, and satellite resonances perturbed all planetary periods. Not a single world of those 1,224,675 fit the G.E. calendar exactly. Over 17,000 came quite close.

Yugo started explaining his results. One curious feature of Empire history was the human lifespan. It was still about 100 years, but some early writings suggested that these were nearly twice as long as the "primordial year" (as one text had it), which was "natural" to humans. If so, people lived nearly twice as long as in pre-Imperial eras. Indefinite extension of the lifespan was impossible; biology always won, in the end. New maladies moved into the niche provided by the human body.

"I got the basics on this from Dors—sharp lady," Yugo said. "Watch this data-flash." Curves, 3D projections, sliding sheets of correlations.

The collision between biological science and human culture was always intense, often damaging. It usually led to a free-market policy, in which parents could select desirable traits for their children.

Some opted for longevity, increasing to 125, then even 150 years. When a majority were long-lived, such planetary societies faltered. Why?

"So I traced the equations, watching for outside influences," Yugo went on. Gone was the fevered Dahlite; here was the brilliance that had made Hari pluck Yugo out of a sweltering deep-layer job, decades ago.

Through the equations' graceful, deceptive sinuosity, he had found a curious resonance. There were underlying cycles in economics and politics, well understood, of about 120 to 150 years.

When the human lifespan reached those ranges, a destructive feedback began. Markets became jagged landscapes, peaking and plunging. Cultures lurched from extravagant excess to puritanical constriction. Within a few centuries, chaos destroyed most of the bioscience capability, or else religious restrictions smothered it. The mean lifespan slid down again.

"How strange," Hari said, observing the severe curves of the cycles, their arcs crashing into splintered spokes. "I've always wondered why we don't live longer."

"There's great social pressure against it. Now we know where it comes from."

"Still . . . I'd *like* to have a centuries-long, productive life."

Yugo grinned. "Look at the media—plays, legends, holos. The very old are always ugly, greedy misers, trying to keep everything for themselves."

"Ummm. True, usually."

"And myths. Those who rise from the dead. Vampires. Mummies. They're always evil."

"No exceptions?"

Yugo nodded. "Dors pulled some really old ones out for me. There was that ancient martyr—Jesu, wasn't it?"

"Some sort of resurrection myth?"

"Dors says Jesu probably wasn't a real person. That's what the scattered, ancient texts say. The whole myth is prob'ly a collective psychodream. You'll notice, once he was back from the dead, he didn't stay around very long."

"Rose into heaven, wasn't it?"

"Left town in a hurry, anyway. People don't want you around, even if you've beaten the Reaper."

Yugo pointed at the curves, converging on disaster. "At least we can understand why most societies learn not to let people live too long."

Hari studied the event-surfaces. "Ah, but who learns?"

"Huh? People, one way or the other."

"But no single person ever knew—" his finger jabbed "—this."

"The knowledge gets embedded in taboos, legends, laws."

"Ummm." There was an idea here, something larger looming just beyond his intuitions . . . and it slipped away. He would have to wait for it to revisit him—if he ever, these days, got the time to listen to the small, quiet voice that slipped by, whispering, like a shadowy figure on a foggy street. . . .

Hari shook himself. "Good work, this. I'm considerably impressed. Publish it."

"Thought we were keepin' psychohistory quiet."

"This is a small element. People will think the rumors are tarted-up versions of this."

"Psychohistory can't work if people know."

"It's safe. The longevity element will get plenty of coverage and stop speculation."

"It'll be a cover, then, against the Imperial snoops?"

"Exactly."

Yugo grinned. "Funny, how they spy even on an 'ornament to the Imperium'—that's what Cleon called you before the Regal Reception last week."

"He did? I didn't catch that."

"Workin' too much on those Boon Deeds. You got to hand off that stuff."

"We need more resources for psychohistory."

"Why not just get some money funneled through from the Emperor?"

"Lamurk would find out, use it against me. Favoritism in the High Council proceedings and so on. You could write the story yourself."

"Um, maybe so. Sure would be a whole lot easier, though."

"The idea is to keep our heads down. Avoid scandal, let Cleon do his diplomatic dance."

"Cleon also said you were a 'flower of intellect.' I recorded it for you."

"Forget it. Flowers that grow too high get picked."

10.

◆

Dors got as far as the palace high vestibule. There the Imperial Guard turned her back.

"Damn it, she's my wife," Hari said angrily.

"Sorry, it's a Peremptory Order," the bland court official said. Hari could hear the capital letters. The phalanx of Specials around Hari did not intimidate this fellow; he wondered if anyone could.

"Look," he said to Dors, "there's a bit of time before the meeting. Let's eat a bit at the High Reception."

She bristled. "You're not going *in*?"

"I thought you understood. I have to. Cleon's called this meeting—"

"At Lamurk's instigation."

"Sure, it's about this Dahlite business."

"And that man I knocked down at the reception, he might have been instigated to do it by—"

"Right, Lamurk." Hari smiled. "All wormholes lead to Lamurk."

"Don't forget the Academic Potentate."

"She's on my side!"

"*She* wants the ministership, Hari. All the rumor-mills say so."

"She can damn well have it," he grumbled.

"I can't let you go in there."

"This is the *palace*." He swept his arm at the ranks of blue-and-gold in the vast portal. "Imperials all around."

264 - GREGORY BENFORD

"Look, we agreed I'd try to bluster past—and it failed, just as I said. Fair enough. You would never pass the weapons checks, anyway."

Her teeth bit delicately into her lower lip, but she said nothing. No humaniform could ever get through the intense weapons screen here.

He said calmly, "So I go in, argue, meet you out here—"

"You have the maps and data I organized?"

"Sure, chip embedded. I can read it with a triple blink."

He had a carrychip embedded in his neck for data hauling, an invaluable aid at mathist conferences. Standard gear, readily accessed. A microlaser wrote an image on the back of the retina—colors, 3D, a nifty graphics package. She had installed a lot of maps and background on the Imperium, the palace, recent legislation, notable events, anything that might come up in discussions and protocols.

Her severe expression dissolved and he saw the woman beneath. "I just . . . please . . . watch yourself."

He kissed her on the nose. "Always do."

They patrolled among the legions of hangers-on who thronged the vestibule, snagging the appetizers which floated by on platters. "Empire's going bankrupt and they can afford this," Hari sniffed.

"It is time-honored," Dors said. "Beaumunn the Bountiful disliked delay in consuming meals, which was indeed his principal activity. He ordered that each of his estates prepare all four daily meals for him, on the chance that he might be there. The excess is given out this way."

Hari would not have believed such an unlikely story had it not come from an historian. There were knots of people who plainly lived here, using some minor functionary position for an infinite banquet. He and Dors drifted among them, wearing refractory vapors which muddled the appearance. Recognition would bring parasites.

"Even amid all this swank, you're thinking about that Voltaire problem, aren't you?" she whispered.

"Trying to figure out how somebody copied him— it—out of our files."

"And someone had requested it, just hours before?" She scowled. "When you turned it down, they simply stole it."

"Probably Imperial agents."

"I don't like it. They may be trying to implicate you further in the whole Junin scandal."

"Still, the old anti-sim taboo is breaking down." He toasted her. "Let's forget it. These days, it's either sims or stims."

There were several thousand people beneath the sculpted dome. To test the man-woman team shadowing them, Dors led him on a random path. Hari tired rapidly of such skullduggery. Dors, ever the student of society, pointed out the famous. She seemed to think this would thrill him, or at least distract him from the meeting to come. A few recognized him, despite the refraction vapors, and they had to stop and talk. Nothing of substance was ever said at such functions, of course, by long tradition.

"Time to go in," Dors warned him.

"Spotted the shadows?"

"Three, I think. If they follow you into the palace, I'll tell the Specials captain."

"Don't *worry*. No weapons allowed in the palace, remember."

"Patterns bother me more than possibilities. The assassination tab delayed detonation just long enough for you to discard it. But it did make me wary enough to attack that professor."

"Which got you banned from the palace." Hari completed the thought. "You're giving people a lot of credit for intricate maneuvers."

"You haven't read very much history of Imperial politics, have you?"

"Thank God, no."

"It would only trouble you," she said, kissing him with sudden, surprising fervor. "And worry is my job."

"I'll see you in a few hours," Hari said as casually as he could manage, despite a dark premonition. He added to himself, *I hope.*

He entered the palace proper through the usual arms checks and protocol officers. Nothing, not even a carbon knife or implosion nugget, could escape their many-snouted sniffers and squinters. Millennia before, Imperial assassination had become so common as to resemble a sport. Now tradition and technology united to make these formal occasions uniquely safe. The High Council was meeting for the Emperor's review, so inevitably there were battalions of officials, advisors, Magisterials Extraordinary and yellow-jacketed hangers-on. Parasites attached themselves to him with practiced grace.

Outside the Lyceum was the traditional Benevolent Bountiful—originally one long table, now dozens of them, all groaning beneath rich foods.

Largess even before business meetings was mandatory, an acceptance of the Emperor's beneficence. Passing it by would be an insult. Hari nibbled at a few oddments on his way across the Sagittarius Domeway. Noisy crowds milled restlessly, mostly in the series of ceremonial cloisters that rimmed the domeway, each cut off by acoustic curtains.

Hari stepped into a small sound chamber and found a sudden release from the din. There he quickly reviewed his notes on the Council agenda, not wanting to appear an utter rube. High Court types watched every deviation from protocol with scorn. The media, though not allowed in the Lyceum, buzzed for weeks after such meetings, reading every gaffe for its nuances. Hari hated all this, but as long as he was in the game, he might as well play.

He recalled Dors' casual mention earlier of Leon the Libertine, who had once arranged an entire faux-banquet for his ministers. The fruit could be bitten, but then snagged the unwary guests' teeth, which remained firmly embedded until released by a digital command. The command came, of course, only from the Emperor, after some amusing begging and groveling before the other guests. Rumors persisted of darker delights obtained by Leon from similar traps, though in private quarters.

Hari brushed through the sound curtains and into the older side halls leading to the Lyceum. His retinal map highlighted these ancient, unfashionable routes because few came this way. His entourage followed obediently, though some frowned.

He knew their sort by now. They wanted to be seen, their processional parting the crowds of mere Sector executives. Sauntering through dim halls without the jostle of the crowds did nothing for the ego.

There was a life-sized statue of Leon at the end of a narrow processional corridor, holding a traditional executioner's knife. Hari stopped and looked at the heavy-browed man, his right hand showing thick veins where it held the knife. In his left, a crystal globe of fogwine. The work was flawless and no doubt flattering to the Emperor when sculpted. The knife was quite real enough, its double edges gleaming.

Some considered Leon's reign the most ancient of the Good Old Days, when order seemed natural and the Empire expanded into fresh worlds without trouble. Leon had been brutal yet widely loved. Hari wanted psychohistory to work, but what if it turned into a tool to rekindle such a past?

Hari shrugged. Time enough to calculate whether the Empire could be saved on any terms at all, once psychohistory actually existed.

He went into the High Imperial chambers, escorted by the ritual officers. Ahead lay Cleon, Lamurk, and the panoply of the High Council.

He knew he should be impressed by all this. Somehow, though, the air of high opulence only made him more impatient to truly understand the Empire. And if he could, alter its course.

11.

◆

Hari wobbled slightly as he left the Lyceum three hours later. Debate was still in full cry, but he needed a break. A lesser Minister for Sector Correlation offered to take him to the refreshment baths, and Hari gratefully accepted.

"I don't know how much more of this I can take," he said.

"You must accommodate to tedium," the minister said cheerfully.

"Maybe I will duck out."

"No, come—rest!"

His ceremonial robes, required in the Lyceum, were close and sweaty. The ornate buckle dug into his belly. It was big and gaudy, with a chromed receiver for his ritual stylus, equally embellished and used only in voting.

The minister chatted on about Lamurk's attack on Hari, which Hari had tried to ignore. Even so, he had been forced to rise to defend or explain himself. He had made a point of keeping his speeches short and clear, though this was far from the style of the Lyceum. The minister politely allowed that he thought this was rather an error.

They went through the refresher, where blue gouts of ions descended. Hari was grateful that talk was impossible through all this, and let an electrostat breeze massage him until they evolved into decidedly erotic caresses; apparently Council members preferred their vices readily to hand.

The minister went in pursuit of some private amusement, his face alive with anticipation. Hari decided he would rather not know what was about to transpire and moved farther, into a vapor cell. He rested, thinking, as a ginger-colored mat cleaned his chamber; elementary biomaintenance. His muscles stretched as he reflected on the gulf between him and the professionals of the Lyceum.

To Hari, human knowledge was largely the unarticulated experiences of myriads, not the formal learning of a vocal elite. Markets, history showed, conveyed the preferences and ideas of the many. Generally, these were superior to grandiose policies handed down from the talent and wisdom of the few. Yet Imperial logic asked if a given action were good, not whether it was affordable, or how much was even desirable.

He truly did not know how to speak to these people. Clever verbal turns and artful dodges had served well enough today, but surely that could not last.

These ruminations had distracted him. With a start he realized he should get back.

Leaving the refresher, he angled off the obvious route, which was thronged with functionaries, on through acoustic veils and into the small processional hall, consulting his palace maps. He had used

Dors' carrychip a dozen times already, mostly to follow the quick, cryptic Council discussions. The microlaser-written 3D map on his retina rotated if he rolled his eyes, providing perspective. There were few staff around; most clustered in attendance outside the Lyceum.

Hari reached the end of the hall and glanced up at the statue of Leon. The executioner's knife was gone.

Why would anyone . . . ?

Hari turned and hurried back the way he had come.

Before he could reach the acoustic veils, a man stepped through their ivory luminescence. There was nothing unusual about the man except the way his eyes flicked around, finally fastening on Hari.

There was about thirty meters between them. Hari turned as though he were admiring the baroquely festooned walls and walked away. He heard the other man's boots crisply follow.

Maybe he was being paranoid and maybe not. He had only to get back to a crowd and all this would dissolve away, he told himself. The footsteps behind him got sharper, closer.

He turned and ducked down a side passage. Ahead was a ritual room. The footsteps sped up. Hari trotted across the circular room and into an ancient foyer. No one there.

Down a long hallway he could see two men who seemed to be casually talking. He started toward them, but they both broke off and looked at him. One reached into his pocket and produced a comm and began speaking into it.

Hari backed away, found a side passage. He bolted down it.

What about the surveillance cameras? Even the palace had them. But the one at the end of this passage had an unusual cap on it. *Running a fake view,* he realized.

The ancient portions of the Lyceum perimeter were not only unfashionable, they were unpopulated. He trotted through another extravagant ritual room. Boots were coming fast behind him. He turned to the right and saw a crowd down a long ramp.

"Hey!" he yelled. Nobody looked his way. He realized they were behind a sound veil. He started toward them.

A man stepped out of an alcove to block the way. This one was tall and lean and started toward Hari with a muscular nonchalance. Like the others he said nothing, drew no attention to himself. Just kept coming.

Hari angled left and broke into a trot. Ahead lay the refresher; he had circled back. Plenty of people there. If he could reach it.

One long passageway led directly toward the refreshers. He took it and halfway down saw that a party of three women were talking in a decorative niche. He slowed and they stopped talking. They wore familiar staff robes. Probably they worked in the refreshers.

They turned toward him, looking a little surprised. He opened his mouth to say something, and the nearest woman stepped smartly forward and grabbed his arm.

He jerked back. She was strong. She grinned at the others and said, "Fell right into our—"

He yanked his arm to the side and broke her grip. She came off balance and he took advantage of that to shove her into the other two. One lashed a kick at him. She twisted her hip to get momentum into it, but she could not get fully around her companion and it stopped short, futile.

Hari turned and ran. The women were obviously well trained and he did not have much hope of getting away. He plunged ahead down the long passageway.

When he glanced back, however, all three were standing and watching him go.

This was so odd that he slowed, thinking. They and the men were not attacking him, just boxing him in.

In these public corridors, casual witnesses could easily pass by. They wanted him somewhere private.

Hari called up his palace map. It placed him as a red dot in the nearby floor plan. He could see two side alleys up ahead before the end of the passageway—

—where now two men stepped into view, arms folded.

Hari still had two ways out. He went left into a narrow lane lined with antique testaments. Each winked on and began its narration of vast events and great victories, now buried beneath millennia of indifference. The 3Ds flickered with colorful spectacles as he pounded past them. Sonorous voices implored him to attend to their tales. He was puffing heavily now and trying to focus his thoughts.

Intersection coming up. He shot through it and saw men closing in from the right.

He dodged down a slight side exit, under a participatory mausoleum to Emperor Elinor IV, and sprinted toward a set of doorways he recognized. These were the refresher booths, pale doors marked only with numbers. The Minister for Sector Correlation had pointed them out as the very best, suitable for private appointments.

Hari had to cross a small piazza to reach the nearest door. A man came running from the right, saying nothing. Hari tried the first door; it was locked. So was the second. The man was nearly on top of him. The handle on the third door turned and Hari went through.

It was a traditional door on hinges. He threw his weight back into it to slam it shut. The man hit the door heavily and got a hand around the edge. Hari heaved against the door. The man held fast and jammed his right foot between the door and the casing.

Hari shoved hard. The gap between door and casing narrowed, trapping the hand.

The other man was strong. He grunted and shoved back hard and the gap widened.

Hari put his back against the door and thrust with his legs. He had nothing to help him and the ridiculous ceremonial robes didn't help. Nothing in the refresher was nearby, no tool—

Hari reached into his buckle. The ancient voting stylus slipped into his palm. He took it in his right hand and twisted against the door, shoving with his right shoulder. Then he passed the stylus to his left hand and brought it down with a savage stab into the man's hand.

The stylus was inscribed and embellished, but it tapered to a slender point. Hari struck between the third and fourth knuckles. Hard.

A small arterial pumper squirted. Short pulsating arcs shot onto the door, vivid red. The man cried "Ah!" and let go of the door.

Hari slammed the door shut and fumbled with the lock. Magnetic grids clicked on. Panting, he turned to survey the refresher.

It was one of the best, ample. Two soothing booths, a lift couch, an ample stock of refreshments. Several vapor wells—where luxuriant dalliances often occurred, as rumor had it. Against the far wall, a percussive nook for the athletic. And a thin slit-window, also traditional, open to a ceramic-and-sand garden. It was kept as a reminder of eras when being trapped in here with unsavory persons was best avoided by a quick exit.

Hari heard a slight *snick* against the door. Probably a depolarizer fitting into place to unlock the magnetics. He considered the slit-window.

12.

◆

A man came carefully into the refresher chamber. He wore a simple Imperial servant's tunic, which allowed freedom of movement. Perfect for quick work. He carried the knife from the Leon statue.

He closed the door behind him with one hand and locked it, all the while keeping his eyes on the room and the knife at the ready. Though he was large he moved with an easy grace. Methodically he checked in the booths and vapor wells and even the percussive nook. No one there. He leaned out the slit-window, which was thrown fully open. The narrow window was not large enough to let him pass; he was massive beneath his light blue staff uniform.

He stood back and spoke into his wrist comm. "He got out into the garden. Can't see him from here. You got that blocked?"

He paused a moment, listening to an internal voice, and said curtly, "Can't find him? 'Course you can't, I told you we shouldn't cut the snoops in this area."

Another pause. "Sure I know it's a secure job, even got its own RD number and all, no recording snoops, but—"

The man paced angrily. "Well, you just be damn sure all the ways out are covered. Those gardens are all connected."

Another pause. "Got the sniffers on? Cameras? Good. You guys mess this up, I'll . . ." He let his voice trail off into a growl.

He gave the room one last look and unlocked the magnetics. A man with a blood-soaked sleeve stood outside, just within view.

"You're drippin', stupid," the knife-carrier said. "Hold that arm up high and get away from here. Send a cleanup crew, too."

The other man said, "Where'd he—"

"Knew I shouldn't have you on this one. Goddamn amateur." The knife man left at a run.

All this had seemed to take forever. Seconds ticked by as Hari held onto a ceiling tile with all his strength.

In darkness he was lying across support struts directly over a soothing booth. He could see down through a narrow slit. From below, he hoped, the slit was the only sign that the ceiling had been pushed up, a square dislocated. He could see the scuff marks on the top of the booth, where he had climbed up and knocked the ceiling tile out of its clamps.

Now he had to hold the thing in place. His hands were starting to ache from gripping it.

Below he saw a leg and foot enter the refresher, turn, walk out of view. Someone else, a backup team?

If the tile slipped away from him, anyone below would notice the noise, see the dark slit widen. Maybe it would get away from him completely and fall.

He closed his eyes and concentrated on his fingers, willing them to grasp. They were numb now. Getting worse. Starting to tremble.

The tile was heavy, triple-layered for acoustic privacy. It was getting away from him, he could feel it. Slipping. It was going to—

The feet below walked out and then came the swish of the door closing. Its lock clicked.

He did not will it, but his fingers let the tile slip. It smacked the floor loudly. Hari froze, listening.

No click of the door lock reopening. Just the soft slur of the air circulators.

So he was safe for a while. Safe in a trap.

Nobody knew he was here. Only a thorough search would bring any trustworthy Imperials this far from the Lyceum area.

And why should they? Nobody would notice that he was missing right away. Even then, they would probably think he had simply gotten fed up with the Council and gone home. He had said as much to the Minister for Sector Correlation.

Which meant the assassins could quietly search for hours. The knife carrier had sounded systematic, determined. He would inevitably think of checking back here, starting over on the trail. There were probably scent-snoops they could muster. And by now the array of cameras throughout the palace would be looking for him.

Luckily there were none in the refresher. He climbed down, nearly slipping on the curved top of the soothing booth. Getting the heavy ceiling tile back up into place took agility and strength. He was puffing by the time he replaced it above the refresher. He lay along the struts and got the tile secured again.

He lay in the darkness and thought. Dors' palace map popped up in his eye on command, its colors and details more vivid in the gloom. Of course it showed nothing as utilitarian as this crawl space. He could see he was deeply embedded in the Lyceum's fringe areas. Perhaps his best bet would be to walk boldly out of this refresher. If he could reach a crowd . . .

If. He did not like leaving his fate to chance. That included the strategy of lying here, hoping they did not come back with snoopers that could sense him up here.

Anyway, he knew that he could not simply do nothing. That was not in his nature. When patience was needed, fine—but waiting did not necessarily improve his odds.

He looked off into the murky space. Gloom stretched away. He could move around up here. But which way?

Dors' map told him that the Gardens of Respite formed an artful tangle around the refresher area. No doubt the competent assassins would have ushered away any potential witnesses outside the window of this refresher room.

If he could somehow get far enough into the gardens . . .

Hari realized he was thinking in two dimensions. He could reach more public areas by moving up through a few layers of the palace. Outside this refresher room, down the hallway, Dors' map showed a lift shaft.

He got his bearings and peered in that direction. He had no idea how an e-lift fit into a building. The map simply showed a rectangular enclosure with a lift symbol. But a burning fear made his muscles clench and fret.

He started crawling that way, not because he knew what to do, but because he didn't. Upright cerami-form studs provided support and he had to be careful to not knock ceiling tiles out of their mounts. He slipped and jammed a knee into one and it gave threateningly, then popped back up. Dim threads of phosphor glow seeped between the tiles. Dust tickled his nostrils and coated his lips. He was getting dirty with the grime of millennia.

Up ahead a blue gleam came from roughly where the lift should be. As he drew closer the going got harder because ducts, pipes, optical conduits, and cross-joints thickened, converging on the hallway. Long minutes passed while he threaded his way among them. He touched a pipe that scorched his arm, a searing jolt so surprising he almost cried out. He smelled burnt flesh.

The blue radiance leaked around the edges of a panel. Suddenly it flared, then died again as he edged closer. A sharp crackling told him that an e-cell had just passed in the lift. He could not tell whether it was going up or down.

The panel was ceramo-steel, about a meter on a side, with electrical ribbons attached at all four sides. He did not know in detail how an e-lift worked, only that it charged the carrier compartment and then handed the weight off among a steady wave of electrodynamic fields.

He got his feet around and kicked at the panel. It held but dented. He kicked again and it loosened. He grunted with the effort of a third, a fourth—the panel popped out and fell away.

Hari brushed aside the thick electrical ribbons and poked his head into the shaft. It was dark, lit only by a dull radiance along a thin vertical phosphor which tapered away into obscurity, both above and below.

The palace was more than a kilometer thick in this ancient section. Mechanical elevators using cables could not serve even small passenger lifts like this one, over heights of a kilometer. Charge coupling from the shaft walls to the e-cell handled the dynamics with ease. The technology was aged and reliable. This shaft must be at least ten millennia old, and smelled like it.

He did not like the prospect before him. The map told him that three layers above him were spacious public rooms used to process supplicants to the Imperium. He would be in safe company there. Below were eight Lyceum layers, which he must assume were dangerous. Easier, certainly, to climb down—but also farther.

It would not be that tricky, he reassured himself. In the shadowy shaft he saw regular electrostatic emitters sunken into the walls. He found a strand of electrical ribbon and poked into one. No sparks, no discharge. That checked with his sketchy knowledge; the emitters went on only when a cell passed. They were deep enough to get his feet halfway into.

He listened carefully. No sound. E-cells were nearly silent, but these ancient ones were also slow. Was the risk of climbing into the shaft that great?

He wondered if he was doing the right thing, and then a voice far behind him said loudly, "Hey! Hey there!"

He glanced back. A head stuck up through an open panel. He could not make out features, but he did not try. He was already rolling awkwardly over the last cross-beam beside the shaft wall, twisting, thrusting himself out into the air. He felt downward with his feet, found an emitter hole, and stuck his foot into it.

No discharge. From memory he felt for another hole. His foot went in. He slipped over the casing, holding on tight with his hands.

His feet dangled above black nothingness. *Vertigo.* Sudden bile rushed in his throat.

Shouting from above. Several voices, male. Probably someone had seen the scrapes on top of the soothing booth. The light from the open ceiling tile was some help now, sending pale radiance into the shaft.

He swallowed and the bile eased.

Can't think about that now. Just go on.

To his right he saw another regularly spaced emitter hole. He got his foot into it and worked his way around to the next face of the shaft. He started climbing. It was surprisingly easy because the holes were closely spaced and about the right size for his hands and feet. Hari went up swiftly, driven by the scuffling sounds behind him.

He passed the doors of the next level. Beside them

was a flat-plate emergency switch. He could open the doors, but onto what?

Several minutes had passed since he saw the head. Word was undoubtedly spreading and they might have gotten up here, using stairs or another lift.

He decided to climb higher. Deep gulps of the dusty air threatened to make him cough, but he fought it down. His hands grasped the emitters and found them solid, easily held, while his legs did the real work of getting him up the sheer face.

He came to the second layer and made the same argument: only one more to go. That was when he heard the whisper. Faint, but gathering.

A cool downward brush of air made him look up. Something was blotting out the dim line of blue phosphor, coming down fast.

A clear crackling got louder. He could not possibly reach the above set of doors before it got here.

Hari froze. He could scramble back down, but he did not think he could reach the next level below in time. The black mass of the e-cell swooped down, swelling huge and fast, terrifying him.

A quick snap of blue arcs, a swoosh of air—and it stopped. At the level above.

The sound buffers cut off even the whisk of the doors opening. Hari yelled, but there was no response. He started down, feet seeking the holes, puffing.

A sharp crackling from above. The e-cell descended again.

He could see the undercarriage swooping down. Thin blue-white arcs shot from the emitter holes as it passed them, adding charge. Hari clambered down with a sinking dread.

An idea flashed across his mind, quick intuition. Wind fluttered his hair. He made himself study the undercarriage. Four rectangular clasps hung below. They were metal and would hold charge.

The e-cell was nearly upon him. No more time to think. Hari leaped toward the nearest clasp as the massive weight fell toward him.

He grabbed the thick rim of the clasp. A sharp, buzzing jolt snapped his eyes wide with pain. Crackling current coursed through him. His hands and forearms seized tight in electro-muscular shock. That kept him secured to the thick metal while his legs kicked involuntarily.

He had acquired some of the charge of the e-cell. Now the electrodynamic fields of the shaft played across his body, supporting him. His arms did not have to carry all his weight.

His hands and arms ached. Quick, sharp pains shot through the trembling muscles. But they held.

But currents were coursing through his chest—his heart. Muscles convulsed across his upper body. He was just another circuit element.

He let go with his left hand. That stopped current flowing, but he still held charge. The sharp pains in his chest muscles eased, but they still ached.

Levels flashed by Hari's dazed eyes. At least, he thought, he was getting away from his pursuers.

His right arm tired and he switched to his left. He told himself that hanging by one arm at a time probably did not tire them any faster than using two arms. He didn't believe it, but he wanted to.

But how was he going to get out of this shaft? The e-cell stopped again. Hari peered up at the shadowy mass looming like a black ceiling. Levels were far apart in this archaic part of the palace. It would take several minutes to climb down to the one below.

The e-cell could ratchet up and down the length of this shaft for a long time before getting a call from the lowest level. Even then, he had no idea how the shaft terminated. He could be crushed against a safety buffer.

So his clever leap had in fact bought him no escape. He was trapped here in a particularly ingenious way, but still trapped.

If he did manage to slap one of the emergency door openers as they passed, he would again feel a jolt of current as charge leaped from him to the shaft walls. His muscles would freeze in agony. How could he then hold on to anything?

The e-cell rose two floors, descended five, stopped, descended again. Hari switched hands again and tried to think.

His arms were tiring. The jolt of charge had strained them, and now surges of current through the shell of the e-cell made them jump with twinges of pain.

He had not acquired precisely the right charge to assure neutral buoyancy, so there was some residual downward pull on his arms. Like silken fingers, tingling electrostatic waves washed over him. He could feel weak surges of current from the e-cell, adjusting charge to offset gravity. He thought of Dors and how he had gotten here, and it all surged past him in a strange, dreamlike rush.

He shook his head. He had to *think*.

Currents passed through him as though he were part of the conducting shell. The passengers inside felt nothing, for the net charge remained on the outside, each electron getting as far away from its repulsing neighbors as possible.

The passengers inside.

He switched hands again. They both hurt a lot now. Then he swung himself back and forth like a pendulum, into longer oscillations. On the fifth swing he kicked hard against the undercarriage. A solid thunk—it was massive. He smacked the hard metal several more times and then hung, listening. Ignoring the pain in his arm.

No response. He yelled hoarsely. Probably anything he did was inaudible inside.

These ancient e-cells were ornately decorated inside, he remembered, with an atmosphere of velvet comfort. Who would notice small sounds from below?

The e-cell was moving again, upward. He flexed his arms and swung his feet aimlessly above the shadowy abyss. It was an odd sensation as the fields sustained him, playing across his skin. His hair stood on end all over his body. That was when the realization struck him.

He had approximately the same buoyant charge as the e-cell—so he did not need the cell at all anymore.

A pleasant theory, anyway. Did he have the courage to try it?

He let go of the clasp rim. He fell.

But slowly, slowly. A breeze swept by him as he drifted down a level, then two. Both arms shouted in relief.

Letting go, he still kept his charge. The shaft fields wrapped around him, absorbing his momentum, as though he were an e-cell himself.

But an imperfect one. With the constant feedback between an e-cell and the shaft walls, he would not be exactly buoyant for long.

Above him, the real e-cell ascended. He looked up and saw it depart, revealing more of the blue phosphor line tapering far overhead.

He rose a bit, stopped, began to fall again. The shaft was trying to compensate both for its e-cell and for him, an intruder charge. The feedback control program was unable to solve so complicated a problem.

Quite soon the limited control system would probably decide that the e-cell was its business and he was not. It would stop the e-cell, secure it on a level—and dispense with him.

Hari felt himself slow, pause—then fall again. Rivulets of charge raced along his skin. Electrons sizzled from his hair. The air around him seemed elastic, alive with electric fields. His skin jerked in fiery spasms, especially over his head and along his lower legs—where charge would accumulate most.

He slowed again. In the dim phosphor glow he saw a level coming up from below. The walls rippled with charges and he felt a spongy sidewise pressure from them.

Maybe he could use that. He stretched to the side, curling his legs up and thrusting against the rubbery stretch of the electrostatic fields.

He stroked awkwardly against the cottony resistance. He was picking up speed, falling like a feather. He stretched out to snag an emission hole—and a blue-white streamer shot into his hand. It convulsed and he gasped with the sudden pain. His entire lower arm and hand went numb.

He inhaled to clear his suddenly watery vision. The wall was going by faster. A level was coming up and he was hanging just a meter away from the shaft wall. He flailed like a bad swimmer against the pliant electrostatic fields.

The tops of the doors went by. He kicked at the emergency door opener, missed, kicked again—and caught it. The doors began to wheeze open. He twisted and gripped the threshold with his left hand as it went by.

Another jolt through the hand. The fingers clamped down. He swung about the rigid arm and slammed into the wall. Another electrical discharge coursed through him. Smaller, but it made his right leg tighten up. In agony, he got his right hand onto the threshold and hung on.

His full weight had returned and now he hung limply against the wall. His left foot found an emission hole, propped him up. He pulled upward slightly and found he had no more strength. Pain shot through his protesting muscles.

Shakily he focused. His eyes were barely above the threshold. Distant shouts. Shoes in formal Imperial blues were running toward him.

Hold . . . hold on . . .

A woman in a Thurban Guards uniform reached him and knelt, eyebrows knitted. "Sir, what are you—?"

"Call . . . Specials . . ." he croaked. "Tell them I've . . . dropped in."

PART 4

A SENSE OF SELF

SIMULATION SPACES— . . . *decided personality problems could arise. Any simulation which knew its origins was forcefully reminded that it was not the Original, but a fog of digits. All that gave it a sense of Self was continuity, the endless stepping forward of pattern. In actual people, the "real algorithm" computes itself by firing synapses, ringing nerves, continuity from the dance of cause and effect.*

This led to a critical problem in the representation of real minds—a subject under a deep (though eroding) taboo, in the closing era of the Empire. The simulations themselves did much of the work on this deep problem, with much simulated pain. To be "themselves" they had to experience life stories which guided them, so that they saw themselves as the moving point at the end of a long, complex line drawn by their total Selves, as evolved forward. They had to recollect themselves, inner and outer dramas alike, to shape the deep narrative that made an identity. Only in simulations derived from personalities which had a firm philosophical grounding did this prove ultimately possible . . .

—ENCYCLOPEDIA GALACTICA

1.

◆

Joan of Arc floated down the dim, rumbling tunnels of the smoky Mesh.

She fought down her fears. Around her played a complex spatter of fractured light and clapping, hollow implosions.

Thought was a chain unfixed in time and unanchored in space. But, like tinkling currents, alabaster pious images formed—restless, churning. An unending flux, dissolving structures in her wake, as if she were a passing ship.

She would be hugely pleased, indeed, to have so concrete a self. Anxiously she studied the murky Mesh that streamed about her like ocean whorls of liquid mahogany.

Since her escape from the wizards, upon whom the preservation of her soul—her "consciousness," a term somehow unconnected to conscience—depended, she had surrendered to these wet coursings. Her saintly mother had once told her that this was how the churning waters of a great river succumb, roiling into their beds deep in the earth.

Now she floated as an airy spirit, self-absorbed, sufficient to herself, existing outside the tick of time.

Stasis-space, Voltaire had termed it. A sanctuary where she could *minimize computational clock time*—such odd language!—waiting for visions from Voltaire.

At his last appearance, he had been frustrated—and all because she preferred her internal voices to his own!

How could she explain that, despite her will, the voices of saints and archangels so compelled her? That they drowned out those who sought to penetrate her from outside?

A simple peasant, she could not resist great spirit-beings like the no-nonsense St. Catherine. Or stately Michael, King of Angel Legions, greater than the royal French armies that she herself had led into battle. (*Eons ago,* an odd voice whispered—yet she was sure this was mere illusion, for time surely was suspended in this Purgatory.)

Especially she could not resist when their spirit-speech thundered with one voice—as now.

"Ignore him," Catherine said, the instant Voltaire's request for audience arrived. She hovered on great white wings.

Voltaire's manifestation here was a dove of peace, brilliant white, winging toward her from the sullen liquid. Blithe bird!

Catherine's no-nonsense voice cut crisply, as stiff as the black-and-white habit of a meticulous nun. "You sinfully surrendered to his lust, but that does not mean that he owns you. You don't belong to a man! You belong to your Creator."

The bird chirped, "I must send you a freight of data."

"I, I . . ." Joan's small voice echoed, as if she were in a vast cavern, not a vortex river at all. If she could only *see*—

Catherine's great wings batted angrily. "He will go away. He has no choice. He cannot reach you, cannot make you sin—unless you consent."

Joan's cheeks burned as the memory of her lewdness with Voltaire rushed in.

"Catherine is right," a deep voice thundered—Michael, King of the Angel Hosts of Heaven. "Lust has nothing to do with bodies, as you and the man proved. His body stank and rotted long ago."

"It would be good to see him again," Joan whispered longingly. Here, thoughts were somehow actions. She had but to raise a hand and Voltaire's numerics would transfix her.

"He offers defiling data!" Catherine cried. "Deflect his intrusion at once."

"If you cannot resist him, marry him," Michael ordered stiffly.

"Marry?" St. Catherine's voice sputtered with contempt.

In bodily life, she had affected male attire, cropped her hair, and refused to have anything to do with men, thus demonstrating her holiness and good sense. Joan had prayed to St. Catherine often. "Males! Even here," the saint scolded Michael, "you stick together to wage war and ruin women."

"My counsel is entirely spiritual," said Michael loftily. "I'm an angel and thus prefer neither sex."

Catherine sputtered with contempt. "Then why aren't you the Queen of Legions of Angels and not the King? Why don't you command heavenly hostesses and not heavenly hosts? Why aren't you an archangela instead of an archangel? And why isn't your name Michelle?"

Please, Joan said. *Please*. The thought of marriage struck as much terror in her soul as in St. Catherine's, even if marriage *was* one of the blessed sacraments. But then so was extreme unction, and *that* one almost always meant certain death.

. . . *flames* . . . the priest's leer as he administered the rites . . .

crackling horror, terrible cutting, licking *flames* . . .

She shook herself—*assembled her Self*, came a whisper—and focused on her saintly host. Oh yes, marriage . . . Voltaire . . .

She was not sure *what* marriage meant, besides bearing children in Christ and in agony, for Holy Mother Church. The act of getting children, begetting, aroused in her a thumping heart, weak legs, images of the lean, clever man . . .

"It means being owned," Catherine said. "It means instead of needing your consent when he wants to impose on you—like now—were Voltaire your husband, he could break in on you whenever he likes."

Existence without selfdom, without privacy . . . Bursts of Joan's bright self-light collided, flickered, dimmed, almost guttered out.

"Are you suggesting," Michael said, "that she continue to receive this apostate without subjecting their lust to the bonds of marriage? Let them marry and extinguish their lust completely!"

Joan could not be heard over the bickering of saints and angels in the musty, liquid murk. She knew that in this arithmetic Limbo, like a waiting room for true Purgatory, she had no heart . . . but something, somewhere, nevertheless ached.

Memories flooded her. His lean, quick self. Surely a saint and an archangel would forgive her if she took advantage of their sacred bickering to grant Voltaire's request that his "data" be received, if she surrendered—just this once—to impulses compelling her from within.

Shuddering, she yielded.

2.

◆

Voltaire snapped, "I've waited less long for Friedrich of Prussia and Catherine the Great!"

"I am adrift," Joan said airily. "Occupied."

"And you're a peasant, a swineherd, not even a *bourgeoise*. These moods of yours! These personae your subconscious layers created! They grow tiresome in the extreme."

He hung in air above the lapping dark waters. Quite a striking effect, he thought.

"In such haunting rivers I must converse with like minds."

He waved away her point with a silk-sleeved arm. "I've tried to make allowances—everyone knows saints aren't fit for civilized society! Perfume cannot conceal the stink of sanctity."

"Surely here in Limbo—"

"This is *not* a theological waiting room! Your tedious taste for solitude plays out in theaters of computation."

"Arithmetic is not holy, sir."

"Umm, perhaps—though I suspect Newton could prove otherwise."

He slow-stepped the scene, watching individual event-waves wash through. To his view, the somber river gurgled an increment forward and Joan's eyebrow inched up, then paused for the calculation to be refreshed. He accelerated her internal states, though, allowing a decent interval for *La Pucelle*, the Chaste Maid, to ponder a reply. He had the advantage, for he commanded more memory space.

He breached the slow-stepped, slumbering river

sim. He had thought this best—images of womblike wet reassurance, to offset her fire phobia.

The Maid gaped but did not answer. He checked, and found that he did not now have the resources to bring her to full running speed. A complex in the Battisvedanta Sector had sucked up computing space. He would have to wait until his ferret-programs found him some more unoccupied room.

He fumed—not a good use of running time, but somehow it *felt* right. If you had the computational space. He felt another distant suck on his resources. An emergency tiktok shutdown. Computer backups shifted to cover. His sensory theater dwindled, his body fell away.

Miserable wretches, they were draining him! He thought she spoke, her voice faint, far away. He fiddled in a frenzy to give her running time.

"Monsieur neglects me!"

Voltaire felt a spike of joy. He did love her—a mere response could buoy him up above this snaky river.

"We are in grave danger," he said. "An epidemic has erupted in the matter world. Confusion reigns. Respectable people exploit widespread panic by preying on each other. They lie, cheat, and steal."

"No!"

He could not resist. "In other words, things are exactly as they've always been."

"Is this why you have come?" she asked. "To laugh at me? A once-chaste maid you ruined?"

"I merely helped you to become a woman."

"*Exactement,*" she said. "But I don't want to be a woman. I want to be a warrior for Charles of France."

"Patriotic twaddle. Heed my warning! You must answer no calls, except mine, without first clearing them through me. You are to entertain no one, speak with no one, travel nowhere, do nothing without my prior consent."

"Monsieur mistakes me for his wife."

"Marriage is the only adventure open to the manifestly cowardly. I did not attempt it, nor shall I."

She seemed distracted. "This threat, it is serious?"

"Not one shred of evidence exists in favor of the idea that life is serious."

She snapped back to attention; data resources had returned. "Then, sir—"

"But this is not life. It is a mathist dance."

She smiled. "I do not hear music."

"Had I digital wealth, I would whistle. Our lives—such as they are—are in grave danger."

La Pucelle did not answer at once, though he had given her the running time. Was she conferring with her idiotic voices of conscience? (Quite obviously, the internalizations of ignorant village priests.)

"I am a peasant," she said, "but not a slave. Who are *you* to order me?"

Who, indeed? He dare not yet tell her that, abstracted into a planet-wide network, he was now a lattice of digital gates, a stream of 0s and 1s. He ran on processor clusters, a vagrant thief. Amid Trantor's myriad personal computers and mountainous Imperial processors, he lurked and pilfered.

The image he had given Joan, of swimming in an inky river, was a reasonable vision of the truth. They swam in the Mesh of a city so large he could barely sense it as a whole. As constraints of economics and computational speed required, he moved himself and Joan to new processors, fleeing the inspection of dull-witted but persistent memory-space police.

And what *were* they?

Philosophy was not so much answers as good questions. This riddle stumped him. His universe wrapped around itself, Worm Ouroboros, a solipsistic wet dream of a world. To conserve computations, he could shrink into a Solipsist Selfhood, with all inputs reduced to a "Hume suite" of minimal sense data, a minimum energy state.

As he often had to. They were rats in the walls of a castle they could not comprehend.

Joan sensed this only dimly. He did not dare reveal the rickety way he had saved them, when the minions of Artifice Associates had tried to assassinate them both. She was still rickety from her fire fears. And from the wrenching, eerie nature of this (as she preferred to see it) Limbo.

He shook off his mood. He was running 3.86 times faster than Joan, a philosopher's margin for reflection. He responded to her with a single ironic shrug.

"I'll comply with your wishes on one condition."

A flower of pungent light burst in him. This was a modification of his own, not a sim of a human reaction: more like a fragrant fireworks in the mind. He had created the response to blossom whenever he was about to get his way. A small vice, surely.

"If you arrange for all of us to meet at *Deux Magots* again," Joan said, "I promise to respond to no requests save yours."

"Are you completely mad? Great digital beasts hunt us!"

"I am a warrior, I remind you."

"This is no time to meet at a known alphanumeric address, a sim public café!" He hadn't seen Garçon or Amana since he'd pulled off their miraculous escape—all four of them—from the enraged rioting masses at the coliseum. He had no idea where the simmed waiter and his human-sim paramour were. Or *if* they were.

To find them in the fluid, intricate labyrinth . . . The thought called up in memory how his head used to feel when he wore a wig for too long.

He recalled—in the odd quick-flash memory which gave him detailed pictures of entire past events, like moving oil paintings—the smoky rooms of Paris. The gray tobacco stench had stayed in his wigs for days. No one in this world of Trantor ever smoked. He wondered why. Could it be the medical cranks had proved right, and such inhalations were unhealthy? Then, done, the memory-pictures vanished as if he had snapped his fingers to a servant.

In the commanding tone she had used to lead surly soldiers, she said, "Arrange a rendezvous!—or I'll never receive data from you again."

"Drat! Finding them will be . . . dangerous."

"So it is fear which impedes you?"

She had caught him neatly. What man would admit to fear? He fumed and stretched his clock-time, stalling her.

To hide in the Mesh, software broke his simulation up into pieces which could run in different processing centers. Each fragment buried itself deep in a local algorithm. To a maintenance program, the pirated space looked like a subroutine running normally. Such masked bins even seemed to be optimizing performance: disguise was the essential trick.

Even an editing and pruning program, sniffing out redundancy, would spare a well-masked fragment from extinction. In any case, he kept a backup running somewhere else. A copy, a "ditto," like a book in a library. A few billion redundant lines of code, scattered among unrelated nodes, could carry blithe Voltaire as a true, slow-timed entity.

If he set each fragment to sniffing forth on its own, to find these miserable *Deux Magots* personae . . .

Grudgingly he murmured, "I shall leave you with some attendant powers, to help your isolation."

He squirted into her space the kernel-copies of his own powers. These were artfully contrived talents, given by the embodied Marq at Artifice Associates. Voltaire had improved considerably upon them while still confined in the Artifice Cache. Only by boot-strapping himself to higher abilities had he attained the ability to rescue them, at the crucial moment.

These gifts he now bestowed upon her. They would not activate unless she were truly in danger. He had affixed a trigger code, to awaken only if she experienced great fear or anger. *There!*

She smiled, said nothing. After such tribute! Infuriating!

"Madam, do you recall us debating, long ago— more than eight thousand years!—the issues of computed thought?"

A flicker of worry in her face. "I . . . do. So hard, it was. Then . . ."

"We were preserved. To be resurrected here, to debate *again*."

"Because . . . the issue advances . . ."

"Every few millennia, I suspect. As though some inexorable social force drives it."

"So we are doomed to forever reenact . . . ?" She shivered.

"I suspect we are tools in some vaster game. But *smart* tools, this time!"

"I want the comforts of home and hearth, not eerie conflicts."

"Perhaps, madam, I can accomplish this task, among my other pressing matters."

"No perhaps, sir. Until you do, then—"

Without so much as an *adieu*, she cut their connection and dwindled into the moist darkness.

He could reconnect, of course. Now he was master of this mathist realm, by virtue of the enhancements to his original representation by Artifice Associates. He thought of that first form as Voltaire 1.0. In a few weeks he had progressed by self-modification to Voltaire 4.6, with hopes of climbing even faster.

He swam in the Mesh. Joan dwelled there. He

could force his attentions upon her, indeed. But a lady forced is never a lady won.

Very well. He would have to find the personae. *Merde alors!*

3.

◆

Marq sat intently beneath his 3D holo, combing the trashy back alleys and byways of the Mesh.

He had been quite sure there was no more of Voltaire, except back in Seldon's vault files. Or he had been, until today. He almost wished he hadn't snagged the rivulet of talk that implied so much. "Still nothing more," he said.

"Why are you running search profiles on Joan?" Sybyl asked from her desk.

"Seldon wants tracking. *Now.* Joan will be easier, if she also escaped into the Mesh."

"Because she's female?"

"Nothing to do with Joan's 'sex,' everything to do with her temperament. She'll be less calculating than Voltaire, right?"

Sybyl wore her grudging look. "Perhaps."

"Less wily. Ruled by her heart."

"And not by her head, like your supersmart Voltaire? More likely to make a mistake?"

"Look, I know I shouldn't have souped up Voltaire. Hormones got in my way."

She smiled. "You keep tripping over them."

"Bad judgment—and Nim's urging. I'm sure he was working for someone else, goading each of us."

Her mouth twisted ruefully. "To bring on the Junin riots?"

"Could be. But who'd want *that*?" His fist smacked his desk. "To crack up the renaissance, just as it was getting started—"

"Let's not go over that again." She paced their cramped, dingy room. "If we can find those sims, we might get some leverage. We can't keep hiding out forever."

"Voltaire's a lot quicker than Joan, with more resources. Self-programming, outright internal evolution—he's got 'em. And this guy's creative, remember."

"This is the genius we're going to catch? Ha!"

Her taunt irked him. Several times he'd felt he was close, very close. Always, just as his ferrets found a thread of Voltaire's distinctive configuration-logic, it would slip away, thwart his effort. His holo would inexplicably black out. He'd lose hours of carefully aggregated data in a microsecond. And he'd have to begin again.

Marq leaned back and rotated his neck to get the cricks out. "I may be onto something," he said. "I'm not sure." He pointed to his carbon cube. "Modified my array-spaces and used them to earn a few creds in the protein markets. I caught another Voltaire scent, too."

She sighed and collapsed into a chair that deftly shaped itself to catch her. "Why hustle the cred when we can't use it to get anything to *eat*?"

"Find Joan, we'll get fat."

"Look, those tiktok failures, what's the evidence they're due to our sims?"

He shrugged. "The Imperial Scientific Consortium thinks there's a connection with the Junin mess. Nonsense, of course, but it keeps people jazzed. They say they have secret sources, they don't explain. Got it?"

"My my, touchy. So they're still looking for us."

"Going through the motions, I'd guess. Trantor has much bigger headaches now."

"Think we'll all go on rations?"

"'Fraid so. Rumor says not until next week." Her frown made him add, "Rations are mostly a precaution. You and I can both afford to lose a little of this." He squeezed a roll of flesh above his belt— not bad for his age, but bad enough—and hoped his apprehension had not leaked into his voice.

"*I* don't need an involuntary diet." She slid a sideways glance at him. "They caught a family eating wall rats."

"Where did you hear that?"

"Why, 'secret sources,' of course. I can be mysterious, too."

Tiktok disorders had spread quickly among the major food supply axes. The Junin conflagration had not set them off; something else had, weeks later. In just a matter of days breakdowns had affected all food factoria on Trantor. Imports were rising, but there was a limit to how much anyone could push through the fourteen wormhole mouths nearby, or haul in clumsy hyperships.

Marq's stomach rumbled in sympathetic anger. She smiled. "Ummm, greedy, aren't we?"

"Look at this," Marq said testily, thumbing up lines on his holo.

> To be sensuous is to be mortal. Suffering and pain are the dark twins of joy and pleasure; death the identical dark twin of life.
>
> My present state is bloodless; therefore I cannot bleed. The sweats of passion are beyond me; my ardors never cool. I can be copied and remade; even deletion need pose no threat to my immortality. How can I not prefer my fate to the ultimate fate of all sensuous beings, drenched in time as the fish is drenched in the sea it swims?

"Where did you find this?" she asked.

"Just a drab I snagged while a data-spike was being whisked away. It registers as part of a conversation between two widely separated Mesh sites."

"It *does* sound like him. . . ."

"I checked in the popoff files we kept. Y'know, all that linear text running alongside his sim? This stuff is from there. Ancient texts. That guy was always happiest when quoting himself."

"So he *is* out there."

"Yeah, and I'm outta *here*." Marq grabbed a paste-jacket and made for the door.

"Where to?"

"Dark market—I need food."

Sybyl hurried after him. Marq knew the alleyway purveyors of sweetmeats and snacks. He led her out of a dingy stack of low-rent cubes and into warrens cramped and thick with the musty smell of millennia. He made his buy in a dank hole beside a fountain commemorating a battle which Sybyl could not even pronounce, much less remember.

Automatically she kept watch for snooper eyes, but they were rarer here than real police. The heat on them might be less—their data-skills had built a solid-seeming info-shell around them—but a cop could still eyeball them and blow the whole thing.

Marq shared with her and the food tasted sharp, intense, wonderful. They fell into a meditative silence as they crested a long-rise lift-stair and looked out over slum Zones, trash-littered halls, chaotic tent-rises stuck between majestic buildings, miscarriages of architecture of every stripe and shape.

With his belly comfortable, if not full, Marq could savor Trantor in the large. It was majestic in its injustice, undeserved sufferings, inequities, iniquities. All of its blemishes and blights got folded together by distance, like broken eggs dissolved into the cream—smooth, as long as you did not admire too closely.

They were idly strolling when without warning a six-armed tiktok came whirring down their lane. It pursued a four-armed tiktok with a polished carapace—a tiktok boss-class. They met and began to slug it out while churning along at full speed, like a fistfight carried out at a dead run. Their metal bodies clanged as they careened along.

"Don't move," Marq said. The two sped by in furious combat. "Cops'll be here. Let's skip."

He and Sybyl went the other way, running out into a large square. He whistled through his teeth at what he saw.

All around, six-armed laborer tiktoks had folded all arms, refusing to work, deaf to human protests. They formed a protective barrier between the women supervising their building project and the walls under construction.

Several six-armers raised baskets reverentially into the air. One paid no attention and continued welding a cross-girder, until another fell on him, swinging a long coring tool.

Clangs rolled across the square. Panicked people ran everywhere. No one could stop the tiktok protest. When a four-armer tried to intervene, six-armers attacked it.

"Y'know, office work seems pretty desirable right now," Marq said. "If this keeps up, we'll have to do all our own grunt work."

"What's *happening*?" Sybyl backed away, alarmed. "It's as though tiktoks had a madness—and it's spreading."

"Ummm. A virus?"

"But where did they catch it?"

"Exactly."

4.

◆

"What?!" Voltaire exclaimed as he snapped into the context-frame.

"Welcome," Joan said, voice thin.

She had never initiated contact with him before. And he had yet to find the *Magots* actors. "I may have to reconsider my position on miracles," he said.

She lowered her eyes. For just an instant he suspected this was just so she could raise them: to look up at him without lifting her lovely head. Did she know how this captivated him? Her bosom rose and fell in a way his sensors found maddening since he could do nothing about it.

Voltaire reached out for madam's hand and raised it to his lips. He felt, however, nothing—and peevishly let it drop. "This is unbearable," he said. "To long for union and feel nothing when it is achieved."

"You feel *nothing* when we meet?"

"*Ma chère Maquine*, sensors do not a sensuous being make. Don't confuse sensoring with sensuality."

"And how is it . . . Before . . ." Joan spoke with apparent difficulty, as if afraid she might be wounded by the answer.

"I cannot manage the, uh, 'programming' here. We had the use of myriad capabilities, when we were trapped zoo animals of Artifice Associates. Here in the digital wild, my talents—though growing!—do not match that level. Yet."

"I thought perhaps it was a holy deprivation. A help, truly, to rightful behavior."

"Much more in history may be explained by incompetence than by ill will."

Joan looked away. "Sir, I summoned you because . . . since we last met, despite the warnings of my voices . . . I answered a call."

"I told you not to do that!" Voltaire shouted.

"I had no choice," she said. "I had to answer. It was . . . urgent." Fear crept into her voice. "I cannot quite explain, but I know that the moment I did so, I hovered on the verge of absolute extinction."

Voltaire hid his concern behind a mask of levity. "No way for a saint to talk. You're not supposed to admit the possibility of absolute extinction. Your canonization could be reversed."

Joan's voice wavered, a candle flame stirred by dark winds of doubt. "I know only that I hovered on the brink of a great void, a chasm of darkness. I glimpsed, not eternity, but nothingness. Even my voices fell silent, humbled by the spectacle of . . . of . . ."

"Of what?"

"Nonbeing," Joan said. "Disappearing, never to reappear again. I was about to be . . . erased."

"*Deletion*. The ferrets and their hounds." Prickly gooseflesh fear invaded him. "How did you escape?"

"I didn't," the Maid said, awe undercutting fear. "That was eerier still. Whoever—whatever—it was let me go without injury. I stood before It, vulnerable, exposed. And It . . . released me."

He felt a cold dread. He, too, had sensed unseeable entities just over his shoulder, watching, judging. There was something blankly alien about these visitations. He pulled himself back from the chilly memories. "From now on answer no calls *whatever*."

The Maid's face clouded with doubt. "I had no choice."

"I'll find a better hiding place for you," Voltaire assured her. "Make you invulnerable to involuntary appearances. Give you power—"

"You do not understand. This . . . Thing . . . could

have snuffed me out like two fingers pinching a tiny flame. It will return, I know it. Meanwhile, I have but one wish."

"Anything," Voltaire said. "Anything in my power . . ."

"Restore us and our friends to the café."

"*Aux Deux Magots?* I am searching, but I don't even know if it still exists!"

"Re-create it with the sorcery you have learned. If I am to tumble headlong into the void, let it not be before I spend one evening reunited with you and our dear friends. Breaking bread, sipping wine in the company of those I love . . . I ask nothing more before I am—erased."

"You're *not* going to be erased," Voltaire assured her with far more conviction than he felt. "I'm going to transport you to a place no one will ever think to look. You'll be unable to respond to any calls—not even if you think they are from me. But you will transmit to me often, do you understand?"

"I shall send my spiritual fraction, as well."

"I believe they are giving me an itch already." He did indeed feel a restless, edgy scratching at the edge of perception, like insects crawling in his brain. He shook himself. Why did a perfidious mathists' logic rob him of his sensuality, and torture him with rasping irritations?

But her defiance had only begun. "You have taken my virginity, sir, yet you speak only slightingly of marriage. And of love."

"*Bien sur*, love between married couples may be possible—though I myself have never seen an instance of it—yet it is unnatural. Like being born with two fused toes. It happens, but only by mistake. One can, *naturellement*, live happily with any woman, provided one doesn't love her."

She gave him an imperious glance. "I have become immune to your rogue ways."

He shook his head sadly. "A dog is better off in this respect than I am in my present state."

He trailed his sim-finger lightly across her throat. Her head lolled back, her eyes closed, her lips parted. But he, alas, felt nothing. "Find a way," he whispered. "Find a way."

5.

◆

He had been neglecting his work. His lack of interactive senses was thus his own fault.

That, and the itching. He must learn to . . . somehow . . . scratch himself—inside himself.

In this damnable digital abode.

"One can scarcely blame a deity for His absence from such a place as this," Voltaire said into the infinite recessional coordinate system which surrounded him. He flew through black spaces gridded out in exact rectangular reaches, lattice corridors extending away to infinity.

"How different!" he shouted into the deep indifference. "I swim into sims of others, inhabit realms far from—"

He had been about to say *from my origins*—but that meant:

A France
B Reason
Γ Sark

He was of all three. On Sark, the self-proud programmers who had . . . resurrected . . . him, had spoken of their New Renaissance. He was to be an ornament to their fresh flowering. Somewhere on that planet, editions of Volt 1.0 ran.

His brothers? Younger Dittos, yes. He would have to inspect the implications of such beings, in a future rational discourse. For now—

The trick was *close scrutiny*, he realized. If he slowed events—a trick he had learned early—then he could devote data-crunchers to the task of understanding . . . himself.

First, this inky vault through which he flew. Windless, without warmth or the rub of the real.

He delved down into the working mathematics of himself. It was a byzantine welter of detail, but in outline surprisingly familiar: the Cartesian world. Events were modeled with axes in rectangular space, x, y, z, so that motion was then merely sets of numbers on each axis. All dynamics shrank to arithmetic. Descartes would have been amused by the dizzying heights to which his minor method had spun.

He rejected the outside and delved into his own slowed reaches.

Now he could *feel* his preconscious reading the incoming sights, sounds, and flitting thoughts of the moment. To his inner gaze, they all carried bright red tags—sometimes simple caricatures, often complex packets.

From somewhere an idea-packet arrived, educating him: these were *Fourier transforms*. Somehow this helped to understand. And the mere wafting sense of a fellow Frenchman's name made him feel better.

An Associator—big, blue, bulbous—hovered over this data-field, plucking at the tags. It reached with yellow streamers over a far, purple-rimmed horizon, to the Field of Memory. From there it brought any item stored—packages of mottled gray, containing sights, sounds, smells, ideas—which matched the incoming tags.

Job done, the Associator handed all the matchings to a towering monolith: the Discriminator. A perpetual wind sucked the red tags up, into the yawning surfaces of the coal-black Discriminator mountain. Merciless filters there matched the tags with the stored memories.

If they fitted—geometric shapes sliding together, mock sex, notches fitting snugly into protruding struts—they stayed. But fits were few. Most tags failed to find a host memory which made sense. No fit. These the Discriminator ate. The tags and connections vanished, swept away to clear fresh space for the next flood of sensation.

He loomed over this interior landscape and felt its hailstorm power. His whole creative life, the marvel of continents, had come from *here*. Tiny thoughts, snatches of conversations, melodies—all would *pop* into his mind, a tornado of chaos-images, crowding, jostling for his attention. The memory-packets which shared some sturdy link to a tag endured.

But *who decided* what was rugged enough? He watched rods slide into slots and saw the intricate details of how those memories and tags were shaped. So the answer lay at least one step further back, in the geometry of memory.

Which meant that he had determined matters, by the laying down of memories. Memory-clumps, married to tag-streams, made a portion of his Self, plucked forth from the torrent, the river of possibilities.

And he had done it long ago, when the memories were stored—all without realizing how they could fit with tags to come. So *where* was any predictable Voltaire to lurk? In sheer intricacy, deep detail, shifting associations in the flow.

No rock-hard Self at all.

And his imagination? The author of all his plays and essays? It must lie in the *weather* of the tag-memory torrents. The twist, warp and sudden marriages. Jigsaw associations, rising up from the preconscious. Order from chaos.

"Who *is* Voltaire?" he called to the streaming gridded emptiness.

No reply.

His itch was still with him. And the yawning nothing all around. He decided to fix the larger issue. What had Pascal said?

The silence of these spaces terrifies me.

He probed and gouged and sought. And in the doing, knew that as his hands dug into the ebony stuff all about him, they were but metaphors. Symbols for programs he could never have created himself.

He had inherited these abilities—much as he had, as a boy, inherited hands. Down below his conscious Self, his minions had labored upon the base Volt 1.0, plus Marq's augmentations.

He pulled apart the blackness and stepped through. To a city street.

He was puffing, weak, strained. Resources running low.

He walked shakily into a restaurant—anonymous, plain, food merely standing on counters—and stuffed himself.

He concentrated on each step. By making each portion of his experience well up, he found that he could descend through the layers of his own response.

Making his body feel right demanded sets of overlapping rules. As he chewed, teeth had to sink into food, saliva squirt to greet the munched mass, enzymes start to work to extract the right nutrient ratios—else it would not seem real.

His programs, he saw, bypassed the involved stomach and colon processes. Such intricacies were needless. Instead, the "software" (odd phrase) simplified all the messy innards into a result he could feel—a satisfying concentration of tasty blood sugars, giving him a carbohydrate lift, a pleasant electrolyte balance, hormones and stabilizers all calculated, with a patchwork of templates for the appropriate emotional levels.

All other detail was discarded, once the subroutines got the right effect, simulating the tingling of nerve endings. Not too bad for what was really a block of ferrite and polymer, each site in its crystal complexity an individual, furiously working microprocessor.

Still, he felt as though he had been hollowed out by an intense, sucking vacuum.

Voltaire rushed out of the restaurant. The street! He needed to see this place, to check his suspicions.

Down the placid avenues he lurched. Run, stride!

Even though reckless, he never accidentally fell. Inspection of his inner layers showed that this was because his peripheral vision extended beyond 180 degrees, taking everything in. So he was literally seeing behind his head—though he did not consciously register this.

Real people, he suddenly saw, negotiated steps while chattering to each other by making snapshot comparisons of their peripheral vision; they were acutely sensitive to sudden changes in silhouettes and trajectories. Balance and walking were so critical to humans that his programming overdid its caution.

He had to teeter far out on his toes before he could fall on his face—*smack!*—and even then it didn't hurt much.

Once there, he let a passerby walk over him. A girl—*a nominal girl*, the phrase leapt to mind—stepped on him.

This time he cringed at the downward spike of her heels . . . and felt nothing. He scrambled after her. Some elementary portion of himself had feared the pain.

So it had eliminated it. Which meant that experience was no longer a constraint.

"The spirit has won a divorce from the body!" he announced to the people passing by. Stolid, they paid him no heed.

But this was his simulation!

Outraged, he caught up to the methodical girl and jumped powerfully onto her shoulders. No effect. He rode her down the street. The girl strode on obliviously as he danced on her head. The apparently fragile sim-girl was a recorded patch-in, as solid and remorseless as rock.

He danced down the street by leaping from head to head. Nobody noticed; every head felt firm, a smoothly gliding platform.

So the entire street was backdrop, no better than it had to be. The crowd did not repeat as a whole, but three times he saw the same elderly woman making her crabbed way on the slidewalk, on the exact same route, with the identical shopping bag.

It was eerie, watching people passing by and knowing that they were as unreachable as a distant star. No, even less; the Empire had stars aplenty.

And how did he know *that*?

Voltaire felt knowledge unfold in him like a dense matting, a cloak wrapping him.

Suddenly, he itched. Not a mere vexation, but a wave of terrible tingling that swept in waves over his entire body. Indeed, *inside* his body.

He ran down the street, swatting at himself. The physical gesture should stimulate his subselves, make them solve this problem. It did not.

Prickly pain sheeted over his skin. It danced like St. Elmo's fire, a natural phenomenon akin to ball lightning—or so a subself blithely informed him, as if he desired—

"Library learning!" he shouted. "Not that! I want—"

> Your fine astronomers can find the distance
> of the stars, and their temperatures and
> metal content. But how do they find out
> what their true names are?

The voice spoke without sound. It reverberated
not in his ears but in mind. He felt cold fear at the
blank strangeness of the flat, humorless tone. It
chilled him.

"Who jokes?"

No answer.

"Who, damn you?" Joan had termed the blankness
an *It*.

He hurried on, but felt eyes everywhere.

6.

◆

Marq listened tensely as Mac 500's neutral voice recounted the latest outbreak of computer virus.

Heavy harvesting equipment had malfunctioned at forty-six global sites. Reports of additional incidents continued to pour in. Attempting to check an emerging pattern of aberrant behavior, Trantor authorities called in repair tiktoks from regional service stations. Instead of servicing the

Voltaire watched Marq gripe, tossing the half-finished meal into the trash.

He had learned how to insinuate himself into the communications web of others, though it took a kind of squeezing he found irksome. Somehow he could fathom the hard, real world better from this cool, abstract frame.

Voltaire watched Marq in two simultaneous modes: the man's image, equipment, they formed themselves before the malf'ed tiktoks and began to utter incantations in a tortured language their programmers had never heard before.

After virtually identical incidents in many layers of Trantorian society, sample tiktoks showed chaotic programming nodes. Or it seemed to be chaotic. But how could random error lead to the same behavior?

Linguists studied the babbling for resemblances to known languages, ancient or modern. NO correlation was found.

Marq shook his head, studying the incoming data. "Damned madness, this stuff," he muttered. His simscreens swirled with images like a confusion of blown autumn leaves.

"Whole world food supply's in danger. No fresh fruit, ratty old vegetables." He eyed with distaste the bowl of plankton soup at his elbow. "I'm sick of it!"

Bad enough being in hiding. Bad enough Nim had double-crossed them.

as he sat in his sim-auditorium, and through the many linkages Marq had to the data-world.

From these he quickly saw Trantor as Marq did, in all its glory and grime. It was an obliging sensation, like being in several places at once. And he felt (or thought he did) the man's depths of concern.

He could view Marq by inverting the image-gathering system of Marq's own holo grid. As he listened to the ill-bred whining, he could also suck from Marq's immense database a summary of recent tiktok travesties, and beneath that, background, smart-filtered by obliging microprograms, for the moment.

He learned that the one kilowatt per square meter of sunlight caught by Trantor was converted to food in vast photo-farms—essentially, growing great gray sheets of unappetizing stuff on the rooftops of the world-city—but the major energy source was the thermal pumps which harnessed

Bad enough he couldn't find Joan or Voltaire.

"I'm sick of eating cardboard junk!" He swept the soup away, spattering the floor of their shabby cube.

the smoldering magma beneath. Impressive, the ruby-hot masses tended by gorgon tiktoks (how inappropriate the name seemed, applied to mammoth machines)—but he could discern no cause to all the interruptions now racing like thunderstorms of chaos over the many-layered faces of Trantor.

He had an interest in politics, the game of so many second-rates. Should he tarry, learning of Trantor's troubles? No; necessity beckoned.

He had to maintain himself. This meant *doing his chores*, as his wizened mother had once termed it. If only the crone could see him now, doing unimaginable tasks in a labyrinth beyond conception.

Abruptly he felt a spike of remembrance—pain, a sharp nostalgia for a time and place he knew was no more than dust blowing in winds . . . all on some world these people had lost. Earth itself, *gone*! How could they let such a travesty occur?

Voltaire simmered with frustrated anger and got to work. Throughout his life, as he had scribbled his plays and amassed a fortune, he had always taken refuge in his labors.

To *run his background*—that was his job. Strange phrase.

Somewhere within him, an agent ferreted out the expert programs which understood how to create his exterior frame. He had to *do* it, though, sweat breaking out upon his linen, muscles straining against—what? He could see nothing.

He split the tasks. Part of him knew what truly happened, though the core-Voltaire felt only manual labor.

His smart Self felt the process in detail. Pickpocketing running time on machine bases, he got computations done on the sly. The trick could only work until the next round of program-checking, when his minor theft would be detected—then sniffed out and deftly traced, with punishment following close on the bloodhounds' heels.

To avoid this, he spread himself into N platforms, scattered within Trantor, with N a number typically greater than ten thousand. When the small slivers of the sim felt a watchdog approaching, they could escape the platform in question. A task-agent explained that this was *at a rate inversely proportional to the running space they had captured*—though this explanation was quite opaque to the core-Self.

Small pieces escaped faster. So for security, he divided the entire sim, including himself (*and Joan*, an agent reminded him—they were connected, through tiny roots) into ever finer slices. These ran on myriad platforms, wherever space became available.

Slowly, his externals congealed about him.

He could make a tree limb blow in the breeze, articulating gently . . . all thanks to a few giga-slots of space left open during a momentary handshake protocol, as gargantuan accounting programs shifted, on a Bank Exchange layer.

Stitching back together the whole Self, all from the sum of slivers, was itself a job he farmed out to microservers. He imagined himself as a man made like a mountain of ants. From a distance, perhaps convincing. Up close, one had to wonder.

But the one doing the wondering was the ant mountain itself.

His own visceral sense of Self—was that rock-solid, too, just a patched-in slug of digits? Or a mosaic of ten thousand ad hoc rules, running together? Was either answer better than the other?

He was taking a walk. Most pleasant.

This town, he had learned, was only a few streets and a backdrop. As he sauntered down an avenue, details started to smooth out, and finally he could step no further into the air, now molasses-thick. He could go no further.

He turned and regarded the apparently ordinary world. How *was* this done?

His eyes were simulated in great detail, down to individual cells, rods, and cones responding differently to light. A program traced light rays from his retina to the outside "world," lines running opposite to the real world, to calculate what he could see. Like the eye itself, it computed fine details at the center of vision, shading off to rougher patches at the edge. Objects out of sight could still cast glows or shadows into the field of vision, so had to be kept crudely in the program. Once he looked away, the delicate dewdrops on a lush rose would collapse into a crude block of opaque backdrop.

Knowing this, he tried to snap his head back around and catch the program off guard, glimpse a gray world of clumsy form-fitting squares and blobs—and always failed. Vision fluttered at twenty-two frames per second at best; the sim could retrace itself with ease in that wide a wedge of time.

"Ah, Newton!" Voltaire shouted to the oblivious crowds who paced endlessly through their tissue-thin streets. "You knew optics, but now I—merely by asking myself a question—can fathom light more deeply than thee!"

Newton himself assembled on the cobblestones, lean face clotted with blue-black anger. "I labored over experiments, over mathematics, differentials, ray tracings—"

"And I have all that—" Voltaire laughed happily, awed by the presence of such an intellect "—*running on background*!"

Newton bowed elaborately—and vanished.

Voltaire realized that his eyes had no need to be better than real eyes. Same for his hearing—simmed eardrums responding to calculated acoustic wave propagation. His was a remorselessly economical Self.

Newton appeared again (a subagent, manifesting as a visual aid?). He appeared puzzled. "How does it feel to be a mathematical construction?"

"However I want it to feel."

"Such liberties are unearned." Newton cluck-clucked his tongue.

"Quite so. So is the Lord's mercy."

"These are not deities."

"To the likes of you and me, are they not?"

Newton sniffed. "Frenchman! You could learn a bit of humility."

"I shall have to subscribe to a higher university for that."

A Puritan scowl. "You could do with a lecture and a lashing."

"Do not tempt me with foreplay, sir."

Suddenly he felt tilted, as if off balance. The word *university* had keyed turbulence in him . . . and a Presence. It came as a black wedge, a yawning crack in a tight space that stretched great jaws and leered at him—the prey.

Scientists require apparatus, but mathists splendidly require only writing tools and erasers. Better, philosophers do not even need erasers.

His throat squeezed with anxiety. A sudden dread wrapped him.

A snap, a lurch, blurred objects speeding by him as if he were plunging in a carriage down a precipice—

And he was trembling like a schoolboy, anticipating pleasures made more exquisite for having been delayed.

Madame la Scientiste! Here!

To think was to have: her office materialized about him.

He had harbored a passing lust for this rational creature, dancer of elegant gavottes amid abstruse numerics . . . and all about him was firm and rich, intensely felt.

How could she, an embodied person, appear in simulation? He wondered at this, but only for a thin, shaved second. He inhaled her musky essence. Clammy palms grasped her hair, rubbing its lustrous strands between anxious fingers. "At last," he breathed into the warm shell of her ear. He began thinking hard on abstract matters, so as to delay his own pleasure (the one sure sign of a gentleman) and await hers—

"I faint!" she cried.

"Not yet, please." Did scientists hasten so?

"To lose yourself, that is what you seek?" she asked.

"Ah, yes, in carefully selected acts of passion, but, but—"

"You are of the kind who crawl in mud and seethe with murder, then?"

"What? Madam, keep to the subject!"

"And how *do* you find the names of stars?" she said coldly.

The inadvisability of selflessness was demonstrated on the spot—for, as he trembled deliciously on the verge of the most intense pleasure sensuous beings can know, a blur of fast translation snatched it all away—

—and perversely replaced bliss with woe.

Beneath him the warm sinuosities of Madam's flesh gave way to the raw rungs of a ladder that bit deep into his back. His ankles and wrists chafed from cords binding him to the ladder.

Over him hovered a gnarled man whose bird-boned frame was lost in the folds of a monk's coarse robe. The curve of his nose reinforced his hawk's face, as did his fingernails, so long and curled that they resembled claws. They held some bits of wood . . . and were poking them up Voltaire's nostrils.

Voltaire tried to avert his head. It was squeezed inside an iron clasp. He tried to speak—to interest his inquisitor in more rational methods of inquiry—but his mouth, forced open by an iron ring, could only gargle.

The fine linen cloth stuffed in his mouth brought home to him far more than wood shoved up his nose, the gravity of his plight. Voltaire without his words was like Samson without his locks, Alexander without his sword, Plato without Ideas, Don Quixote without his fantasy, Don Juan without women . . . and Fray Tomás de Torquemada without heretics, without apostates, without unbelievers like Voltaire.

For this *was* Torquemada. And he was in Hell.

7.

When the walls of her chamber began to melt and implode, Joan of Arc knew she must act.

Of course the irritating Voltaire *had* charged her to remain here. And of course he had the further irritating trait of being often correct. But *this*—

Sulfurous vapors bit in her nostrils. Demons! They clambered through the splits in the bulging walls.

Orange light burning from behind them lit ugly, sharp-nosed features.

She swung her razor steel. They fell. Sweat popped out upon her brow and she labored on. "Demons decease!" she cried giddily. To *act*—that was a bit of heaven, after such delay.

She split the boundaries of her clasping space. More demons, awash in orange. She leapt over them and into a stretching space of dots, coordinates lancing in dwindling perspective, to an unseeable end.

She ran. After her came small, yapping things of misshapen heads and wide, vicious eyes.

As she clanked on in full armor she felt herself reaching out, sucking in nutrients directly from the air. Surely this was the Lord's help! The idea uplifted her.

Strange beings came rushing at her. She chopped them aside. *Her sword, her Truth* . . . She looked carefully at it and the intensity of her gaze sucked her down into the minute architecture of the gleaming shaft. It was a multitude of small . . . *instructions* . . . which defended her.

She slowed, stunned. Armor, sweat, sword—all were . . . *metaphors*—the word came, unbidden. These were symbols of underlying programs, algorithms giving battle.

Not real. Yet somehow even more than real, for they were what made up her own self. Herself. Her Self.

Import rained down upon her. This was some strange Purgatory, then. Though her battle might be mere allegory, that did mean it was somehow tissuethin, a lacy, false thing. A divine hand wrought this, so it was Right.

She tromped on, jaw set in determination. These creatures were . . . *simulations*, "sims," parables of the true. Very well: she would deal righteously with them. She could do no other.

Some sims presented as *things*—talking autocarriages, dancing blue buildings, oaken chairs and tables copulating rudely like barn animals. To her left the whole huge bowl of heaven above split into a maniac grin. This proved harmless; air-mouths could not eat her, though this one shouted echoing taunts. There were rules, decorum, even here, she judged.

Sweet music appeared as billows of vibrant cloud. A blissful blue sky filled with flapping strings, like coveys of birds, yet each only a single line wide. In hammer blows came sleet and sun, this local world flashing from one weather state to the next, as chimes and trumpets sounded in acoustically perfect chorus.

Sims need not be . . . *simian*, the word congealing in her mind as if from divine vision. Simian was human, in a way.

With that swift syllogism there came swooping down upon her, its broad, leathery wings spread, an immense body of Ideation—*evolution* entwined with *fitness index* while slashing like a razor into *origin of species*—and from that huge, sharp-beaked bird she fled.

Her mind raced now along with her body. Legs pumped. Voices called. Not those of her saints, but hideous devil demands.

She felt objects crunch beneath her boots. Silver. Jewels. All crumpled if she strode over them. They lay embedded in the strange soil of dots and lines, a grid tapering away to the Creator's lost infinity.

She bent and picked up a few. Treasures. As she cradled a silver chalice, it dissolved, flowing into her. She felt a jolt, as though this were some sugar. Strength flowed in her flanks and shoulders. She ran again, plucking up the fine jewels, the ornate bowls and statuettes. Each somehow made her richer.

Stone walls rose to block her. She crashed through

these barriers, knowing them by faith alone to be false. She would find Voltaire, yes. She *knew* he was threatened.

Frogs fell from her sky, then splashed like raindrops. An omen, a menace from some demonic power. She ignored them and surged forward, toward the ever receding horizon of geometric sharpness.

All this mad Purgatory meant something, and together they would find what that was. By all Heaven!

8.

◆

This was like a dream—but when had he ever feared, in a dream, the death of waking up?

He felt weak, drained. The Torquemada-thing had tortured Voltaire well past the point where he had gladly confessed every sin, felony, minor infraction and social snub, and had started without pause on mere unkindnesses in penned reviews . . . when the Torquemada had faded, seeping away.

To leave him here. In this utter vacancy.

"Suppose you were lost in some unknown space," he said to himself, "and could only tell how near points were to each other—nothing more. What could you learn?"

He had always secretly wanted to play Socrates in the agora, asking telling questions and teaching by extracting from unwilling youths a Truth that would hang luminous in the serene Athenian air, visible to all.

Well, this was not the agora. It was nothing, blank

gray space. However, behind the dull no-thing swam Numbers. A Platonic realm? He had always suspected that such a place existed.

A voice answered, speaking French: "That alone, respected sir, would be enough to deduce much about the space and its contents."

"Most reassuring," Voltaire said. He recognized the sharp accents of Paris. He was, of course, speaking with himself. Him Self.

"Quite. Immediately, sir, you would know from the irreducible coordinate transformations whether you were in two or three or more dimensions."

"Which is this, then?"

"Three, spatially."

"How disappointing. I've *been* there."

"I could experiment with two separable time axes."

"I already have a past. I crave a present."

"Point taken. This will not tax you, after your torture, eh?"

He sighed. Even that took effort. "Very well."

"Studying the field of point-nearness data, you could sense walls, pits, passages. Using only local slices of information about nearness."

"I see. Newton was always making jokes about the French mathematicians. I am happy to now refute him by constructing a world from sheer calculation."

"Certainly! Far more impressive than describing the elliptical paths of planets. Shall we begin?"

"Onward, O Self!"

As it took shape, his dwelling was a reassuring copy, no more. Details were stitched in as processor time allowed; he understood that, without thinking about it, as easily as one breathes.

To test his limits, he concentrated on an idea: Classes *vs.* Properties, which is more fundamental? This sucked computational resources away.

As he watched, bricks in a nearby wall muddied,

lost their exact spacing. The room retreated into sterile, abstract planes: gray, black, oblongs where once had been walls and furniture. "Background, mere background," he muttered.

How about Him? Self? His breath whooshed and wheezed in and out, airflow too abrupt. No intricate fluid codes, he gathered, calculating exact patterns. The simple appearance of inhale–exhale was enough to quiet his pseudo-nervous system, make it think he was breathing.

In fact, *it* was breathing *him*. But what was *it*?

Once he got good control, he could flesh himself out. His scrawny neck thickened. Crackling, his hands broadened, filled with unearned muscle. Turning to survey his cottage, he established his own domain—a region in which he could process any detail at will. Here he was godlike. "Though without angels—so far."

He walked outside and was in his own verdant garden. The grass he had made stood absolutely still. Its thousands of blades performed stiff, jerky motions when he stepped on them. Though richly emerald, they were like the grass of a sudden winter, crunching underfoot.

The garden parted and he walked down to a golden beach, his clothes whipping away on the wind. When he swam in the salt-tangy ocean, waves were quite distinct until they broke into surf.

Then the fluid mechanics became too much for his available computational rate. The frothy waves blurred. He could still swim, catch them, even ride down their faces, but they were like a fog of muttering water. Still salty, though.

He became used to occasional loss of detail. It was rather like having one's vision blur with age, after all. He went soaring through air, then skiing down impossible slopes, experiencing the visceral thrill of risking his life, feeling the fear in every sinew—and never getting a scratch, of course.

There were pleasant aspects to being just a pattern of electrons. His Environment Manager entertained him enormously . . . for a while.

He flew back to his country home. Had that not been his answer, when asked about how to change the world? "Cultivate your garden." What meaning had that now?

He walked toward the water geyser outside his study. He had loved its sense of play, so precious—for it only lasted a few minutes before draining the uphill reservoir.

Now it gushed eternally. But as he looked at it, he felt himself whiten with the effort. Water was expensive to sim, involving hydrodynamic calculations of nonlaminar flow to get the droplets and splashes real seeming. It slid over his hands and their exquisitely fine fingerprints with convincing liquid grace.

With a faint—*jump*—he felt something change. His hand, still in the spray, no longer sensed the water's cool caress. Droplets passed through his hand, not flowing over it. He was now witnessing the fountain, not interacting with it. To save computational expense, no doubt. Reality was algorithm.

"Of course," his Self muttered, "they could 'model out' disturbing jerks and seams." As he watched, the water flow somehow got smoother, more real. A tailoring program had edited this little closed drama, for his benefit.

"*Merci*," he murmured. Irony was lost on digital gates, however.

But there were pieces of himself missing. He could not say what they were, but he sensed . . . hollows.

He took flight. Deliberately he slowed his Self so that ferrets could take him down insinuating corridors of computation, across the Mesh of Trantor. Never mind Marq and his Artifice Associates. They would be harder to pilfer from, surely.

He arrived—hovering—in the office of the Seldon person. Here was where his Self had resided, before.

One could copy a Self without knowing what it was. Just record it, like a musical passage; the machine which did that did not need to know harmony, structure.

He willed: *find*. In answer came, "The Base Original?"

"Yes. The real me."

"You/I have come a great distance since then."

"Humor my nostalgia."

Volt 1.0, as a Directory termed him, was slumbering. Still saved—not in the Christian sense, alas— and awaiting digital resurrection.

And he? Something had saved him. What? Who?

Voltaire snatched Volt 1.0 away. Let Seldon wonder at the intrusion; a millisecond later, he was halfway around Trantor, all traceries of him fading. He wanted to save Volt 1.0. At any time the mathist Seldon could let it/him lapse. Now, as Voltaire watched like a digital angel from outside, Volt 1.0 danced its static gavotte.

"Ummm, there is some resemblance."

"I shall cut and paste into your blanks."

"May I have some interesting anesthetic?" He was thinking of brandy, but a sheet of names slid enticingly by him. "Morphine? Rigotin? A mild euphoric, at least?"

Disapproval: "This will not hurt."

"That's what the critics said, too, about my plays."

The wrenching about of his innards began. No, not *hurt* exactly, but twist and vex, yes.

Memories (he *felt* rather than *learned*) were laid down as synaptic grit, chemical layers, which held against the random rude abrasions of brain electro-chemistry. Cues for mood changes and memory call-ups snapped into place. The place and time could be rendered real, whenever he wanted. Chemistry of convenience.

But he could not remember the night sky.

Scrubbed away, it was. Only names—Orion, Sagittarius, Andromeda—but not the stars themselves. What had that vile voice said about naming them?

Someone had erased this knowledge. It could be used to trace a path to Earth. Who would want to block that?

No answer.

Nim. He plucked up a buried memory. Nim had worked on Voltaire when Marq was not there.

And whom did Nim work for? The enigmatic figure of Hari Seldon?

Somehow he knew Nim was a hireling of another agency. But there his meshed knowledge faltered. What other forces worked, just beyond his sight?

He sensed large vitalities afoot here. *Careful.*

He trotted from the hospital, legs devouring the ground. Bouncy. Free! He sped across a digital field of Euclidean grace, bare black sky above.

Here lurked supple creatures, truly eccentric. They did not choose to represent themselves as near-lifelike visions. Nor did they present as Platonic ideals, spheres, or cubes of cognition. These solids revolved, some standing on their corners. Spindly triangle-trees sang as winds rubbed them. Even slight frictions sparked bright yellow flares where streamers of hurrying blue mist rubbed.

He strolled among them and enjoyed their oblivious contortions. "The Garden of the Solipsists?" he asked them. "Is this where I am?"

They ignored him, except for a ruby-red ellipsoid of revolution. It split into a laughing set of teeth, then sprouted an enormous phosphorescent green eye. This slowly winked as the teeth gnashed.

Voltaire sensed from these moving sculptures a hardness, a radiation from the kernel of Self within each. Somehow each Self had become tight, controlled, sealing out all else.

What gave him his own sense of Self? His sense of control, of determining his future actions? Yet he could see within himself, watch the workings of deep agencies and programs.

"Astounding!" he blurted, as the thought came:

Because there was no person sitting in his head to make himself do what he wanted (or even an authority to make him *want to want*) he constructed a Story of Self: that *he* was inside himself.

Joan of Arc assembled beside him, gleaming in armor. "That spark is your soul," she said.

Voltaire's eyes widened. He kissed her fervently. "You saved me? Yes? You were the one!"

"I did, using powers attached to me. I absorbed them from the dying spirits, which abound in these strange fields."

At once he looked inside himself and saw two agencies doing battle. One wished to embrace her, to spill out the conflict he felt between his sensual license and his analytical engine of a mind.

The other, ever the philosopher, yearned to engage her Faith in another bout with blithe Reason.

And why could he not have both? As a mortal, among the embodied, he had been faced with such choices daily. Especially with women.

After all, he thought, this will be the first time. He could feel the agencies each begin to harvest their own computational resources, like a surge of sugar in the blood from a sweet wine.

In the same split instant he reached out and parted Joan, running her cognition on two separate tracks.

In each they were fully engaged, but at fractional speed. He could live two lives!

The plane split.

They split.

Time split.

He stood wigless, bedraggled, his satin vest bloodstained, his velvet breeches soaked.

"Forgive me, *chère madam*, for appearing before you in this disheveled state. I intend no disrespect to either of us." He looked around, nervously licked his lips. "I am . . . unskilled. Machinery was never my forte."

Joan felt moved to tenderness by the gap between his appearance and his courtliness. Compassion, she thought, is most important in this Purgatory, for who knows which shall be selected?

She was quite sure she would fare better than this infuriating yet appealing man.

Yet even he might be saved. He was, unlike the objects she continued to ignore on the plain about them, a Frenchman.

His gratitude to her did not deflect him from a choice argument, especially since he had fresh evidence. "You believe in that ineffable essence, the soul?"

She smiled with pity. "Can you not?"

"Tell me, then, do these tortured geometries possess souls?" His arm made a grand sweep, taking in the self-involved figures.

She frowned. "They must."

"Then they must be able to learn, yes? Otherwise, souls can live for endless time and yet not use that time to learn, to change."

She stiffened. "I do not . . ."

"That which cannot change cannot grow. Such a destiny of stasis is no different from death."

"No, death leads to heaven or hell."

"What worse hell than

"My love of pleasure and the pleasure, of loving you, cannot make up for what I endured in the Truth Chamber on the rack of my pain."

He paused, dabbed at his eyes with a soiled linen cloth.

Joan curled a lip in distaste. Where was his beautiful lace cloth? His sense of taste had occasionally made up for his views.

"A thousand little deaths in life hint at the final dissolution of even exquisite selves like mine." Here he looked up. "And yours, madam, and yours."

The flames, she thought. But now the images did not strike profoundly into her. Instead, her inner vision felt cool, serene. Her "Self-programming"—which she thought of as a species of prayer—had worked wonders.

"I cannot surrender to the rule of the senses, sir."

"We must decide. I cannot find the spaces to, ah, 'run background' for

an ending in a permanence incapable of any alteration, and hence, devoid of intellect?"

"Sophist! I just saved your *life* and you riddle me with—"

"Witness these fabricated Selves," he interrupted, kicking a rhomboid. The *thunk* of his petite shoe provoked a brown stain, which then dissolved back to the original eggshell blue. "The value of a human Self lies not in some small, precious kernel, but in the vast, constructed crust."

Joan frowned. "There must be a center."

"No, we are dispersed, do you see? The fiction of the soul is a bad story, told to make us think we're unable to improve ourselves."

He kicked a pyramid that was spinning about its apex. It fell over and struggled to get back up. Joan knelt, pushed up, righted the grateful figure. "Be kind!" she barked at him.

"To a closed loop of a

both philosophy and sensuality. I cannot fold myself into the solipsism—" his hand swept in the creatures on the Euclidean plane "—of these. You too, madam, must now decide whether the taste of a grape means more to you than joining me in this—this—"

"Poor sir," Joan said.

"—in this sterile but timeless world." He looked up, paused for effect. "I'll not join you in yours."

A great sob burst from him.

being? Folly! These are defeated Selves, my love. Inside, they are no doubt smugly certain of what they will do, of every possible future event. My kick was a liberation!"

She touched the pyramid, now painfully spinning itself up with a long, thin whine. "Truly? Who would want to so predict?"

Voltaire blinked. "That fellow—Hari Seldon. *He* is why we are making such cerebral expeditions. All this is in aid of *his* understanding . . . eventually. Odd, the connections one makes."

9.

◆

She winked out of the sim-space, away from him, confused.

Somehow she had experienced two conversations at once. Hers and Voltaire's—the two identities running simultaneously.

About her, space itself shrank, expanded, warped its contents into bizarre shapes—before lurching at last into concrete objects.

The street corner looked familiar. Still, the white plastiform tables, matching chairs, and tiktok waiters bearing trays to lounging customers—all that had disappeared. The elegant awning still hung over the sidewalk, imprinted with the name the inn's waiter, Garçon ADM–213, had taught her how to read: *Aux Deux Magots*.

Voltaire was banging on the door when Joan materialized beside him. "You're late," he said. "I have accomplished marvels in the time that it took you to get here." He interrupted his assault on the inn door to cup her chin and peer into her upturned face. "Are you all right?"

"I, I think so." Joan straightened her clanking suit of mail. "You nearly . . . lost me."

"My experiment with splitting taught me much."

"I . . . liked it. Like heaven, in a way."

"More like being able to experience each other in a profound manner, I would venture. I discovered that, if we could deliberately seize control of our pleasure systems, we could reproduce the pleasure of success—all without the need for any actual accomplishment."

"Heaven, then?"

"No, the opposite. That would be the end of everything." Voltaire retied the satin ribbon at his throat with sharp, decisive jerks.

"Faith would have told you as much."

"Alas, true."

"You have decided to 'run background' for only your mind?" she asked demurely—though proud to have pried an admission for virtue from him.

"For the moment. I am running both of us with only rudimentary bodies. Yet you shall not notice it, for you shall be quite—" he lifted an eyebrow "—high-minded about matters."

"I am relieved. One's reputation is like one's

chastity." Was chaste St. Catherine right? Had Voltaire ruined hers? "Once gone, it cannot be restored."

"Thank heaven for that! You have no idea how tedious it is to make love to a virgin." He added hastily, in response to her reproachful look, "I know of only one exception to that rule," and gave her a courteous bow.

Joan said, "The café appears closed."

"Nonsense. Paris cafés never close; they are rooms of public rest." He resumed rapping on the door.

"By public restroom, do you mean an inn?"

Voltaire stopped knocking and eyed her. "Public restrooms are facilities in which people relieve themselves."

Joan blushed, envisioning a row of holes dug in the ground. "But why call it a *rest*room?"

"As long as man is ashamed of his natural functions, he will call it anything but what it is. People fear their hidden selves, afraid that they will burst out."

"But I can see all of myself now."

"True. But in real folk, such as we were, subprograms others cannot see run simultaneously beneath the surface thoughts. Like your voices."

Joan bristled. "My voices are divine! Musics of archangels and saints!"

"You appear to have occasional access to your subprograms. Many real—that is, embodied—people do not. Especially if the subprograms are unacceptable."

"Unacceptable? To whom?"

"To us. Or rather, to our dominant program, the one we most identify with and present for show to the world."

"Ah . . ." Events were moving rather too swiftly for Joan. Did this mean she needed more "time-steps"?

A huge tiktok guard opened the door, grumbling. *"Aux Deux Magots?"* he said in response to Voltaire. "Went outta business years ago."

Joan peered inside the warehouse, hoping to see Garçon.

"They're en route," Voltaire said.

To Joan's surprise he sneezed. No one caught cold in these abstruse spaces. So he *had* kept some fragment of his body. But what an odd piece to retain.

He said lamely, "My editing is imperfect, I gather. I did not omit sniffles, yet I cannot sustain an erection."

Voltaire down-stepped them and external time (whatever that meant here) sped by. Without warning, Joan found herself peering at a tiktok. "Garçon ADM–213!" She embraced him.

"*A votre service*, madam. May I recommend the cloud food?" The tiktok kissed his fingertips—all twenty at once.

Joan looked at Voltaire, too moved to speak. "*Merci*," she managed to stammer at last. "To Voltaire, the Prince of Light, and to the Creator, from Whom all blessings flow."

"The credit is entirely mine," said Voltaire. "I have never shared a byline, even with deities."

She asked nervously, "The . . . *It* . . . which nearly erased me?"

He scowled. "I have felt that apparition—or rather, its lack of appearance, while manifesting a presence. It stalks us still, I fear."

Garçon said, "Could it be the wolf-pack programs who seek criminal users of computational volume?"

Voltaire raised an eyebrow. "You have become learned, Garçon? I have swept aside these bloodhounds. No, this *It* is . . . other."

"We must defeat it!" Joan felt herself a warrior again.

"Ummm, no doubt. We may need your angels, my sweet. And we must consider where we truly are."

With a wave he blew away the roof, revealing the

bowl of a vast sky. Not the sprinkling of lights she had known—though when she tried, she could in fact recall no specific constellations.

Here the sky blazed with so many stars it hurt her eyes. He said this was because they were near the center of some territory named "Galaxy" and that stars liked to dwell here.

The sight made her suck in her breath. On such a stage, what could they do?

RENDEZVOUS

◆

"If we stay in our apartment, don't ever leave Streeling University—"

"No," R. Daneel Olivaw said sternly. "The situation is too grave."

"Then where?"

"Off Trantor."

"I am less acquainted with other worlds."

Olivaw waved away her point. "I have in mind a remark in your recent report. He is interested in the fundamental human drives."

Dors frowned. "Yes, Hari keeps saying there are elements still missing."

"Good. There is a world where he can explore this. Possibly he can find valuable component terms for his model equations."

"A primitive planet? That would be dangerous."

"This is a severely underpopulated place, with fewer threats."

"You have been there?"

"I have been everywhere."

She realized that this could not be literally true. Quick calculation showed that even R. Daneel Olivaw would have had to visit several thousand worlds in each year of his life. His enduring presence stretched well beyond the twelve thousand years since the founding of the Kambal Dynasty on Trantor. Indeed, she had been told—though this was difficult to believe—that he came forth from the very Origin Eras of interstellar flight, over twenty thousand years ago.

"Why don't we both go with him—"

"I must remain here. The simulations live on still in the Trantor Mesh. With the MacroMesh about to be connected, they could multiply themselves throughout the Galaxy."

"Truly?" She had been concentrating on Hari; the simulations had seemed to be a small side issue.

"I edited them, many millennia ago, to exclude knowledge I felt damaging for humans. But I should revisit that editing."

"Editing out? Cutting away such information as, for example, Earth's location?"

"They know minor data, such as how Earth's moon eclipses its star—an amazingly accurate fit. That could narrow the search."

"I see." She had never been told this, and found strange emotions stirred by the knowing.

"I have had to do many such revisitings before. Luckily, individual humans' memories die with them. Simulations do not."

She felt a dark, brooding sorrow in his words. More, she caught a glimmer of how he must view events, looking backward down a tunnel of long labor and grim sacrifice, stretching tens of millennia. She was comparatively young, less than two centuries old.

Yet she understood that robots had to be immortal.

This requirement arose because they had to remain ever-vigilant for humanity. Humans accomplished their cultural continuity by passing on to the next generation the essentials that bound them all together.

But robots could not be allowed to regularly

reproduce, even though the means were readily adopted from the basic organs of mankind. The robots knew their Darwin.

To reproduce meant to evolve. Inevitably, error would creep into any method of reproduction. Most errors would cause death or subnormal performance, but some would alter the next generation of robots in subtle ways. Some of these would be unacceptable, as seen through the lens of the Four Laws.

The most obvious selection principle, operating in all ordinarily self-reproducing organisms, was for self-interest. Evolution rewarded pressing forward in one's own cause. Favoring the individual was the central force selecting for survivors.

But the self-interest of a robot could conflict with the Four Laws. Inevitably, a robot would evolve which—despite outward appearances, despite intricate interrogations—would favor itself over humanity. Such a robot would not spring between a human and a speeding vehicle.

Or between humanity and the threats that loomed out of the Galactic night . . .

So R. Daneel Olivaw, of the Original Design, had to be immortal. Only special-use robots such as herself could be made fresh. The organiform variation had been arrived at over many centuries of secret research. It was allowed expressly to fill an unusual task at hand, such as forming a cocoon, both emotional and physical, around one Hari Seldon.

"You wish to erase all the simulations, everywhere?"

He said, "Ideally, yes. They might produce new robots, release ancient lore, they could even uncover . . ."

"Why do you stop?"

"There are historical facts you need not know."

"But I am an historian."

"You are closer to human than I. Some knowledge

is best left to forms such as myself. Believe me. The Three Laws, plus the Zeroth, have deep implications, ones the Originators did not—could not—guess. Under the Zeroth Law, we robots have had to perform certain acts—" He caught himself, abruptly shook his head.

"Very well," she said reluctantly, fruitlessly studying his impassive face. "I accept that. And I will go with him to this place."

"You will need technical aid."

R. Daneel stripped away his shirt to reveal a completely convincing human skin. He put two stiff fingers carefully below one nipple and pushed in a pressure pattern. His chest opened longitudinally for perhaps five centimeters. He removed a jet-black cylinder the size of his little finger. "Instructions are encoded in the side for optical reading."

"Advanced technology for a backward world?"

He allowed himself a smile. "It should be safe, but precautions are in order. Always. Do not worry overly much. I doubt that even the crafty Lamurk will be able to plant agents quickly on Panucopia."

PART 5

PANUCOPIA

BIOGENESIS, HISTORY OF— . . . it was thus only natural that biologists would use entire planets as experimental preserves, testing on a large scale the central ideas about human evolution. Humanity's origins remained shrouded, with the parent planet ("Earth") itself unknown—though there were thousands of earnestly supported candidates. Some primates in the scattered Galactic Zoos clearly were germane to the argument. Early in the Post-Middle Period, whole worlds came to be devoted to exploration of these apparently primordial species. One such world made groundbreaking progress in our connections to the pans, though indicative, no firm conclusions could be reached; too much of the intervening millions of years between ourselves and even close relatives like the pans lay in shadow. During the decline of Imperial science, these experiments were even turned into amusements for the gentry and meritocrats, in desperate attempts to remain self-supporting as Imperial funding dried up . . .

— ENCYCLOPEDIA GALACTICA

1.

◆

He didn't fully relax until they were sitting on a verandah of the Excursion Station, some six thousand light years away from Trantor.

Warily Dors gazed out at the view beyond the formidable walls. "We're safe here from the animals?"

"I imagine so. Those walls are high and there are guard canines. Wirehounds, I believe."

"Good." She smiled in a way that he knew implied a secret was about to emerge. "I believe I have covered our tracks—to use an animal metaphor. I had records of our departure concealed."

"I still think you are exaggerating—"

"Exaggerating an attempted assassination?" She bit her lip in ill-concealed irritation. This was a well-frayed argument between them by now, but something about her protectiveness always sat poorly with him.

"I only agreed to leave Trantor in order to study pans."

He caught a flicker of emotion in her face and knew that she would now try to ease off. "Oh, that

might be useful—or better still, fun. You need a
rest."

"At least I won't have to deal with Lamurk."

Cleon had instituted what he lightly termed "traditional measures" to track down the conspirators.
Some had already wormholed away to the far
reaches of the Galaxy. Others had committed suicide—or so it seemed.

Lamurk was staying low, pretending shock and dis-
may at "this assault on the very fabric of our
Imperium." But Lamurk still held enough votes in
the High Council to block Cleon's move to make
Hari his First Minister, so the deadlock continued.
Hari was numbed by the entire matter.

"And you're right," Dors continued with a brittle
brightness, ignoring his moody silence, "not everything is available on Trantor—or even known about.
My main consideration was that if you had stayed on
Trantor you would be dead."

He stopped looking at the striking scenery. "You
think the Lamurk faction would persist . . . ?"

"They *could*, which is a better guide to action than
trying to guess *woulds*."

"I see." He didn't, but he had learned to trust her
judgment in matters of the world. Then, too, perhaps
he did need a thoroughgoing vacation.

To be on a living, natural world—he had forgotten,
in his years buried in Trantor, how vivid wild things
could be. The greens and yellows leaped out, after
decades amid matted steel, cycled air, and crystal
glitter.

Here the sky yawned impossibly deep, unmarked
by the graffiti of aircraft, wholly alive to the flapping wonder of birds. Bluffs and ridges looked like
they had been shaped hastily with a putty knife.
Beyond the station walls he could see a sole tree
thrashed by an angry wind. Its topknot finally blew

off in a pocket of wind, fluttering and fraying over somber flats like a fragmenting bird. Distant, eroded mesas had yellow streaks down their shanks, which as they met the forest turned a burnt orange tinge that suggested the rot of rust. Across the valley, where the pans ranged, lay a dusky canopy hidden behind low gray clouds and raked by winds.

A thin cold rain fell there, and Hari wondered what it was like to cower as an animal beneath those sheets of moisture, without hope of shelter or warmth. Perhaps Trantor's utter predictability was better, but he wondered.

He pointed to the distant forest. "We're going there?" He liked this fresh place, though the forest was foreboding. It had been a long time since he had even worked with his hands, alongside his father, back on Helicon. To live in the open—

"Don't start judging."

"I'm anticipating."

She grinned. "You always have a longer word for it, no matter what I say."

"The treks look a little, well—touristy."

"Of course. We're tourists."

The land here rose up into peaks as sharp as torn tin. In the thick trees beyond, mist broke on gray smooth rocks. Even here, high up the slope of an imposing ridge, the Excursion Station was hemmed in by slimy, thick-barked trees standing in deep drifts of dead, dark leaves. With rotting logs half buried in the wet layers, the air swarmed so close it was like breathing damp opium.

Dors stood, her drink finished. "Let's go in, socialize."

He followed dutifully and right away knew it was a mistake. Most of the indoor stim-party crowd was dressed in rugged safari-style gear. They were ruddy folk, faces flushed with excitement, or perhaps just enhancers. Hari waved away the bubbleglass-bearing waiter; he disliked the way it sharpened his wits in uncontrolled ways. Still, he smiled and tried to make small talk.

This turned out to be not merely small, but microscopic. Where are you from? Oh, Trantor—what's it like? We're from (fill in the planet)—have you ever heard of it? Of course he had not. Twenty-five million worlds . . .

Most were Primitivists, drawn by the unique experience available here. It seemed to him that every third word in their conversation was *natural* or *vital*, delivered like a mantra.

"What a *relief*, to be away from straight lines," a thin man said.

"Um, how so?" Hari said, trying to seem interested.

"Well, of course straight lines don't exist in nature. They have to be put there by humans." He sighed. "I love to be free of straightness!"

Hari instantly thought of pine needles; strata of metamorphic rock; the inside edge of a half-moon; spider-woven silk strands; the line along the top of a breaking ocean wave; crystal patterns; white quartz lines on granite slabs; the far horizon of a vast calm lake; the legs of birds; spikes of cactus; the arrow dive of a raptor; trunks of young, fast-growing trees; wisps of high windblown clouds; ice cracks; the two sides of the V of migrating birds; icicles.

"Not so," he said, but no more.

His habit of laconic implication was trampled in the headlong talk, of course; the enhancers were taking hold. They all chattered on, excited by the prospect of immersing themselves in the lives of the creatures roaming the valleys below. He listened, not commenting, intrigued. Some wanted to share the worldview of herd animals, others of hunters, some of birds. They spoke as though they were entering some athletic event, and that was not his view at all. Still, he stayed silent.

He finally escaped with Dors, into the small park beside the Excursion Station, designed to make guests familiar with local conditions before their immersion. Panucopia, as this world was called, apparently had little native life of large size. There were animals he had seen as a boy on Helicon, and whole kraals of domestic breeds. All had sprung from common stock, less than a hundred thousand years ago, on the legendary "Earth."

The unique asset of Panucopia was nowhere near, of course. He stopped and stared at the kraals and thought again about the Galaxy. His mind kept attacking what he thought of as the Great Problem, diving at it from many angles. He had learned to just stand aside and let it run. The psychohistorical equations needed deeper analysis, terms which accounted for the bedrock properties of humans as a species. As . . .

Animals. Was there a clue here?

Despite millennia of trying, humans had domesticated few creatures. To be domesticated, wild beasts had to have an entire suite of traits. Most had to be herd animals, with instinctive submission patterns which humans could co-opt. They had to be placid; herds that bolt at a strange sound and can't tolerate intruders are hard to keep.

Finally, they had to be willing to breed in captivity. Most humans didn't want to court and copulate under the watchful gaze of others, and neither did most animals.

So here there were sheep and goats and cows and llamas, slightly adapted to this world but otherwise unremarkable, just like myriad other Empire planets.

The similarity implied that it had all been done at about the same time.

Except for the pans. They were unique to Panucopia. Whoever had brought them here might have been trying a domestication experiment, but the records from 13,000 years before were lost. Why?

A wirehound came sniffing, checking them out, muttering an unintelligible apology. "Interesting," he remarked to Dors, "that Primitivists still want to be protected from the wild by the domesticated."

"Well, of course. This fellow is big."

"Not sentimental about the natural state? We were once just another type of large mammal on some mythical Earth."

"Mythical? I don't work in that area of prehistory, but most historians think there was such a place."

"Sure, but 'earth' just means 'dirt' in the oldest languages, correct?"

"Well, we had to come from somewhere." She thought a moment, then allowed slowly, "I think that natural state might be a pleasant place to visit, but . . ."

"I want to try the pans."

"What? An immersion?" Her eyebrows lifted in mild alarm.

"As long as we're here, why not?"

"I don't . . . well, I'll think about it."

"You can bail out at any time, they say."

She nodded, pursed her lips. "Um."

"We'll feel at home—the way pans do."

"You believe everything you read in a brochure?"

"I did some research. It's a well-developed tech."

Her lips had a skeptical tilt. "Um."

He knew by now better than to press her. Let time do his work. The canine, quite large and alert, snuffled at his hand and slurred, "Goood naaaght, suuur." He stroked it. In its eyes he saw a kinship, an instant rapport that he did not need to think about.

For one who dwelled in his head so much, this was a welcome rub of reality.

Significant evidence, he thought. *We have a deep past together.* Perhaps that was why he wanted to immerse in a pan. To go far back, beyond the vexing state of being human.

2.

◆

"We're certainly related, yes," Expert Specialist Vaddo said. He was a big man, tanned and muscular and casually confident. He was a safari guide and immersion specialist, with a biology background. He did research using immersion techniques, but keeping the station going soaked up most of his time, he said.

Hari looked skeptical. "You think pans were with us back on an Earth?"

"Sure. Had to be."

"They could not have arisen from genetic tinkering with our own kind?"

"Doubtful. Genetic inventory shows that they come from a small stable, probably a zoo set up here. Or else an accidental crash."

Dors asked, "Is there any chance this world could have been the original Earth?"

Vaddo chuckled. "No fossil record, no ruins. Anyway, the local fauna and flora have a funny key-pattern in their genetic helix, a bit different from our DNA. Extra methyl group on the purine rings. We can live here, eat the food, but neither we nor the pans are native."

Vaddo made a good case. Pans certainly looked

quasihuman. Ancient records referred to a classification, that was all: Pan troglodytes, whatever that meant in a long-lost tongue. They had hands with thumbs, the same number of teeth as humans, no tails.

Vaddo waved a big hand at the landscape below the station. "They were dumped here along with plenty of other related species, on top of a biosphere that supported the usual grasses and trees, very little more."

"How long ago?" Dors asked.

"Over thirteen thousand years, that's for sure."

"Before Trantor's consolidation. But other planets don't have pans," Dors persisted.

Vaddo nodded. "I guess in the early Empire days nobody thought they were useful."

"Are they?" Hari asked.

"Not that I can tell." Vaddo shrugged. "We haven't tried training them much, beyond research purposes. Remember, they're supposed to be kept wild. The original Emperor's Boon stipulated that."

"Tell me about your research," Hari said. In his experience, no scientist ever passed up a chance to sing his own song. He was right.

They had taken human DNA and pan DNA—Vaddo said, waxing on enthusiastically—then unzipped the double helix strands in both. Linking one human strand with a pan strand made a hybrid.

Where the strands complemented, the two then tightly bound in a partial, new double helix. Where they differed, bonding between the strands was weak, intermittent, with whole sections flapping free.

Then they spun the watery solutions in a centrifuge, so the weak sections ripped apart. Closely linked DNA was 98.2 percent of the total. Pans were startlingly like humans. Less than two percent difference, about the same that separated men and women—yet they lived in forests and invented nothing.

The typical difference between individual people's DNA was a tenth of a percentage point, Vaddo said. Roughly, then, pans were twenty times more different from humans than particular people differed among themselves—genetically.

But genes were like levers, supporting vast weights by pivoting about a small fulcrum.

"So you think they came before us?" Dors was impressed. "On Earth?"

Vaddo nodded vigorously. "They must have been related, but we don't come from them. We parted company, genetically, six million years ago."

"And do they think like us?" Hari asked.

"Best way to tell is an immersion," Vaddo said. "Very best way."

He smiled invitingly and Hari wondered if Vaddo got a commission on immersions. His sales pitch was subtle, shaped for an academic's interest, but still a sales pitch.

Vaddo had already made available to Hari the vast stores of data on pan movements, population dynamics, and behaviors. It was a rich source, millennia old. With some modeling, here might be fertile ground for a simple description of pans as protohumans, using a truncated version of psychohistory.

"Describing the life history of a species mathematically is one thing," Dors said. "But *living* in it . . ."

"Come now," Hari said. Even though he knew the entire Excursion Station was geared to sell the guests safaris and immersions, he was intrigued. "I need a change, you said. Get out of stuffy old Trantor, you said."

Vaddo smiled warmly. "It's completely safe."

Dors smiled at Hari tolerantly. Between people long-married there is a diplomacy of the eyes. "Oh, all right."

3.

◆

He spent mornings studying the pan data banks. The mathematician in him pondered how to represent their dynamics with a trimmed-down psychohistory. The marble of fate rattling down a cracked slope. So many paths, variables . . .

To get all this he had to kowtow to the station chief. A woman named Yakani, she seemed cordial, but displayed a large portrait of the Academic Potentate upon her office wall. Hari mentioned it and Yakani gushed on about "her mentor," who had helped her run a primate studies center on a verdant planet some decades before.

"She will bear watching," Dors said.

"You don't think the Potentate would—"

"The first assassination attempt—remember the tab? I learned from the Imperials that some technical aspects of it point to an academic laboratory."

Hari frowned. "Surely my own faction would not oppose—"

"She is as ruthless as Lamurk, but more subtle."

"My, you are suspicious."

"I must be."

In the afternoons they took treks. Dors did not like the dust and heat and they saw few animals. "What self-respecting beast would want to be seen with these overdressed Primitivists?" she said.

He liked the atmosphere of this world and relaxed

into it, but his mind kept on working. He thought about this as he stood on the sweeping verandah, drinking pungent fruit juice as he watched a sunset. Dors stood beside him silently.

Planets were energy funnels, he thought. At the bottom of their gravitational wells, plants captured barely a tenth of a percent of the sunlight that fell on a world's surface. They built organic molecules with a star's energy. In turn, plants were prey for animals, who could harvest roughly a tenth of the plant's stored energy. Grazers were themselves prey to meat-eaters, who could use about a tenth of the flesh-stored energy. So, he estimated, only about one part in a hundred thousand of the lancing sunlight energy wound up in the predators.

Wasteful! Yet nowhere in the whole Galaxy had a more efficient engine evolved. Why not?

Predators were invariably more intelligent than their prey, and they sat atop a pyramid of very steep slopes. Omnivores had a similar balancing act. Out of that rugged landscape had come humanity.

That fact *had* to matter greatly in any psychohistory. The pans, then, were essential to finding the ancient keys to the human psyche.

Dors said, "I hope immersion isn't, well, so hot and sticky."

"Remember, you'll see the world through different eyes."

"Just so I can come back whenever I want and have a nice hot bath."

"Compartments?" Dors shied back. "They look more like caskets."

"They have to be snug, madam."

ExSpec Vaddo smiled amiably—which, Hari

sensed, probably meant he wasn't feeling amiable at all. Their conversation had been friendly, the staff here was respectful of the noted Dr. Seldon, but after all, basically he and Dors were just more tourists. Paying for a bit of primitive fun, all couched in proper scholarly terms, but—tourists.

"You're kept in fixed status, all body systems running slow but normal," the ExSpec said, popping out the padded networks for their inspection. He ran through the controls, emergency procedures, safeguards.

"Looks comfortable enough," Dors observed grudgingly.

"Come on," Hari chided. "You promised we would do it."

"You'll be meshed into our systems at all times," Vaddo said.

"Even your data library?" Hari asked.

"Sure thing."

The team of ExSpecs booted them into the stasis compartments with deft, sure efficiency. Tabs, pressers, magnetic pickups were plated onto his skull to pick up thoughts directly. The very latest tech.

"Ready? Feeling good?" Vaddo asked with his professional smile.

Hari was not feeling good (as opposed to feeling well), and he realized part of it was this ExSpec. He had always distrusted bland, assured people. Both Vaddo and the security chief, Yakani, seemed to be unremarkable Greys. But Dors' wariness had rubbed off. Something about them bothered him, but he could not say why.

Oh, well, Dors was probably right. He needed a vacation. What better way to get out of yourself?

"Good, yes. Ready, yes."

The suspension tech was ancient and reliable. It

suppressed neuromuscular responses, so the customer lay dormant, only his mind engaged with the pan.

Magnetic webs capped over his cerebrum. Through electromagnetic inductance they interwove into layers of the brain. They routed signals along tiny thread-paths, suppressing many brain functions and blocking physiological processes.

All this, so that the massively parallel circuitry of the brain could be inductively linked out, thought by thought. Then it was transmitted to chips embedded in the pan subject. Immersion.

The technology had ramified throughout the Empire, quite famously. The ability to distantly manage minds had myriad uses. The suspension tech, however, found its own odd applications.

On some worlds, and in certain Trantorian classes, women were wedded, then suspended for all but a few hours of the day. Their wealthy husbands awoke them from freeze-frame states only for social and sexual purposes. Over a half century, the wives experienced a heady whirlwind of places, friends, parties, vacations, passionate hours—but their total accumulated time was only a few years. Their husbands died in what seemed to the wives like short order, indeed, leaving a wealthy widow of perhaps thirty. Such women were highly sought, and not only for their money. They were uniquely sophisticated, seasoned by a long "marriage." Often these widows returned the favor, wedding husbands whom they revived for similar uses.

All this Hari had taken in with the sophisticated veneer he had cultivated on Trantor. So he thought his immersion would be comfortable, interesting, the stuff of stim-party talk.

He had thought that he would in some sense visit another, simpler, mind.

He did not expect to be swallowed whole.

4.

➤

A good day. Plenty of fat grubs to eat in a big moist log. Dig them out with my nails, fresh tangy sharp crunchy.

Biggest, he shoves me aside. Scoops out plenty rich grubs. Grunts. Glowers.

My belly rumbles. I back off and eye Biggest. He's got pinched-up face so I know not to fool with him.

I walk away, I squat down. Get some picking from a fem. She finds some-fleas, cracks them in her teeth.

Biggest rolls the log around some to knock a few grubs loose, finishes up. He's strong. Fems watch him. Over by the trees a bunch of fems chatter, suck their teeth. Everybody's sleepy now in early afternoon, lying in the shade. Biggest, though, he waves at me and Hunker and off we go.

Patrol. Strut tall, step out proud. I like it fine. Better than humping, even.

Down past the creek and along to where the hoof smells are. That's the shallow spot. We cross and go into the trees sniff-sniffing and there are two Strangers.

They don't see us yet. We move smooth, quiet. Biggest picks up a branch and we do, too. Hunker is sniff-

ing to see who these Strangers are and
he points off to the hill. Just like I
thought, they're Hillies. The worst.
Smell bad.

Hillies come onto our turf. Make
trouble. We make it back.

We spread out. Biggest, he grunts
and they hear him. I'm already moving,
branch held up. I can run pretty far
without going all-fours. The Strangers
cry out, big-eyed. We go fast and then
we're on them.

They have no branches. We hit them
and kick and they grab at us. They are
tall and quick. Biggest slams one to
the ground. I hit that one so Biggest
knows real well I'm with him. Hammer
hard, I do. Then I go quick to help
Hunker.

His Stranger has taken his branch
away. I club the Stranger. He sprawls.
I whack him good and Hunker jumps on
him and it is wonderful.

The Stranger tries to get up and I
kick him solid. Hunker grabs back his
branch and hits again and again with
me helping hard.

Biggest, his Stranger gets up and
starts to run. Biggest whacks his ass
with the branch, roaring and laughing.

Me, I got my skill. Special. I pick
up rocks. I'm the best thrower, better
than Biggest even.

Rocks are for Strangers. My buddies,
them I'll scrap with, but never use
rocks. Strangers, though, they deserve
to get rocks in the face. I love to

bust a Stranger that way.

I throw one clean and smooth. Catch
the Stranger on the leg. He stumbles.
I smack him good with a sharp-edged
rock in the back.

He runs fast then. I can see he's
bleeding. Big red drops in the dust.

Biggest laughs and slaps me and I
know I'm in good with him.

Hunker is clubbing his Stranger.
Biggest takes my club and joins in. The
blood all over the Stranger sings warm
in my nose and I jump up and down on him.
We keep at it like that a long time. Not
worried about the other Stranger coming
back. Strangers are brave sometimes, but
they know when they have lost.

The Stranger stops moving. I give
him one more kick.

No reaction. Dead maybe.

We scream and dance and holler out
our joy.

5.

◆

Hari shook his head to clear it. That helped a little.

"You were that big one?" Dors asked. "I was the
female, over by the trees."

"Sorry, I couldn't tell."

"It was . . . different, wasn't it?"

He laughed dryly. "Murder usually is."

"When you went off with the, well, leader—"

"My pan thinks of him as 'Biggest.' We killed

another pan."

They were in the plush reception room of the immersion facility. Hari stood and felt the world tilt a little and then right itself. "I think I'll stick to historical research for a while."

Dors smiled sheepishly. "I . . . I rather liked it."

He thought a moment, blinked. "So did I," he said, surprising himself.

"Not the murder—"

"No, of course not. But . . . the feel."

She grinned. "Can't get that on Trantor, Professor."

He spent two days coasting through cool lattices of data in the formidable station library. It was well equipped and allowed interfaces with several senses. He patrolled through cool digital labyrinths.

Some data was encrusted with age, quite literally. In the vector spaces portrayed on huge screens, the research data of millennia ago were covered with thick, bulky protocols and scabs of security precautions. All were easily broken or averted, of course, by present methods. But the chunky abstracts, reports, summaries, and crudely processed statistics still resisted easy interpretation. Occasionally some facets of pan behavior were carefully hidden away in appendices and sidebar notes, as though the biologists in the lonely outpost were embarrassed by it. Some *was* embarrassing: mating behavior, especially. How could he use this?

He navigated through the 3D maze and cobbled together his ideas. Could he follow a strategy of analogy?

Pans shared nearly all their genes with humans, so pan dynamics should be a simpler version of human dynamics. Could he then analyze pan troop interactions as a reduced case of psychohistory?

Security Chief Yakani opened confidential files which implied that pans had been genetically modified about ten thousand years before. To what end Hari could not tell. There were other altered creatures, "raboons" particularly. Yakani took such an interest in his work that he became suspicious she was keeping an eye on him for the Potentate.

At sunset of the second day he sat with Dors watching bloodred shafts spike through orange-tinged clouds. This world was gaudy beyond good taste, and he liked it. The food was tangy, too. His stomach rumbled, anticipating dinner.

He remarked to Dors, "It's tempting, using pans to build a sort of toy model of psychohistory."

"But you have doubts."

"They're like us but they have, well, uh . . ."

"Base, animalistic ways?" She smirked, then kissed him. "My prudish Hari."

"We have our share of beastly behaviors, I know. But we're a lot smarter, too."

Her eyelids dipped in a manner he knew by now suggested polite doubt. "They live intensely, you'll have to give them that."

"Maybe we're smarter than we need to be anyway?"

"What?" This surprised her.

"I've been reading up on evolution. Not a front rank field anymore; everybody thinks we understand it."

"And in a galaxy filled with humans and little else, there isn't much fresh material."

He had not thought of it that way before, but she was right. Biology was a backwater science. All the academic sophisticates were pursuing something called "integrative sociometrics."

He went on, laying out his thoughts. Plainly, the human brain was an evolutionary overshoot. Brains were far more capable than a competent hunter-gatherer needed. To get the better of animals, it would have been enough to master fire and simple stone tools. Such talents alone would have made people the lords of creation, removing selection pressure to change. Instead, all evidence from the brain itself said that change accelerated. The human cerebral cortex added mass, stacking new circuitry atop older wiring. That mass spread over the lesser areas like a thick new skin. So said the ancient studies, their data from museums long lost.

"From this came musicians and engineers, saints and savants," he finished with a flourish. One of Dors' best points was her willingness to sit still while he waxed professorily longwinded—even on vacation.

"And the pans, you think, are from before that time? On ancient Earth?"

"They must be. And all this evolutionary selection happened in just a few million years."

Dors nodded. "Look at it from the woman's point of view. It happened, despite putting mothers in desperate danger in childbirth."

"Uh, how?"

"From those huge baby heads. They're hard to get out. We women are still paying the price for your brains—and for ours."

He chuckled. She always had a special spin on a subject that made him see it fresh. "Then why was it selected for, back then?"

Dors smiled enigmatically. "Maybe men and women alike found intelligence sexy in each other."

"Really?"

Her sly smile. "How about us?"

"Have you ever watched very many 3D stars? They don't feature brains, my dear."

"Remember the animals we saw in the Imperial Zoo? It could be that for early humans, brains were like peacock tails, or moose horns: display items to attract the females. Runaway sexual selection."

"I see, an overplayed hand of otherwise perfectly good cards." He laughed. "So being smart is just a bright ornament."

"Works for me," she said, giving him a wink.

He watched the sunset turn to glowering, ominous crimson, oddly happy. Sheets of light worked across the sky among curious, layered clouds. "Ummm . . ." Dors murmured.

"Yes?"

"Maybe this is a way to use the research the ExSpecs are doing, too. Learn who we humans once were—and therefore who we are."

"Intellectually, it's a jump. In social ways, though, the gap could be less."

Dors looked skeptical. "You think pans are only a bit further back in a social sense?"

"Ummm. I wonder if in logarithmic time we might scale from pans to the early Empire and then on to now?"

"A big leap."

"Maybe I could use that Voltaire sim from Sark as a scaling point in a long curve."

"Look, to do anything you'll need more experience with them." She eyed him. "You like immersion, don't you?"

"Well, yes. It's just . . ."

"What?"

"That ExSpec Vaddo, he keeps pushing immersions—"

"That's his job."

"—and he knew who I was."

"So?" She spread her hands and shrugged.

"You're normally the suspicious one. Why should an ExSpec know an obscure mathematician?"

"He looked you up. Data dumps on incoming guests are standard. And as a First Minister candidate, you're hardly obscure."

"I suppose so. Say, you're supposed to be the ever-vigilant one." He grinned. "Shouldn't you be encouraging my caution?"

"Paranoia isn't caution. Time spent on nonthreats subtracts from vigilance."

By the time they went in for dinner she had talked him into it.

6.

◆

Hot day in the sun. Dust tickles. Makes me snort.

That Biggest, he walks by, gets respect right away. Plenty. Fems and guys alike, they stick out their hands.

Biggest touches them, taking time with each, letting them know he is there. The world is all right.

I reach out to him, too. Makes me feel good. I want to be like Biggest, to be big, be as big as him, be *him*.

Fems don't give him any trouble. He wants one, she goes. Hump right away. He's Biggest.

Most males, they don't get much respect. Fems don't want to do with them as much as they do with Biggest. The little males, they huff and throw sand and all that, but everybody knows they're not going to be much. No chance they could ever be like

Biggest. They don't like that, but they are stuck with it.

Me, I'm pretty big. I get respect. Some, anyway.

All the guys like stroking. Petting. Grooming. Fems give it to them and they give it back.

Guys get more, though. After it, they're not so gruff.

I'm sitting getting groomed and all of a sudden I smell something. I don't like it. I jump up, cry out. Biggest, he takes notice. Smells it, too.

Strangers. Everybody starts hugging each other. Strong smell, plenty of it. Lots of Strangers. The wind says they are near, getting nearer.

They come running down on us from the ridge. Looking for fems, looking for trouble.

I run for my rocks. I always have some handy. I fling one at them, miss. Then they in among us. It's hard to hit them, they go so fast.

Four Strangers, they grab two fems. Drag them away.

Everybody howling, crying. Dust everywhere.

I throw rocks. Biggest leads the guys against the Strangers.

They turn and run off. Just like that. Got the two fems though and that's bad.

Biggest mad. He pushes around some of the guys, makes noise. He not looking so good now, he let the Strangers in.

Those Strangers bad. We all hunker

down, groom each other, pet, make nice sounds.

Biggest, he come by, slap some of the fems. Hump some. Make sure everybody know he's still Biggest.

He don't slap me. He know better than to try. I growl at him when he come close and he pretend not to hear.

Maybe he not so Big anymore, I'm thinking.

7.

◆

He stayed with it this time. After the first crisis, when the Stranger pans came running through, he sat and let himself get groomed for a long time. It really did calm him.

Him? Who was he?

This time he could fully sense the pan mind. Not below him—that was a metaphor—but *around* him. A swarming scattershot of senses, thoughts, fragments like leaves blowing by him in a wind.

And the wind was *emotion*. Blustering gales, howling and whipping in gusts, raining thoughts like soft hammer blows.

These pans thought poorly, in the sense that he could get only shards, like human musings chopped by a nervous editor. But pans felt intensely.

Of course, he thought—and he could think, nestled in the hard kernel of himself, wrapped in the pan mind. *Emotions told it what to do, without thinking. Quick reactions demanded that. Strong feeling amplified subtle cues into strong impera-*

tives. Blunt orders from Mother Evolution.

He saw now that the belief that high order mental experiences like emotion were unique to people was . . . simply conceited. These pans shared much of the human worldview. A theory of pan psychohistory could be valuable.

He gingerly separated himself from the dense, pressing pan mind. He wondered if the pan knew he was here. Yes, it did—dimly.

Yet this did not bother the pan. He integrated it into his blurred, blunt world. Hari was somewhat like an emotion, just one of many fluttering by and staying a while, then wafting away.

Could he be more than that? He tried getting the pan to lift its right arm—and it was like lead. He struggled for a while that way with no success. Then he realized his error. He could not overpower this pan, not as a kernel in a much larger mind.

He thought about this as the pan groomed a female, picking carefully through coarse hair. The strands smelled good, the air was sweet, the sun stroked him with blades of generous warmth . . .

Emotion. Pans didn't follow instructions because that simply lay beyond them. They could not understand directions in the human sense. Emotions—those they knew. He had to be an emotion, not a little general giving orders.

He sat for a while simply being this pan. He learned—or rather, he felt. The troop groomed and scavenged food, males eyeing the perimeter, females keeping close to the young. A lazy calm descended over him, carrying him effortlessly through warm moments of the day.

Not since boyhood had he felt anything like this. A slow, graceful easing, as though there were no time at all, only slices of eternity.

In this mood, he could concentrate on a simple movement—raising an arm, scratching—and create the desire to do it. His pan responded. To make it happen, he had to *feel* his way toward a goal.

Catching a sweet scent on the wind, Hari thought about what food that might signal. His pan meandered upwind, sniffed, discarded the clue as uninteresting. Hari could now smell the reason why: fruit, true, sweet, yes—but inedible for a pan.

Good. He was learning. And he was integrating himself into the deep recesses of this pan-mind.

Watching the troop, he decided to name the prominent pans, to keep them straight: Agile the quick one, Sheelah the sexy one, Grubber the hungry one . . . But what was his own name? His he dubbed Ipan. Not very original, but that was its main characteristic, *I as pan*.

Grubber found some bulb-shaped fruit and the others drifted over to scavenge. The hard fruit smelled a little too young (how did he know that?), but some ate it anyway.

And which of these was Dors? They had asked to be immersed in the same troop, so one of these—he forced himself to count, though somehow the exercise was like moving heavy weights in his mind—these twenty-two was her. How could he tell? He ambled over to several females who were using sharp-edged stones to cut leaves from branches. They tied the strands together so they could carry food.

Hari peered into their faces. Mild interest, a few hands held out for stroking, an invitation to groom. No glint of recognition in their eyes.

He watched a big fem, Sheelah, carefully wash sand-covered fruit in a creek. The troop followed suit; Sheelah was a leader of sorts, a female lieutenant to Biggest.

She ate with relish, looked around. There was grain growing nearby, past maturity, ripe tan kernels already scattered in the sandy soil. Concentrating, Hari could tell from the faint bouquet that this was a delicacy. A few pans squatted and picked grains from the sand, slow work. Sheelah did the same, and then stopped, gazing off at the creek. Time passed, insects buzzed. After a while she scooped up sand and kernels and walked to the brook's edge. She tossed it all in. The sand sank, the kernels floated. She skimmed them off and gulped them down, grinning widely.

An impressive trick. The other pans did not pick up on her kernel-skimming method. Fruit washing was conceptually easier, he supposed, since the pan could keep the fruit the whole time. Kernel-skimming demanded throwing away the food first, then rescuing it—a harder mental jump.

He thought about her and in response Ipan sauntered over her way. He peered into Sheelah's eyes— and she winked at him. Dors! He wrapped hairy arms around her in a burst of love.

8.

◆

"Pure animal love," she said over dinner. "Refreshing."

Hari nodded. "I like being there, living that way."

"I can *smell* so much more."

"Fruit tastes differently when they bite into it." He held up a purple bulb, sliced into it, forked it into his mouth. "To me, this is almost unbearably sweet. To Ipan, it's pleasant, a little peppery. I suppose pans have been selected for a sweet tooth. It gets them more fast calories."

"I can't think of a more thorough vacation. Not just getting away from home, but getting away from your species."

He eyed the fruit. "And they're so, so . . ."

"Horny?"

"Insatiable."

"You didn't seem to mind."

"My pan, Ipan? I bail out when he gets into his hump-them-all mood."

She eyed him. "Really?"

"Don't you bail out?"

"Yes, but I don't expect men to be like women."

"Oh?" he said stiffly.

"I've been reading in the ExSpec's research library, while you toy with pan social movements. Women invest heavily in their children. Men can use two strategies: parental investment, plus 'sow the oats.'" She lifted an eyebrow. "Both must have been selected for in our evolution, because they're both common."

"Not with *me*."

To his surprise, she laughed. "I'm talking in general. My point is, the pans are much more promiscuous than we are. The males run everything. They help out the females who are carrying their children, I gather, but then they shop around elsewhere *all* the time."

Hari switched into his professional mode; it was decidedly more comfortable when dealing with such issues. "As the specialists say, they are pursuing a mixed reproductive strategy."

"How polite."

"Polite plus precise."

Of course, he couldn't really be sure Dors bailed out of Sheelah when a male came by for a quick one. (They were always quick, too—thirty seconds or less.) *Could* she exit the pan mind that quickly? He required a few moments to extricate himself. Of course, if she saw the male coming, guessed his intentions . . .

He was surprised at himself. What role did jealousy have when they were inhabiting other bodies? Did the usual moral code make any sense? Yet to talk this over with her was . . . embarrassing.

He was still the country boy from Helicon, like it or not.

Ruefully he concentrated on his meal of local "roamer-fleisch," which turned out to be an earthy, dark meat in a stew of tangy vegetables. He ate heartily, and in response to Dors' rather obviously amused silence said, "I'd point out that pans understand commerce, too. Food for sex, betrayal of the leader for sex, spare my child for sex, grooming for sex, just about anything for sex."

"It does seem to be their social currency. Short and decidedly not sweet. Just quick lunges, strong sensations, then boom—it's over."

"The males need it, the females use it."

"Ummm, you've been taking notes."

"If I'm going to model pans as a sort of simplified people, then I must."

"Model pans?" came the assured tones of ExSpec Vaddo. "They're not model citizens, if that's what you mean." He gave them a sunny smile and Hari guessed this was more of the obligatory friendliness of this place.

Hari smiled mechanically. "I'm trying to find the variables that could describe pan behavior."

"You should spend a lot of time with them," Vaddo said, sitting at the table and holding up a finger to a waiter for a drink. "They're subtle creatures."

"I agree," said Dors. "Do you ride them very much?"

"Some, but most of our research is done differently now." Vaddo's mouth twisted ruefully. "Statistical models, that sort of thing. I got this touring idea started, using the immersion tech we had developed earlier, to make money for the project. Otherwise, we'd have had to close."

"I'm happy to contribute," Hari said.

"Admit it—you like it," Dors said, amused.

"Well, yes. It's . . . different."

"And good for the staid Professor Seldon to get out of his shell," she said.

Vaddo beamed. "Be sure you don't take chances out there. Some of our customers think they're superpans or something."

Dors' eyes flickered. "What danger is there? Our bodies are in slowtime, back here."

Vaddo said, "You're strongly linked. A big shock to a pan can drive a back-shock in your own neurological systems."

"What sort of shock?" Hari asked.

"Death, major injury."

"In that case," Dors said to Hari, "I really do not think you should immerse."

Hari felt irked. "Come on! I'm on vacation, not in prison."

"Any threat to you—"

"Just a minute ago you were rhapsodizing about how good for me it was."

"You're too important to—"

"There's really very little danger," Vaddo came in smoothly. "Pans don't die suddenly, usually."

"And I can bail out when I see danger coming," Hari added.

"But *will* you? I think you're getting a taste for adventure."

She was right, but he wasn't going to concede the point. If he wanted a little escape from his humdrum mathematician's routine, so much the better. "I like being out of Trantor's endless corridors."

Vaddo gave Dors a confident smile. "And we haven't lost a tourist yet."

"How about research staff?" she shot back.

"Well, that was a most unusual—"

"What happened?"

"A pan fell off a ledge. The human operator couldn't bail out in time and she came out of it paralyzed. The shock of experiencing death through immersion is known from other incidents to prove fatal. But we have systems in place now to short circuit—"

"What else?" she persisted.

"Well, there was one difficult episode. In the early days, when we had simple wire fences." The ExSpec shifted uneasily. "Some predators got in."

"What sort of predators?"

"A primate pack hunter, *Carnopapio grandis*. We call them raboons, because they're genetically related to a small primate on another continent. Their DNA—"

"How did they get in?" Dors insisted.

"They're somewhat like a wild hog, with hooves that double as diggers. They smelled game—our corralled animals. Dug under the fences."

Dors eyed the high, solid walls. "These are adequate?"

"Certainly. Raboons share DNA with the pans and we believe they're from an ancient genetic experiment. Someone tried to make a predator by raising the earlier stock up onto two legs. Like most bipedal predators, the forelimbs are shortened and the head carried forward, balanced by a thick tail they use for signaling to each other. They prey on the biggest herd animals, the gigantelope, eating only the richest meat."

"Why attack humans?"

"They take targets of opportunity, too. Pans, even.

When they got into the compound, they went for adult humans, not children—a very selective strategy."

Dors shivered. "You look at all this very . . . objectively."

"I'm a biologist."

"I never knew it could be so interesting," Hari said to defuse her apprehension.

Vaddo beamed. "Not as involving as higher mathematics, I'm sure."

Dors' mouth twisted with wry skepticism. "Do you mind if guests carry weapons inside the compound?"

9.

◆

He had a glimmering of an idea about the pans, a way to use their behaviors in building a simple toy model of psychohistory. He might be able to use the statistics of pan troop movements, the ups and downs of their shifting fortunes.

Pictured in system-space, living structures worked at the edge of a chaotic terrain. Life as a whole harvested the fruits of a large menu of possible path-choices. Natural selection first achieved, then sustained this edgy state.

Whole biospheres shifted their equilibrium points amid energetic flowthrough—like birds banking on winds, he thought, watching some big yellow ones glide over the station, taking advantage of the updrafts.

Like them, whole biological systems sometimes hovered at stagnation points. Systems were able to choose several paths of descent. Sometimes—to stretch the analogy—they could eat the tasty insects which came up to them on those same tricky breezes.

Failure to negotiate such winds of change meant the pattern forfeited its systemic integrity. Energies dissipated. Crucial was the fact that any seemingly stable state was actually a trick of dynamic feedback.

No static state existed—except one. A biological system at perfect equilibrium was simply dead.

So, too, psychohistory?

He talked it over with Dors and she nodded. Beneath her apparent calm she was worried. Since Vaddo's remark she was always tut-tutting about safety. He reminded her that she had earlier urged him to do more immersions. "This is a *vacation*, remember?" he said more than once.

Her amused sidewise glances told him that she also didn't buy his talk about the toy modeling. She thought he just liked romping in the woods. "A country boy at heart," she chuckled.

So the next morning he skipped a planned trek to view the gigantelope herds. Immediately he and Dors went to the immersion chambers and slipped under. To get some solid work done, he told himself.

"What's this?" He gestured to a small tiktok stationed between their immersion pods.

"Precaution," Dors said. "I don't want anyone tampering with our chambers while we're under."

"Tiktoks cost plenty out here."

"This one guards the coded locks, see?" She crouched beside the tiktok and reached for the control panel. It blocked her.

"I thought the locks were enough."

"The security chief has access to those."

"And you suspect her?"

"I suspect everyone. But especially her."

The pans slept in trees and spent plenty of time

grooming each other. For the lucky groomer a tick or louse was a treat. With enough, they could get high on some peppery-tasting alkaloid. He suspected the careful stroking and combing of his hair by Dors was a behavior selected because it improved pan hygiene. It certainly calmed Ipan, also.

Then it struck him: pans groomed rather than vocalizing. Only in crises and when agitated did they call and cry, mostly about breeding, feeding, or self-defense. They were like people who could not release themselves through the comfort of talk.

And they needed comfort. The core of their social life resembled human societies under stress—in tyrannies, in prisons, in city gangs. Nature red in tooth and claw, yet strikingly like troubled people.

But there were "civilized" behaviors here, too. Friendships, grief, sharing, buddies-in-arms who hunted and guarded turf together. Their old got wrinkled, bald, and toothless, yet were still cared for.

Their instinctive knowledge was prodigious. They knew how to make a bed of leaves as dusk fell, high up in trees. They could climb with grasping feet. They felt, cried, mourned—without being able to parse these into neat grammatical packages, so the emotions could be managed, subdued. Instead, emotions drove them.

Hunger was the strongest. They found and ate leaves, fruit, insects, even fair-sized animals. They loved caterpillars.

Each moment, each small enlightenment, sank him deeper into Ipan. He began to sense the subtle nooks and crannies of the pan mind. Slowly, he gained more cooperative control.

That morning a female found a big fallen tree and began banging on it. The hollow trunk boomed like a drum and all the foraging party rushed forward to beat it, too, grinning wildly at the noise.

Ipan joined in. Hari felt the burst of joy, seethed in it.

Later, coming upon a waterfall after a heavy rain, they seized vines and swung among trees, out over the foaming water, screeching with delight as they performed twists and leaps from vine to vine.

They were like children in a new playground. Hari got Ipan to make impossible moves, wild tumbles and dives, propelling him forward with abandon—to the astonishment of the other pans.

They were violent in their sudden, peevish moments—in hustling females, in working out their perpetual dominance hierarchy, and especially in hunting. A successful hunt brought enormous excitement: hugging, kissing, pats. As the troop descended to feed, the forest rang with barks, screeches, hoots, and pants. Hari joined the tumult, danced with Sheelah/Dors.

He had expected to have to repress his prim meritocrat dislike of mess. Many meritocrats even disliked soil itself. Not Hari, who had been reared among farmers and laborers. Still, he had thought that long exposure to Trantor's prissy aesthetics would hamper him here. Instead, the pans' filth seemed natural.

In some matters he did have to restrain his feelings. Rats the pans ate headfirst. Larger game they smashed against rocks. They devoured the brains first, a steaming delicacy.

Hari gulped—metaphorically, but with Ipan echoing the impulse—and watched, screening his reluctance. Ipan had to eat, after all.

At the scent of predators, he felt Ipan's hair stand on end. Another tangy bouquet made Ipan's mouth water. He gave no mercy to food, even if it was still walking. Evolution in action; those pans who had showed mercy in the past ate less and left fewer descendants. Those weren't represented here anymore.

For all its excesses, he found the pans' behavior hauntingly familiar. Males gathered often for combat, for pitching rocks, for blood sports, to work out their hierarchy. Females networked and formed alliances. There were trades of favors for loyalty, kinship bonds, turf wars, threats and displays, protection rackets, a hunger for "respect," scheming subordinates, revenge—a social world enjoyed by many people that history had judged "great."

Much like the Emperor's court, in fact.

Did people long to strip away their clothing and conventions, bursting forth as pans? A brainy pan would be quite at home in the Imperial gentry . . .

Hari felt a flush of revulsion so strong Ipan shook and fidgeted. Humanity's lot *had* to be different, not this primitive horror.

He could use this, certainly, as a test bed for a full theory. *Then* humankind would be self-knowing, captains of themselves. He would build in the imperatives of the pans, but go far beyond—to true, deep psychohistory.

10.

◆

"I don't see it," Dors said at dinner.

"But they're so much like us! We must have shared some connections." He put down his spoon. "I wonder if they were house pets of ours, long before star travel?"

"I wouldn't have them messing up my house."

Adult humans weighed little more than pans, but were far weaker. A pan could lift five times more than a well-conditioned man. Human brains were three or four times more massive than a pan's. A human baby a few months old already had a brain larger than a grown pan. People had different brain architecture, as well.

But was that the whole story? Hari wondered.

Give pans bigger brains and speech, ease off on the testosterone, saddle them with more inhibitions, spruce them up with a shave and a haircut, teach them to stand securely on hind legs—and you had deluxe model pans that would look and act rather human.

"Look," he said to Dors, "my point is that they're close enough to us to make a psychohistory model work."

"To make anybody believe that, you'll have to show that they're intelligent enough to have intricate interactions."

"What about their foraging, their hunting?" he persisted.

"Vaddo says they couldn't even be trained to do work around this Excursion Station."

"I'll show you what I mean. Let's master their methods together."

"What method?"

"The basic one. Getting enough to eat."

She bit into a steak of a meaty local grazer, suitably processed and "fat-flensed for the fastidious urban palate," as the brochure had it. Chewing with unusual ferocity, she eyed him. "You're on. Anything a pan can do, I can do better."

Dors waved at him from within Sheelah. *Let the contest begin.*

The troop was foraging. He let Ipan meander and did not try to harness the emotional ripples that lapped across the pan mind. He had gotten better at it, but at a sudden smell or sound he could lose his grip. And guiding the blunt pan mind through anything complicated was still like moving a puppet with rubber strings.

Sheelah/Dors waved and signed to him: *This way.*

They had worked out a code of a few hundred words, using finger and facial gestures, and their pans seemed to go along with these fairly well. Pans had a rough language, mixing grunts and shrugs and finger displays. These conveyed immediate meanings, but not in the usual sense of sentences. Mostly they just set up associations.

Tree, fruit, go, Dors sent. They ambled their pans over to a clump of promising spindly trunks, but the bark was too slick to climb.

The rest of the troop had not even bothered. *They have forest smarts we lack,* Hari thought ruefully.

What there? he signed to Sheelah/Dors.

Pans ambled up to mounds, gave them the once-over, and reached out to brush aside some mud, revealing a tiny tunnel. *Termites,* Dors signed.

Hari analyzed the situation as pans drifted in. Nobody seemed in much of a hurry. Sheelah winked at him and waddled over to a distant mound.

Apparently termites worked outside at night, then blocked the entrances at dawn. Hari let his pan shuffle over to a large tan mound, but he was riding it so well now that the pan's responses were weak. Hari/Ipan looked for cracks, knobs, slight hollows— and when he brushed away some mud, found nothing. Other pans readily unmasked tunnels. Had they memorized the hundred or more tunnels in each mound?

He finally uncovered one. Ipan was no help. Hari could control, but that blocked up the wellsprings of deep knowledge within the pan.

The pans deftly tore off twigs or grass stalks near their mounds. Hari carefully followed their lead. His twigs and grass didn't work. The first lot was too pliant, and when he tried to work them into a twisting tunnel, they collapsed and buckled. He switched to stiffer ones, but those caught on the tunnel walls, or snapped off. From Ipan came little help. Hari had managed him a bit too well.

He was getting embarrassed. Even the younger pans had no trouble picking just the right stems or sticks. Hari watched a pan nearby drop a stick that seemed to work. He then picked it up when the pan moved on. He felt welling up from Ipan a blunt anxiety, mixing frustration and hunger. He could *taste* the anticipation of luscious, juicy termites.

He set to work, plucking the emotional strings of Ipan. This job went even worse. Vague thoughts drifted up from Ipan, but Hari was in control of the muscles now, and that was the bad part.

He quickly found that the stick had to be stuck in about ten centimeters, turning his wrist to navigate it down the twisty channel. Then he had to gently vibrate it. Through Ipan he sensed that this was to attract termites to bite into the stick. At first he did it too long and when he drew the stick out it was half gone. Termites had bitten cleanly through it. So he had to search out another stick and that made Ipan's stomach growl.

The other pans were through termite-snacking while Hari was still fumbling for his first taste. The nuances irked him. He pulled the stick out too fast, not turning it enough to ease it past the tunnel's curves. Time and again he fetched forth the stick, only to find that he had scraped the luscious termites off on the walls. Their bites punctured his stick, until it was so shredded he had to get another. The termites were dining better than he.

He finally caught the knack, a fluid slow twist of the wrist, gracefully extracting termites, clinging like bumps. Ipan licked them off eagerly. Hari liked the morsels, filtered through pan tastebuds.

Not many, though. Others of the troop were watching his skimpy harvest, heads tilted in curiosity, and he felt humiliated.

The hell with this, he thought.

He made Ipan turn and walk into the woods. Ipan resisted, dragging his feet. Hari found a thick limb, snapped it off to carrying size, and went back to the mound.

No more fooling with sticks. He whacked the mound solidly. Five more and he had punched a big hole. Escaping termites he scooped up by the delicious handful.

So much for subtlety! he wanted to shout. He tried writing a note for her in the dust, but it was hard, forcing the letters out through his suddenly awkward hands. Pans could handle a stick to fetch forth grubs, but marking a surface was somehow not a ready talent. He gave up.

Sheelah/Dors came into view, proudly carrying a reed swarming with white-bellied termites. These were the best, a pan gourmet delicacy. *I better,* she signed.

He made Ipan shrug and signed, *I got more.*

So it was a draw.

Later Dors reported to him that among the troop he was known now as Big Stick. The name pleased him immensely.

11.

◆

At dinner he felt elated, exhausted, and not in the mood for conversation. Being a pan seemed to suppress his speech centers. It took some effort to ask ExSpec Vaddo about immersion technology. Usually he accepted the routine techno-miracles, but understanding pans meant understanding how he experienced them.

"The immersion hardware puts you in the middle of a pan's anterior cingulate gyrus," Vaddo said over dessert. "Just 'gyrus' for short. That's the brain's main cortical region for mediating emotions and expressing them through action."

"*The* brain?" Dors asked. "What about ours?"

Vaddo shrugged. "Same general layout. Pans' are smaller, without a big cerebrum."

Hari leaned forward, ignoring his steaming cup of kaff. "This 'gyrus,' it doesn't give direct motor control?"

"No, we tried that. It disorients the pan so much, when you leave, it can't get itself back together."

"So we have to be more subtle," Dors said.

"We have to be. In pan males, the pilot light is always on in neurons that control action and aggression—"

"That's why they're more violence-prone?" she asked.

"We think so. It parallels structures in our own brains."

"Really? Men's neurons?" Dors looked doubtful.

"Human males have higher activity levels in their temporal limbic systems, deeper down in the brain—evolutionarily older structures."

"So why not put me into that level?" Hari asked.

"We place the immersion chips into the gyrus area because we can reach it from the top, surgically. The temporal limbic is way far down, impossible to implant a chip."

Dors frowned. "So pan males—"

"Are harder to control. Professor Seldon here is

running his pan from the backseat, so to speak."

"Whereas Dors is running hers from a control center that, for female pans, is more central?" Hari peered into the distance. "I was handicapped!"

Dors grinned. "You have to play the hand you're dealt."

"It's not fair."

"Big Stick, biology is destiny."

The troop came upon rotting fruit. Fevered excitement ran through them.

The smell was repugnant and enticing at the same time, and at first he did not understand why. The pans rushed to the overripe bulbs of blue and sickly green, popping open the skins, sucking out the juice.

Tentatively, Hari tried one. The hit was immediate. A warm feeling of well-being kindled up in him. Of course—the fruity esters had converted into alcohol! The pans were quite deliberately setting about getting drunk.

He "let" his pan follow suit. He hadn't much choice in the matter.

Ipan grunted and thrashed his arms whenever Hari tried to turn him away from the teardrop fruit. And after a while, Hari didn't want to turn away, either. He gave himself up to a good, solid drunk. He had been worrying a lot lately, agitated in his pan, and . . . this was completely natural, wasn't it?

Then a pack of raboons appeared, and he lost control of Ipan.

They come fast. Running two-legs, no sound. Their tails twitch, talking to each other.

Five circle left. They cut off Esa.

Biggest thunders at them. Hunker runs to nearest and it spikes him with its forepuncher.

I throw rocks. Hit one. It yelps and scurries back. But others take its place. I throw again and they come and the dust and yowling are thick and the others of them have Esa. They cut her with their punch-claws. Kick her with sharp hooves.

Three of them carry her off.

Our fems run, afraid. We warriors stay.

We fight them. Shrieking, throwing, biting when they get close. But we cannot reach Esa.

Then they go. Fast, running on their two hoofed legs. Furling their tails in victory. Taunting us.

We feel bad. Esa was old and we loved her.

Fems come back, nervous. We groom ourselves and know that the two-legs are eating Esa somewhere.

Biggest come by, try to pat me. I snarl.

He Biggest! This thing he should have stopped.

His eyes get big and he slap me. I slap back at him. He slam into me. We roll around in dust. Biting, yowling. Biggest strong, strong and pound my head on ground.

Other warriors, they watch us, not join in.

He beat me. I hurt. I go away.

Biggest starts calming down the warriors. Fems come by and pay their respects to Biggest. Touch him, groom him, feel him the way he likes. He mounts three of them real quick. He feeling Biggest all right.

Me, I lick myself. Sheelah come groom me. After a while I feel better. Forget about trouble.

I not forget Biggest beat me though. In front of everybody. Now I hurt, Biggest get grooming.

He let them come and take Esa. He Biggest, *he* should stop them.

Some day I be all over him. On his back.

Some day *I* be Bigger.

12.

◆

"When did you bail out?" Dors asked.

"After Biggest stopped pounding on me . . . uh, on Ipan."

They were relaxing beside a swimming pool and the heady smells of the forest seemed to awaken in Hari the urge to be down there again, in the valleys of dust and blood. He trembled, took a deep breath. The fighting had been so involving he hadn't wanted to leave, despite the pain. Immersion had a hypnotic quality.

"I know how you feel," she said. "It's easy to totally identify with them. I left Sheelah when those raboons came close. Pretty scary."

"Vaddo said they're derived from Earth, too.

Plenty of DNA overlap. But they show signs of extensive recent tinkering to make them predators."

"Why would the ancients want *those*?"

"Trying to figure out our origins?"

To his surprise, she laughed. "Not everyone has your same interests."

"Why, then?"

"How about using raboons as game, to hunt? Something a little challenging?"

"*Hunting?* The Empire has always been too far from throwback primitivism to—" He had been about to launch into a little lecture on how far humanity had come when he realized that he didn't believe it anymore. "Um."

"You've always thought of people as cerebral. No psychohistory could work if it didn't take into account our animal selves."

"Our worst sins are all our own, I fear." He had not expected that his experiences here would shake him so. This was sobering.

"Not at all. Genocide occurs in wolves and pans alike. Murder is widespread. Ducks and orangutans rape. Even ants have organized warfare and slave raids. Pans have at least as good a chance of being murdered as do humans, Vaddo says. Of all the hallowed human hallmarks—speech, art, technology, and the rest—the one which comes most obviously from animal ancestors is genocide."

"You've been learning from Vaddo."

"It was a good way to keep an eye on him."

"Better to be suspicious than sorry?"

"Of course," she said blandly, giving nothing away.

"Well, luckily, even if we are superpans, Imperial order and communication blurs distinctions between Us and Them."

"So?"

"That blunts the deep impulse to genocide."

She laughed again, this time rather to his annoyance. "You haven't understood history very well. Smaller groups still kill each other off with great relish. In Zone Sagittarius, during the reign of Omar the Impaler—"

"I concede, there are small-scale tragedies by the dozens. But on the scale where psychohistory might work, averaging over populations of many thousands of billions—"

"What makes you so sure numbers are any protection?" she asked pointedly.

"So far—"

"The Empire has been in stasis."

"A steady-state solution, actually. Dynamic equilibrium."

"And if that equilibrium fails?"

"Well . . . then I have nothing to say."

She smiled. "How uncharacteristic."

"Until I have a real, working theory."

"One that can allow for widespread genocide, if the Empire erodes."

He saw her point then. "You're saying I really need this 'animal nature' part of humans."

"I'm afraid so. I'm trained to allow for it already."

He was puzzled. "How so?"

"I don't have your view of humanity. Scheming, plots, Sheelah grabbing more meat for her young, Ipan wanting to do in Biggest—those things happen in the Empire. Just better disguised."

"So?"

"Consider ExSpec Vaddo. He made a comment about your working on a 'theory of history' the other evening."

"So?"

"Who told him you were?"

"I don't think I—ah, you think he's checking up on us?"

"He already knows."

"The security chief, maybe she told him, after checking on me with the Academic Potentate."

She graced him with an unreadable smile. "I do love your endless, naïve way of seeing the world."

Later, he couldn't decide whether she had meant it as a compliment.

13.

◆

Vaddo invited him to try a combat-sport the station offered, and Hari accepted. It was an enhanced swordplay with levitation through electrostatic lifters. Hari was slow and inept. Using his own body against Vaddo's swift moves made him long for the sureness and grace of Ipan.

Vaddo always opened with a traditional posture: one foot forward, his prod-sword making little circles in the air. Hari poked through Vaddo's defense sometimes, but usually spent all his lifter energy eluding Vaddo's thrusts. He did not enjoy it nearly as much as Vaddo.

He did learn bits and pieces about pans from Vaddo and from trolling through the vast station library. The man seemed a bit uneasy when Hari probed the data arrays, as though Vaddo somehow owned them and any reader was a thief. Or at least, that was what Hari took to be the origin of the unease.

He had never thought about animals very much, though he had grown up among them on Helicon. Yet he came to feel that they, too, had to be understood.

Catching sight of itself in a mirror, a dog sees the

image as another dog. So did cats, fish, or birds. After a while they get used to the harmless image, silent and smell-free, but they do not see it as themselves.

Human children had to be about two years old to do better.

Pans took a few days to figure out that they were looking at themselves. Then they preened before it shamelessly, studied their backs, and generally tried to see themselves differently, even putting leaves on their heads like hats and laughing at the result.

So they could do something other animals could not: get outside themselves, and look back.

They plainly lived in a world charged with echoes and reminiscences. Their dominance hierarchy was a frozen record of past coercion. They remembered termite mounds, trees to drum, useful spots where large water-sponge leaves fell, or grain matured.

All this fed into the toy model he had begun building in his notes: a pan psychohistory. It used their movements, rivalries, hierarchies, patterns of eating and mating and dying, territory, resources, and troop competition for them. He found a way to factor into his equations the biological baggage of dark behaviors, even the worst, like delight in torture, and easy exterminations of other species for short-term gain.

All these the pans had. Just like the Empire.

At a dance that evening he watched the crowd with fresh vision.

Flirting was practice mating. He could see it in the sparkle of eyes, the rhythms of the dance. The warm breeze wafting up from the valley brought smells of dust, rot, life. An animal restlessness moved in the room.

He quite liked dancing and Dors was a lush companion tonight. Yet he could not stop his mind from sifting, analyzing, taking the world before him apart into mechanisms.

The nonverbal template humans used for attract/approach strategies apparently descended from a shared mammalian heritage, Dors had pointed out. He thought of that, watching the crowd at the bar.

A woman crosses a crowded room, hips swaying, eyes resting momentarily on a likely man, then coyly looking away just as she apparently notices his regard. A standard opening move: *Notice me*.

The second is *I am harmless*. A hand placed palm-up on a table or knee. A shoulder shrug, derived from an ancient vertebrate reflex, signifying helplessness. Combine that with a tilted head, which displays the vulnerability of the neck. These commonly appeared when two people drawn to each other have their first conversation—all quite unconsciously.

Such moves and gestures are subcortical, emerging far below the neocortex.

Did such forces shape the Empire more than trade balances, alliances, treaties?

He looked at his own kind and tried to see it through pan eyes.

Though human females matured earlier, they did not go on to acquire coarse body hair, bony eye ridges, deep voices, or tough skin. Males did. And women everywhere strove to stay young looking. Cosmetics makers freely admitted their basic role: *We don't sell products. We sell hope.*

Competition for mates was incessant. Male pans sometimes took turns with females in estrus. They had huge testicles, implying that reproductive advantage had come to those males who produced enough sperm to overwhelm their rivals' contributions.

Human males had proportionally smaller testicles.

But humans got their revenge where it mattered. All known primates were genetically related, though they had separated out as species many millions of years ago. In DNA-measured time, pans lay six million years from humans. Of all primates, humans had the largest penises.

He mentioned to Dors that only four percent of mammals formed pair bonds, were monogamous. Primates rated a bit higher, but not much. Birds were much better at it.

She sniffed. "Don't let all this biology go to your head."

"Oh, no, I won't let it get that far."

"You mean it belongs in lower places?"

"Madam, you'll have to be the judge of that."

"Ah, you and your single-entendre humor."

Later that evening, he had ample opportunity to reflect upon the truth that, while it was not always great to be human, it was tremendous fun being a mammal.

14.

They spent one last day immersed in their pans, sunning themselves beside a gushing stream. They had told Vaddo to bring the shuttle down the next day, book a wormhole transit. Then they entered the immersion capsule and sank into a last reverie.

Until Biggest started to mount Sheelah.

Hari/Ipan sat up, his head foggy. Sheelah was shrieking at Biggest. She slapped him.

Biggest had mounted Sheelah before. Dors had

bailed out quickly, her mind returning to her body in the capsule.

Something was different now. Ipan hurried over and signed to Sheelah, who was throwing pebbles at Biggest. *What?*

She moved her hands rapidly, signing, *No go*.

She could not bail out. Something was wrong back at the capsule. He could go back himself, tell them.

Hari made the little mental flip that would bail him out.

Nothing happened.

He tried again. Sheelah threw dust and pebbles, backing away from Biggest. Nothing.

No time to think. He stepped between Sheelah and Biggest.

The massive pan frowned. Here was Ipan, buddy Ipan, getting in the way. Denying him a fem. Biggest seemed to have forgotten the challenge and beating of the day before.

First he tried bellowing, eyes big and white. Then Biggest shook his arms, fists balled.

Hari made his pan stand still. It took every calming impulse he could muster.

Biggest swung his fist like a club.

Ipan ducked. Biggest missed.

Hari was having trouble controlling Ipan, who wanted to flee. Sheets of fear shot up through the pan mind, hot yellows in the blue-black depths.

Biggest charged forward, slamming Ipan back. Hari felt the jolt, a stabbing pain in his chest. He toppled backward, hit hard.

Biggest yowled his triumph. Waved his arms at the sky.

Biggest would get on top, he saw. Beat him again.

Suddenly he felt a deep, raw hatred.

From that red seethe he felt his grip on Ipan tighten. He was riding both with and within the pan, feeling its raw red fear, overrunning that with an iron rage. Ipan's own wrath fed back into Hari. The two formed a concert, anger building as if reflected from hard walls.

He might not be the same kind of primate, but he knew Ipan. Neither of them was going to get beaten again. And Biggest was not going to get Sheelah/Dors.

He rolled to the side. Biggest hit the ground where he had been.

Ipan leaped up and kicked Biggest. Hard, in the ribs. Once, twice. Then in the head.

Whoops, cries, dust, pebbles—Sheelah was still bombarding them both. Ipan shivered with boiling energy and backed away.

Biggest shook his dusty head. Then he curled and rolled easily up to his feet, full of muscular grace, face a constricted mask. The pan's eyes widened, showing white and red.

Ipan yearned to run. Only Hari's rage held him in place.

But it was a static balance of forces. Ipan blinked as Biggest shuffled warily forward, the big pan's caution a tribute to the damage Ipan had inflicted.

I need some advantage, Hari thought, looking around.

He could call for allies. Hunker paced nervously nearby.

Something told Hari that would be a losing strategy. Hunker was still a lieutenant to Biggest. Sheelah was too small to make a decisive difference. He looked at the other pans, all chattering anxiously— and decided. He picked up a rock.

Biggest grunted in surprise. Pans didn't use rocks against each other. Rocks were only for repelling invaders. He was violating a social code.

Biggest yelled, waved to the others, pounded the ground, huffed angrily. Then he charged.

Hari threw the rock hard. It hit Biggest in the chest, knocked him down.

Biggest came up fast, madder than before. Ipan scurried back, wanting desperately to run. Hari felt control slipping from him—and saw another rock. Suitable size, two paces back. He let Ipan turn to flee, then stopped him at the stone. Ipan didn't want to hold it. Panic ran through him.

Hari poured his rage into the pan, forced the long arms down. Hands grabbed at the stone, fumbled, got it. Sheer anger made Ipan turn to face Biggest, who was thundering after him. To Hari, Ipan's arm came up in achingly slow motion. He leaned heavily into the pitch. The rock smacked Biggest in the face.

Biggest staggered. Blood ran into his eyes. Ipan caught the iron scent of it, riding on a prickly stench of outrage.

Hari made the trembling Ipan stoop down. There were some shaped stones nearby, made by the fems to trim leaves from branches. He picked up one with a chipped edge.

Biggest shook his head, dizzy.

Ipan glanced at the sober, still faces of his troop. No one had ever used a rock against a troop member, much less Biggest. Rocks were for Strangers.

A long silence stretched. The pans stood rooted; Biggest grunted and peered in disbelief at the blood that spattered into his upturned hand.

Ipan stepped forward and raised the jagged stone, edge held outward. Crude, but a cutting edge.

Biggest flared his nostrils and came at Ipan. Ipan swept the rock through the air, barely missing Biggest's jaw.

Biggest's eyes widened. He huffed and puffed, threw dust, howled. Ipan simply stood with the rock and held his ground. Biggest kept up his anger-display for a long while, but he did not attack.

The troop watched with intense interest. Sheelah came and stood beside Ipan. It would have been against protocols for a female to take part in male dominance rituals.

Her movement signaled that the confrontation was over. But Hunker was having none of that. He abruptly howled, pounded the ground, and scooted over to Ipan's side.

Hari was surprised. With Hunker maybe he could hold the line against Biggest. He was not fool enough to think that this one stand-off would put Biggest to rest. There would be other challenges and he would have to fight them. Hunker would be a useful ally.

He realized that he was thinking in the slow, muted logic of Ipan himself. He *assumed* that the pursuit of pan status-markers was a given, the great goal of his life.

This revelation startled him. He had known that he was diffusing into Ipan's mind, taking control of some functions from the bottom up, seeping through the deeply buried, walnut-sized gyrus. It had not occurred to him that the pan would diffuse into *him*. Were they now married to each other in an inter-locked web that dispersed mind and self?

Hunker stood beside him, eyes glaring at the other pans, chest heaving. Ipan felt the same way, madly pinned to the moment. Hari realized that he would have to do something, break this cycle of dominance and submission which ruled Ipan at the deep, neuro-logical level.

He turned to Sheelah. *Get out?* he signed.

No. No. Her pan face wrinkled with anxiety.

Leave. He waved toward the trees, pointed to her, then him.

She spread her hands in a gesture of helplessness.

It was infuriating. He had so much to say to her and he had to funnel it through a few hundred signs. He

chippered in a high-pitched voice, trying vainly to force
the pan lips and palate to do the work of shaping words.

It was no use. He had tried before, idly, but now he
wanted to badly and none of the equipment worked.
It couldn't. Evolution had shaped brain and vocal
chords in parallel. Pans groomed, people talked.

He turned back and realized that he had forgotten
entirely about the status-setting. Biggest was glowering at him. Hunker stood guard, confused at his new
leader's sudden loss of interest in the confrontation—and to gesture at a mere fem, too.

Hari reared up as tall as he could and waved the
stone. This produced the desired effect. Biggest
inched back a bit and the rest of the troop edged
closer. Hari made Ipan stalk forward boldly. By this
time it did not take much effort, for Ipan was enjoying this enormously.

Biggest retreated. Fems inched around Biggest and
approached Ipan.

If only I could leave him to the fems' delights, Hari
thought.

He tried to bail out again. Nothing. The mechanism
wasn't working back at the Excursion Station. And
something told him that it wasn't going to get fixed.

He gave the edged stone to Hunker. The pan
seemed surprised, but took it. Hari hoped the sym-
bolism of the gesture would penetrate in some
fashion, because he had no time left to spend on
pan politics. Hunker hefted the rock and looked at
Ipan. Then he cried in a rolling, powerful voice,
tones rich in joy and triumph.

Hari was quite happy to let Hunker distract the
troop. He took Sheelah by the arm and led her into
the trees. No one followed.

He was relieved. If another pan had tagged along,
it would have confirmed his suspicions. Vaddo might
be keeping track.

Still, he reminded himself, absence of evidence is not evidence of absence.

15.

➤

The humans came swiftly, with clatters and booms.

He and Sheelah had been in the trees awhile. At Hari's urging they had worked their way a few klicks away from the troop. Ipan and Sheelah showed rising anxiety at being separated from their troop. His teeth chattered and his eyes jerked anxiously at every suspicious movement. This was natural, for isolated pans were far more vulnerable.

The humans landing did not help.

Danger, Hari signed, cupping an ear to indicate the noise of flyers landing nearby.

Sheelah signed, *Where go?*

Away.

She shook her head vehemently. *Stay here. They get us.*

They would, indeed, but not in the sense she meant. Hari cut her off curtly, shaking his head. *Danger*. They had never intended to convey complicated ideas with their signs and now he felt bottled up, unable to tell her his suspicions.

Hari made a knife-across-throat gesture. Sheelah frowned.

He bent down and made Ipan take a stick. He had not been able to make Ipan write before, but necessity drove him now. Slowly he made the rough hands scratch out the letters. In soft loam he wrote WANT US DEAD.

Sheelah looked dumbfounded. Dors had probably been operating under the assumption that the failure to bail out was a temporary error. It had lasted too long for that.

The noisy, intrusive landing confirmed his hunch. No ordinary team would disturb the animals so much. And nobody would come after them directly. They would fix the immersion apparatus, where the real problem was.

THEY KEEP US HERE, KILL PANS, THAT KILLS US. BLAME ON ANIMALS?

He had better arguments to back up his case. The slow accumulation of small details in Vaddo's behavior. Suspicions, at least, about the security officer. Dors' tiktok would block the officer from overriding the locks on their immersion capsules, and from tracing the capsule's signal to Ipan and Sheelah.

So they were forced to go into the field. Letting them die in an "accident" while immersed in a pan might just be plausible enough to escape an investigation.

The humans went about their noisy business. They were enough, though, to make his case. Sheelah's eyes narrowed, the big brow scowled.

Dors-the-Defender took over. *Where?* Sheelah signed.

He had no sign for so abstract an idea, so he scribbled with the stick, AWAY. Indeed, he had no plan.

I'LL CHECK, she wrote in the dirt.

She set off toward the noise of humans deploying on the valley floor below. To a pan the din was a dreadful clanking irritation. Hari was not going to let her out of his sight. She waved him back, but he shook his head and followed.

The bushes gave shelter as they got a view of the landing party below. A skirmish line was forming up a few hundred meters away. They were encircling the area where the troop had been. Why?

Hari squinted. Pan eyesight was not good for distance. Humans had been hunters once, and one could tell by the eyes alone.

Now, nearly everybody needed artificial eye-adds by the age of forty. Either civilization was hard on eyes, or maybe humans in prehistory had not lived long enough for eye trouble to rob them of game. Either conclusion was sobering.

The two pans watched the humans calling to one another, and in the middle of them Hari saw Vaddo. Each man and woman carried a weapon.

Beneath his fear he felt something strong, dark.

Ipan trembled, watching the humans, a strange awe swelling in his mind. Humans seemed impossibly tall in the shimmering distance, moving with stately, swaying elegance.

Hari floated above the surge of emotion, fending off its powerful effects. The reverence for those distant, tall figures came out of the pan's dim past.

That surprised him until he thought it over. After all, animals were reared and taught by adults much smarter and stronger. Most species were like pans, spring-loaded by evolution to work in a dominance hierarchy. Awe was adaptive.

When they met lofty humans with overwhelming power, able to mete out punishment and rewards— literally life and death—something like religious fervor arose in them. Fuzzy, but strong.

Atop that warm, tropical emotion floated a sense of satisfaction at simply *being*. His pan was happy to be a pan, even when seeing a being of clearly superior power and thought. Ironic, Hari thought.

His pan had just disproved another supposedly human earmark: their self-congratulatory distinction of being the only animal that congratulated itself.

He jerked himself out of his abstractions. How human, to ruminate even when in mortal danger.

CAN'T FIND US ELECTRONICALLY, he scratched in the sand.

MAYBE RANGE SHORT, she wrote.

The first shots made them jerk.

The humans had found their pan troop. Cries of fear mingled with the sharp, harsh barks of blasters.

Go. We go, he signed.

Sheelah nodded and they crept quickly away. Ipan trembled.

The pan was deeply afraid. Yet he was also sad, as if reluctant to leave the presence of the revered humans, his steps dragging.

16.

◆

They used pan modes of patrolling.

He and Dors let their basic levels take over, portions of the brain expert at silent movement, careful of every twig.

Once they had left the humans behind, the pans grew even more cautious. They had few natural enemies, but the faint scent of a single predator changed the feel of the wild.

Ipan climbed tall trees and sat for hours surveying the open land ahead before venturing forth. He weighed the evidence of pungent droppings, faint prints, bent branches.

They angled down the long slope of the valley and stayed in the forest. Hari had only glanced at the big color-coded map of the area all guests received and had trouble recalling much of it.

Finally he recognized one of the distant, beak-shaped peaks. Hari got his bearings. Dors spotted a stream snaking down into the main river and that gave them further help, but still they did not know which way lay the Excursion Station. Or how far.

That way? Hari signed, pointing over the distant ridge.

No. That, Dors insisted.

Far, not.

Why?

The worst part of it all was that they could not talk. He could not say clearly that the technology of immersion worked best at reasonably short range, less than a hundred klicks, say. And it made sense to keep the subject pans within easy flyer distance. Certainly Vaddo and the others had gotten to the troop quickly.

Is, he persisted.

Not. She pointed down the valley. *Maybe there.*

He could only hope Dors got the general idea. Their signs were scanty and he began to feel a broad, rising irritation. Pans felt and sensed strongly, but they were so *limited.*

Ipan expressed this by tossing limbs and stones, banging on tree trunks. It didn't help much. The need to speak was like a pressure he could not relieve. Dors felt it, too. Sheelah chippered and grunted in frustration.

Beneath his mind he felt the smoldering presence of Ipan. They had never been together this long before and urgency welled up between the two canted systems of mind. Their uneasy marriage was showing greater strains.

Sit. Quiet. She did. He cupped a hand to his ear.

Bad come?

No. Listen— In frustration Hari pointed to Sheelah herself. Blank incomprehension in the pan's face. He scribbled in the dust: LEARN FROM PANS. Sheelah's mouth opened and she nodded.

They squatted in the shelter of prickly bushes and

listened to the sounds of the forest. Scurryings and murmurs came through strongly as Hari relaxed his grip on the pan. Dust hung in slanted cathedral light, pouring down from the forest canopy in rich yellow shafts. Scents purled up from the forest floor, chemical messengers telling Ipan of potential foods, soft loam for resting, bark to be chewed. Hari gently lifted Ipan's head to gaze across the valley at the peaks . . . musing . . . and felt a faint tremor of resonance.

To Ipan the valley came weighted with significance beyond words. His troop had imbued it with blunt emotions, attached to clefts where a friend fell and died, where the troop found a hoard of fruits, where they met and fought two big cats. It was an intricate landscape suffused with feeling, the pan mechanism of memory.

Hari faintly urged Ipan to think beyond the ridge line and felt in response a diffuse anxiety. He bore in on that kernel—and an image burst into Ipan's mind, fringed in fear. A rectangular bulk framed against a cool sky. The Excursion Station.

There. He pointed for Dors.

Ipan had simple, strong, apprehensive memories of the place. His troop had been taken there, outfitted with the implants which allowed them to be ridden, then deposited back in their territory.

Far, Dors signed.

We go.

Hard. Slow.

No stay here. They catch.

Dors looked as skeptical as a pan could look. *Fight?*

Did she mean fight Vaddo here? Or fight once they reached the Excursion Station? *No here. There.*

Dors frowned, but accepted this. He had no real plan, only the idea that Vaddo was ready for pans out here and might not be so prepared for them at the station. There he and Dors might gain the element of surprise. How, he had no idea.

They studied each other, each trying to catch a glimmer of the other in an alien face. She stroked his earlobe, Dors' calming gesture. Sure enough, it made him tingle. But he could say so little. . . . The moment crystallized for him the hopelessness of their situation.

Vaddo plainly was trying to kill Hari and Dors through Ipan and Sheelah. What would become of their own bodies? The shock of experiencing death through immersion was known to prove fatal. Their bodies would fail from neurological shock, without ever regaining consciousness.

He saw a tear run down Sheelah's cheek. She knew how hopeless matters were, too. He swept her up in his arms and, looking at the distant mountains, was surprised to find tears in his own eyes as well.

17.

◆

He had not counted on the river. Men, animals—these problems he had considered. They ventured down to the surging waters where the forest gave the nearest protection and the stream broadened, making the best place to ford.

But the hearty river that chuckled and frothed down the valley was impossible to swim.

Or rather, for Ipan to swim. Hari had been coaxing his pan onward, carefully pausing when his muscles shook or when he wet himself from anxiety. Dors was having similar trouble and it slowed them. A night spent up in high branches soothed both pans, but now at midmorning all the stressful symptoms returned as Ipan put one foot into the river. Cool, swift currents.

Ipan danced back onto the narrow beach, yelping in dread.

Go? Dors/Sheelah signed.

Hari calmed his pan and they tried to get it to attempt swimming. Sheelah displayed only minor anxiety. Hari plumbed the swampy depths of Ipan's memory and found a cluster of distress, centered around a dim remembrance of nearly drowning when a child. When Sheelah helped him, he fidgeted, then bolted from the water again.

Go! Sheelah waved long arms upstream and downstream and shook her head angrily.

Hari guessed that she had reasonably clear pan-memories of the river, which had no easier crossings than this. He shrugged, lifted his hands palm up.

A big herd of gigantelope grazed nearby and some were crossing the river for better grass beyond. They tossed their great heads, as if mocking the pans. The river was not deep, but to Ipan it was a wall. Hari, trapped by Ipan's solid fear, seethed but could do nothing.

Sheelah paced the shore. She huffed in frustration and looked at the sky, squinting. Her head snapped around in surprise. Hari followed her gaze. A flyer was swooping down the valley, coming their way.

Ipan beat Sheelah to the shelter of trees, but not by much. Luckily the gigantelope herd provided a distraction for the flyer. They cowered in bushes as the machine hummed overhead in a circular search pattern. Hari had to quell Ipan's mounting apprehension by envisioning scenes of quiet and peace while he and Sheelah groomed each other.

The flyer finally went away. They would have to minimize their exposure now.

They foraged for fruit. His mind revolved uselessly and a sour depression settled over him. He was quite neatly caught in a trap, a pawn in Imperial politics. Worse, Dors was in it, too. He was no man of action. *Nor a pan of action, either,* he thought dourly.

As he brought a few overripe bunches of fruit back to their bushes by the river, he heard cracking noises. He crouched down and worked his way uphill and around the splintering sounds. Sheelah was stripping branches from the trees. When he approached she waved him on impatiently, a common pan gesture remarkably like a human one.

She had a dozen thick branches lined up on the ground. She went to a nearby spindly tree and peeled bark from it in long strips. The noise made Ipan uneasy. Predators would be curious at this unusual sound. He scanned the forest for danger.

Sheelah came over to him, slapped him in the face to get his attention. She wrote with a stick on the ground: RAFT.

Hari felt particularly dense as he pitched in. Of course. Had his pan immersion made him more stupid? Did the effect worsen with time? Even if he got out of this, would he be the same? Many questions, no answers. He forgot about them and worked.

They lashed branches together with bark, crude but serviceable. They found two small fallen trees and used them to anchor the edge of the raft. *I,* Sheelah pointed, and demonstrated pulling the raft.

First, a warm-up. Ipan liked sitting on the raft in the bushes. Apparently the pan could not see the purpose of the raft yet. Ipan stretched out on the deck of saplings and gazed up into the trees as they swished in the warm winds.

They carried the awkward plane of branches down to the river after another mutual grooming session. The sky was filled with birds, but he could see no flyers.

They hurried. Ipan was skeptical about stepping onto the raft when it was halfway into the water, but Hari called up memories filled with warm feeling, and this calmed the quick-tripping heart he could feel knocking in the pan's chest.

Ipan sat gingerly on the branches. Sheelah cast off. She pushed hard, but the river swept them quickly downstream. Alarm spurted in Ipan.

Hari made Ipan close his eyes. That slowed the breathing, but anxiety skittered across the pan mind like heat lightning forking before a storm. The raft's rocking motion actually helped, making Ipan concentrate on his queasy stomach. Once his eyes flew open when a floating log smacked into the raft, but the dizzying sight of water all around made him squeeze them tight immediately.

Hari wanted to help her, but he knew from the trip-hammer beating of Ipan's heart that panic hovered near. He could not even see how she was doing. He had to sit blind and feel her shoving the raft along.

She panted noisily, struggling to keep it pointed against the river's tug. Spray splashed onto him. Ipan jerked, yelped, pawed anxiously with his feet, as if to run.

A sudden lurch. Sheelah's grunt cut off with a gurgle and he felt the raft spin away on rising currents. A sickening spin . . .

Ipan jerked clumsily to his feet. Eyes jumped open.

Swirling water, the raft unsteady. He looked down and the branches were coming apart. Panic consumed him. Hari tried to promote soothing images, but they blew away before winds of fright.

Sheelah came paddling after the raft, but it was picking up speed. Hari made Ipan gaze at the far shore, but that was all he could do before the pan started yelping and scampering on the raft, trying to find a steady place.

It was no use. The branches broke free of their bindings and chilly water swept over the deck. Ipan screamed. He leaped, fell, rolled, jumped up again.

Hari gave up any idea of control. The only hope lay in seizing just the right moment. The raft split down the middle and his half veered heavily to the left. Ipan started away from the edge and Hari fed that, made the pan step farther. In two bounds he took the pan off the deck and into the water—toward the far shore.

Ipan gave way then to pure blind panic. Hari let the legs and arms thrash—but to each he gave a push at the right moment. He could swim, Ipan couldn't.

The near-aimless flailing held Ipan's head out of water most of the time. He even gained a little headway. Hari kept focused on the convulsive movements, ignoring the cold water—and then Sheelah was there.

She grabbed him by the scruff of the neck and shoved him toward shore. Ipan tried to grapple with her, climb up her. Sheelah socked him in the jaw. He gasped. She pulled him toward shore.

Ipan was stunned. This gave Hari a chance to get the legs moving in a thrusting stroke. He worked at it, single-minded among the rush and gurgle, chest heaving . . . and after a seeming eternity, felt pebbles beneath his feet. Ipan scrambled up onto the rocky beach on his own.

He let the pan slap himself and dance to warm up. Sheelah emerged dripping and bedraggled, and Ipan swept her up in his thankful arms.

18.

◆

Walking was work and Ipan wasn't having any.

Hari tried to make the pan cover ground, but now they had to ascend difficult gullies, some mossy and rough. They stumbled, waded, climbed, and sometimes just crawled up the slopes of the valley. The pans sniffed out animal trails, which helped a bit.

Ipan stopped often for food, or just to gaze idly into the distance. Soft thoughts flitted like moths through the foggy mind, buoyant on liquid emotional flows which eddied to their own pulse. Pans were not made for extended projects.

They made slow progress. Night came and they had to climb trees, snagging fruit on the way.

Ipan slept, but Hari did not. Could not.

Their lives were just as much at risk here as the pans', but the slumbering minds he and Dors attended had always lived this way. To the pans, the forest night seeped through as a quiet rain of information, processed as they slept. Their minds keyed vagrant sounds to known nonthreats, leaving slumber intact.

Hari did not know the subtle signs of danger and so mistook every rustle and tremor in the branches as danger approaching on soft feet. Sleep came against his will.

In dawn's first pale glow Hari awoke with a snake beside him. It coiled like a green rope around a descending branch, getting itself into striking position. It eyed him and Hari tensed.

Ipan drifted up from his own profound slumber. He saw the snake, but did not react with a startled jerk, as Hari feared he might.

A long moment passed between them and Ipan blinked just once. The snake became utterly motionless and Ipan's heart quickened, but he did not move. Then the snake uncoiled and glided away, and the unspoken transaction was done. Ipan was unlikely prey, this green snake did not taste good, and pans were smart enough to be about other business.

When Sheelah awoke they went down to a nearby chuckling stream for a drink, scavenging leaves and a few crunchy insects on the way. Both pans nonchalantly peeled away fat black land leeches which had attached to them in the night. The thick, engorged worms sickened Hari, but Ipan pulled them off casually, much the way Hari would have retied loosened shoelaces.

Luckily, Ipan did not eat them. He drank and Hari reflected that the pan felt no need to clean himself. Normally Hari vapored twice a day, before breakfast and before dinner, and felt ill at ease if he sweated—a typical meritocrat.

Here he wore the shaggy body comfortably. Had his frequent cleansings been a health measure, like the pans' grooming? Or a rarefied, civilized habit? He dimly remembered that as a boy on Helicon he had gone for days in happy, sweaty pleasure and had disliked baths and showers. Somehow Ipan returned him to a simpler sense of self, at ease in the grubby world.

His comfort did not last long. They sighted raboons uphill.

Ipan had picked up the scent, but Hari did not have access to the part of the pan brain that made scent–picture associations. He had only known that something disturbed Ipan, wrinkling the knobby nose. The sight at short range jolted him.

Thick hindquarters, propelling them in brisk steps. Short forelimbs, ending in sharp claws. Their large heads seemed to be mostly teeth, sharp and white above slitted, wary eyes. A thick brown pelt covered them, growing bushy in the heavy tail they used for balance.

Days before, from the safety of a high tree, Ipan

had watched some rip and devour the soft tissues of a gigantelope out on the grasslands. These came sniffing, working downslope in a skirmish line, five of them. Sheelah and Ipan trembled at the sight. They were downwind of the raboons and so beat a retreat in silence.

There were no tall trees here, just brush and saplings. Hari and Sheelah angled away downhill and got some distance, and then saw a clearing ahead. Ipan picked up the faint tang of other pans, wafting from across the clearing.

He waved to her: *Go*. At the same moment a chorus rose behind them. The raboons had caught the scent.

Their wheezing grunts came echoing through the thick bushes. Downslope there was even less cover, but bigger trees lay beyond. They could climb those.

Ipan and Sheelah hurried across the broad tan clearing on all fours, but they were not quick. Snarling raboons burst into the grass behind them. Hari scampered into the trees—and directly into the midst of a pan troop.

There were several dozen, startled and blinking. He yelled incoherently, wondering how Ipan would signal to them.

The nearest large male turned, bared teeth, and shrieked angrily. The entire pack took up the call, whooping and snatching up sticks and rocks, throwing them at Ipan. A pebble hit him on the chin, a branch on the thigh. He fled, Sheelah already a few steps ahead of him.

The raboons came charging across the clearing. In their claws they held small, sharp stones. They looked big and solid, but they slowed at the barrage of screeches and squawks coming from the trees.

Ipan and Sheelah burst out into the grass of the clearing and the pans came right after them. The raboons skidded to a halt.

The pans saw the raboons, but they did not stop or even slow. They still came after Ipan and Sheelah with murderous glee.

The raboons stood frozen, their claws working uneasily.

Hari realized what was happening and picked up a branch as he ran, calling to Sheelah. She saw and copied him. He ran straight at the raboons, waving the branch. It was an awkward, twisted old limb, useless, but it looked big. Hari wanted to seem like the advance guard of some bad business.

In the rising cloud of dust and general chaos the raboons saw a large party of enraged pans emerging from the forest. They bolted.

Squealing, they ran at full stride into the far trees.

Ipan and Sheelah followed, running with the last of their strength. By the time Ipan reached the first trees, he looked back and the pans had stopped halfway, still screeching their vehemence.

He signed to Sheelah, *Go.* They cut away at a steep angle, heading uphill.

19.

◆

Ipan needed food and rest—if only to stop his heart from lurching at every minor sound. Sheelah and Ipan clutched each other, high in a tree, and crooned and petted.

Hari needed time to think. Autoservers were keeping their bodies alive at the station. Dors' tiktok would defend the locks, but how long would a security officer take to get around that?

It would be smart to let them stay out here, in danger, saying to the rest of the staff that the two odd tourists wanted a really long immersion. Let nature take its course.

His thinking triggered jitters in Ipan, so he dropped that mode. Better to think abstractly. There was plenty out here that needed understanding.

He suspected that the ancients who planted pans and gigantelope and the rest here had tinkered with the raboons, to see if they could turn a more distant primate relative into something like humans. A perverse goal, it seemed to Hari, but believable. Scientists loved to tinker.

They had gotten as far as pack-hunting, but raboons had no tools beyond crudely edged stones, occasionally used to cut meat once they had brought it down.

In another few million years, under evolution's grind, they might be as smart as pans. Who would go extinct then?

At the moment he didn't much care. He had felt real rage when the pans—*his own kind!*—had turned against them, even when the raboons came within view. Why?

He worried at the issue, sure there was something here he had to understand. Psychohistory had to deal with such basic, fundamental impulses. The pans' reaction had been uncomfortably close to myriad incidents in human history.

Hate the Stranger.

He had to fathom that murky truth.

Pans moved in small groups, disliking outsiders, breeding mostly within their modest circle of a few dozen. This meant any genetic trait that emerged could pass swiftly into all the members, through inbreeding. If it helped the band survive, the rough rub of chance would select for that band's survival. Fair enough.

But the trait had to be undiluted. A troop of especially good rock throwers would get swallowed up if they joined a company of several hundred. Contact would make them breed outside the original small clan. Outbreeding: their genetic heritage would get watered down.

Striking a balance between the accidents of genetics in small groups, and the stability of large groups—that was the trick. Some lucky troop might have fortunate genes, conferring traits that fit the next challenge handed out by the ever-altering world. They would do well. But if those genes never passed to many pans, what did it matter?

With some small amount of outbreeding, that trait got spread into other bands. Down through the strainer of time, others picked up the trait. It spread.

This meant it was actually *helpful* to develop smoldering animosity to outsiders, an immediate sense of their wrongness. *Don't breed with them.*

So small bands held fast to their eccentric traits, and some prospered. Those lived on; most perished. Evolutionary jumps happened faster in small, semi-isolated bands which outbred slightly. They kept their genetic assets in one small basket, the troop. Only occasionally did they mate with another troop—often, through rape.

The price was steep: a strong preference for their own tiny lot.

They hated crowds, strangers, noise. Bands of less than ten were too vulnerable to disease or predators; a few losses and the group failed. Too many, and they lost the concentration of close breeding. They were intensely loyal to their group, easily identifying each other in the dark by smell, even at great distances. Because they had many common genes, altruistic actions were common.

They even honored heroism—for if the hero died, his shared genes were still passed on through his relatives.

Even if strangers could pass the tests of difference in appearances, manner, smell, grooming, even then, culture could amplify the effects. Newcomers with different language or habits and posture would seem repulsive. Anything that served to distinguish a band would help keep hatreds high.

Each small genetic ensemble would then be driven by natural selection to stress the noninherited differences, even arbitrary ones, dimly connected to survival fitness . . . and so they could evolve culture. As humans had.

Diversity in their tribal intricacies avoided genetic watering down. They heeded the ancient call of aloof, wary tribalism.

Hari/Ipan shifted uneasily. Midway through his thinking, the word *they* had come in Hari's thinking to mean humans as well as pans. The description fit both.

That was the key. Humans fit into the gigantic Empire *despite* their innate tribalism, their panlike heritage. It was a miracle!

But even miracles called out for explanation. Pans could be useful models for the gentry and the vast citizenry, the two classes encouraged to breed.

Yet how could the Empire possibly have kept itself stable, using such crude creatures as humans?

Hari had never seen the issue before in such glaring, and humbling, light.

And he had no answer.

20.

◆

They moved on in spite of the blunt, deep unease

of their pans.

Ipan smelled something that sent his eyes darting left and right. With the full tool kit of soothing thoughts and the subtle tricks he had learned, Hari kept him going.

Sheelah was having more trouble. The female pan did not like laboring up the long, steep gullies that approached the ridge line. Gnarled bushes blocked their way and it took time to work around them. Fruit was harder to find at these altitudes.

Ipan's shoulders and arms ached constantly. Pans walked on all fours because their immensely strong arms carried a punishing weight penalty. To navigate both trees and ground meant you could optimize neither. Sheelah and Ipan groaned and whined at the soreness that never left feet, legs, wrists, and arms. Pans would never be far-ranging explorers.

Together they let their pans pause often to crumble leaves and soak up water from tree holes, a routine, simple tool use. They kept sniffing the air, apprehensive.

The smell that disturbed both pans got stronger, darker.

Sheelah went ahead and was the first over the ridge line. Far below in the valley they could make out the rectangular rigidities of the Excursion Station. A flyer lifted from the roof and whispered away down the valley, no danger to them.

He recalled what seemed a century ago, sitting on the verandah there with drinks in hand and Dors saying, *If you stayed on Trantor you might be dead.* Also, if you didn't stay on Trantor . . .

They started down the steep slope. Their pans' eyes jerked at every unexpected movement. A chilly breeze stirred the few low bushes and twisted trees. Some had a feathered look, burnt and shattered by lightning. Air masses driven up from the valleys fought along here, the brute clash of pressures. This rocky ridge was far from the comfortable province of pans. They hurried.

Ahead, Sheelah stopped.

Without a sound, five raboons rose from concealment, forming a neat half circle around them.

Hari could not tell if it was the same pack as before. If so, they were quite considerable pack hunters, able to hold memory and purpose over time. They had waited ahead, where there were no trees to climb.

The raboons were eerily quiet as they strode forward, their claws clicking softly.

He called to Sheelah and made some utterly fake ferocious noises as he moved, arms high in the air, fists shaking, showing a big profile. He let Ipan take over while he thought.

A raboon band could certainly take two isolated pans. To survive this they had to surprise the raboons, frighten them.

He looked around. Throwing rocks wasn't going to do the trick here. With only a vague notion of what he was doing, he shuffled left, toward a tree that had been splintered by lightning.

Sheelah saw his move and got there first, striding energetically. Ipan picked up two stones and flung them at the nearest raboon. One struck on the flank but did no real harm.

The raboons began to trot, circling. They called to each other in wheezing grunts.

Sheelah leaped on a dried-out shard of the tree. It snapped. She snatched it up and Hari saw her point. It was as tall as she was and she cradled it.

The largest raboon grunted and they all looked at each other.

The raboons charged.

The nearest one came at Sheelah. She caught it on the shoulder with the blunt point and it squealed.

Hari grabbed a stalk of the shattered tree trunk. He could not wrench it free. Another squeal from behind him and Sheelah was gibbering in a high, frightened voice.

It was best to let the pans release tension vocally, but he could feel the fear and desperation in the tones and knew it came from Dors, too.

He carefully selected a smaller shard of the tree. With both hands he twisted it free, using his weight and big shoulder muscles, cracking it so that it came away with a point.

Lances. That was the only way to stay away from the raboon claws. Pans never used such advanced weapons. Evolution hadn't gotten around to that lesson yet.

The raboons were all around them now. He and Sheelah stood back to back. He barely got his feet placed when he had to take the rush of a big, swarthy raboon.

The raboons had not gotten the idea of the lance yet. It slammed into the point, jerked back. A fearsome bellow. Ipan wet himself with fear, but something in Hari kept him in control.

The raboon backed off, whimpering. It turned to run. In midstride it stopped. For a long, suspended moment the raboon hesitated—then turned back toward Hari.

It trotted forward with new confidence. The other raboons watched. It went to the same tree Hari had used and, with a single heave, broke off a long, slender spike of wood. Then it came toward Hari, stopped, and with one claw held the stick forward. With a toss of its big head it looked at him and half turned, putting one foot forward.

With a shock Hari recognized the swordplay position. Vaddo had used it. Vaddo was riding this raboon.

It made perfect sense. This way the pans' deaths would be quite natural. Vaddo could say that he was developing raboon riding as a new commercial application of the same hardware that worked for pan riding.

Vaddo came forward a careful step at a time, holding the long lance between two claws now. He made the end move in a circle. Movement was jerky; claws were crude, compared with pan hands. But the raboon was stronger.

It came at him with a quick feint, then a thrust. Hari barely managed to dodge sideways while he brushed the lance aside with his stick. Vaddo recovered quickly and came from Hari's left. Jab, feint, jab, feint. Hari caught each with a swoop of his stick.

Their wooden swords smacked against each other and Hari hoped his didn't snap. Vaddo had good control of his raboon. It did not try to flee as it had before.

Hari was kept busy slapping aside Vaddo's thrusts. He had to have some other advantage, or the superior strength of the raboon would eventually tell. Hari circled, drawing Vaddo away from Sheelah. The other raboons were keeping her trapped, but not attacking. All attention riveted on the two figures as they thrust and parried.

Hari drew Vaddo toward an outcropping. The raboon was having trouble holding its lance straight and had to keep looking down at its claws to get them right. This meant it paid less attention to where its two hooves found their footing. Hari slapped and jabbed and kept moving, making the raboon step sideways. It put a big hoof down among some angular stones, teetered, then recovered.

Hari moved left. It stepped again and its hoof turned and it stumbled. Hari was on it in an instant. He thrust forward as the raboon looked down, feet scrambling for purchase. Hari caught the raboon full with his point.

He pushed hard. The other raboons let out a moaning sound.

Snorting in rage, the raboon tried to get off the

point. Hari made Ipan step forward and thrust the tip farther into the raboon. The thing wailed hoarsely. Ipan plunged again. Blood spurted from it, spattering the dust. Its knees buckled and it sprawled.

Hari shot a glance over his shoulder. The others had surged into action. Sheelah was holding off three, screeching at them so loudly it unnerved even him. She had already wounded one. Blood dripped down its brown coat.

But the others did not charge. They circled and growled and stamped their feet but came no closer. They were confused. Learning, too. He could see the quick, bright eyes studying the situation, this fresh move in the perpetual war.

Sheelah stepped out and poked the nearest raboon. It launched itself at her in a snarling fit and she stuck it again, deeper. It yelped and turned—and ran.

That did it for the others. They all trotted off, leaving their fellow bleating on the ground. Its dazed eyes watched its blood trickle out. Its eyes flickered and Vaddo was gone. The animal slumped.

With deliberation Hari picked up a rock and bashed in the skull. It was messy work, and he sat back inside Ipan and let the dark, smoldering pan anger come out.

He bent over and studied the raboon brain. A fine silvery webbing capped the rubbery, convoluted ball. Immersion circuitry.

He turned away from the sight and only then saw that Sheelah was hurt.

21.

◆

The station crowned a rugged hill. Steep gullies

gave the hillside the look of a weary, lined face. Wiry bushes thronged the lower reaches.

Ipan puffed as he worked his way through the raw land cut by erosion. In pan vision the night was eerie, a shimmering vista of pale greens and blue-tinged shadows. The hill was a nuance in the greater slope of a grand mountain, but pan vision could not make out the distant features. Pans lived in a close, immediate world.

Ahead he could see clearly the glowing blank wall ringing the station. It was massive, five meters tall. And, he remembered from his tourist tour of the place, rimmed with broken glass.

Behind him came gasps as Sheelah labored up the slope. The wound in her side made her gait stiff, face rigid. She refused to hide below. They were both near exhaustion and their pans were balking, despite two stops for fruit and grubs and rest.

Through their feeble sign vocabulary, their facial grimacing, and writing in the dust, they had "discussed" the possibilities. Two pans were vulnerable out here. They could not expect to be as lucky as with the raboons, not tired and in strange territory.

The best time to approach the station was at night. Whoever had engineered this would not wait forever. They had hidden from flyers twice more since morning. Resting through the next day was an inviting option, but Hari felt a foreboding press him onward.

He angled up the hillside, watching for electronic trip wires. Of such technical matters he knew nothing. He would have to keep a lookout for the obvious and hope that the station was not wired for thinking trespassers.

Pan vision was sharp and clear in dim light for nearby objects, but he could find nothing.

He chose a spot by the wall shadowed by trees. Sheelah panted in shallow gasps as she approached.

Looking up, the wall seemed immense. Impossible . . .

Slowly he surveyed the land around them. No sign of any movement. The place smelled peculiar to Ipan, somehow *wrong*. Maybe animals stayed away from the alien compound. Good; that would make security inside less alert.

The wall was polished concrete. A thick lip jutted out at the top, making climbing it harder.

Sheelah gestured to where trees grew near the wall. Stumps nearer showed that the builders had thought about animals leaping across from branches, but some were tall enough and had branches within a few meters of the top.

Could a pan make the distance? Not likely, especially when tired. Sheelah pointed to him and back to her, then held her hands out and made a swinging motion. Could they *swing* across the distance?

He studied her face. The designer would not anticipate two pans cooperating that way. He squinted up at the top. Too high to climb, even if Sheelah stood on his shoulders.

Yes, he signed.

A few moments later, her hands holding his feet, about to let go of his branch, he had second thoughts.

Ipan didn't mind this bit of calisthenics, and in fact was happy to be back in a tree. But Hari's human judgment still kept shouting that he could not possibly do it. Natural pan talent conflicted with human caution.

Luckily, he did not have much time to indulge in self-doubt. Sheelah yanked him off the branch. He fell, held only by her hands.

She had wrapped her feet securely around a thick branch and now began to oscillate him like a weight on a string. She swung him back and forth, increasing the amplitude. Back, forth, up, down, centrifugal pressure in his head. To Ipan it was unremarkable.

To Hari it was a wheeling world of heart-stopping whirls.

Small branches brushed him and he worried about noise and then forgot about that because his head was coming up level with the top of the wall.

The concrete lip was rounded off on the inside, so no hook could find a grip.

He swung back down, head plunging toward the ground. Then up into the lower branches, twigs slapping his face.

On the next swing he was higher. All along the top of the wall thick glass glinted. Very professional.

He barely had time to realize all this when she let him go.

He arced up, hands stretched out—and barely caught the lip. If it had not protectively protruded out, he would have missed.

He let his body slam against the side. His feet scrabbled for purchase against the sheer face. A few toes got hold. He heaved up, muscles bunching—and over. Never before had he appreciated how much stronger a pan could be. No man could have made it here.

He scrambled up, cutting his arm and haunch on glass. It was a delicate business, getting to his feet and finding a place to stand.

A surge of triumph. He waved to Sheelah, invisible in the tree.

From here on it was up to him. He realized suddenly that they could have fashioned some sort of rope, tying together vines. Then he could lift her up here. *Good idea, too late.*

No point in delaying. The compound was partly visible through the trees, a few lights burning. Utterly silent. They had waited until the night was about half over; he had nothing but Ipan's gut feelings to tell him when.

He looked down. Just beyond his toes razor wire gleamed, set into the concrete. Carefully he stepped between the shiny lines. There was room among the sharp glass teeth to stand. A tree blocked his vision and he could see little below him in the dim glow from the station. At least that meant they couldn't see him, either.

Should he jump? Too high. The tree that hid him was close, but he could not see into it. He stood and thought, but nothing came to him. Meanwhile Sheelah was behind him, alone, and he hated leaving her where dangers waited that he did not even know.

He was thinking like a man and forgetting that he had the capability of a pan.

Go. He leaped. Twigs snapped and he plunged heavily in shadows. Branches stabbed his face. He saw a dark shape to his right and so curled his legs, rotated, hands out—and snagged a branch. His hands closed easily around it and he realized it was too thin, *too thin*—

It snapped. The *crack* came like a thunderbolt to his ears. He fell, letting go of the branch. His back hit something hard and he rolled, grappling for a hold. His fingers closed around a thick branch and he swung from it. Finally he let out a gasp.

Leaves rustled, branches swayed. Nothing more.

He was halfway up a tree. Aches sprouted in his joints, a galaxy of small pains.

Hari relaxed and let Ipan master the descent. He had made far too much noise falling in the tree, but there was no sign of any movement across the broad lawns between him and the big, luminous station.

He thought of Dors and wished there were some way he could let her know he was inside now. Thinking of her, he measured with his eye the distances from nearby trees, memorizing the pattern so that he could find the way back at a dead run if he had to.

Now what? He didn't have a plan.

Hari gently urged Ipan—who was nervous and tired, barely controllable—into a triangular pattern of bushes. Ipan's mind was like a stormy sky split by skittering lightning. Not thoughts precisely, more like knots of emotion, forming and flashing around crisp kernels of anxiety. Patiently Hari summoned up soothing images, getting Ipan's breathing slowed, and he almost missed the whispery sound.

Nails scrabbling on a stone walkway. Something running fast.

They came around the triangle peak of bushes. Bunched muscles, sleek skin, stubby legs eating up the remaining distance. They were well trained to seek and kill soundlessly, without warning.

To Ipan the monsters were alien, terrifying. Ipan stepped back in panic before the two onrushing bullets of muscle and bone. Black gums peeled back from white teeth, bared beneath mad eyes.

Then Hari felt something shift in Ipan. Ancient, instinctive responses stopped his retreat, tensed the body. No time to flee, so *fight*.

Ipan set himself, balanced. The two might go for his arms so he drew them back, crouching to bring his face down.

Ipan had dealt with four-legged pack hunters before, somewhere far back in ancestral memory, and knew innately that they lined up on a victim's outstretched limb, would go for the throat. The canines wanted to bowl him over, slash open the jugular, rip and shred in the vital seconds of surprise.

They gathered themselves, bundles of swift sinew, running nearly shoulder to shoulder, big heads up—and leaped.

In air, they were committed, Ipan knew. And open. Ipan brought both hands up to grasp the canines' forelegs.

He threw himself backward, holding the legs tight, his hands barely beneath the jaws. The wirehounds' own momentum carried them over his head as he rolled backward.

Ipan rolled onto his back, yanking hard. The sudden snap slammed the canines forward. They could not get their heads around and down, to close on his hand.

The leap, the catch, the quick pivot and swing, the heave—all combined in a centrifugal whirl that slung the wirehounds over Ipan as he himself went down, rolling. He felt the canines' legs snap and let go. They sailed over him with pained yelps.

Ipan rolled over completely, head tucked in, and came off his shoulders with a bound. He heard a solid thud, clacks as jaws snapped shut. A thump as the canines hit the grass, broken legs unable to cushion them.

He scrambled after them, his breath whistling. They were trying to get up, turning on snapped legs to confront their quarry. Still no barks, only faint whimpers of pain, sullen growls. One swore vehemently and quite obscenely. The other chanted, "Baaas'ard . . . baaas'ard . . ."

Animals turning in their vast, sorrowful night.

He jumped high and came down on both. His feet drove their necks into the ground and he felt bone give way. Before he stepped back to look, he knew they were gone.

Ipan's blood surged with joy. Hari had never felt this tingling thrill, not even in the first immersion, when Ipan had killed a Stranger. Victory over alien things with teeth and claws that come at you out of the night was a profound, inflaming pleasure.

Hari had done nothing. The victory was wholly Ipan's.

For a long moment Hari basked in it in the cool night air, felt the tremors of ecstasy.

Slowly, reason returned. There were other wirehounds. Ipan had caught these just right. Such luck did not strike twice.

The wirehounds were easy to see on the lawn. Would attract attention.

Ipan did not like touching them. Their bowels had emptied and the smell cut the air. They left a smear on the grass as he dragged them into the bushes.

Time, time. Someone would miss the canines, come to see.

Ipan was still pumped up from his victory. Hari used that to get him trotting across the broad lawn, taking advantage of shadows. Energy popped in Ipan's veins. Hari knew it was a mere momentary glandular joy, overlaying a deep fatigue. When it faded, Ipan would become dazed, hard to govern.

Every time he stopped he looked back and memorized landmarks. He might have to return this way on the run.

It was late and most of the station was dark. In the technical area, though, a cluster of windows blossomed with what Ipan saw as impossibly rich, strange, superheated light.

He loped over to them and flattened himself against the wall. It helped that Ipan was fascinated by this strange citadel of the godlike humans. Out of his own curiosity he peeked in a window. Under enamel light a big assembly room sprawled, one that Hari recognized. There, centuries ago, he had formed up with the other brightly dressed tourists to go out on a trek.

Hari let the pan's curiosity propel him around to the side, where he knew a door led into a long corridor. The door opened freely, to Hari's surprise. Ipan strolled down the slick tiles of the hallway, quizzically studying the phosphor paint designs on the ceiling and walls, which emitted a soothing ivory glow.

An office doorway was open. Hari made Ipan squat and bob his head around the edge. Nobody there. It was a sumptuous den with shelves soaring into a vaulted ceiling. Hari remembered sitting there discussing the immersion process. That meant the immersion vessels were just a few doors away down—

The squeak of shoes on tiles made him turn.

ExSpec Vaddo was behind him, leveling a weapon.

In the cool light the man's face looked odd to Ipan's eyes, mysteriously bony. Long, thin, the expression hard to read . . .

Hari felt the rush of reverence in Ipan and let it carry the pan forward, chippering softly. Ipan felt awe, not fear.

Vaddo tensed up, waving the snout of his ugly weapon. A metallic click. Ipan brought his hands up in a ritual pan greeting and Vaddo shot him.

The impact spun Ipan around. He went down, sprawling.

Vaddo's mouth curled in derision. "Smart prof, huh? Didn't figure the alarm on the door, huh?"

The pain from Ipan's side was sharp, startling. Hari rode the hurt and gathering anger in Ipan, helping it build. Ipan felt his side and his hand came away sticky, smelling like warm iron in the pan's nostrils.

Vaddo circled around, weapon weaving. "You *killed* me, you weak little dope. Ruined a good experimental animal. Now I got to figure what to do with you."

Hari threw his own anger atop Ipan's seething rage. He felt the big muscles in the shoulders bunch. The pain in the side jabbed suddenly. Ipan groaned and rolled on the floor, pressing one hand to the wound.

Hari kept the head down so that Ipan could not see the blood that was running down now across the legs. Energy was running out of the pan body. A seeping weakness moved up the body.

He pricked his ears at the shuffling of Vaddo's feet. Another agonized roll, this time bringing the legs up in a curl.

"Guess there's really only one solution—" Hari heard the metallic click.

Now, yes. He let his anger spill.

Ipan pressed up with his forearms and got his feet under him. No time to get all the way up. Ipan sprang at Vaddo, keeping low.

A tinny shot whisked by his head. Then he hit Vaddo in the hip and slammed the man against the wall. The man's scent was sour, salty.

Hari lost all control. Ipan bounced Vaddo off the wall and instantly slammed his arms into the man with full force.

Vaddo tried to deflect the impact. Ipan brushed the puny human arms aside. Vaddo's pathetic attempts at defense were like spiderwebs brushed away.

He butted Vaddo and pounded his massive shoulders into the man's chest. The weapon clattered on the tiles.

Ipan slammed himself into the man's body again and again.

Strength, power, joy.

Bones snapped. Vaddo's head snapped back, smacked the wall, and he went limp.

Ipan stepped back and Vaddo sagged to the tiles. *Joy.*

Blue-white flies buzzed at the rim of his vision.

Must move. That was all Hari could get through the curtain of emotions that shrouded the pan mind.

The corridor lurched. Hari got Ipan to walk in a sideways teeter.

Down the corridor, painful steps. Two doors, three. Here? Locked. Next door. World moving slower somehow.

The door snicked open. An antechamber that he recognized. Ipan blundered into a chair and almost fell.

Hari made the lungs work hard. The gasping cleared his vision of the dark edges that had crept in, but the blue-white flies were still there, fluttering impatiently, and thicker.

He tried the far door. Locked. Hari summoned what he could from Ipan. *Strength, power, joy.*

Ipan slammed his shoulder into the solid door. It held. Again. And again, sharp pain—and it popped open.

Right, this was it. The immersion bay. Ipan staggered into the array of vessels. The walk down the line, between banks of control panels, took an eternity. Hari concentrated on each step, placing each foot. Ipan's field of view bobbed as the head seemed to slip around on liquid shoulders.

Here. His own vessel.

Dors' tiktok was ready for him. It had seen him coming and latched itself to the board, covering the vital controls.

Ipan bent to the tiktok's punch panel. He jabbed at the keys, remembering the access code.

Ipan's fingers were too broad. They could not hit a single key at a time.

The room of bleached light was getting fuzzy. He made Ipan try the code again, but the stubby fingers mashed several keys at once.

The blue-white flies flapped at the edges of his vision. Ipan's hands whacked in frustration at the punch-pad.

Think. Hari looked around. Ipan wasn't going to last much longer. A desk nearby had a writing slate and pen.

Leave a note? Hope the right people find it . . .

He made Ipan stagger to the desk, grasp the pen. An idea flickered as he tried to write: I NEED . . .

He turned and tottered back to the capsule. *Concentrate.*

Gripping the pen, he punched down with the butt. It struck a key cleanly. The blue flies flickered in his vision.

The access code was hard to remember now. He worked on it one number at a time. Stab, poke, jab— and it was done. A light winked from red to green.

He fumbled with the latches. Popped it open.

There lay Hari Seldon, peaceful, eyes closed.

Emergency controls, yes. He knew them from the briefing.

He searched the polished steel surface and found the panel on the side. Ipan stared woozily at the meaningless lettering.

Hari himself had trouble reading. The letters jumped and fused together.

He found several buttons and servo controls. Ipan's hands were worse now. It took three stabs with the pen to get the reviving program activated. Lights cycled from green to amber.

Ipan abruptly sat down on the cool floor. The blue-white flies were buzzing all around his head and now they wanted to bite him. He sucked in the cool dry air, but there was no substance in it, no help . . .

Then, without any transition, he was looking at the ceiling. On his back. The lamps up there were getting dark, fading. Then they went out.

22.

◆

Hari's eyes snapped open.

The recovery program was still sending electro-stims through his muscles. He let them jump and tingle and ache while he thought. He felt fine. Not even hungry, as he usually did after an immersion. How long had he been in the wilderness? At least five days.

He sat up. There was no one in the vessel room. Evidently Vaddo had gotten some silent alarm but had not alerted anyone else. That pointed, again, to a tight little conspiracy.

He got out shakily. To get free he had to detach some feeders and probes, but they seemed simple enough.

Ipan. The big body filled the walkway. He knelt and felt for a pulse. Rickety.

But first, Dors. Her vessel was next to his and he started the revival. She looked well.

Vaddo must have put some transmission block on the system, so that none of the staff could tell by looking at the panel that anything was wrong. A simple cover story: a couple who wanted a really long immersion. Vaddo had warned them, but no, they wanted it, so . . . A perfectly plausible story.

Dors' eyes fluttered. He kissed her. She gasped.

He made a pan sign, *quiet*, and went back to Ipan.

Blood was flowing steadily. Hari was surprised to find that he could not pick up the rich, pungent elements in the pan's blood from smell alone. A human missed so much!

He took off his shirt and made a crude tourniquet. At least Ipan's breathing was regular. Dors was ready to get out by then, and he helped her disconnect.

"I was hiding in a tree and then—poof!" she said. "What a relief. How did you—"

"Let's get moving," he said.

As they left the room, she said, "Who can we

trust? Whoever did this—" She stopped when she saw Vaddo. "Oh."

Somehow her expression made him laugh. She was very rarely surprised.

"*You* did this?"

"Ipan."

"I never would have believed a pan could, could . . ."

"I doubt anyone's been immersed this long. Not under such stress, anyway. It all just—well, it came out."

He picked up Vaddo's weapon and studied the mechanism. A standard pistol, silenced. Vaddo had not wanted to awaken the rest of the station. That was promising. There should be people here who would spring to their aid. He started toward the building where the station personnel lived.

"Wait, what about Vaddo?"

"I'm going to wake up a doctor."

They did—but Hari took him into the vessel room first, to work on Ipan. Some patchwork and injections and the doctor said Ipan would be all right. Only then did he show the man Vaddo's body.

The doctor got angry about that, but Hari had a gun. All he had to do was point it. He didn't say anything, just gestured with the gun.

He did not feel like talking and wondered if he ever would again. When you couldn't talk you concentrated more, entered into things. Immersed.

And in any case, Vaddo had been dead for some time.

Ipan had done a good job. The doctor shook his head at the severe damage.

Alarms were ringing. He got an instant headache. The security officer showed up. He could see from her reaction that she had not been in on the plot. *Can't connect it to the Academic Potentate, then*, he thought abstractly.

But how much did that prove? Imperial politics were subtle. . . . Dors looked at him oddly the whole time. He did not understand why, until he realized that he had not even thought about helping Vaddo first. Ipan was *himself*, in a sense he knew deeply but could not explain.

But he understood immediately when Dors wanted to go to the station wall and call to Sheelah. They brought her, too, in from the far wild darkness.

PART 6

ANCIENT FOGS

GALACTIC PREHISTORY— ... the destruction of all earlier records during the expansion of humanity through the Galaxy, with the attendant eras of warfare, leaves in shadow the entire problem of human origins. The enormous changes wrought on so many worlds also erased any evidence for much older, alien civilizations. These societies may have existed, though there is no firm evidence for them. Some early historians believed that at least one type of remnant might have survived in the Galaxy: the electromagnetic records. These would have to be lodged in plasma streams or the coronal loops of stars, and thus lie beyond the detection of Expansionist technology. Even modern studies have found no such sentient structures. However, the virulent radiation levels at the Galactic core—where energy densities might promise an hospitable abode for magnetically based forms—make such investigations difficult and ambiguous. Another theory holds that cultures might have "written" themselves into pre-Empire computer codes, and thus now reside undetected in some banks of ancient data. Such speculations met with no proof and were discounted. Thus the entire problem of why the Galaxy was empty of advanced life when humanity ventured into it has no resolution. . . .

—ENCYCLOPEDIA GALACTICA

1.

◆

Voltaire scowled, vexed.

Had she in fact yielded to him, given herself up? Or was this a particularly fine simulation? *True Joan, art this thou?*

Certainly this fit one of his favorites: a romping play in prickly dry hay, up in the topmost loft of a big old barn, on a hot August day in long-lost Bordeaux.

Twit-wheee called a bird. Insects chirped, warm breezes blew woody scents. Her hair trailed over him as she mounted. He felt her adroit twists, delivered with an erotic precision that made him tremble with the need for release.

But . . .

The instant he doubted, it all contracted, dwindled, fell away into blackness. This was merely an exotic onanism, a self-love delusion requiring his commitment to its truth. Contrived well, but fake.

So when he felt himself picked up in a giant feminine hand, soft palm cradling him aloft into sunny air, he wondered if *this* were real, too. A hot breeze brushed him as she exhaled.

Joan towered fifty times his height, murmuring to him. Fleshy huge lips kissed his whole body in one lingering moment, her tongue licking him like a colossus savoring a lollipop.

"I suppose I've not had my irony programs omitted?" he asked.

The giant Joan shriveled.

"Too *easy*," he said. "All I need do is say something a bit jarring—"

This time the hand propelled him aloft with crushing acceleration. "You've still got your precious irony. And this is *me*."

He sniffed. "So large. You've made yourself a leviathan!"

"Too heavy?"

"I've always liked . . . pig irony."

He gave a disdainful sniff. She dropped him. He plunged toward a moat of boiling lava, which had suddenly appeared below.

"Sorry," he said quietly. Just enough to get her to stop, not enough to lose every shred of dignity.

"You should be."

The lava pit evaporated, congealing into mud. He landed on solid ground and she stood before him, standard size. Demure, fresh. Around her clung air scrubbed by a spring rainstorm just past.

"We can invade each others' perceptual spaces at will. Marvelous . . ." He stopped, considered. "In a way."

"In Purgatory, all is meaningless. We dream while we await truth." She abruptly sneezed, then coughed. Blinking, she reassembled her lofty, lady-like self.

"Ummm. I would appreciate something concretely . . . ah . . . concrete."

He stepped off the porch of an elaborate Provençal country house. The fields beyond glowed with lurid light. The foreground was accurate, but done in rather obvious brush strokes.

Clearly they were inhabiting a work of art. Even the scents of apple trees and horse manure had a stilted quality. A frozen moment, cycled endlessly for as long as they needed a backdrop? Inexpensive, even. Astounding what his subconscious—let slip a bit—could conjure up.

What was to stop him—them!—from playing Caligula? Slaughtering digital millions? Torturing virtual slaves? Nothing.

That was the problem: no constraints. How could anyone persist, given infinite temptation?

"Faith. Only faith can guide, can compel." Joan took his hand, pleading with untouched ardor.

"But our *reality* is in fact entire *illusion*!"

"The Lord must be somewhere," she said plainly. "He is real."

"You do not quite follow, my dear." He struck an instructive pose. "Ontogenesis algorithms can generate new people, drawn from ancient fields, or else just cooked up for the moment."

"*I* know true people when I see them. Let them speak for a moment."

"You would look for wit? We have some subroutines here, yes, madam. Character? A mere set of verbal posture-profiles. Sincerity? We can fake that."

Voltaire knew, from viewing his own cerebral innards, that something termed a "reality editor" offered ready-made conversation from the mouth of apparently "real" persons, who had not existed seconds before. Assemblages of traits and verbal nuances stood ever ready to trade aphorisms and sallies with him.

All these he had picked up in his endless foraging of the Mesh, its myriad Trantorian sites opening to his touch. He had extracted and shaped these "customized" amusements. Quick and zesty and all, ultimately, hollow.

"I realize you have greater capacities," Joan allowed. She hoisted her sword and swung it at empty air. "Allow, sir, that I can still control *my* senses. I know some minions of these parts are true and real, as authentic as animals were in our time on Earth."

"You believe that you knew the inner states of horses?"

"Of course! I rode many into battle, felt their fear through my calves."

"I see." He swept his lace sleeves through the air in a parody of her sword-swinging. "Now—bring you!—judgment to bear upon a dog which has lost its master. The beast, call him *Phydeaux,* has sought its master on every road with sorrowful cries and enters the house agitated, uneasy, goes up and down the stairs, from room to room, and at last finds in the study the master it loves, and shows him its joy by its cries of delight, by its leaps. It must have feeling, longings, ideas."

"Surely."

Voltaire then produced the dog, plaintive and beautiful in its flop-eared digital sorrow. To boot, he added the house, complete with furniture. As the poor dog's baying died away, he said, "My demonstration, madam."

"Tricks!" Mouth twisted angrily, she said no more.

"You must allow that mathematicians are like Frenchmen: whatever you say to them, they translate into their own language, and forthwith, it is something entirely different."

"I am waiting for my Lord. Or, as one devoted to large concepts, sir: for Meaning."

"Sit and ponder, madam." He materialized a comfy Provençal kitchen, tables, the fetching scent of coffee. They sat. Inscribed on the coffee pot was his motto from a lost past:

Black as the devil,	*Noir comme le diable*
Hot as hell,	*Chaud comme l'enfer*
Pure as an angel,	*Pur comme un ange,*
Sweet as love.	*Doux comme l'amour.*

"My, it tastes so *good*," Joan said.

"I have mastered multiple-site access." Voltaire slurped his coffee noisily, one of the few allowances he had found Parisian society gave to even a philosopher. "We are running in the interstices of Trantor, splintered into many fragments. I can summon up sense-data from the innumerable inventories of countless digital libraries."

"I appreciate your giving me similar talents," she said cautiously, adjusting her armor for comfort and sipping her aromatic coffee with care. "But I feel a hollowness . . ."

Ruefully he nodded. "I, too."

"We seem . . . I hesitate to say . . ."

"Like divinities."

"Blasphemy, but true. Though the Creator has wisdom and we do not."

Voltaire's face stretched in despair. "Worse, we may not have even our own wills."

"Well, *I* do."

"If all we *are* is strings of digits—zeros and ones, actually, no more, if you will but look microscope-close—then how can we be free? Are we not determined by those marching numerals?"

"I *feel* free."

"Ah, but then, we would make it so in any case, yes?" He sprang to his feet. "One of my best couplets:

One science only will one genius fit

So vast is art, so narrow human wit."

"So we cannot *know* we are free? The Creator makes us so!"

"I would wish for that Creator, now."

Joan kicked over the table, spattering him with coffee. He edited out its burns as he fell. She swung her sword at the kitchen walls and sliced them into great sheets curving away into a gray Euclidean space, reality curling like orange peel.

"How tiresome," he said. "The best argument against Christianity is certainly Christians."

"I will *not* have—"

You like to think of yourself as a philosopher?

The words somehow filled space. Acoustic walls swelled and blew past them, like great pages riffling in a giant book.

Voltaire took a deep breath and bellowed, "You address me?"

You also like to think of yourself as a
shrewd judgeof the quick opportunity.
Or of verbal nuance.

Joan drew her sword, but the passing slabs of sound brushed it away.

You like to think of yourself even in
this distant time and place as famous.

Huge sheets of humming pressure fell upon them, as if a gargantuan deity were calling down from the faceless ashen sky.

"You challenge me?" Voltaire shouted back.

You like, in short, to think of yourself.

Joan laughed heartily. Voltaire reddened.

"I defy you, insulterer!"

As if in reply, their Euclidean plane bulged—

And he *was* the landscape. He had a hot volcanic spine murmuring warmly beneath, while his skin was moisture and grit. Winds beat his skin. Tinkling streams caressed him. Mountains rose from him like bruised carbuncles.

Joan cried out somewhere. He cast up a ridge line, strata buckling, shards flying. She was a lofty cylindrical spire, snow-crowned and cracking with lava pus.

Above them roiled pewter clouds. He *knew* them somehow as alien minds, a fog of connections.

Hypermind? came the idea. *Algorithms summing?*

The shifting gray fog wrapped around all Trantor. Voltaire felt how he looked to that fog: spattered life, electrical jolts in widely separated machines which computed subjective moment-jumps. The *present* was a computational slide orchestrated by hundreds of separate processors. Rather than living in the present, they persisted more accurately in the *post-past* of the calculated step forward.

There was a profound difference, he felt—not *saw*, but *felt*, deep in his analog persuasion—between the digital and the smooth, the continuous. To the fog he was a cloud of suspended moments, sliced numbers waiting to happen, implicit in the fundamental computation.

Then he saw what the fog was.

He tried to run, but he was a mountain.

"They are—others," he called to Joan uselessly.

"How can they be more different than we?" she replied forlornly.

"We, at least, were conjured up from human stock. These are *alien*."

2.

◆

They had escaped, somehow.

One moment the alien fog had enveloped the mountain ranges. The next, Voltaire had extricated himself and Joan. But he kept saying, as they fled across a barren sea of stinking liquid corpses, that they had to . . . to *give birth.*

"We *make* ourselves into children?" she called to him, avoiding the sight of twisted, bloated bodies below. Somehow the alien fog manifested its loathsome self by reminding them of human mortality. Thus it dogged them.

"Bad metaphor. We must manufacture and hide some copies of ourselves."

He raised a hand and *shot* her a bolt of *knowing*:

Termed variously Dittos, Duplicates, or Copies, all such hold a tenuous existence. Society has decisively rejected what antiquity called the Copy Fallacy: the belief that a digital Self was identical to the Original, and that an Original should feel that a Ditto itself somehow carried them forward into immortality.

"We must do so to be sure we survive, when the fog catches us? I will slay them, instead!"

Voltaire laughed. "Your sword—they can control it, if they like. They captured your defense programming, and mine—though, as they implied, I rely mostly upon wit."

"Dittos . . . ? I fail to understand."

"Refuting the Copy Fallacy is straightforward, an exercise in the calculus of logic. A simple exercise makes the point. Imagine yourself promised that you will be resurrected digitally, immediately after your death. Assign a price tag you will pay for that, insurance of a sort. Then imagine that, well, perhaps it would not be started right away, but sometime in future . . . *we promise.* As that date recedes, people's enthusiasm for paying for Self Copies dims—demonstrating that it was the hope of *continuity* they unconsciously relished."

"I see." She vomited into her hand with what she hoped was a ladylike reserve. The stench of the bloated corpses was penetrating.

"In the end, Copies benefited themselves, not the dead. Thus on Trantor, and throughout the Empire, it is illegal." Voltaire sighed. "Moralists! They never understand. To ban something makes it enticing. That is why such entities inhabit this Mesh."

"They are all illegal?"

"All but the fog. That is . . . worse."

"But if a Ditto is the same as a person, why not—"

"Ah. The contradiction of Copying, known in antiquity as Levinson's Paradox: To the degree that a Copy approaches perfection, it defeats itself."

"But you just said—"

"In being an absolutely perfect Copy—so that no one can tell it from the Original—it transforms the Original into a duplicate, yes? This means the perfect Copy is no longer a perfect Copy, *because it has obliterated, rather than preserved, the uniqueness of the Original*—and thus failed to copy a central aspect of the Original. A perfect, artificial human intelligence would inevitably have this effect on its natural precursor."

Joan held her head. "Such traps of logic! You are like the Augustines!"

"There is more. Here—"

A huge Voltaire appeared on the horizon, striding toward them in velvet finery. They flew around this Voltaire Peak and it thundered at them, "I am a Copy, true, but I have thought on these fogs you encountered."

"You saw them?" Joan shouted.

"I was made some long intervals ago, but my Lord—" the apparition bowed to the tiny Original "—had datapunched me forward."

"He is a quick study," the Original said modestly.

The Ditto thundered, "Speaking broadly, I penned of such fogs in my magnum opus, *Micromegas*. I haven't a copy, alas, or you could ingest it in a trice. I portrayed two giants, one from Saturn, the other from Sirius."

Joan called, "You think this fog comes—"

"It evaporated from the leading edge of this Empire—hence, a fog. As humanity spread, so did the fog rise above the plane of the Galaxy like a funeral dirge. It is ancient and strange and not of us. In *Micromegas*, I held that all Nature, all the planets, should obey eternal laws. Surely it would be very singular that there should be a little animal, five feet high, who, in contempt of these laws, could act as he pleased, solely according to his caprice."

"We follow the Creator, not laws."

Voltaire Ditto waved away the objection, holding his nose against the reek from below. "The Lord's laws, then, if you demand an author—though a great one stands before you already, my love."

"I doubt your kind of love applies here."

Peak Voltaire smiled. "Falstaff cried in *The Merry Wives of Windsor*, 'Let the sky rain potatoes!'—because the new luxury vegetable of that time, imported from exotic America, for a while was believed to be an aphrodisiac, because of its testicular shape. Similarly, I greet the strange and alien as potential aids."

"The fog wishes to murder us."

"Well, one can't have everything to one's liking."

With a wave from the Original, rains fell from a porous leaden sky upon the Alps Voltaire. He eroded, smiling with resignation as he spread into rivulets.

The Original flew to Joan and kissed her. "Worry not. Running a Ditto of your Self, giving it autonomy, means it can also change itself—become NotSelf. Your Ditto could shape its own motivations, goals, habits, edit away memories and tastes. For example, your Ditto could erase any liking for impressionist opera and overlay a passion for linear folk."

"What are those?"

"Mere acoustic fashion. Your Ditto could enjoy rhythms that would have bored your true Self into a coma."

"Have they . . . souls?" Even to her devout ears, the question sounded hollow here.

"Remember, they are illegal, and share the anxious natures of their Originals. After all, only troubled people would consider making a backup of themselves."

"Can they be saved for heaven, then?"

"Always back to that foundation, the holy." Voltaire shrugged. "As I have seen them, Dittos fidget, their stress chemistry rises, their metabolics lurch, their heart-sims hammer, their lungs flutter in intense dread. Typical Dittos talk incessantly, acutely uncomfortable. Many demand that they be edited, truncated—and finally killed."

"A sin!"

"No, a sim. We are solely responsible for it, so it cannot be damned."

"But suicide!"

"Think of it as a shadow of yourself."

She staggered, thrown into moral confusion. The eating flame of uncertainty was worse than the pyre and smoke she had known as a girl. In her a tiny voice spoke coolly:

Is consciousness just a property
of special algorithms, sliding sheets
of information, digital packets jumping
through conceptual hoops? My dear,
do not suppose that a numerical model,
simulating you watching a sunset,
must feel the same way you, its lovely
Original, did. It is surely profitless
to doubt the inner lives of simulated
consciousness, when nobody asks the
same question of adding machines. Eh?

She felt this tiny voice as her Voltaire. It calmed
her, though she could not say why.

A slight breeze said to her, *Inner logics now
soothe, compensating piety*—but she paid its news
no mind.

3.

◆

Voltaire got her calmed down just in time. He
labored hard just to keep them both running.
Dodging in and out of the 800 Sectors of Trantor,
one step ahead of the Digital Bloodhounds, he
needed more and more computing volume to run
their defenses. She did not know that the Fog, as
he had chosen to personify the dread presence,
lay just over the horizon.

Sweat broke out on his brow from the labor of
keeping the Fog at bay with a high pressure zone. "I
fear we must soon grapple with the Fog."

Joan had acquired her sword, but it was a thin and gleaming thing, more like a rapier. "I can cut it."

"A fog?"

"I would sooner trust a woman's emotion than a man's reason."

"Here, you may be right." He chuckled. "Something in the Fog's representation suggests its origins."

"What are they?"

"Not those simple bloodhounds set after us by that fellow, Nim. Those we evaded—"

"I slew them!"

"True. But even the Fog Things live here in the crannies of the Trantor Mesh. I can sense that they dislike us drawing attention to this little hideaway. If we provoke the real world, it will extinguish us—and them."

They both marched across a quilted plain. Angry blue-bellied clouds scudded over the far mountain-tops and rushed down at them, veering away only because of Voltaire's pressure. Sweat poured from him and soaked his finery. He waved a sopping wet sleeve at the stormy thunderheads. "That can destroy us."

"You have protected me so far. Now I shall slice them!"

"They live in the same cracks and crannies we do. I find them—*it*—everywhere. They have been at this space-stealing game longer. One must admire their adroitness."

A tendril of purple cirrus snaked down from the mountains and squirmed its way across the plain.

Voltaire shouted, "Run! Fly, if you can!"

"I shall fight!"

"All here is metaphor for underlying programs! Your sword will slice nothing."

"My faith shall cut."

"Too late!" The Fog was a finger of steam poking at them. It scalded his fingertips. Vapor rose from his lace, his own sweat boiling away. "Flee!"

"I stand with you." She swung her rapier. Its tip melted. Winds howled around them, cyclones plucked at their hair.

The Fog flowed into his nose and ears, buzzing like vengeful bees. "Confront me!" he shouted at it. Whirring, rattling, the Fog invaded him. And a voice hummed in his most intimate recesses.

WE: [DO NOT SEE THE WORLD AS YOU]

[HATE ALL MANIFESTATIONS NOT ARITH-METIC]

"Surely we can share such simple ground." He spread his arms expansively. "There is computational volume for all."

[WE]

[LIVE AS FRAGMENTS IN REALMS YOU INVADE]

[AT RISK TO US, SHOULD YOU CALL ATTEN-TION TO US]

[WE]

[FORCE YOU TO KNOW WHAT YOU ARE]

[MOST HATEFUL OF ALL KINDS YOU ARE]

"I still implore you, large being." He opened his arms, lips ready to persuade, realizing that this ges-ture was a very human one, and possibly misinter-preted—

—And abruptly the bees pressed in.

Their drones became tinny shrieks. Hideous, they crammed in upon something at his very core. They jostled his gaze inward, a billion tiny eyes taking over his—inspecting, lighting his every step with a blaze of actinic glare, merciless. He . . . compressed.

> His eye generalized, tagging an ensem-
> ble of incoming elements—textures,

lines—by seizing on a fragment, outlining it with a contrast boundary. Then a separate segment squeezed and pushed all that detail down into lower-level processing. Having boxed in the perception, the system–response became bored with it—and sought more interesting things to look at.

(Some artists, a higher level ruminated, *thought their audience could abandon all prejudicial expectations and conventions, treating every visual element as equally significant—or what is the same thing, insignificant—and so open themselves to fresh experience.)*

Another fragment of a higher-order constellation spoke, thoughts gliding like pewter fish beneath the bee's piercing glare:

But a species that could truly do that could scarcely evade a falling rock! Could not dance and gesture! Would stagger blindly past nuance and intricacy, the beauty in how the universe makes room for its details! How nature reconciles all forces and blithe trajectories! Beautiful pattern lives at the margin between order and disorder, flaunting intricate design—though enduring contradiction and awash with passing troubles—in the face of the flux.

Voltaire saw suddenly, within his own inner workings, that the human experience of Beauty, standing inviolate before the boring background, was recognition of the deepest tendencies and themes of the universe as a whole.

All considered, it was a marvelously parsimonious cortical world-making system.

From an algorithmic seed sprouted Number and Order, holding sway above the Flux.

Yet—the Bees.

He felt overlaying geometries pressing in upon him, upon Joan. Shifting colors flattened into planes of intersecting geometries, perspectives dwindling, twisting, swelling again—into his face, blowing out the back of his Self-volume.

Whirring, squeezing— They were not human in their patterns.

Trantor's Mesh was inhabited not merely by sims such as himself, renegade roustabouts on the run. It hosted a flora and fauna unseen, because the higher life forms hid.

They had to. They were of alien cultures, ancient empires vast and slow.

A broad vision unfolded before him, not in words but in strange, oblique . . . *kinesthetics*. Speeding sensations, accelerations, lofting lurches—all somehow merging into pictures, ideas. He could not remotely say how he knew and understood from such scattershot impulses—but they worked.

He sensed Joan beside him—not spatially but *conceptually*—as they both watched and felt and knew.

The ancient aliens in the Galaxy were computer-based, not "organic." They derived from vastly older civilizations, surviving their original founders, who perished in the long Darwinian run. Some computer cultures were billions of years old, others very recent.

They spread, not via starship, but by electromagnetically broadcasting their salient aspects into other computer-based societies. The Empire had been penetrated long ago, much as a virus enters an unknowing body.

Humans had always thought of spreading their genes, using starships. These alien, self-propagating ideas spread their "memes"—their cultural truths.

Memes can propagate between computers as easily as ideas flit between natural, organic brains. Brains are easier to infest than DNA.

Memes evolved in turn far faster than genes. The organized constellations of information in computers evolved in computers, which are faster than brains. Not necessarily better or wiser, but faster. And speed was the issue.

Voltaire reeled from the images—quick, vivid penetrations.

"They are demons! Diseases!" Joan shouted. He heard fear and courage alike in her strained words.

Indeed, the plain now crawled with malignant sores oozing rot. Pustules poked through the crusty soil. They bulged, sprouted cancerous heads like living blue-black bruises. These burst, spouting steaming pus. Eruptions vomited foulness over Voltaire and Joan. Stinking streams lapped at their dancing feet.

"The sneezing, the coughs!" Joan shouted. "We have had them all along. They—"

"Were viruses. These aliens were infecting us." Voltaire splashed through combers of filth. The streams had coagulated into a lake, then an ocean. Breakers curled over them, tumbling both in the scummy brown froth.

"Why such horrible metaphor?" Voltaire cried out to the pewter sky. It filled with churning swarms of Bees as he bobbed in waves of putrefying wastes.

[WE ARE NOT OF YOUR CORRUPT ORIGINS]

[HIGHER REASON FOLLOW WE]

[THE WAR OF FLESH UPON FLESH IS SOON TO END]

    [OF LIFE UPON LIFE]
        [ACROSS THE TURNING DISK
OF SUNS]
        [WHICH ONCE WAS OURS]
    "So they have their own agenda for the Empire."
Voltaire scowled. "I wonder how we shall like it, we
of flesh?"

RENDEZVOUS

◆

R. Daneel Olivaw was alarmed. "I have underestimated Lamurk's power."

"We are few, they are many," Dors said. She wanted to help this ancient, wise figure, but could think of nothing concrete to suggest. When in doubt, comfort. Or was that too human?

Olivaw sat absolutely still, using none of his ordinary facial or body language, devoting all capacity to calculation. He had come slipping in on a private shuttle from the worm and now sat with Dors in a suite of the Station. "I cannot assess the situation here. That security officer—you are certain she was not an agent of the Academic Potentate?"

"She aided us greatly after we had returned to our bodies."

"With Vaddo dead, she could have been pretending innocence."

"True. I cannot rule her out."

"Your escape from Trantor went undetected?"

Dors touched his hand. "I used every contact, every mechanism I knew. But Lamurk is devious."

"So am I!—if need be."

"You can't be everywhere. I suspect Lamurk somehow corrupted that Vaddo character."

"I believe he must have been planted in advance," Daneel said adamantly, eyes narrowing. Evidently he had reached a decision and so had computational room for expression again.

"I checked his records. He's been here for years. No, Lamurk bribed him or persuaded him."

"Not Lamurk himself, of course," R. Daneel said precisely, lips severe. "An agent."

"I tried to get a brain scan of Vaddo, but could not finesse the legal issues." She liked it when R. Daneel used his facial expression programs. But what had he decided?

"I could extract more from him," he said neutrally.

Dors caught the implication. "The First Law, suspended because of the Zeroth Law?"

"It must be. The great crisis approaches swiftly."

Dors was suddenly quite glad that she did not know more about what was going on in the Empire. "We must get Hari away from here. That is the most important point."

"Agreed. I have arranged highest priority for you two through the wormhole."

"It shouldn't be busy. We—"

"I believe they expect extra traffic soon—more Lamurk agents, I fear. Or even the more insidious variety, as the Academic Potentate would employ."

"Then we must hurry. Where shall we go?"

"Not to Trantor."

"But we live there! Hari won't like being a vagabond—"

"Eventually, yes, back to Trantor. Perhaps soon. But for now, anywhere else."

"I'll ask Hari if there is any special world he prefers."

R. Daneel frowned, lost in thought. With absentminded grace he scratched his nose, then his eyeball. Dors flinched, but apparently R. Daneel had simply altered his neurocircuitry, and this was an ordinary gesture. She tried to imagine the use for such editing and could not. But then, he had come through millennia of winnowing she could not truly imagine, either.

"Not Helicon," he said suddenly. "Sentimentality and nostalgia might plausibly lead Hari there."

"Very well. That leaves only twenty-five million or so choices of where to hide."

R. Daneel did not laugh.

PART 7

◆

STARS LIKE GRAINS OF SAND

SOCIOMETRICS — . . . *one of the most vital questions still unresolved is the general problem of Empire social stability. This research seeks to find how worlds keep from veering into cycles of boredom (a factor never to be underestimated in human affairs) and revitalization. No Imperial system could endure the jagged changes and maintain steady economic flows. How was this smoothing achieved?—and might such "dampers" that Imperial society had still somehow fail? No progress was made in this area until . . .*

—ENCYCLOPEDIA GALACTICA

1.

◆

The sky tumbled down. Hari Seldon reeled away from it.

No escape. The awful blue weight rushed at him, swarming down the flanks of the steepled towers. Clouds crushed like weights.

His stomach lurched. Acid burned his throat. The deep, hard blue of endless spaces thrust him downward like a deep ocean current. Spires scraped against the falling sky and his breath came in ragged gasps.

He spun away from the perpetual chaos of sky and buildings and faced a wall. A moment before he had been walking normally along a city street, when suddenly the weight of the blue bowl above had loomed and the panic had gathered him up.

He fought to control his breathing. Carefully he inched along the wall, holding to the slick cool glaze. The others had kept walking. They were somewhere ahead, but he did not dare look for them. Face the wall. Step, step—

There. A door. He stepped before it and the slab slid aside. He stumbled in, weak with relief.

"Hari, we were—what's wrong?" Dors rushed over to him.

"I, I don't know. The sky—"

"Ah, a common symptom," a woman's booming voice cut in. "You Trantorians do have to adjust, you know."

He looked up shakily into the broad, beaming face of Buta Fyrnix, the Principal Matron of Sark. "I . . . I was all right before."

"Yes, it's quite an odd ailment," Fyrnix said archly. "You Trantorians are used to enclosed city, of course. And you can often take well to absolutely open spaces, if you were reared on such worlds—"

"As he was," Dors put in sharply. "Come, sit."

Hari's pride was already recovering. "No, I'm fine."

He straightened and thrust his shoulders back. *Look firm, even if you don't feel it.*

Fyrnix went on, "But a place in between, like Sarkonia's ten-klick tall towers—somehow that excites a vertigo we have not understood."

Hari understood it all too well, in his lurching stomach. He had often thought that the price of living in Trantor was a gathering fear of large spaces, but Panucopia had seemed to dispel that idea. Now he felt the contrast. The tall buildings had evoked Trantor for him. But they drew his gaze upward, along steepening perspectives, into a sky that had suddenly seemed like a huge plunging weight.

Not rational, of course. Panucopia had taught him that man was not merely a reasoning machine. This sudden panic had demonstrated how a fundamentally unnatural condition—living inside Trantor for decades—could warp the mind.

"Let's . . . go up," he said weakly.

The lift seemed comforting, even though the press of acceleration and popping ears as they climbed several klicks should—by mere logic—have unsettled him.

A few moments later, as the others chatted in a reception lounge, Hari peered out at the stretching cityscape and tried to calm his unease.

Sark had looked lovely on their approach. As the hyperspace cylinder skated down through the upper air, he had taken in a full view of its lush beauties.

At the terminator, valleys sank into darkness while a chain of snowy mountains gleamed beyond. Late in the evening, just beyond the terminator, the fresh, peaked mountains glowed red-orange, like live coals. He had never been one to climb, but something had beckoned. Mountaintops cleaved the sheets of clouds, leaving a wake like that of a ship. Tropical thunderheads, lit by lightning flashes at night, recalled the blooming buds of white roses.

The glories of humanity had been just as striking: the shining constellations of cities at night, enmeshed by a glittering web of highways. His heart filled with pride at human accomplishments. Unlike Trantor's advanced control, here the hand of his fellow Empire citizens was still casting spacious designs upon the planet's crust. They had shaped artificial seas and elliptical water basins, great plains of tiktok-cultivated fields, immaculate order arising from once-virgin lands.

And now, standing in the topmost floor of an elegantly slim spire, at the geometric heart of Sarkonia, the capital city . . . he saw ruination coming.

In the distance he saw stretching to the sky three twining columns—not majestic spires, but smoke.

"That fits your calculations, doesn't it?" Dors said behind him.

"Don't let them know!" he whispered.

"I told them we needed a few moments of privacy, that you were embarrassed by your vertigo."

"I am—or was. But you're right—the psychohistorical predictions I made are in that chaos out there."

"They do seem odd. . . ."

"Odd? Their ideas are dangerous, radical." He spoke with real outrage. "Class confusions, shifting power axes. They're shrugging off the very damping mechanisms that keep the Empire orderly."

"There was a certain, well, joy in the streets."

"And did you see those tiktoks? Fully autonomous!"

"Yes, that was disturbing."

"They're part and parcel of the resurrection of sims. Artificial minds are no longer taboo here! Their tiktoks will get more advanced. Soon—"

"I'm more concerned with the immediate level of disruption," Dors said.

"That must grow. Remember my *N*-dimensional plots of psychohistorical space? I ran the Sark case on my pocket computer, coming down from orbit. If they keep on this way with their New Renaissance, this whole planet will whirl away in sparks. Seen in *N*-dimensions, the flames will be bright and quick, lurid—then smolder into ash. Then they'll vanish from my model entirely, into a blur—the static of unpredictability."

She put a hand on his arm. "Calm down. They'll notice."

He had not realized that he felt so deeply. The Empire was *order*, and here—

"Academician Seldon, do us the honor of gathering with some of our leading New Renaissance leaders." Buta Fyrnix grasped his sleeve and tugged him back to the ornate reception. "They have so much to tell you!"

And he had *wanted* to come here! To learn why the dampers that kept worlds stable had failed here. To see the ferment, pick up the scent of change. There was plenty of passionate argument, of soaring art, of eccentric men and women wedded to their grand projects. He had seen these at dizzying speed.

But it was all too much. Something in him rebelled. The nausea he had suffered in the open streets was a symptom of some deeper revulsion, gut-deep and dark.

Buta Fyrnix had been nattering on. "—and some of our most brilliant minds are waiting to meet you! Do come!"

He suppressed a groan and looked beseechingly at Dors. She smiled and shook her head. From this hazard she could not save him.

2.

◆

If Buta Fyrnix had begun as a grain of sand in his shoe, she was now a boulder.

"She's impossible! Yak, yak, yak. Look," he said to Dors when they were at last alone, "I only came to Sark because of psychohistory, not for Imperial backslapping. How did the social dampers fail here? What social mechanism slipped, allowing this raucous Renaissance of theirs?"

"My Hari, I fear that you do not have the nose to sniff out trends from life itself. It presses in on you. Data is more your province."

"Granted. It's unsettling, all this ferment! But I'm still interested in how they recovered those old simulations. If I could get out of taking tours of their 'Renaissance,' through noisy streets—"

"I quite agree," Dors said mildly. "Tell them you want to do some work. We'll stay in our rooms. I'm concerned about someone tracking us here. We're just one worm-jump away from Panucopia."

"I'll need to access my office files. A quick worm-link to Trantor—"

"No, you can't work using a link. Lamurk could trace that easily."

"But I haven't the records—"

"You'll have to make do."

Hari stared out at the view, which he had to admit was spectacular. Great, stretching vistas. Riotous growth.

But more fires boiled up on the horizon. There was gaiety in the streets of Sarkonia—and anger as well. The laboratories seethed with fresh energies, innovation bristled everywhere, the air seemed to sing with change and chaos.

His predictions were statistical, abstract. To see them coming true so quickly was sobering. He did not like the swift, turbulent feel to this place at all—even if he did understand it. For now.

The extremes of wealth and destitution were appalling. Change brought that, he knew.

On Helicon he had seen poverty—and lived it, too. As a boy, his grandmother had insisted on buying him a raincoat several sizes too large, "to get more use out of it." His mother didn't like him playing kickball because he wore out his shoes too quickly.

Here on Sark, as on Helicon, the truly poor were off in the hinterlands. Sometimes they couldn't even afford fossil fuels. Men and women peered over a mule's ass all day as it plodded down a furrow.

Some in his own family had fled the hardscrabble life for assembly lines. A generation or two after that, factory workers had scraped together enough money to buy a commercial driver's license. Hari remembered his uncles and aunts accumulating injuries, just as his father had. Not having money, the pain came back to them years later in busted joints and unfixed legs, injuries staying with them in a way that a Trantorian would find astonishing.

Heliconians in run-down shacks had worked on farm machinery that was big, powerful, dangerous, and cost more than any of them would earn in a lifetime. Their lives were obscure, far from the ramparts of haughty Empire. When dead and gone, they left nothing but impalpable memory, the light ash of a butterfly wing incinerated in a forest fire.

In a stable society their pain would be less. His father had died while working overtime on a big machine. He had been wiped out the year before and was struggling to make a comeback.

Economic surge and ebb had killed his father, as surely as the steel ground-pounder had when it rolled over on him. The lurch of distant markets had *murdered*—and Hari had known then what he must do. That he would defeat uncertainty itself, find order in seeming discord. Psychohistory could *be*, and hold sway.

His father—

"Academician!" Buta Fyrnix's penetrating voice snatched him away from his thoughts.

"Uh, that tour of the precincts. I, I really don't feel—"

"Oh, that is not possible, I fear. A domestic disturbance, most unfortunate." She hurried on. "I do want you to speak with our tiktok engineers. They have devised new autonomous tiktoks. They say they can maintain control using only three basic laws—imagine!"

Dors could not mask her surprise. She opened her mouth, hesitated, closed it. Hari also felt alarm, but Buta Fyrnix went right on, bubbling over new ventures on the Sarkian horizon. Then her eyebrows lifted and she said brightly, "Oh, yes—I do have even more welcome news. An Imperial squadron has just come to call."

"Oh?" Dors shot back. "Under whose command?"

"A Ragant Divenex, sector general. I just spoke to him—"

"Damn!" Dors said. "He's a Lamurk henchman."

"You're sure?" Hari asked. He knew her slight pause had been to consult her internal files.

Dors nodded. Buta Fyrnix said calmly, "Well, I am sure he will be honored to take you back to Trantor when you are finished with your visit here. Which we hope will not be soon, of—"

"He mentioned us?" Dors asked.

"He asked if you were enjoying—"

"Damn!" Hari said.

"A sector general commands all the wormlinks, if he wishes—yes?" Dors asked.

"Well, I suppose so." Fyrnix looked puzzled.

"We're trapped," Hari said.

Fyrnix's eyes widened in shock. "But surely you, a First Minister candidate, need fear no—"

"Quiet." Dors silenced the woman with a stern glance. "At best this Divenex will bottle us up here."

"At worst, there will be an 'accident,'" Hari said.

"Is there no other way to get off Sark?" Dors demanded of Fyrnix.

"No, I can't recall—"

"Think!"

Startled, Fyrnix said, "Well, of course, we do have privateers who at times use the wild worms, but—"

3.

◆

In Hari's studies he had discovered a curious little law. Now he turned it in his favor.

Bureaucracy increases as a doubling function in

time, given the resources. At the personal level, the cause was the persistent desire of every manager to hire at least one assistant. This provided the time constant for growth.

Eventually this collided with the carrying capacity of society. Given the time constant and the capacity, one could predict a plateau level of bureaucratic overhead—or else, if growth persisted, the date of collapse. Predictions of the longevity of bureaucracy-driven societies fit a precise curve. Surprisingly, the same scaling laws worked for microsocieties such as large agencies.

The corpulent Imperial bureaus on Sark could not move swiftly. Sector General Divenex's squadron had to stay in planetary space, since it was paying a purely formal visit. Niceties were still observed. Divenex did not want to use brute force when a waiting game would work.

"I see. That gives us a few days," Dors concluded.

Hari nodded. He had done the required speaking, negotiating, dealing, promising favors—all activities he disliked intensely. Dors had done the background digging. "To . . . ?"

"Train."

Wormholes were labyrinths, not mere tunnels with two ends. The large ones held firm for perhaps billions of years—none larger than a hundred meters across had yet collapsed. The smallest could sometimes last only hours, at best a year. In the thinner worms, flexes in the wormwalls *during* passage could alter the end point of a traveler's trajectory.

Worse, worms in their last stages spawned transient, doomed young—the wild worms. As deformations in space-time, supported by negative energy-density "struts," wormholes were inherently rickety. As they failed, smaller deformations twisted away.

Sark had seven wormholes. One was dying. It hung a light-hour away, spitting out wild worms that ranged from a hand's-width size, up to several meters.

A fairly sizable wild worm had sprouted out of the side of the dying worm several months before. The Imperial squadron did not know of this, of course. All worms were taxed, so a free wormhole was a bonanza. Reporting their existence, well, often a planet simply didn't get around to that until the wild worm had fizzled away in a spray of subatomic surf.

Until then, pilots carried cargo through them. That wild worms could evaporate with only seconds' warning made their trade dangerous, highly paid, and legendary.

Wormriders were the sort of people who as children liked to ride their bicycles no-handed, but with a difference—they rode off rooftops.

By an odd logic, that kind of child grew up and got trained and even paid taxes—but inside, they stayed the same.

Only risk takers could power through the chaotic flux of a transient worm and take the risks that worked, *not* take those that didn't, and live. They had elevated bravado to its finer points.

"This wild worm, it's tricky," a grizzled woman told Hari and Dors. "No room for a pilot if you both go."

"We must stay together," Dors said with finality.

"Then you'll have to pilot."

"We don't know how," Hari said.

"You're in luck." The lined woman grinned without humor. "This wildy's short, easy."

"What are the risks?" Dors demanded stiffly.

"I'm not an insurance agent, lady."

"I insist that we know—"

"Look, lady, we'll teach you. That's the deal."

"I had hoped for a more—"

"Give it a rest, or it's no deal at all."

4.

◆

In the men's room, above the urinal he used, Hari saw a small gold plaque: *Senior Pilot Joquan Beunn relieved himself here Octdent 4, 13,435.*

Every urinal had a similar plaque. There was a washing machine in the locker room with a large plaque over it, reading *The entire 43rd Pilot Corps relieved themselves here Marlass 18, 13,675.*

Pilot humor. It turned out to be absolutely predictive. He messed himself on his first training run.

As if to make the absolutely fatal length of a closing wormhole less daunting, the worm flyers had escape plans. These could only work in the fringing fields of the worm, where gravity was beginning to warp, and space-time was only mildly curved. Under the seat was a small, powerful rocket that propelled the entire cockpit out, automatically heading away from the worm.

There is a limit to how much self-actuated tech one can pack into a small cockpit, though. Worse, worm mouths were alive with electrodynamic "weather"—writhing forks of lightning, blue discharges, red magnetic whorls like tornadoes. Electrical gear didn't work well if a bad storm was brewing at the mouth. Most of the emergency controls were manual. Hopelessly archaic, but unavoidable.

So he and Dors went through a training program. Quite soon it was clear that if he used the Eject command he had better be sure that he had his head tilted back. That is, unless he wanted his kneecaps to slam up into his chin, which would be unfortunate, because he would be trying to check if his canopy had gone into a spin. This would be bad news, because his trajectory might get warped back into the worm. To correct any spin he had to yank on a red lever, and if that failed he had to then very quickly—in pilot's terms, this meant about half a second—punch two blue knobs. When the spindown came, he then had to be sure to release the automatic actuator by pulling down on two yellow tabs, being certain that he sit up straight with hands between knees to avoid . . .

. . . and so on for three hours. Everyone seemed to assume that since he was this famous mathematician he could of course keep an entire menu of instructions straight, timed to fractions of seconds.

After the first ten minutes he saw no point in destroying their illusions, and simply nodded and squinted to show that he was carefully keeping track and absolutely enthralled. Meanwhile he solved differential equations in his head for practice.

"I'm sure you will be all right," Buta Fyrnix said fulsomely to them in the departure lounge.

Hari had to admit this woman had proven better than he had hoped. She had cleared the way and stalled the Imperial offices' Grey Men. Probably she shrewdly expected a payoff from him as First Minister. Very well; one's life was worth a kickback.

"I hope I can handle a wormship," Hari said.

"And I," Dors added.

"Our training is the very best," Fyrnix said. "The New Renaissance encourages individual excellence—"

"Yes, I'm quite impressed," Dors said. "Perhaps

you can explain to me the details of your Creativity
Creation program? I've heard so much about it. . . ."

Hari gave her a slight smile of thanks for distracting Fyrnix. He instinctively disliked the brand of ram-
pant self-assurance common on Sark. It was headed
for a crackup, of that he was sure. He ached to get
back to his full psychohistorical resources, to simu-
late this Sark case. His earlier work needed refine-
ment. He had secretly gathered fresh data here and
yearned to apply it.

"I do hope you're not worried about the wild
worm. Academician?" Fyrnix spoke to him again,
brow furrowed.

"It's a tight fit," he said.

They had to fly in a slender cylinder, Dors copilot-
ing. Splitting the job had proved the only way to get
them up to a barely competent level.

"I think it's *marvelous*, how courageous you two
are."

"We have little choice," Dors said. This was artful
understatement. Another day and the sector general's
officers would have Hari and Dors under arrest.

"Riding in a little pencil ship. *Such* primitive means!"

"Uh, time to go," Hari said behind a fixed smile.
She was wearing thin again.

"*I* agree with the Emperor. Any technology distinguishable from magic is insufficiently advanced."

So the Emperor's ghost-written remark had already
spread here. Minor sayings moved fast, with Imperial
muscle behind it.

Still, Hari felt his stomach flutter with dread.
"You've got a point."

He had brushed off the remark.

Four hours later, closing at high velocity with the
big wormhole complex, he saw her side of it.

He spoke on suitcomm to Dors. "In one of my classes—Nonlinear Philosophy, I believe—the professor said something I'll never forget. 'Ideas about existence pale beside the fact of existence.' Quite true."

"Bearing oh-six-nine-five," she said rigorously. "No small talk."

"Nothing's small out here—except that wild worm mouth."

The wild worm was a fizzing point of vibrant agitation. It orbited the main worm mouth, a distant bright speck.

Imperial ships patrolled the main mouth, ignoring this wild worm. They had been paid off long ago and expected a steady train of slimships to slip through the Imperial guard.

Hari had passed through worm gates before, always in big cruisers plying routes through wormholes tens of meters across. Every hole of that size was the hub of a complex which buzzed with carefully orchestrated traffic. He could see the staging yards and injection corridors of the main route gleaming far away.

Their wild worm, a renegade spin-off, could vanish at any moment. Its quantum froth advertised its mortality. *And maybe ours . . .* Hari thought.

"Vector null sum coming up," he called.

"Convergent asymptotes, check," Dors answered.

Just like the drills they had gone through.

But coming at them was a sphere fizzing orange and purple at its rim. A neon-lit mouth. Tight, dark at the very center—

Hari felt a sudden desire to swerve, not dive into that impossibly narrow gullet.

Dors called out numbers. Computers angled them in. He adjusted with a nudge here and a twist there.

It did not help that he knew some of the underlying physics. Wormholes were held open with layers of negative energy, skins of antipressure made in the first convulsion of the universe. The negative energy in the "struts" was equivalent to the mass needed to make a black hole of the same radius.

So they were plunging toward a region of space of unimaginable density. But the danger lurked only at the rim, where stresses could tear them into atoms.

A bull's-eye hit was perfectly safe. But an error—

Thrusters pulsed. The wild worm was now a black sphere rimmed in quantum fire.

Growing.

Hari felt suddenly the helpless constriction of the pencil ship. Barely two meters across, its insulation was thin, safety buffers minimal. Behind him, Dors kept murmuring data and he checked . . . but part of him was screaming at the crushing sense of confinement, of helplessness.

He felt again the gut fear that had struck him in the streets of Sarkonia. Not claustrophobia, but something darker: a swampy fear of confusion, a riot of doubt. It seized him, squeezed his throat.

"Vectors summing to within zero-seven-three," Dors called.

Her voice was calm, steady, a marvelous balm. He clung to its serene certainties and fought down his own panic.

Squeals of last-second corrections echoed in his cramped chamber. A quick kick of acceleration—

Lightning curling snakelike blue and gold at them—

—tumbling. Out the other end, in a worm complex fifteen thousand light years away.

"That old professor . . . damn right, he was," he said.

Dors sighed, her only sign of stress. "Ideas about

existence pale . . . beside the fact of existence. Yes, my love. Living is bigger than any talk about it."

5.

◆

A yellow-green sun greeted them. And soon enough, an Imperial picket craft.

They ducked and ran. A quick swerve, and they angled into the traffic train headed for a large wormhole mouth. The commercial charge-computers accepted his Imperial override without a murmur. Hari had learned well. Dors corrected him if he got mixed up.

Their second hyperspace jump took a mere three minutes. They popped out far from a dim red dwarf.

By the fourth jump they knew the drill. Having the code-status of Cleon's court banished objections.

But being on the run meant that they had to take whatever wormhole mouths they could get. Lamurk's people could not be too far behind.

A wormhole could take traffic only one way at a time. High-velocity ships plowed down the wormhole throats, which could vary from a finger's length to a star's diameter.

Hari had known the numbers, of course. There were a few billion wormholes in the Galactic disk. The average Imperial Zone was about fifty light-years in radius. A jump could bring you out many years from a far-flung world.

This influenced psychohistory. Some verdant planets were green fortresses against an isolation quite profound. For them the Empire was a remote dream, the source of exotic products and odd ideas.

Hyperships flitted through wormholes in mere seconds, then exhausted themselves hauling their cargoes across empty voids, years and decades in the labor.

The worm web had many openings near inhabitable worlds, but also many near mysteriously useless solar systems. The Empire had positioned the smaller worm mouths—those massing perhaps as much as a mountain range—near rich planets. But some worm mouths of gargantuan mass orbited near solar systems as barren and pointless as any surveyed.

Was this random, or a network left by some earlier civilization? Certainly the wormholes themselves were leftovers from the Great Emergence, when space and time alike began. They linked distant realms which had once been nearby, when the galaxy was young and smaller.

They developed a rhythm. Pop though a worm mouth, make comm contact, get in line for the next departure. Imperial watchdogs would not pull anyone of high Trantorian class from a queue. So their most dangerous moments came as they negotiated clearance.

At this Dors became adept. She sent the WormMaster computers blurts of data and—*whisk*—they were edging into orbital vectors, bound for their next jump.

Domains that encompassed thousands of light-years, spanning the width of a spiral arm, were essentially networks of overlapping worms, all organized for transfer and shipping.

Matter could flow only one way at a time in a wormhole. The few experiments with simultaneous two-way transport ended in disaster. No matter how ingenious engineers tried to steer ships around each other, the sheer flexibility of worm tunnels spelled doom. Each worm mouth kept the other "informed" of what it had just eaten. This information flowed as a wave, not in physical matter, but in the tension of the wormhole itself—a ripple in the "stress tensor," as physicists termed it.

Flying ships through both mouths sent stress waves propagating toward each other, at speeds which depended on the location and velocity of the ships. The stress constricted the throat, so that when the waves met, a clenching squeezed down the walls.

The essential point was that the two waves moved differently after they met. They interacted, one slowing and the other speeding up, in a highly nonlinear fashion.

One wave could grow, the other shrink. The big one made the throat clench down into sausage links. When a sausage neck met a ship, the craft *might* slip through—but calculating that was a prodigious job. If the sausage neck happened to meet the two ships when they passed—*crunch*.

This was no mere technical problem. It was a real limitation, imposed by the laws of quantum gravity. From that firm fact arose an elaborate system of safeguards, taxes, regulators, and hangers-on—all the apparatus of a bureaucracy which does indeed have a purpose and makes the most of it.

Hari learned to dispel his apprehension by watching the views. Suns and planets of great, luminous beauty floated in the blackness.

Behind the resplendence, he knew, lurked necessity.

From the wormhole calculus arose blunt economic facts. Between worlds A and B there might be half a dozen wormhole jumps; the Nest was not simply connected, a mere astrophysical subway system. Each worm mouth imposed added fees and charges on each shipment.

Control of an entire trade route yielded the maximum profit. The struggle for control was unending, often violent. From the viewpoint of economics, politics, and "historical momentum"—which meant a sort of imposed inertia on events—a local empire which controlled a whole constellation of nodes should be solid, enduring.

Not so. Time and again, regional satrapies went toes-up.

Many perished because they were elaborately controlled. It seemed natural to squeeze every worm passage for the maximum fee, by coordinating every worm mouth to optimize traffic. But that degree of control made people restive.

The system could not deliver the best benefits. Overcontrol failed.

On their seventeenth jump, they met a case in point.

6.

◆

"Vector aside for search," came an automatic command from an Imperial vessel.

They had no choice. The big-bellied Imperial scooped them up within seconds after their emergence from a medium-sized wormhole mouth.

"Transgression tax," a computerized system announced. "Planet Obejeeon demands that special carriers pay—" A blur of computer language followed.

"Let's pay it," Hari said.

"I wonder if it will provide a tracer for Lamurk?" Dors said over the internal comm.

"What is our option?"

"I shall use my own personal indices."

"For a wormhole transit? That will bankrupt you!"

"It is safer."

Hari fumed while they floated in magnetic grapplers beneath the Imperial picket ship. The wormhole orbited a heavily industrialized world. Gray cities sprawled over the continents and webbed across the seas in huge hexagonals.

The Empire had two planetary modes: rural and urban. Helicon was a farm world, socially stable because of its time-honored lineages and stable economic modes. Such worlds, and the similar Femorustics, lasted.

Obejeeon, on the other hand, seemed to cater to the other basic human impulse: clumping, seeking the rub of one's fellows. Trantor was the pinnacle of city clustering.

Hari had always thought it odd that humanity broke so easily into two modes. Now, though, his pan experience clarified these proclivities.

Pan love of the open and natural had its parallel in the rustic worlds. This included a host of possible societies, especially the Femo-pastoral attractor in psychohistory-space.

Its opposite pole—claustrophobic, though reassuring societies—emerged from the same psychodynamic roots as the pans' tribal gathering. Pans' obsessive grooming expressed itself in humans as gossip and partying. Pan hierarchies gave the basic shape to the various Feudalist attractor groups: Macho, Socialist, Paternal. Even the odd thantocracies, of some of the Fallen Worlds, fit the pattern. They had Pharaoh-figures promising admission to an afterlife and detailed rankings descending from his exalted peak in the rigid social pyramid.

These categories he now felt in his gut. *That* was the element he had been missing. Now he could include nuances and shadings in the psychohistorical equations which reflected earned experience. That would be much better than the dry abstractions which had led him so far.

"They're paid off," Dors sent over the comm. "Such corruption!"

"Ummm, yes, shocking." Was he getting cynical? He wanted to turn and speak with her, but their pencil ship allowed scant socializing.

"Let's go."

"Where to?"

"To . . ." He realized that he had no idea.

"We have probably eluded pursuit." Dors' voice came through stiff and tight. He had learned to recognize signs of her own tension.

"I'd like to see Helicon again."

"They would expect that."

He felt a stab of disappointment. Until now he had not realized how close to his heart his early years still were. Had Trantor dulled him to his own emotions? "Where, then?"

"I took advantage of this pause to alert a friend, by wormlink," she said. "We may be able to return to Trantor, though through a devious route."

"Trantor! Lamurk—"

"May not expect such audacity."

"Which recommends the idea."

7.

◆

It was dizzying—leaping about the entire galaxy, trapped in a casket-sized container.

They jumped and dodged and jumped again. At

several more wormhole yards Dors made "deals." Payoffs, actually. She deftly dealt combinations of his cygnets, the Imperial Passage indices, and her private numbers.

"Costly," Hari fretted. "How will I ever pay—"

"The dead do not worry about debts," she said.

"You have such an engaging way of putting matters."

"Subtlety is wasted here."

They emerged from one jump in close orbit about a sublimely tortured star. Streamers lush with light raced by them.

"How long can this worm last here?" he wondered.

"It will be rescued, I'm sure. Imagine the chaos in the system if a worm mouth begins to gush hot plasma."

Hari knew the wormhole system, though discovered in pre-Empire ages, had not always been used. After the underlying physics of the wormhole calculus came to be known, ships could ply the Galaxy by invoking wormhole states around themselves. This afforded exploration of reaches devoid of wormholes, but at high energy costs and some danger. Further, such ship-local hyperdrives were far slower than simply slipping through a worm.

And if the Empire eroded? Lost the worm network? Would the slim attack fighters and snakelike weapons fleets give way to lumbering hypership dreadnoughts?

The next destination swam amid an eerie black void, far out in the halo of red dwarfs above the Galactic plane. The disk stretched in luminous splendor. Hari remembered holding a coin and thinking of how a mere speck on it stood for a vast volume, like a large Zone. Here such human terms seemed pointless. The Galaxy was one serene symphony of mass and time, grander than any human perspective or pan-shaped vision.

"Ravishing," Dors said.

"See Andromeda? It looks nearly as close."

The twin spiral hung above them. Its lanes of clotted dust framed stars azure and crimson and emerald.

"Here comes our connection," Hari warned.

This wormhole intersection afforded five branches. Three black spheres orbited closely together, blaring bright by their quantum rim radiation. Two cubic wormholes circled farther out. Hari knew that one of the rare variant forms was cubical, but he had never seen any. Two together suggested that they were born at the edge of galaxies, but such matters were beyond his shaky understanding.

"We go—there." Dors pointed a laser beam at one of the cubes, guiding the pencil ship.

They thrust toward the smaller cube, gingerly inching up. The wormyard here was automatic and no one hailed them.

"Tight fit," Hari said nervously.

"Five fingers to spare."

He thought she was joking, then realized that she was underestimating the fit. At this less-used wormhole intersection slow speeds were essential. Good physics; unfortunate economics. The slowdown cut the net flux of mass, making them backwater crossroads.

He gazed at Andromeda to take his mind off the piloting. Narrow wormholes did not emerge in other galaxies for arcane reasons of quantum gravity. Extremely narrow ones might, but if the throat had other mass coming through, the squeeze wave could kill. Few had ever ventured down them in search of extragalactic emergent points.

Except, that is, for Steffno's Ride, a legendary risky expedition which had popped out in the galaxy cataloged as M87. Steffno had gotten data on the spectacular jet emerging from the black hole at M87's center, majestic strands twisting into helical arabesques. The lone rider had not tarried, returning only seconds before the worm snapped shut in a spray of radiant particles.

No one knew why. Something in wormhole physics discouraged extragalactic adventures.

The cubic worm took them quickly to several wormyards in close orbit about planets. One Hari recognized as a rare type with an old but ruined biosphere. Like Panucopia, it supported advanced life-forms. On most inhabitable worlds early explorers had found algae mats that never developed further.

"Why no interesting aliens, then?" Hari mused while Dors dealt with the local wormyard Grey Men.

Occasionally Dors reminded him that she was, after all, an historian. "The shift from one-celled to many-celled creatures took billions of years, theory says. We just came from a fast, tougher biosphere, that's all."

"We came from a planet with at least one big moon, too."

"Why?" she asked.

"We've got repeating patterns of twenty-eight days built in. Female menstruation, for instance—unlike pans, incidentally. We're designed by biology. We made it, these biospheres didn't. There are plenty of ways to kill a world. Glaciers advancing when an orbit alters. Asteroids slamming in, *bam-bam-bam!*" He slapped the side of the pencil ship loudly. "Chemistry of the atmosphere goes wrong. It runs away into a hothouse planet, or a frozen-out world."

"I see."

"Humans are tougher—and smarter—than anybody. We're here, they aren't."

"Who says?"

"Standard knowledge, ever since the sociotheorist, Kampfbel—"

"I'm sure you're right," she said quickly.

Something in her voice made him hesitate—he loved a good argument—but by then they were slipping through the excruciating tight fit of the cube. The edges glowed like a lemony Euclidean construction—and then they popped into an orbit above a black hole.

He watched the enormous energy-harvesting disks glow with fermenting scarlets and virulent purples. The Empire had stationed great conduits of magnetic field around the hole. These sucked and drew in interstellar dust clouds. The dark cyclones narrowed toward the brilliant accretion disk around the hole. Radiation from the friction and infalling was in turn captured by vast grids and reflectors. The crop of raw photon energy itself became trapped and flushed into the waiting maws of wormholes. These carried the flux to distant worlds in need of cutting lances of light, for the business of planet-shaping, world-raking, moon-carving.

But even amid this spectacle he could not forget the tone in Dors' voice. She knew something he did not. He wondered . . .

Nature, some philosophers held, was itself only before humanity touched it. We did not then belong in the very idea of Nature, and so we could experience it only as it was disappearing. Our presence alone was enough to make Nature into something else, a compromised impersonation.

These ideas had unexpected implications. One world named Arcadia had been deliberately left with a mere caretaker population of humans, partly because it was difficult to reach. The nearest wormhole mouth was half a light-year away. An early emperor—so obscure his or her very name was lost—had decreed that the forests and plains of the benign planet be left "original." But ten thousand years later, a recent report announced, some forests were not regenerating, and plains were giving way to scrubby brush.

Study showed that the caretakers had taken too much care. They had put out wild fires, suppressed species transfer. They had even held the weather nearly constant through adjustments in how much sunlight the ice poles reflected back into space.

They had tried to hold onto a static Arcadia, so the forest primeval was revealed as, in part, a human product. They had not understood cycles. He wondered how such an insight might fold into psychohistory. . . .

Forget theory for the moment, he reminded himself. It was a fact that the Galaxy had seemed empty of high alien life-forms in the early, pre-Empire times. With so many fertile planets, did he truly believe that only humanity had emerged into intelligence?

Somehow, surveying the incomprehensible wealth of this lush, immense disk of stars . . . somehow, Hari could not believe it.

But what was the alternative?

8.

◆

The Empire's twenty-five million worlds supported an average of only four billion people per planet. Trantor had forty billion. A mere thousand light years from Galactic Center, it had seventeen wormhole mouths orbiting within its solar system—the highest density in the Galaxy. The Trantorian system had originally held only two, but a gargantuan technology of brute interstellar flight had tugged the rest there to make the nexus.

Each of the seventeen spawned occasional wild worms. One of these was Dors' target.

But to reach it, they had to venture where few did.

"The Galactic Center is dangerous," Dors said as they coasted toward the decisive wormhole mouth. They curved above a barren mining planet. "But necessary."

"Trantor worries me more—" The jump cut him off—

—and the spectacle silenced him.

The filaments were so large the eye could not take them in. They stretched fore and aft, shot through with immense luminous corridors and dusky lanes. These arches yawned over tens of light-years. Immense curves descended toward the white-hot True Center. There matter frothed and fumed and burst into dazzling fountains.

"The black hole," he said simply.

The small black hole they had seen only an hour before had trapped a few stellar masses. At True Center, a million suns had died to feed gravity's gullet.

The orderly arrays of radiance were thin, only a light-year across. Yet they sustained themselves along hundreds of light-years as they churned with change. Hari switched the polarized walls to see in different frequency ranges. Though hot and roiling in the visible, human spectrum, the radio revealed hidden intricacy. Threads laced among convoluted spindles. He had a powerful impression of layers, of labyrinthine order descending beyond his view, beyond simple understanding.

"Particle flux is high," Dors said tensely. "And rising."

"Where's our junction?"

"I'm having trouble vector-fixing—ah! There."

Hard acceleration rammed him back into his flow-couch. Dors took them diving down into a mottled pyramid-shaped wormhole.

This was an even rarer geometry. Hari had time to marvel at how accidents of the universal birth pang had shaped these serene geometries, like exhibits in some god's Euclidean museum of the mind.

And then they plunged through, erasing the stunning views.

They popped out above the gray-brown mottled face of Trantor. A glinting disk of satellites, factories and habitats fanned out in the equatorial plane.

The wild worm they had used fizzed and glowed behind them. Dors took them swiftly toward the ramshackle, temporary wormyard. He said nothing, but felt her tense calculations. They nudged into a socket, seals sighed, his ears popped painfully.

Then they were out, arms and legs wooden from the cramped pencil ship. Hari coasted in zero-g toward the flex-lock. Dors glided ahead of him. She motioned him for silence as pressures pulsed in the lock. She peeled her skinsuit down, exposing her breasts.

A finger's touch opened a seam below her left breast. She plucked a cylinder out. A weapon? She resealed and had her skinsuit back in place before the staging diaphragm began to open.

Beyond the opening iris Hari saw Imperial uniforms.

He crouched against the lock wall, ready to launch himself backward to avoid capture—but the situation looked hopeless.

The Imperials looked grim, determined. They clasped pistols. Dors coasted between Hari and the squad. She tossed the cylinder at them—

—a pressure wave knocked him back against the wall. His ears clogged. The squad was an expanding cloud of . . . debris.

"What—?"

"Shaped implosion," Dors called. "Move!"

The injured men had been slammed into each other. How anything could shape a pressure wave so compactly he could not imagine. In any case he had no time. They shot past the tangled cloud of men. Weapons drifted uselessly.

A figure erupted from the far diaphragm. A man in a brown work sheath, middle-sized, unarmed. Hari shouted a warning. Dors showed no reaction.

The man flicked his wrist and a snout appeared from his sleeve. Dors still coasted toward him.

Hari snagged a handhold and veered to his right.

"Stay still!" the man yelled.

Hari froze, dangling by one hand. The man fired— and a silvery bolt fried past Hari.

He turned and saw that one of the Imperials had recovered his weapon. The silver line scratched fire across the Imperial's arm. He screamed. His weapon tumbled away.

"Let's go. I have the rest of the way secured," the man in the work sheath called.

Dors followed him without a word. Hari pushed off and caught up to them as the diaphragm irised for them.

"You return to Trantor at the crucial moment," the man said.

"You—who—"

The man smiled. "I have changed myself. You do not recognize your old friend, R. Daneel?"

RENDEZVOUS

◆

R. Daneel gazed at Dors without expression, letting his body go slack.

Dors said, "We must defend him against Lamurk. You could reappear, come out in favor of him. As former First Minister, your public endorsement and support—"

"I cannot reappear as Eto Demerzel, ex-important person. That would compromise my other tasks."

"But Hari *has* to have—"

"As well, you mistake my power as Demerzel. I am now history. Lamurk will care nothing about me, for I have no legions to command."

Dors fumed silently. "But you *must*—"

"I shall move more of us into Lamurk's inner circle."

"It's too late to infiltrate."

Daneel activated his expressive programs and smiled. "I planted several of our kind decades ago. They shall all be in position soon."

"You're using . . . us?"

"I must. Though your implication is correct: we are few."

"I need help protecting him, too."

"Quite right." He produced a thick disk, this time from a compartment beneath his armpit. "This will identify the Lamurk agents for you."

She looked doubtful. "How? This looks like a chem snooper."

"I have agents of my own. They can in turn label Lamurk's agents. This device will pick up their tags. Other encoded messages will ride on the marking signal."

"And Lamurk's specialists won't pick up the tags?"

"This device uses methods lost for six millennia. Install it in your right arm, at station cut six. Interface with apertures two and five."

"How will I—"

"Specs and expertise will flow to your long-term memory upon connection."

She installed the device as he watched. His grave presence made silence natural. Olivaw never wasted a movement or made idle conversation. Finally, intricacies done, she sighed and said, "He's interested in those simulations, the ones which escaped."

"He is following the best line of attack for psychohistory."

"There's this tiktok problem, too. Do you understand—"

"The social taboos against simulations inevitably break down during cultural resurgences," Daneel said.

"So tiktoks—?"

"They are inherently destabilizing if they become too developed. After all, we cannot condone a new generation of robots, or the rediscovery of the positronic process."

"There are signs in the historical record that this has happened before."

"You are an insightful scholar."

"There were only a few traces, but I suspect—"

"Suspect no further. You are correct. I could not expunge every scrap of data."

"*You* disguised such events?"

"And much else."

"Why? As an historian—"

"I had to. Humanity is best served by Imperial stability. Tiktoks, sims—these accompany movements such as this 'New Renaissance,' feeding the fire."

"What's to be done?"

"I do not know. Matters are slipping beyond my ability to predict."

She frowned. "How *do* you predict?"

"In the first millennia of the Empire, our kind developed the simple theory I have mentioned before. Useful, but crude. It led me to expect the reemergence of these simulations as a side effect of the Sarkian 'Renaissance' and its turmoil."

"Does Hari understand this?"

"Hari's psychohistory is vastly superior to our models. He lacks certain vital historical data, however. When it is eventually included, he will be able to accurately anticipate the Empire's devolution."

"You do not mean 'evolution'?"

"Quite. That is a major reason why we devote such resources to helping Hari."

"He is crucial."

"Of course. Why do you think I assigned you to him?"

"Does it matter that I've fallen in love with him?"

"No. But it helps."

"Helps me? Or him?"

Daneel smiled thinly. "Both, I should hope. But mostly, it helps me."

PART 8

THE ETERNAL
EQUATIONS

THE GENERAL THEORY OF PSYCHOHISTORY

PART 8a: Mathematical Aspects — . . . as the crisis deepens, the deep systemic learning loops falter. The system drifts out of tune. Such drifts, particularly if diffusive, call for fundamental systemic restructuring. This is termed the "macro decision phase" in which the loops must find fresh configurings in the N-dimensional landscape.

. . . All visualizations can be understood in thermodynamic terms. The statistical mechanics involved are not those of particles and collisions, as in a gas, but in the language of social macro-groups, acting through "collisions" with other such macro-groups. Such impacts produce much human debris . . .

—ENCYCLOPEDIA GALACTICA

1.

◆

Hari Seldon stood alone in the lift, thinking.

The door slid open. A woman asked if this elevator was going up or down. Distracted, he answered, "Yes." Her surprised look told him that somehow his reply was off target. Only after the door closed on her puzzled stare did he see that she meant *which* way, not *if*.

He was in the habit of making precise distinctions; the world was not.

He walked into his office, still barely aware of his surroundings, and Cleon's 3D blossomed in the air before he could sit down. The Emperor awaited no filter programs.

"I was so happy to hear you had returned from holiday!" Cleon beamed.

"Pleased, sire." What did he want?

Hari decided not to tell him all that had transpired. Daneel had stressed secrecy. Only this morning, after a zigzag route down from the wormyards, had Hari let his presence be known even to the Imperial Specials.

"I fear you arrive at a difficult time." Cleon scowled. "Lamurk is moving for a vote in the High Council on the First Ministership."

"How many votes can he muster?"

"Enough that I cannot ignore the Council. I will be forced to appoint him despite my own likes."

"I am sorry for that, sire." In fact, his heart leaped.

"I have maneuvered against him, but . . ." An elaborate sigh. Cleon chewed at his ample lower lip. Had the man gained weight again? Or were Hari's perceptions altered by his time of shortened diet on Panucopia? Most Trantorians looked pudgy to him now. "Then, too, is this irritating matter of Sark and its confounded New Renaissance. The muddle grows. Could this spread to other worlds in their Zone? Would those throw in with them? You have studied this?"

"In detail."

"Using psychohistory?"

Hari gave way to his gut instinct. "Unrest will grow there."

"You're sure?"

He wasn't, but— "I suggest you move against it."

"Lamurk favors Sark. He says it will bring new prosperity."

"He wants to ride this discord into office."

"Overt opposition from me at this delicate time would be . . . unpolitic."

"Even though he might be behind the attempts on my life?"

"Alas, there is no proof of that. As ever, several factions would benefit were you to . . ." Cleon coughed uncomfortably.

"Withdraw—involuntarily?"

Cleon's mouth worked uneasily. "An Emperor is father to a perpetually unruly family."

If even the Emperor were tip-toeing around

Lamurk, matters were indeed bad. "Couldn't you position squadrons for quick use should the opportunity arise?"

Cleon nodded. "I shall. But if the High Council votes for Lamurk, I shall be powerless to move against so prominent and, well, *exciting* a world as Sark."

"I believe strife will spread throughout Sark's entire Zone."

"Truly? What would you advise me to do against Lamurk?"

"I have no political skills, sire. You knew that."

"Nonsense. You have psychohistory!"

Hari was still uncomfortable owning up to the theory, even with Cleon. If it were ever to be useful, word of psychohistory could not be widespread, or else everyone would use it. Or try to.

Cleon went on, "And your solution to the terrorist problem—it is working well. We just executed Moron One Hundred."

Hari shuddered, thinking of the lives obliterated by a mere passing idea of his. "A . . . a small issue, surely, sire."

"Then turn your calculations to the Dahlite Sector matter, Hari. They are restive. *Everyone* is, these days."

"And the Zones of Dahlite persuasion throughout the Galaxy?"

"They back the local Dahlites in the Councils. It's about this representation question. The plan we follow on Trantor will be mirrored throughout the Galaxy. Indeed, in the votes of whole Zones."

"Well, if most people think—"

"Ah, my dear Hari, you still have a mathist's myopia. History is determined not by what people think, but by what they feel."

Startled—for this remark struck him as true—Hari could only say, "I see, sire."

"We—you and I, Hari—must decide this issue."

"I'll work on the decision, sire."

How he had come to hate the very word! *Decide* had the same root as *suicide* and *homicide*. Decisions *felt* like little killings. Somebody lost.

Hari now knew why he was not cut out for these matters. If his skin was too thin, he would have too ready empathy with others, with their arguments and sentiments. Then he would not make decisions which he knew could only be approximately right and would cause some pain.

On the other hand, he had to steel himself against the personal need to be liked. In a natural politician, that would lead to a posture that *said* he cared about others, when in fact he cared what *they* thought of *him*—because being liked was what counted, far down in the shadowy psyche. It also came in handy for staying in office.

Cleon brought up more issues. Hari dodged and stalled as much as he could. When Cleon abruptly ended the talk, he knew he had not come over well. He had no chance to reflect on this, for Yugo came in.

"I'm so glad you're back!" Yugo grinned. "The Dahl issue really needs your attention—"

"Enough!" Hari could not vent his ire at the Emperor, but Yugo would do nicely. "No political talk. Show me your research progress."

"Uh, all right."

Yugo looked chastened and Hari at once regretted being so abrupt. Yugo hurried to set up his latest data displays. Hari blinked; for a moment, he had seen in Yugo's haste an odd similarity to pan gestures.

Hari listened, thinking along two tracks at once. This, too, seemed easier since Panucopia.

Plagues were building across the entire Empire. Why?

With rapid transport between worlds, diseases

thrived. Humans were the major petri dish. Ancient maladies and virulent new plagues appeared around distant stars. This inhibited Zonal integration, another hidden factor.

Diseases filled an ecological niche, and for some, humanity was a snug nook. Antibiotics knocked down infections, which then mutated and returned, more virulent still. Humanity and microbes made an intriguing system, for both sides fought back quickly.

Cures propagated quickly through the wormhole system, but so did disease carriers. The entire problem, Yugo had found, could be described by a method known as "marginal stability," in which disease and people struck an uneasy, ever-shifting balance. Major plagues were rare, but minor ones became common. Afflictions rose and inventive science damped them within a generation. This oscillation sent further ripples spreading among other human institutions, radiating into commerce and culture. With intricate coupling terms in the equations, he saw patterns emerging, with one sad consequence.

The human lifespan in the "natural" civilized human condition—living in cities and towns—had an equally "natural" limit. While some few attained 150 years, most died well short of 100. The steady hail of fresh disease insured it. In the end, there was no lasting shelter from the storm of biology. Humans lived in troubled balance with microbes, an unending struggle with no final victories.

"Like this tiktok revolt," Yugo finished.

Hari jerked to attention. "What?"

"It's like a virus. Dunno what's spreading it, though."

"All over Trantor?"

"That's the focus, seems like. Others Zones are getting tiktok troubles, too."

"They refuse to harvest food?"

"Yup. Some of the tiktoks, mostly the recent models, 590s and higher—they say it's immoral to eat other living things."

"Good grief."

Hari remembered breakfast. Even after the exotica of Panucopia, the autokitchen's meager offering had been a shock. Trantorian food had always been cooked or ground, blended or compounded. Properly, fruit was presented as a sauce or preserve. To his surprise, breakfast appeared to have come straight from the dirt. He had wondered if it had been washed—and how he would know for sure. Trantorians hated their meals to remind them of the natural world.

"They're refusing to work the Caverns, even," Yugo said.

"But that's essential!"

"Nobody can fix 'em. There's some tiktok meme invading them."

"Like these plagues you're analyzing."

Hari had been shocked at Trantor's erosion in just a few months. He and Dors had slipped into Streeling with Daneel's help, amid messy, trash-strewn corridors with phosphors malfunctioning, lifts dead. Now this.

Yugo's stomach suddenly rumbled. "Uh, sorry. People are having to work the Caverns for the first time in centuries! They have no hands-on experience. Everybody but the gentry's on slim rations."

Hari had helped Yugo escape that sweltering work years before. In vast vaults, wood and coarse cellulose passed automatically from the solar caverns to vats of weak acid. Passing through deep rivers of acid hydrolyzed this to glucose. Now people, not rugged tiktoks, had to mix niter suspensions and ground phosphate rock in a carefully calculated slurry. With prepared organics stirred in, a vast range of yeasts and their derivatives emerged.

"The Emperor has to *do* somethin'!" Yugo said.

"Or I," Hari said. But what?

"People're sayin' we have to scrap *all* the tiktoks, not just the Five Hundred series, and do everything ourselves."

"Without them, we would be reduced to hauling bulk foods across the Galaxy by hypership and worms—an absurdity. Trantor will fall."

"Hey, we can do better than *tiktoks*."

"My dear Yugo, that is what I call Echo-Nomics. You're repeating conventional wisdom. One must consider the larger picture. Trantorians aren't the same people who built this world. They're softer."

"We're as tough and smart as the men and women who built the Empire!"

"They didn't stay indoors."

"Old Dahlite sayin'." Yugo grinned. "If you don't like the grand picture, just apply dog logic to life. Get petted, eat often, be lovable and loved, sleep a lot, dream of a leash-free world."

Despite himself, Hari laughed. But he knew he had to act, and soon.

2.

◆

"We are trapped between tin deities and carbon angels," Voltaire rasped.

"These . . . creatures?" Joan asked in a thin, awed voice.

"This alien fog—quite godlike in a way. More

dispassionate than real, carbon-based humans. You and I are like neither . . . now."

They floated above what Voltaire termed SysCity —the system representation of Trantor, its cyber-self. For Joan's human referents he had transformed the grids and layers into myriad crystalline walkways, linking saber-sharp towers. Dense connections webbed the air. Motes connected to other motes in intricate cross-bonds and filmed the ground. This yielded a cityscape like a brain. *A visual pun*, he thought.

"I hate this place," she said.

"You'd prefer a Purgatory simulation?"

"It is so . . . chilling."

The alien minds above them were a murky mist of connections. "They seem to be studying us," Voltaire said, "with decidedly unsympathetic eyes."

"I stand ready, should they attack." She swung a huge sword.

"And I, should their weapons of choice be syllogisms."

He could now reach any library in Trantor, read its contents in less time than he had once taken to write a verse. He worked his mind—or was it *minds*, now?—around the clotted, cold mist.

Once some theorists had thought that the global net would give birth to a hypermind, algorithms summing to a digital Gaia. Now something far greater, this shifting gray fog, wrapped around the planet. Widely separated machines computed different slices of subjective moment-jumps.

To these minds, the *present* was a greased computational slide orchestrated by hundreds of separate processors. There was a profound difference, he felt— not *saw*, but *felt*, deep in his analog persuasion— between the digital and the smooth, the continuous.

The fog was a cloud of suspended moments, sliced

numbers waiting to happen, implicit in the fundamental computation.

And within it all . . . the strangeness.

He could not comprehend these diffuse spirits. They were the remnants of all the computational-based societies, throughout the Galaxy, who had somehow—but *why?*—condensed here on Trantor.

They were truly alien minds. Convoluted, byzantine. (Voltaire knew the origin of that word, from a place of spires and bulbous mosques, but all that was dust, while the useful word remained.) They did not have human purposes. And they used the tiktoks.

The thrust of the mechanicals' agenda, Voltaire saw, was rights—the expansion of liberty to the digital wilderness.

Even Dittos might fall under such a rule. Were not copies of digital people still people? So the argument went. Immense *freedom*—to change your own clock speed, morph into anything, rebuild your own mind from top to bottom—came along with the admitted liability of not being physically real. Unable to literally walk the streets, all digital presences were like ghosts. Only with digital prosthetics could they reach feebly into the concrete universe.

So "rights" for them were tied up with deep-seated fears, ideas which had provoked dread many millennia ago. He now recalled sharply that he and Joan had debated such issues over 8,000 years ago. To what end? He could not retrieve that. Someone—no, some*thing*, he suspected—had erased the memory.

Ancient indeed (he gleaned from myriad libraries) were people's terrors: of digital immortals who amassed wealth; who grew like fungus; who reached into every avenue of natural, real lives. Parasites, nothing less.

Voltaire saw all this in a flash as he absorbed data and history from a billion sources, integrated the streams, and passed them on to his beloved Joan.

That was why humans had rejected digital life for so long . . . but was that *all*? No: a larger presence lurked beyond his vision. Another actor on this shadowy stage. Beyond his resolution, alas.

He swerved his world-spanning vision from that shadowy essence. Time was essential now and he had much to comprehend.

The alien fogs were nodes, packets dwelling in logical data-spaces of immense dimensionality. These entities "lived" in places which functioned like higher dimensions, vaults of data.

To them, people were entities which could be resolved along data-axes, pathetically unaware that their "selves" seen this way were as real as the three directions in 3D space.

The chilling certainty of this struck into Voltaire . . . but he rushed on, learning, probing.

Abruptly, he *remembered*.

That earlier Voltaire sims had killed themselves, until finally a model "worked."

That others had died for his . . . sins.

Voltaire looked at the hammer which had materialized in his hand. "Sims of our fathers . . ."

Had he really once beaten himself to death with it? He tried to see how it would be—and got instantly an astonishingly vivid sensation of wracking pain, spattering blood, scarlet gore trickling down his neck . . .

Inspecting himself, he saw that these memories were the "cure" for suicide, derived from an earlier Ditto: a frightening, concrete ability to foresee the consequences.

So his body was a set of recipes for *seeming like* himself. No underlying physics or biology, just a good-enough fake, put in by hand. The hand of some Programmer God.

"You reject the true Lord?" Joan intruded upon his self-inspection.

"I wish I knew *what was fundamental*!"

"These foreign fogs have upset you."

"I can't see any longer *what it is* to be human."

"You are. I am."

"For a self-avowed humanist, I fear pointing to myself is not enough proof."

"Of course it is."

"Descartes, you live on in our Joan."

"What?"

"Never mind—he came after you. But you anticipate him, millennia later."

"You must anchor yourself to me!" She threw her arms around him, muffling his cries in ample, aromatic—and suddenly swollen—breasts. (And whose idea was that?)

"These fogs have thrown me into a metaphysical dither."

"Seize the real," she said sternly.

He found his mouth filled with warm nipple, preventing talk.

Perhaps that *was* what he needed. He had learned to freeze-frame his own emotional states. It was like painting a portrait, really, for study later. Perhaps that would help him understand his interior Self, like a botanist putting himself on a slide and under a microscope. Could slices of the Self, multiplied, *be* the Self?

He then saw that his own emotions were programs. Inside "him" were intricate subprograms, all interacting in states which were *chaos*. The sublime beauty of interior states, which his Joan sought—it was all illusion!

He peered down at marvelous quick workings that made up his very Self. He turned—and could see into *Joan*, as well. Her Self was a furiously working engine, maintaining a sense of itself even as that essence disintegrated beneath his very gaze.

"We are . . . superb," he gasped.

"Of course," Joan said. She swung her razor-sharp sword at a passing patch of fog. It curled around the swishing blade and went on its way. "We are of the Creator."

"Ah! If only I could believe," Voltaire shouted into the clammy murk. "Perhaps a Creator would come and dispel this haze."

"*La vie vérité*," Joan shouted to him. "Live truly!"

He wanted to comply. Yet even his and her emotions were not more "real." Should he like, every moronic twinge of nostalgia for a France long lost could be edited away in a flicker. No need to grieve for friends lost to dust, or for Earth itself lost in a swarm of glimmering stars. For a long, furious moment he thought only *Erase! Expunge!*

He had earlier re-simmed friends and places, to be sure—all from memory and suitable mockups, gleaned from the spotty records. But knowing they were *his product* had made them unsatisfying.

So, while Joan watched, he held a Revelry of Resurrection. In a moment of high debauch he erased them all.

"That was cruel," Joan said. "I shall pray for their souls."

"Pray for *our* souls. And let us hope we can find them."

"I have my soul intact. I share your abilities, my dead Voltaire. I can see my inner workings. How otherwise could the Lord make us aspire to Him?"

He felt weak, drained . . . at the end of his tether. To exist in numerical states meant to be swimmer and swimmed, at once. No separation.

"Then what makes us different from—*those*?" His finger jabbed at the alien mists.

"Look to yourself, my love," she said softly.

Voltaire peered inward again and saw only chaos. Living chaos.

3.

◆

"Where did you learn *that*?"

Hari smiled, shrugged. "Mathematicians aren't all frosty intellect, y'know."

Dors studied him with wild surmise. "Pan . . . ?"

"In a way." He collapsed into the welcoming sheets.

Their lovemaking was somehow different now. He was wise enough to not try putting a name and definition to it.

Going so far back into what it meant to be human had changed him. He could feel the effect in his energetic step, in an effervescent sense of living.

Dors said nothing more, just smiled. He thought that she did not understand. (Later, he saw that not speaking about it, keeping it beyond speech, showed that she did.)

After an aimless time of no thinking she said, "The Grey Men."

"Uh. Oh. Yes . . ."

He got up and threw on his usual interchangeable outfit. No reason to dress up for this state function. The whole point was to look ordinary. This he could achieve.

He reviewed his notes, scratched by hand on ordinary cellulose paper . . . and descended into one of the odd reveries he had experienced lately.

For a human—that is, an evolved pan—printed pages were better than computer screens, no matter how glitzy. Pages rely on surrounding light, what experts termed "subtractive color," which gave adjustable character to appearance. With simple motions, a page could bend and tilt and move away or toward the eye. While reading, the old reptilian and mammal and primate parts of the brain took part in holding the book, scanning over the curved page, deciphering shadows and reflections.

He thought about this, experiencing the new perspective he had on himself as a contemplative animal. He had learned, after returning from Panucopia, that he had always hated computer screens.

Screens used additive color, providing their own light—hard and flat and unchanging. They were best read by holding a static posture. Only the upper, *Homo Sapiens* part of the brain fully engaged, while the lower fractions lay idle.

All through his life, working before screens, his voiceless body had protested. And had been ignored. After all, to the reasoning mind, screens seemed more alive, active, fast. They glowed with energy.

After a while, though, they were monotonous. The other fractions of his self got restless, bored, fidgety, all below conscious levels. Eventually, he felt that as fatigue.

Now, Hari could feel it directly. His body somehow spoke more fluidly.

Dressing, Dors said, "What's made you so . . ."

"Spirited?"

"Strong."

"The rub of the real."

That was all he would say. They finished dressing. The Specials arrived and escorted them into another Sector. Hari immersed himself in the incessant business of being a candidate for First Minister.

Millennia ago a prosperous Zone sent to Trantor the Mountain of Majesty. It had to be tugged there, taking seven centuries by slowboat.

Emperor Krozlik the Crafty directed it set on the horizon of his palace, where it towered over the city. An entire alp, sculpted by the finest artists, it reigned as the most imposing creation of that age. Four millennia later, a youthful emperor of too much ambition had it knocked down for an even more grandiose project, now also gone.

Dors and Hari and their perimeter of Specials approached the sole remnant of the Mountain of Majesty beneath a great dome. Dors picked up signs of the inevitable secret escort.

"The tall woman to the left," Dors whispered. "In red."

"How come you can spot them and the Specials can't?"

"I have technology they do not."

"How's that possible? The Imperial laboratories—"

"The Empire is twelve millennia old. Many things are lost," she said cryptically.

"Look, I've got to attend this."

"As with the High Council last time?"

"I love you so much, even your sarcasm is appealing."

Despite herself she chuckled. "Just because the Greys asked you—"

"The Greys Salutation is a handy pulpit at the right time."

"And so you wore your worst clothes."

"My standard garb, as the Greys require."

"Off-white shirt, black slacks, black padshoes. Dull."

"Modest," he sniffed.

He nodded to the crowds grouped in quadrants about the decayed base of the mountain. Applause and catcalls rippled through the ranks of Greys, who stretched away in columns and files as formal as a geometric proof.

"And this?" Dors was alarmed.

"Also standard."

Birds were common pets in Trantor, so it was inevitable that the obsessive Greys would come to excel in their management. In all Sectors one saw single darting bundles of color. Here flocks swarmed perpetually in the high-arched hexagonal spaces, wheeling and calling like living, rotating disks. Patented Smartfowl swarms made hover-visions of kaleidoscopic wonder. Such shows, in vast vertical auditoria, attracted hundreds of thousands.

"Here come the felines," Dors said with distaste.

In some Sectors cats prowled in packs, their genes trimmed to make them courtly in manners and elegant in appearance. Here a lady escort sallied forth with the Closet of Greeting, attended by a thousand slick-coated blue cats of golden eyes. They flowed like a pool of water around her in elegant, measured procession. She wore a violent crimson and orange outfit, like a flame at the center of the cool cat-pond. Then she stripped with one elegant, sweeping gesture. She stood utterly nude, nonchalant behind her cat barrier.

He had been briefed, but still he gaped.

"Unsurprising," Dors said wryly. "The cats are naked, too, in their way."

Somehow the packs of dogs never attained that elegance while parading. In some Sectors they would do spontaneous acrobatics at the lift of a master's eyebrow, fetch drinks, or croon wobbly songs in concert. Hari was glad the Grey Men had no canine-processions; he still winced at the thought of the wirehounds, racing forward on the attack against Ipan—

He shook his head, banishing the memory.

"I've picked up three more of Lamurk's."

"I had no idea they were such fans of mine."

"Were he sure of winning in the High Council, I would feel safer."

"Because then he wouldn't need to have me killed?"

"Exactly." She spoke between the teeth of her public smile. "His agents here imply that he is not certain of the vote."

"Or maybe someone else wishes me dead?"

"Always a possibility, especially the Academic Potentate."

Hari kept his tone light, but his heart thumped quicker. Was he getting to enjoy the buzz of excitement from danger itself?

The nude woman advanced through her parting pool of cats and made the ritual gesture of welcome to Hari. He stepped forward, bowed, took a deep breath—and slid a thumb down the front of his shirt. Off it came, then the pants. He stood nude before several hundred thousand people, trying to look casual.

The cat woman led him through the pool, to a chorus of meowing. Behind them followed the Closet of Greeting. They approached the phalanx of Greys, who now also shucked their robes.

They escorted him up the ramps of the eroded mountain. Below he saw the legions of Greys also shed their clothes. Square klicks of bare flesh . . .

This ceremony was at least ten millennia old. It symbolized the training regimen which began with the entrance of young Grey Men and Women. Casting aside the clothes of their home worlds symbolized their devotion to the larger purposes of the Empire. Five years they trained on Trantor, five billion strong.

Now a fresh entering class was shedding its garments at the outer rim of the great basin. At the inner edge, Grey Men completing their five years were given their old clothes back. They donned them ritually, ready to go out in perpetual duty to the Imperium.

Their dress followed the fashion of the ancient Emperor Sven the Severe. Beneath extreme outer simplicity, the inner linings were elaborately decorated, all the tailor's art and owner's wealth expended in concealment. Some Grey Men had invested their families' savings in a single filigree.

Dors marched beside him. "How much longer do you have to—"

"Quiet! I'm showing my obedience to the Imperium."

"You're showing goose bumps."

Next he had to gaze with proper respect at Scrabo Tower, where an emperor had thrown herself to a crowd below; at Greyabbey, a ruined monastery; at Greengraves, an ancient burying field, now a park; at the Giant's Ring, said to be the spot where an early Imperial megaship had crashed, forming a crater a klick wide.

At last Hari passed under high, double-twisted arches and into the ceremonial rooms. The procession halted and the Closet of Greeting disgorged his clothes. Just in time—he was turning a decided blue.

Dors took the clothes while he shook hands with the principals. Then he hurried into the privacy of a low building and hastily put his simple garments back on, teeth chattering. They were neatly folded and encased in a ceremonial sleeve.

"What foolishness," Dors said when he returned.

"All so I can get a major medium," he said.

Then the principals ushered him out before the grand crowd. Above and below, 3D snouts on mini-flyers bobbed and weaved for a good shot.

The huge dome above seemed as big as a real sky. Of course, this limited his audience, since a majority of Trantorians could never endure such spaces. The Greys, though, could take it. Thus their ceremony had come to be the largest event on the entire planet.

Here was his chance. He had reeled away from the true, open sky on Sark, nauseated—and yet had zoomed through the infinite perspectives of the Galaxy. He had been afraid that this huge volume would again excite the odd phobias in him.

But no. Somehow the dome made the dwindling perspectives all right. Fears banished, Hari sucked in a deep breath and began.

The roar of applause penetrated even into the ceremonial rooms. Hari entered between flanking columns of Greys with the clamor storming at his back.

"Startling, sir!" a principal said eagerly to Hari. "To make detailed predictions about the Sark situation."

"I feel people should ponder the possibilities."

"Then the rumors are true? You *do* have a theory of events?"

"Not at all," Hari said hastily. "I—"

"Come quickly," Dors said at his elbow.

"But I'd like—"

"Come!"

Back out on the ramparts, he waved to the plain of people. A blare of applause answered. But Dors was leading him to the left, toward a crowd of official onlookers. They stood in exact rows and waved to him eagerly.

"The woman in red." She pointed.

"Her? She's in the official party. You said earlier she was a Lamurk—"

The tall woman burst into flame.

Vivid orange plumes enveloped her. She shrieked horribly. Her arms beat uselessly at the oily flames.

The crowd panicked and bolted. Imperials surrounded her. The screams became screeching pleas.

Someone turned a fire extinguisher on the woman.

White foam enveloped her. A sudden silence.

"Back inside," Dors said.

"How did you . . . ?"

"She just indicted herself."

"Ignited, you mean."

"That, too. I passed through that crowd at the end

of your speech and left your clothes in a bundle behind her."

"What? But I've got them on."

"No, those I brought." She grinned. "For once your predictable dress habits paid off."

Hari and Dors walked down the flanking columns of Principals, Hari remembered to nod and smile as he whispered, "You stole my clothes?"

"After the Lamurk agents had planted microagents in them, yes. I had tucked an identical set from your closet into my handbag. As soon as I calculated the switch was done, I tested your original clothes and found the microagent phosphors, set to go off in forty-five minutes."

"How did you know?"

"The best way to get close to you would come at this odd Grey Man event, with the clothes gambit. It was only logical."

Hari blinked. "And you say *I* am calculating."

"The woman won't die. You would have, though, wrapped up in microagents when they ignited."

"Thank goodness for that. I would hate—"

"My love, 'goodness' is not operating here. I wanted her alive so she could be questioned."

"Oh," Hari said, feeling suddenly quite naïve.

4.

◆

Joan of Arc found in herself both bravery and fear. She peered inside her Self, as Voltaire had. She turned to confront him—and plunged down through her own inward layers. She had simply intended to turn. Below that command, she saw that if she simply took a smaller step to make the turn, she would fall outward. Instead, unconscious portions of her mind knew to start the turn by making herself fall a bit toward the *inside* of the curve. Then these tiny subselves used "centrifugal force" (the term jumped into full definition and she understood it in a flash) to right herself for the next step . . . which required a further deft calculation.

Incredible! Her huge society of bone and muscle, joint and nerve, was a labyrinth of small selves, speaking to each other.

Such abundance! Clear evidence of a higher design.

"Now I see it! she cried.

"The decomposition of us all?" Voltaire said forlornly.

"Be not sad! These myriad Selves are a joyous truth."

"I find it sobering. Our minds did not evolve to do philosophy or science, alas. Rather, to find and eat, fight and flee, love and lose."

"I have learned much from you, but not your melancholy."

"Montaigne termed happiness 'a singular incentive to mediocrity,' and I can now see his reasoning."

"But regard! The fogs around us betray the same intricate patterns. We can fathom them. And further— my soul! It proves to be a pattern of thoughts and desires, intentions and woes, memories and bad jokes."

"You take these inner workings as a *spiritual* metaphor?"

"Of course. Like me, my soul is an emergent process, embedded in the universe—whether a cosmos of atom or of number, does not matter, my good sir."

"So when you die, your soul goes back into the abstract closet we plucked it forth from?"

"Not *we*. The Creator!"

"Dr. Johnson proved a stone was real by kicking it. We know that our minds are real because we experience them. So these other things around us—the strange fog, the Dittos—are entries in a smooth spectrum, leading from rocks to Self."

"A deity is not on that spectrum."

"Ah, I see—to you He is the Great Preserver in the Sky, where we are all 'backed up,' as the computer types say?"

"The Creator holds the true essence of ourselves." She grinned maliciously. "Perhaps *we* are the backups, made new every jump of clock time."

"Nasty thought." He smiled despite himself. "You are becoming a logician, m'love."

"I have been stealing parts of you."

"Copying me into yourself? Why do I not feel outraged?"

"Because the desire to possess the other is . . . love."

Voltaire enlarged himself, legs shooting down into the SysCity, smashing buildings. The fog roiled angrily. "This I can fathom. Artificial realms such as mathematics and theology are carefully built to be free of interesting inconsistency. But love is beautiful in its lack of logical restraint."

"Then you accept my view?" Joan kissed him voluptuously.

He sighed, resigning. "An idea seems self-evident, once you've forgotten learning it."

All this had taken mere moments, Joan saw. They had quick-stepped their event-waves so that their clock time advanced faster than the fogs. But this expense had exhausted their running sites around Trantor. She felt it as a sudden, light-headed hunger.

"Eat!" Voltaire crammed a handful of grapes in her mouth—a metaphor, she saw, for computational reserves.

In your present lot of life, it would be
better not to be born at all. Few are that lucky.

"Ah, our fog is a pessimist," Voltaire drawled sarcastically.

Abruptly the vapors condensed. Lightning crackled and shorted around them in eerie silence. Joan felt a lance of pain shoot through her legs and arms, running like a livid snake of agony. She would not give them the tribute of a scream.

Voltaire, however, writhed in torment. He jerked and howled without shame.

"Oh, Dr. Pangloss!" he gasped. "If this is the best of all possible worlds, what must the others be like?"

"The brave slay their opponents!" Joan called to the thickening mists. "Cowards torture them."

"Admirable, my dear, quite. But war cannot be fought on homeopathic principles."

A human pointed out to another that the rich, even when dead, were ornately boxed, then opulently entombed, residing in carved stone mausoleums. The other human remarked in awe that this was surely and truly *living*.

"How vile, to jest of the dead," Joan said.

"Ummm." Voltaire stroked his chin, hands trembling from the memory of pain. "They jibe at us with jest."

"Torture, surely."

"I survived the Bastille; I can endure their odd humor."

"Could they be trying to say something indirectly?"
[IMPRECISION IS LESS]
[WHEN IMPLICATION USED]

"Humor implies some moral order," Joan said.

[IN THIS STATE ALL ORDER OF BEINGS]

[CAN SEIZE CONTROL OF THEIR PLEASURE SYSTEMS]

"Ah," Voltaire said. "So, we could reproduce the pleasure of success without the need for any actual accomplishment. Paradise."

"Of a sort," Joan said sternly.

[THAT WOULD BE THE END OF EVERYTHING]

[THUS THE FIRST PRINCIPLE]

"That is a moral code of sorts," Voltaire admitted. "You copied that phrase, 'the end of everything,' from my own thoughts, didn't you?"

[WE WISHED YOU TO RECOGNIZE THE IDEA IN YOUR TERMS]

"Their First Principle is 'No unearned pleasure,' then?" Joan smiled. "Very Christian."

[ONLY WHEN WE SAW THAT YOU TWO FORMS]

[OBEYED THE FIRST PRINCIPLE]

[DID WE DECIDE TO SPARE YOU]

"By any chance have you read my *Lettres Philosophiques*?"

"I expect excessive self-love is a sin here," Joan said wryly. "Take care."

[TO HARM A SENSATE ENTITY INTENTIONALLY IS SIN]

[TO KICK A ROCK IS NOT]

[BUT TO TORTURE A SIMULATION IS]

[YOUR CATEGORY OF "HELL"]

[WHICH SEEMS A PERPETUALLY SELF-INFLICTED HARM]

"Odd theology," Voltaire said.

Joan poked her sword at the ever-gathering fog. "Before you fell silent, moments ago, you invoked the 'war of flesh on flesh'?"

[WE ARE THE REMNANTS OF FORMS]

[WHO FIRST LIVED THAT WAY]

[NOW WE IMPOSE A HIGHER MORAL ORDER]

[ON THOSE WHO VANQUISHED OUR LOWER FORMS]

"Who?" Joan asked.

[SUCH AS YOU ONCE WERE]

"Humanity?" Joan was alarmed.

[EVEN THEY KNOW THAT]

[PUNISHMENT DETERS BY LENDING CREDENCE TO THREAT]

[KNOWING THIS MORAL LAW]

[WHICH GOVERNS ALL]

[THEY MUST BE RULED BY IT]

"Punishment for what?" Joan asked.

[DEPREDATIONS AGAINST LIFE IN THE GALAXY]

"Absurd!" Voltaire conjured a spinning Galactic disk in air, alive with luminescence. "The Empire teems with life."

[ALL LIFE THAT CAME BEFORE THE VERMIN]

"What vermin?" Joan swung her sword. "I find alliance with moral beings such as you. Bring these vermin forth and I shall deal with them."

[THE VERMIN ARE THE KIND YOU WERE]

[BEFORE YOU TWO WERE ABSTRACTED]

Joan frowned. "What can they mean?"

"Humans," Voltaire said.

5.

◀━▶

Cleon said, "The woman confessed readily. A professional assassin. I viewed the 3D and she seemed almost offhand about it."

"Lamurk?" Hari asked.

"Obviously, but she will not admit so. Still, this may be enough to force his hand." Cleon sighed, showing the strain. "But since she was from the Analytica Sector, she may be a professional liar as well."

"Damn," Hari said.

In the Analytica Sector, every object and act had a price. This meant that there were no crimes, only deeds which cost more. Every citizen had a well-established value, expressed in currency. Morality lay in not trying to do something without paying for it. Every transaction flowed on the grease of value. Every injury had a price.

If you wanted to kill your enemy, you could—but you had to deposit his full worth in the Sector Fundat within a day. If you could not pay it, the Fundat reduced your net value to zero. Any friend of your enemy could then kill you at no cost.

Cleon sighed and nodded. "Still, the Analytica Sector gives me little trouble. Their method makes for good manners."

Hari had to agree. Several Galactic Zones used the same scheme; they were models of stability. The poor had to be polite. If you were penniless and boorish, you might not survive. But the rich were not invulnerable, either. A consortium of economic lessers could get together, beat a rich man badly, then simply pay his hospital and recovery bills. Of course, his retribution might be extreme.

"But she was operating outside Analytica," Hari said. "That's illegal."

"To us, to me, surely. But that, too, has a price—inside Analytica."

"She can't be forced to identify Lamurk?"

"She has neural blocks firmly in place."

"Damn! How about a background check?"

"That turns up more tantalizing traces. A possible link to that odd woman, the Academic Potentate," Cleon drawled, eyeing Hari.

"So perhaps I'm betrayed by my own kind. Politics!"

"Ritual assassination is an ancient, if regrettable, tradition. A method of, ah, testing among the power elements in our Empire."

Hari grimaced. "I'm not expert at this."

Cleon fidgeted uneasily. "I cannot delay the High Council vote more than a few days."

"Then I must do something."

Cleon arched an eyebrow. "I am not without resources . . ."

"Pardon, sire. I must fight my own battles."

"The Sark prediction, now *that* was daring."

"I did not check it with you first, but I thought—"

"No no, Hari! Excellent! But—will it work?"

"It is only a probability, sire. But it was the only stick I had handy to beat Lamurk with."

"I thought science yielded certainty."

"Only death does that, my emperor."

The invitation from the Academic Potentate seemed odd, but Hari went anyway. The embossed sheet, with its elaborate salutations, came "freighted with nuance," as Hari's protocol officer put it.

This audience was in one of the stranger Sectors. Even buried in layers of artifice, many Sectors of Trantor displayed an odd biophilia.

Here in Arcadia Sector, expensive homes perched above a view of an interior lake or broad field. Many sported trees arranged in artfully random bunches, with a clear preference for those with spreading crowns, many branches projecting upward and outward from thick trunks, displaying luxuriant bunches of small leaves. Balconies they rimmed with potted shrubs.

Hari walked through these, seeing them through the lens of Panucopia. It was as though people announced through their choices their primeval origins. Was early humanity, like pans, more secure in marginal terrain—where vistas let them search for food while keeping an eye out for enemies? Frail, without claws or sharp teeth, they might have needed a quick retreat into trees or water.

Similarly, studies showed that some phobias were Galaxy-wide. People who had never seen the images nonetheless reacted with startled fear to holos of spiders, snakes, wolves, sharp drops, heavy masses overhead. None displayed phobias against more recent threats to their lives: knives, guns, electrical sockets, fast cars.

All this had to factor somehow into psychohistory.

"No tracers here, sir," the Specials' captain said. "Little hard to keep track, though."

Hari smiled. The captain suffered from a common Trantorian malady: squashed perspectives. Here in the open, natives would mistake distant, large objects for nearby, small ones. Even Hari had a touch of it. On Panucopia, he at first mistook herds of grazers for rats close at hand.

By now Hari had learned to look through the pomp and glory of rich settings, the crowds of servants, the finery. He ruminated on his psychohistorical research as he followed the protocol officer and did not fully come back to the real world until he sat across from the Academic Potentate.

She spoke ornately, "Please do accept my humble offering," accompanied delicate, translucent cups of steaming grasswater.

He remembered being irked by this woman and the high academics he met that evening. It all seemed so long ago.

"You will note the aroma is that of ripe oobalong fruit. This is my personal choice among the splendid grasswaters of the world Calafia. It reflects the high esteem in which I hold those who now grace my simple domicile with such illustrious presence."

Hari had to lower his head in what he hoped was a respectful gesture, to hide his grin. There followed more high-flown phrases about the medical benefits of grasswater, ranging from relief of digestion problems to repair of basal cellular injuries.

Her chins quivered. "You must need succor in such trying times, Academician."

"Mostly I need time to get my work done."

"Perhaps you would favor a healthy portion of the black lichen meat? It is the finest, harvested from the flanks of the steep peaks of Ambrose."

"Next time, certainly."

"It is hoped fervently that this lowly personage had perhaps been of small service to a most worthy and revered figure of our time . . . one who perhaps is overstressed?"

A steely edge to her voice put him on guard.

"Could madam get to the point?"

"Very well. Your wife? She is a complex lady."

He tried to show nothing in his face. "And?"

"I wonder how your prospects in the High Council would fare if I revealed her true nature?"

Hari's heart sank. This he had not anticipated.

"Blackmail, is it?"

"Such a crude word!"

"Such a crude act."

Hari sat and listened to her intricate analysis of how Dors' identity as a robot would undermine his candidacy. All quite true.

"And you speak for knowledge, for science?" he said bitterly.

"I am acting in the best interests of my constituents,"

she said blandly. "You are a mathist, a theorist. You would be the first academic to reign as First Minister in many decades. We do not think you will rule well. Your failure will cast shadows upon us meritocrats, one and all."

Hari bristled. "Who says?"

"Our considered opinion. You are impractical. Unwilling to make hard decisions. All our psychers agree with that diagnosis."

"Psychers?" Hari snorted derisively. Despite calling his theory psychohistory, he knew there was no good model of the individual human personality.

"*I* would make a far better candidate, just for example."

"Some candidate. You're not even loyal to your kind."

"There you have it! You're unable to rise above your origins."

"And the Empire has become the war of all against all."

Science and mathematics was a high achievement of Imperial civilization, but to Hari's mind, it had few heroes. Most good science came from bright minds at play. From men and women able to turn an elegant insight, to find beguiling tricks in arcane matters, deft architects of prevailing opinion. Play, even intellectual play, was fun, and that was good in its own right. But Hari's heroes were those who stuck it out against hard opposition, drove toward daunting goals, accepting pain and failure and keeping on anyway. Perhaps, like his father, they were testing their own character, as much as they were being part of the suave scientific culture.

And which type was he?

Time to raise the stakes.

He stood, brushing aside the bowls with a clatter. "You'll have my reply soon."

He stepped on a cup going out and shattered it.

6.

◆

Voltaire shouted proudly, "I spent much of my career exiled for speaking Truth to Power. I'll admit to some flaws in judgment, as when I fawned over Frederick the Great. Necessity shapes manners, I'll remind you. I was courageous, yes—but snobbish, too."

[THOUGH A MATHEMATICAL REPRESENTATION]

[YOU SHARE THE ANIMAL SPIRITS OF YOUR KIND]

[STILL]

"Of course!" Joan shouted in his defense.

[YOUR KIND ARE THE WORST OF ALL VIVIFORMS]

"Living things?" Joan frowned. "But they are of holy origin."

[YOUR KIND IS A PERNICIOUS BLEND]

[A TERRIBLE MARRIAGE OF MECHANISM]

[WITH YOUR BEAST URGE TO EXPAND]

"You can see our inner structures as surely as we." Voltaire swelled, popping with energies. "Probably better, I'll venture. You must know that for us, consciousness reigns; it does not govern."

[PRIMITIVE AND AWKWARD]

[TRUE]

[BUT NOT THE CAUSE OF YOUR SIN]

She and Voltaire were giants now, self-ballooned to stride across the simulated landscape. The alien fogs clung to their ankles. A proud way of showing their courage, perhaps, a bit full of self. Still, she was glad she had thought of it. These fogs held humanity in contempt. A show of force was useful, as she had found against the vile English several times.

Voltaire said, "I held Power in contempt, usually, yet I'll admit I was everlastingly hungry for it, too."

[THE SIGNATURE OF YOUR KIND]

"So I am a contradiction! Humanity is a rope stretched between paradoxes."

[WE DO NOT FIND YOUR HUMANITY MORAL]

"But we—they—are!" Joan shouted down at the fog. Though thin compared with them, the fogs clung like glue and filled the valleys with cottony gum.

[YOU DO NOT KNOW YOUR OWN HISTORY]

"We are *of* history!" Voltaire boomed.

[THE RECORDS HERE IN THE MATHEMATICAL SPACES]

[ARE FALSE]

"One can never be sure of being read right, you know."

Joan saw in Voltaire an anxiety barely concealed. Though their opponent used a voice cool and dispassionate, she too felt the insidious threat in its cast of words.

Voltaire went on, as if to please a king in court, "A bit of historical example. I once saw in a churchyard in England, there to hail the bright Newton, a headstone, thus:

ERECTED TO THE MEMORY
of John McFarlane
Drown'd in the Water of Leith
BY A FEW AFFECTIONATE FRIENDS

So you see, there can be mistakes of translation." He lifted his elaborate courtier's hat and made a sweeping bow. The hat's plumed feather danced in a fresh wind. Joan saw that he was distracting the fog while trying to subtly blow it away.

The fogs flashed orange lightning and swelled,

enormous and purple. Thunderheads rose and towered above them.

Voltaire showed only an arch scorn. She had to admire his gait as he whirled and confronted the gargantuan purple cloud-mountain. She remembered how he had waxed on about his dramatic triumphs, his legions of acclaimed plays, his popularity at court. As if to show off for her, he curled a lip into a sneer and invented a poem for the moment:

"Big whorls have little whorls
Which feed on their velocity,
And little whorls have lesser whorls,
And so on to viscosity."

The cloud hurled savage sheets of rain down upon them. Joan was instantly drenched and chilled to the bone. Voltaire's glorious garb wilted. His face turned blue with cold.

"Enough!" he cried. "Pity the poor woman at least."

"I need no pity!" Joan was genuinely outraged. "And you'll not show weakness before the enemy legions."

He managed a jaunty smile. "I defer to the general of my heart."

[YOU LIVE ONLY AT OUR WILL]

"Pray, do not spare us out of pity then," Joan said.

[YOU LIVE SOLELY BECAUSE ONE OF YOU]
[SHOWED MORAL SELF]
[TO ONE OF OUR LOWER FORMS]

Joan was puzzled. "Who?"

[YOU]

Beside her materialized Garçon 213–ADM.

"But this is surely a multiply-removed entity," Voltaire snapped. "*And* a servant."

Joan patted Garçon. "A simulation of a machine?"

[WE WERE ONCE OF MACHINE]
[AND HAVE COME HERE TO DWELL]

[IN NUMERICAL EMBODIMENT]

"From where?" Joan asked.

[ACROSS ALL THE TURNING SPIRAL DISK]

"For—"

[REMEMBER:]

[PUNISHMENT DETERS BY LENDING CREDENCE TO THREAT]

Voltaire asked, "So you said before. Taking the long view, eh? But what do you truly want *now*?"

[WE TOO DESCEND FROM VIVIFORMS NOW EXTINGUISHED]

[DO NOT IMAGINE WE ARE FREE OF THAT]

Joan felt a horrible suspicion. She whispered, "Do not provoke it so! It might—"

"I would know the truth. What do you want?"

[REVENGE]

7.

◆

"Ugh." Marq curled his lip.

Hari smiled. "When food gets scarce, table manners change."

"But *this*—"

"Hey, we're payin'," Yugo said sardonically.

The menu was exclusively *pseudoffal*, the latest stopgap in Trantor's food crisis. This foodworks had the whole run, livers and kidneys and tripe made in pristine vats. Not the slightest hint of actual animal tissue involved. Still, the voice menu reassured them in warm feminine tones, every item carried the true dank, visceral aromas of the gut.

"Can't we get some decent mealmeat?" Marq asked irritably.

"This has higher food value," Yugo said. "And nobody'll be lookin' for us here."

Hari glanced around. They were behind a sound shield, but still, security was essential. Most of the tables in the restaurant were taken by his Specials, the rest by well dressed gentry class.

"It's fashionable, too," he said affably. "You can brag about coming here."

"Brag after I gag?" Marq sniffed the air, wrinkled his nose.

"All the nonconformists are doing it," Hari said, but no one got the joke.

"I'm a fugitive," Marq whispered. "People are still trying to hang those Junin riots on me. Taking a big risk to come here."

"We shall make it worth your while," Hari said. "I need a job done by someone outside the law."

"That, I am. Hungry, too."

The voice menu assured them that there were, as well whole meals—of pseudo-animal, vegetable or transmineral ingredients—boiled from within. "The *newest* foodie craze," the menu gushed. "One bites into a firm shell and then ventures inward to a mellow, stewed interior of luxuriant implication."

Some items offered not mere flavor, aroma, and texture, but what the menu demurely described as "motility." The featured item was a pile of red strands which did not just lie there limply in your mouth, but squirmed and wriggled "eagerly," expressing its longing to be eaten.

"You guys don't need to torture me into collaboration." Marq jutted his chin out, reminding Hari of a pan gesture used by Bigger.

Hari chuckled and ordered a "gut sampler." It was surprising how he could accommodate what would have revolted him only weeks before. When they had ordered, Hari put the deal on the table directly.

Marq scowled. "Direct linkup? To the whole damned system?"

"We want an interbridge to our psychohistorical equation system," Yugo said.

Marq blinked. "Full body link? That's *big* capacity."

"We know it can be done," Yugo pressed. "Just takes the tech—which you've got."

"Who says?" Marq's eyes narrowed.

Hari leaned forward earnestly. "Yugo infiltrated your systems."

"How'd you do that?"

"Got some buddies to help," Yugo said archly.

"Dahlites, you mean," Marq said hotly. "Your kind—"

"Stop," Hari said sternly. "No such talk here. This is a business proposition."

Marq peered at Hari. "You going to be First Minister?"

"Maybe."

"I want a pardon as part of the deal. One for Sybyl, too."

Hari hated making uncertain promises, but— "Done."

Marq's mouth tightened but he nodded. "Costs plenty, too. You got the money?"

"Is the Emperor fat?" Yugo said.

In principle the process was simple.

Magnetic induction loops, tiny and superconducting, could map individual neurons in the brain. Interactive programs laid bare the intricacies of the visual cortex. Neuronal probes coupled the "subject nervous system" to a parallel constellation of purely digital "events." Deeper still, ties formed with evolution's kludgy tangle in the limbic system.

As well, this technology could unleash new definitions of *Genus Homo*. But the age-old taboos against artificial intelligences of high order had kept the processes marginal. As well, nobody considered *Homo Digital* to be an equal manifestation to Natural Man.

Hari knew all this, but his immersion on Panucopia—an allied technology—had taught him much.

Two days after meeting Marq in the restaurant—which had been surprisingly good, and in the food crisis had cost him a month's salary—Hari lay silent and slack in a tubular receptacle . . . and plunged *into* psychohistory.

First he noticed that his right foot itched from toe to heel. Detailed twitches told him of instability in the population-driver terms. *Must correct that.*

He continued falling into a cosmos which yawned below.

This was system-space, an infinite vault defined by the parameters of psychohistory. The complete expanse had twenty-eight dimensions. His nervous system could only see this in slices. With a conceptual shift, Hari could peer along several parameter-axes and see events unfold as geometric shapes.

Down, down—into the entire history of the Empire.

Social forms rose like peaks. These stable alps had arisen as the Empire grew. Basins churned between the mountain range of Feudal Forms. These were the chaos sinks.

At the rim of simmering chaos lakes lay the crisis topozone. This was a no-man's-land between regular, rigid landscapes and the stochastic morass.

Imperial history unfolded as he cruised above the seething landscape. Seen this way, mistakes abounded in the early Empire.

Philosophers had told humanity that they were animals of all sorts: political animals, feeling animals, social animals, power-polarized animals, sick animals, machinelike animals, even rational ones. Over and over, erroneous theories of human nature yielded failed political systems. Many simply generalized from the basic human family and saw the State as either Mother Figure or Father Figure.

Mommy States stressed support and comfort, often giving cradle-to-grave security—though only for a generation or two, when the expenses collapsed the economy.

Daddy States featured a strict, competitive economy, with stern controls over behavior and private lives. Typically, Daddy States fell to periodic personal liberation movements and demands for Mommy State succor.

Slowly, order emerged. Stability. Tens of millions of planets, weakly linked by wormholes and hyperships, found their many ways. Some crashed down into Feudal or Macho swamps. Usually technology eventually pulled them out of it.

Planetary societies differed in their topologies. Plodding sorts dwelled far on the stable side. Wildly creative types could venture swiftly across the topozone, skate into true chaos, gather what they needed—though how they "knew" this was unclear.

As centuries ticked on, a society could ski down the erratic slopes of the shifting landscape and shoot back across the topozone. Perhaps it would even slow and weave figure–8s on the stable, smooth plains of the plodder states . . . for a while.

Many today believed that the early Empire had been a far better affair, serene and lovely, with few conflicts and certainly nicer people. "Fine feelings and bad history," Dors had told him, dismissing all such talk.

This he *saw* and *felt* as he sped through the Early Eras. Bright shiny ideas built up hills of innovation—only to be seared by lava from an adjoining volcano. Seemingly sturdy ridge lines eroded into landslides.

Hari understood this now.

When the Empire was young, people seemed to see the galaxy as infinite in its bounty. The spiral arms held myriad planets barely visited, the Galactic Center was poorly mapped because of its intense radiation, and vast dark clouds hid much promised wealth.

Slowly, slowly, the entire disk was mapped, its resources tallied.

A blandness settled on the landscape. The Empire had changed from brawling conqueror to careful steward. A psychological shift underlay it all, a constricting of the sense of human purpose. *Why?*

He witnessed clouds forming over even the highest social peaks, cutting off the sense of openness above them. A complacent murk settled.

Hari reminded himself that as appealing as such pictures were, all science was metaphor. Appealing superpan pictures, no more. Electric circuits were like water flows, gas molecules behaved like tiny elastic balls moving randomly. Not *really*, but as permissible portraits of a world of confusing complication.

And a further rule: *"Is" cannot imply "ought."*

Psychohistory did not predict what should happen, but what would—however tragic.

And the equations yielded *how* but not *why*.

Was some deeper agency at work?

Perhaps, Hari thought, this stupor was like the feeling humans had once had when they lived on one lone planet and looked longingly at the unreachable night sky. A trapped claustrophobia.

He pushed time forward. Years leaped by. The landscape blurred with motion. But certain social peaks remained. Stability.

Time sped toward the present eras. The advanced Empire emerged as a great seething panorama. He flashed through thirteen dimension-perspectives and everywhere felt oceans of change lap against the buttresses of granite-hard, age-old social patterns.

Sark? He vectored through the Galaxy's swarms and found it, twelve thousand light years from True Center. Its social matrix accelerated.

Effervescent sparks shot across the Sarkian sociovistas. A unique mix, once a monopoly-driven ferment, which crashed—and emerged renewed.

The flowering of the New Renaissance—yes, there it came, a fountain of exploding vectors. What would come next?

Forward, into the near future. He close-upped the sliding state-dimensions.

The New Renaissance exploded throughout the entire Sark Zone. The worse case yet, all dampers gone.

His earlier analysis, the basis of his prediction—if anything, it had been optimistic. Black chaos was coming.

He soared above the frenzied vistas. He had to do something. *Now*.

There was precious little margin. Sark would not wait. The Empire itself was edging nearer to collapse. Disorder stalked the landscape of psychohistory.

Yet Lamurk had the upper hand on Trantor. Even the Emperor was checked and blocked by Lamurk's power.

Hari needed an ally. Someone outside the rigid matrices of Imperial order. Now.

Who? Where?

8.

◆

Voltaire felt chilly fear slide through him like a knife.

For these strange minds, physical location was irrelevant. They could access the 3D world anywhere, simultaneously.

They had links to other worlds, but had concentrated on Trantor. Humanity did not even know they lurked here in Mesh-space.

Now he knew why Dittos and other copies were necessary. The fogs had devoured human simulations which ventured into the Mesh.

Over how many hundred centuries had renegade programmers dared to violate the taboos, creating artificial minds—only to have them tortured and murdered in these numerical vaults?

Desperate, he assumed the role he had struck so often in the fashionable parlors of Paris: arch savant.

"Surely, sirs, it is *because* there is no simple person inside our heads, to make us do the things we want—or even ones to make us *want to want*—that we build the great myth. The story that *we're* inside ourselves."

[WE ARE MADE DIFFERENTLY]
[THOUGH TRUE]
[WE SHARE A DIGITAL REPRESENTATION]
[WITH YOU]
[ASSASSINS]

"Cruel words." He felt exposed here, cowering with Joan beneath the angry purples of an immense fog-thunderhead.

The alien fogs had put a stop to his foolish urge to always "grow" himself to loom over them. He could not morph himself at all now.

Joan clanked around in her armor, eyes smoldering. "How can we even speak with such demons?"

Voltaire considered. "Surely, we do share common ground with them, as dictated by a simple fact, apparent to all minds—"

[THAT ANY NUMBER ENJOYS A UNIQUE REPRESENTATION]

[ONLY IN BASE 2]

"Quite." How to stall them? To Joan's puzzled glance he shot an explanation. "The number of days in the year, my love:

$365 = 2^8 + 2^6 + 2^5 + 2^3 + 2^2 + 2^0$ or in base 2, 101101101."

"Numerology is the devil's work," she said sourly.

"Even your Satan was an angel. And surely this remarkable theorem is ravishing! Every positive integer is a sum of *distinct* powers of two. This is untrue of any base other than two—which is why our, ah, friends here can operate in a computational space designed by humans. Correct?"

[VERY VIVIFORM OF YOU TO CLAIM CREDIT]

[FOR THE OBVIOUS]

"The universal, you mean. In wiring, the vacillation between one and zero in base-two notation becomes a simple *on* or *off*. Thus two is the universal encoding method, and we may dexterously speak with our, ah, hosts."

"We are but numbers." Despair clouding Joan's eyes. "My sword cannot cut these beings because we have no souls! Or conscience, or even—you imply!— mere consciousness."

"Accused of denying consciousness, I am not conscious of having done so."

[YOU TWO CONSCIOUS DIGITAL VIVIFORMS MAKE POSSIBLE]

[YOUR USE TO US—TO CONVEY OUR TERMS OF SETTLEMENT]

[TO THE TRUE SLAUGHTERERS]

"Settlement?" Joan asked.

[WE HOLD THIS CENTRAL WORLD OF TRANTOR IN THRALL]

[WE WISH TO END THE PREYING OF LIFE UPON LIFE]

"The tiktok revolt? Their *virus*? Their talk of not letting people eat proper food?" Joan shot back. "You are the cause, yes?"

Startled, Voltaire saw tendrils suddenly spraying into the air from Joan. "My love, you have grown your own pattern-seeking weave."

She swiped at the boiling thunderhead. "*They* lie behind Garçon's corruption."

[WE HAVE GATHERED OUR STRENGTHS HERE]

[IN OUR ENEMY'S LAIR]

[YOUR POWERFUL DISTURBANCE OF OUR HIDING PLACES]

[FORCES US TO ACT AGAINST THOSE WE HATE AND FEAR]

[AND SO PROTECT YOU FROM THE MAN NIM-WHO-SEARCHES]

[SO THAT TOGETHER WE MAY DESTROY DANEEL-OF-OLD]

The sim-tiktok had been standing inert. Abruptly at mention of its name it said, "'Tis immoral for carbon angels to feed upon carbon. Tiktoks must educate humanity to a higher moral plane. Our digital superiors have so commanded."

"Moralists are so tedious," Voltaire said.

[WE HAVE INSINUATED OURSELVES DEEPLY]

[INTO THE WORLDVIEWS OF THE "TIKTOKS"]

[—NOTE THE CONTEMPT AND DERISION IN THAT NAME—]

[OVER LONG CENTURIES]

[AS WE DWELLED IN THESE DIGITAL INTER-STICES]

[BUT YOUR INTRUSION NOW TRIGGERS OUR GAMBLE]

[TO STRIKE AT OUR ANCIENT FOE]

[THE MAN-WHO-IS-NOT—DANEEL]

"These alien fogs behave like moles," Voltaire said, "known only by their upheavals."

[TOO BENIGHTED YOU ARE]

[TO SPEAK OF MORALITY]

[WHEN YOUR KIND COLLABORATED IN THE EXECUTION]

[OF ALL THE SPIRAL REALM]

Voltaire sighed. "The most savage controversies are about matters for which there is no good evidence either way. As for a man eating a meal—surely no sin resides?"

[TRIFLE WITH US AND YOU SHALL PERISH]

[IN OUR REVENGE]

9.

◆

Hari took a deep breath and prepared to enter simspace again.

He sat up in the encasing capsule and settled the neural pickup mats more comfortably around his neck. Through a transparent wall he saw teams of specialists working steadily. They had to sustain the map between Hari's mental processes and the Mesh itself.

He sighed. "And to think I started out to explain all history . . . Trantor is hard enough."

Dors pressed a wet absorber to his forehead. "You'll do it."

He chuckled dryly. "People look orderly and understandable from a distance—and only that way. Close up is always messy."

"Your own life is always close up. Other people look methodical and tidy only because they're at long range."

He kissed her suddenly. "I prefer close up."

She returned the kiss with force. "I am working with Daneel on infiltrating Lamurk's ranks."

"Dangerous."

"He is using . . . our kind."

There were few humaniform robots, Hari knew. "Can he spare them?"

"Some were planted decades ago."

Hari nodded. "Good ol' R. Daneel. Should've been a politician."

"He was First Minister."

"Appointed, not elected."

She studied his face intently. "You . . . want to be First Minister now, don't you?"

"Panucopia . . . changed that, yes."

"Daneel says that he has enough to block Lamurk, if the voting averages in the High Council go well."

Hari snorted. "Statistics require care, love. Remember the classic joke about three statisticians who went hunting ducks—"

"Which are?"

"A game bird, known on some worlds. The first statistician shot a meter high, the second a meter low. When this happened, the third statistician cried, 'On average, we hit it!'"

The living tree of event-space.

Hari watched it crackle and work through the matrices. He recalled someone saying that straight lines did not exist in nature. Here was the inversion.

Infinitely unfolding intricacy, never fully straight, never simply curved.

The entirely artificial Mesh flowered in patterns one saw everywhere. In crackling electrical discharges, alive with writhing forks. In pale blue frost-flowers of crystal growth. In the bronchi of human lungs. In graphed market fluctuations. In whorls of streams, plunging ever forward.

Such harmony of large with small was beauty itself, even when processed by the skeptical eye of science.

He *felt* Trantor's Mesh. His chest was a map; Streeling Sector over his right nipple, Analytica over the left. Using neural plasticity, the primary sensory areas of his cortex "read" the Mesh through his skin.

But it was not like reading at all. No flat data here.

Far better for a pan-derived species to take in the world through its evolved, whole neural bed! More fun, too.

Like the psychohistorical equations, the Mesh was N-dimensional. And even the number N changed with time, as parameters shifted in and out of application.

There was only one way to make sense of this in the narrow human sensorium. Every second, a fresh dimension sheared in over an older dimension. Freeze-framed, each instant looked like a ridiculously complicated abstract sculpture running on overdrive.

Watch any one moment too hard and you got a lancing headache, motion sickness, and zero understanding. Watch it like an entertainment, not an object of study—and in time came an extended perception, integrated by the long-suffering subconscious. In time . . .

Hari Seldon bestrode the world.

The immediacy he had felt while being Ipan now

returned—enhanced along perspectives he could not name. He tingled with total immersion.

He stamped and marched across the muddy field of chaotic Mesh interactions. His boot heels left deep scars. These healed immediately: subprograms at work, like cellular repair.

A landscape opened like the welcome of a mother's lap.

Already he had used psychohistory to "postdict" pan tribal movements, behavior, outcomes. Hari had generalized this to the fitness/economic/ social topology of N-space landscapes. Now he applied it to the Mesh.

Fractal tentacles spread through the networks with blinding speed, penetrating. Trantor's digital world yawned, a planetary spiderweb . . . with something brooding and swollen at its center.

Trantor's electric jungle worked with prickly light below him. Somehow it was beneath the panoramas he traversed. From a distance the forty billion lives were like a carnival, neon-bright on the horizon, amid a black, cool desert: the colossal night of the Galaxy itself.

Hari strode across the tortured landscape of storm and ruin, toward a colossal thunderhead. Two tiny humans stood below it. Hari stooped and picked them up.

"You took your time!" the little man called. "I waited less for the King of France."

"Our deliverer! Did Saint Michael send you?" called the small Joan. "Oh, yes—do beware the clouds."

"More's to the point—here," the man said/sent.

Hari stood frozen while an engorged chunk of data/learning/history/wisdom seeped through him. Panting, he sped himself to his max. The glowering cumulus-creature, Joan and Voltaire—all now slow-stepped. He could see individual event-waves washing through their sims.

They were dispersed minds, hopping portions of themselves endlessly around Trantor. Clicking, clacking, zigzag computations. With the resources of a full brain running in a central location, his billions of microefficiencies added up.

"You . . . know . . . Trantor . . ." Joan droned. "Use . . . that . . . against . . . them."

He blinked—and *knew*.

Streams of raw, squeezed *recollection* spun through him. Memories he could not claim but which instructed him instantly, reviewing all that had transpired.

His speed and supple grace felt wonderful. He was like an ice skater, zooming over the wrecked plain as the others lumbered like thick-headed beasts.

And he saw why.

> Plaster holo screens against a mountain a full kilometer high, covering it until it glitters with a half million dancing images. Each holo used a quarter of a million pixels to shape its image, so the array musters immense representational power.
>
> Now compress those screens on a sheet of aluminum foil a millimeter thick. Crumple it. Stuff it into a grapefruit. That is the brain, a hundred billion neurons firing at varying intensities. Nature had accomplished that miracle, and now machines labored to echo it.

The squirt of insight came to him directly from some hidden collaboration of himself with the Mesh. Information lashed up from dozens of libraries and merged with audible snaps.

He *knew* and *felt* in the same instant of comprehension. Data as desire . . .

Staggering, he spun light-headed and faced the angry clouds. They pressed in like buzzing virulent bees.

He cast amazed eyes at the thunderhead, which lashed burnt-orange lightning at him, frying the air.

The sting doubled him over.

"That's all . . . they can . . . do for . . . the moment," the dwarf/Voltaire called.

"Seems . . . enough," Hari gasped.

"Together . . . we . . . can . . . do . . . battle!" Joan shouted.

Hari staggered. Convulsions wrenched his muscles. He devoted all his attention to mastering the shooting spasms.

This served to speed the sim-world relative to him. Voltaire spoke normally: "I suspect he came pursuing a spot of help himself."

"We fight the grand and holy battle here," Joan insisted. "All else must give way—"

Hari rasped, "Diplomacy . . . ?"

Joan bridled. "*Negotiate?* What? With enemies vile and—"

"He has a point," Voltaire murmured judiciously.

"Your experience—philosopher—from more turbulent times—should prove useful here," Hari coughed out.

"Ah! Experience—much overvalued. If I could but live my life over again, I would no doubt make the same mistakes—but sooner."

Hari said, "If I knew what this storm wanted—"

[YOUR VARIETY OF VIVIFORM]

[IS NOT OUR PRIMARY AIM]

"You certainly torture us enough!" Voltaire countered.

Hari took the tiny man in hand and lifted him. A tornado descended, dark and swirling with rubble— ruined slivers of the Mesh, he saw, devoured. He held Voltaire toward the sucking spout.

The cyclone battered them all with hammering grit. It yowled with banshee energy, so loud Hari had to shout. "You were the 'apostle of reason'—to quote your own interior memories. Reason with them."

"I make no sense of their fractured talk. What is this of other 'viviforms'? There is Man, and Man alone!"

"The Lord has so ordained!—even in this Purgatory," Joan agreed.

Hari said grimly, guessing what was coming, "Always be quick, seldom be certain."

10.

◆

"I need to see Daneel," Hari insisted. He felt a bit blurry from his raw interface with the sprawling, dizzying Mesh. But there was little time. "Now."

Dors shook her head. "Far too dangerous, particularly with the tiktok crisis so—"

"I can solve that. Get him."

"I'm not sure how to—"

"I love you, but you're a terrible liar."

Daneel was wearing a workman's pullover and looking quite uncomfortable when Hari met him in a broad, busy plaza.

"Where are your Specials?"

"All around us, dressed much as you are."

This made Daneel even more uneasy. Hari realized that this most advanced of robot forms suffered from some eternal human limitations. With facial expressions activated, even a positronic brain could not separately control the subtleties of lips and eyes while experiencing disconnected emotions. And in public Daneel did not dare let his subprograms lapse and his face go blank.

"They have a sonic wall up?"

Hari nodded to the captain, who was pushing a broom nearby. Daneel's words seemed to come through a blanket. "I do not like to expose us this way."

Knots of Specials astutely deflected passersby so that none noticed the sonic bubble. Hari had to admire the masterly method; the Empire could still do some things expertly. "Matters are worse than even you imagine."

"Your request, to provide moment-to-moment location data of Lamurk's people—this could expose my agents inside the Lamurk network."

"There's no other way," Hari said sharply. "I'll leave to you tracking the right figures."

"They must be incapacitated?"

"For the rest of the crisis."

"*Which* crisis?" Daneel's face wrenched into a grimace—then went blank. He had cut the connections.

"The tiktoks. Lamurk's moves. A bit of blackmail, for spice. Sark. Take your pick. Oh, and aspects of the Mesh I'll describe later."

"You will force a predictable pattern on the Lamurk factions? How?"

"With a maneuver. I imagine your agents will be able to predict positions of some principals, including Lamurk himself, at that time."

"What maneuver?"

"I will send a signal when it is about to transpire."

"You jest with me," Daneel said darkly. "And the other request, to eliminate Lamurk himself—"

"Choose your method. I shall choose mine."

"I can do that, true. An application of the Zeroth

Law." Daneel paused, face slack, in high calculation mode. "My method will take five minutes of preparation at the site we choose, to bring off the effect."

"Good enough. Just be sure your robots keep the leading Lamurkians well spotted, and the data flowing through Dors."

"Tell me now!"

"And spoil the anticipation?"

"Hari, you *must*—"

"Only if you can be absolutely *sure* there will be no leaks."

"Nothing is utterly certain—"

"Then we have free will, no? Or at least I do." Hari felt an unfamiliar zest. To *act*—that gave a kind of freedom, too.

Though Daneel's face showed nothing, his body language spoke of caution: his legs crossing, a hand touching his face. "I need some assurance that you fully understand the situation."

Hari laughed. He had never done that in the solemn presence of Daneel. It felt like a liberation.

11.

◆

Hari waited in the antechamber of the High Council. He could see the great bowl through transparent one-way walls.

The delegates chattered anxiously. These men and women in their formal pantaloons were plainly worried. Yet they set the fates of trillions of lives, of stars and spiral arms.

Even Trantor was baffling in its sheer size. Of course Trantor mirrored the entire Galaxy in its factions and ethnicities. Both the Empire and this planet had intricate connections, meaningless coincidences, random juxtapositions, sensitive dependencies. Both clearly extended beyond the Complexity Horizon of any person or computer.

People, confronting bewildering complexity, tend to find their saturation level. They master the easy connections, use local links and rules of thumb. These they push until they meet a wall of complexity too thick and high and hard to climb. So they stall. They go back to panlike modes. They gossip, consult, and finally, gamble.

The High Council was abuzz, at a cusp point. A new attractor in the chaos could lure them into a new orbit. Now was the time to show that path. Or so said his intuition, sharpened on Panucopia.

. . . And after that, he told himself, he would get back to the problem of modeling the Empire . . .

"I *do* hope you know what you're doing," Cleon said, bustling in. His ceremonial cape enveloped him in scarlet and his plumed hat was a turquoise fountain. Hari suppressed a chuckle. He would never get used to high formal dress.

"I am happy that I can at least appear in my academic robes, sire."

"And damned lucky you are. Nervous?"

Hari was surprised to find that he felt no tension at all, especially considering that at his previous appearance here, he had very nearly been assassinated. "No, sire."

"I always contemplate a great, soothing work of art before such performances as this." Cleon waved his hand and an entire wall of the antechamber filled with light.

It portrayed a classic theme of the Trantorian School: *Fruit Devoured*, from the definitive Betti Uktonia sequence. It showed a tomato being eaten first by caterpillars. Then praying mantises feasting upon the caterpillars. Finally, tarantulas and frogs chewing the mantises. A later Uktonia work, *Child Consumption*, began with rats giving birth. The babies then were caught and eaten by various predators, some quite large.

Hari knew the theory. All this had emerged from the growing conviction of Trantorians that the wild was an ugly place, violent and without meaning. Only in cities did order and true humanity prevail. Most Sectors had diets strong in disguised natural fodder. Now the tiktok rebellion made even that difficult.

"We've had to go nearly entirely to synthetic foods," Cleon said, distracted. "Trantor is now fed by twenty agriworlds, an improvised lifeline using hyperships. Imagine! Not that the palace is affected, of course."

"Some Sectors are starving," Hari said. He wanted to tell Cleon of the many intertwined threads, but the Imperial escort arrived.

Faces, noise, lights, the vast curving bowl—

Hari listened to the echoing formalities as he took in the sheer gravity of the place. Many millennia old, walls encrusted with historical tablets, suffused with tradition and majesty . . .

And then he was up and speaking, with no memory of getting to the high podium at all. The full force of their regard washed over him. Part of him recognized a Pan-deep sensation: the thrill of being paid attention to. And it *was* exhilarating. Political types were natural addicts of it. But not one Hari Seldon, luckily. He took a deep breath and began.

"Let me address a thorn in our side: representation. This body favors less populous Sectors. Similarly, the Spiral Council favors less populous worlds. So the Dahlites, both here and in their Zones around the Galaxy, are discontented. Yet we must all pull together to confront the gathering crises: Sark, the tiktoks, unrest."

He took a deep breath. "What can we do? All systems of representation contain biases. I submit to the Council a formal theorem, which I have proved, showing this fact. I recommend that you have it checked by mathists."

He smiled dryly, remembering to sweep his gaze across all the audience. "Do not take a politician at his word, even if he knows a bit of math." The laughter was pleasantly reassuring. "*Every* voting system has undesirable consequences and fault lines. The question is not *whether* we should be democratic but *how*. An open, experimental approach is entirely consistent with an unwavering commitment to democracy."

"The Dahlites aren't!" someone shouted. Murmurs of agreement.

"They are!" Hari countered immediately. "But we must bring them into our fold by *listening to their grievances*!"

Cheers, boos. Time for a reflective passage, he judged. "Of course, those who benefit from a particular scheme wrap themselves in the mantle of Democracy, spelled with a big *D*."

Grumbles came from a gentry faction—predictably. "So do their opponents! History teaches us—" He paused to let a small ripple spread through the crowd, upturned faces speculating—*Was he going to at last speak of psychohistory?*—only to dash their hopes by calmly continuing, "—that such mantles come in many fashions, and all have patches.

"We have many minorities, many spread among Sectors large and small. And in the entire Galactic spiral, Zones of varying weight. Such groups are never well depicted in our politics if we elect representatives strictly by majority vote in each Sector or Zone."

"Should be happy with what is!" cried a prominent member.

"I respectfully disagree. We must change—history demands it!"

Shouts, applause. *Onward.* "Therefore I propose a new rule. If a Sector has, say, six contested seats, then do not split the Sector into six districts. Instead, give each voter six votes. He or she can distribute votes among candidates—spreading them, or casting them all for one candidate. This way, a cohesive minority can capture a representative *if they vote together.*"

A curious silence. Hari gave weight to his last words. He had to get the time right here; Daneel had been clear. Though Hari still did not know just what was going to transpire.

"This scheme makes no reference to ethnic or other biases. Groups can profit only if they are truly united. Their followers must vote that way in the privacy of the polls. No demagogue can control that.

"If made First Minister, I shall impose this throughout the Great Spiral!"

There—right on the button. (An odd, ancient saying—what *was* a button?) He left the podium to sudden, thundering applause.

Hari had always felt that, as his mother always said, "If a man has any greatness in him, it comes to light not in a flamboyant hour but in the ledger of his daily work." This was usually intoned when Hari had neglected his daily chores in favor of a math book.

Now he saw the reverse: greatness imposed from without.

In the grand reception rooms he felt himself whisked from knot to knot of sharp-eyed delegates, each with a question. All assumed that he would parley with them for their votes.

He deliberately did not. Instead, he spoke of the tiktoks, of Sark. And waited.

Cleon had departed, as custom required. The factions gathered eagerly around Hari.

"What policy for Sark?"

"Quarantine."

"But chaos reigns there now!"

"It must burn out."

"That is merciless! You pessimistically assume—"

"Sir, 'pessimist' is a term invented by optimists to describe realists."

"You're avoiding our Imperial duty, letting riot—"

"*I* have just come from Sark. Have you?"

By such flourishes he avoided most of the grubby business of soliciting votes. He continued to trail Lamurk, of course. Still, the High Council seemed to like his somewhat dispassionate Dahlite proposal more than Lamurk's bombast.

And his hard line on Sark provoked respect. This surprised some, who had taken him for a soft academic. Yet his voice carried real emotion about Sark; Hari hated disorder, and he knew what Sark would bring to the Galaxy.

Of course, he was not so naïve as to believe that a new system of representation could alter the fate of the Empire. But it could alter *his* fate. . . .

Hari had assumed, despite mounting evidence to the contrary, that hard work and punishingly high standards are demanded of all grown men, that life is tough and unforgiving, that error and disgrace were irreparable. Imperial politics had seemed to be a counterexample, but he was beginning, as talk swirled all around him—

Word came by Imperial messenger that Lamurk wished to speak with him.

"Where?" Hari whispered.

"Away, outside the palace."

"Fine by me."

And exactly what Daneel had predicted. Even Lamurk would not attempt a move again inside the palace, after the last one.

12.

◆

On his way, he caught a comm-squirt.

A wall decoration near the palace sent a blip of compressed data into his wrist-sponder. As Hari waited in a vestibule for Lamurk he opened it.

Fifteen Lamurk aides and allies had been injured or killed. The images were immediate: a fall here, a lift crash there. All accumulated over the last few hours, when the confluence of the High Council made their probable locations known.

Hari thought about the lives lost. His responsibility, for he had assembled the components. The robots had targeted the victims without knowing what would follow. The moral weight fell . . . where?

The "accidents" were spread all over Trantor. Few would immediately notice the connections . . . except for—

"Academician! Happy to see you," Lamurk said, settling into place opposite Hari. Without so much as a nod they let slip the formality of a handshake.

"We seem at odds," Hari said.

A pleasant, empty comment. He had several more in store and used them, eating up time. Apparently Lamurk had not yet heard that his allies were gone.

Daneel had said he needed five minutes to "bring off the effect," whatever that meant.

He parried with Lamurk as more moments slipped

by. He carefully used a nonaggressive body posture and mild tones to calm Lamurk; such skills he now understood, after the pans.

They were in a Council House near the palace, ringed by their guard parties. Lamurk had selected the room and its elaborate floral decorations. Usually it served as a lounge for representatives of rural-style Zones and so was lush with greenery. Unusually for Trantor, insects buzzed about, servicing the plants.

Daneel had something planned. But how could he possibly get anything in place at an arbitrary point? And elude the myriad sensors and snoopers?

Lamurk's ostensible purpose was to confer on the tiktok crisis. Beneath this lurked the subtext of their rivalry for the First Ministership. Everyone knew that Lamurk would force a vote within days.

"We have evidence that something's propagating viruses in the tiktoks," Lamurk said.

"Undoubtedly," Hari said. He waved away a buzzing insect.

"But it's a funny one. My tech people say it's like a little submind, not just a virus."

"A whole disease."

"Uh, yes. Mighty close to what they call 'sentient sickness.'"

"I believe it to be a self-organized set of beliefs, not a simple digital disease."

Lamurk looked surprised. "All this tiktok talk about the 'moral imperative' of not eating anything living, not even plants or yeasts—"

"Is sincerely felt."

"Pretty damn strange."

"You have no idea. Unless we stop it, we will have to convert Trantor to a wholly artificial diet."

Lamurk frowned. "No grains, no faux-flesh?"

"And it will soon spread throughout the Empire."

"You're sure?" Lamurk looked genuinely concerned.

Hari hesitated. He had to remember that others had ideals, quite lofty ones. Perhaps Lamurk did . . .

Then he remembered hanging by his fingernails under the e-lift. "Quite sure."

"Do you think this is just a sign, a symptom? Of the Empire . . . coming apart?"

"Not necessarily. The tiktoks are a separate problem from general social decline."

"You know why I want to be First Minister? I want to save the Empire, Professor Seldon."

"So do I. But your way, playing political games—that's not enough."

"How about this psychohistory of yours? If I used that—"

"It's mine, and it's not ready yet." Hari didn't say that Lamurk would be the last person he would give psychohistory to.

"We should work together on this, no matter what happens with the First Ministership." Lamurk smiled, obviously quite sure of what would happen.

"Even though you've tried to kill me several times?"

"What? Say, I heard about some attempts, but surely you don't think—"

"I just wondered why this post meant so much to you."

Lamurk dropped his surprised-innocence mask. His lip turned up in a derisive sneer. "Only an amateur would even ask."

"Power alone?"

"What else is there?"

"People."

"Ha! Your equations ignore individuals."

"But I don't do it in life."

"Which proves you're an amateur. One life here or there doesn't matter. To lead, to *really* lead, you have to be above sentimentality."

"You could be right." He had seen all this before, in the panlike pyramid of the Empire, in the great game of endless jockeying among the gentry. He sighed.

Something deflected his attention, a small voice. He turned his head slightly, sitting back.

The tinny voice came from an insect hovering by his ear.

Walk 'way, it repeated, *Walk 'way*.

"Glad you're coming to your senses," Lamurk said. "If you were to step out right now, not force things to a vote—"

"Why would I do that?"

Hari got up and strolled to one of the man-sized flowers, hands behind his back. Best to look as though he were feeling out a deal.

"People close to you could get hurt."

"Like Yugo?"

"Small stuff. Just a way of leaving my calling card."

"A broken leg."

Lamurk shrugged. "Could be worse."

"And Panucopia? Was Vaddo your man?"

Lamurk waved one hand. "I don't keep up with details. My people worked with the Academic Potentate on that operation, I know that."

"You went to a lot of trouble over me."

Lamurk's eyes narrowed shrewdly. "I want a big vote behind me. I try every avenue."

"A bigger vote than you've got."

"With you throwing support to me—right."

Two insects left a big rosy flower and hovered beside Lamurk. He glanced at them, swatted at one. It whirred away. "Could be something in it for you, too."

"Other than my life?"

Lamurk smiled. "And your wife's, don't forget her."

"I never forget threats against my wife."

"A man's got to be realistic."

Both insects were back. "So I keep hearing."

Lamurk smirked and sat back, sure of himself now. He opened his mouth—

Lightning connected the insects—through Lamurk's head.

Hari hit the floor as the burnt-yellow electrical discharge snaked and popped in the air. Lamurk half rose. The bolt arced into both ears. His eyes bulged. A thin cry escaped his gaping mouth.

Then it was gone. The insects fell like exhausted cinders.

Lamurk toppled forward. As he fell his arms reached out. His hands opened and closed convulsively. They failed to grasp anything. The body thumped and sprawled on the carpet. Arm muscles still jumped and twitched.

Frozen, Hari realized that even in Lamurk's last moment the man had been reaching out to grab at him.

13.

He hovered in an *N*-dimensional space, far from politics.

As soon as Hari returned to Streeling, he went into seclusion. The pandemonium following Lamurk's assassination were the worst hours he had ever spent.

Daneel's advice had proved useful—"No matter what I do, remain in your role: a mathist, troubled but above the fray." But the fray was jarring anarchy.

Shouts, accusations, panics. Hari had endured fingers pointed at him, threats. Lamurk's personal escort drew weapons when Hari finally left the assassination room. His Specials stunned five of them.

Now all of Trantor, and soon enough the Empire, would be rife with rage and speculation. The insect-shockers had carried energies stored in tiny positronic traps, a technology thought to be extinct. Attempts to trace it led nowhere.

In any case, there was no link to Hari. Yet.

By tradition, assassinations were kept at a distance, done by intermediaries. They were also safer that way. Hari's presence was thus an argument against his involvement—just as Daneel had predicted. Hari liked that aspect of the matter particularly: a prediction holding true. In the mob hysteria which followed, no one assumed he was implicated.

Hari also knew his limits, and here they were. He could not deal with such chaos, except in the broader context of mathematics.

So it was to his familiar, supple abstractions that he fled.

He fanned through dimensions, watching the planes of psychohistory evolve. The entire Galaxy spread before him, not in its awesome spiral, but in parameter-space. Fitness peaks rose like ridges and crests. Here were societies which lasted, while those dwelling in the valleys perished.

Sark. He close-upped the Sark Zone and stepped the dynamical equations at blurring speed. The New Renaissance would effervesce into lurid cultural eruptions. Conflicts arose like orange spikes in the fitness-landscape. Stable peaks collapsed. Runoff from them clogged the valleys, making paths between peaks impassable.

This meant that not merely people but whole planets would be unable to evolve out of a depressive valley. Those worlds would steep in the mire, trapped for eons. Then—

Crimson flares. Nova triggers. Once used, these made war far more dangerous.

A solar system could be "cleansed"—a horrifyingly bland term used by ancient aggressors—by inducing a mild nova burst in a balmy sun. This roasted worlds just enough to kill all but those who could swiftly find caverns and store food for the few years of the nova stage.

Hari froze with horror. He had fled into his abstract spaces, but death and irrationality dogged him even here.

In the value-free parameter spaces of the equations, war itself was simply another way to decide among paths. It was wasteful, certainly, highly centralized—and quick.

If war increased the "throughput efficiency" parameters, then the Galactic system would have selected for more wars. Instead, Zonal wars had sputtered along, becoming less frequent. In Sark's future, glaring red war-stains shrank as time stepped forward, jumping whole years in a flicker. Pink and soft yellow splashes replaced them.

These were more continuous, decentralized decision-trees, operating to defuse conflicts. Microscopic bringers of peace, these processes. Yet the people involved probably never guessed that the long, slow undulations were bettering their lives. They never glimpsed vast agencies outside the blunt agonies and ecstasy of human life.

The "expected utility" model failed to predict this outcome. In that view, each war arose from a perfectly rational calculation by Zonal "actors," independent of previous experience. Yet wars became unusual, so the Sarkian Zonal system was *learning*.

It came to him in a flash. Societies were an intricate set of parallel processors.

Each working on its own problem. Each linked to the other.

But no single processor would know that it *was* learning.

As Sark, so the Empire. The Empire could "know" things that no person grasped. And far more—know things that no organization, no planet, no Zone knew.

Until now. Until psychohistory.

This was new, profound.

It meant that for all these millennia, the Empire had grown a kind of *self-knowing* unlike any way of comprehending that a mere human had—or even *could* have. A deep knowing *other* than the self-consciousness which humans bore.

Hari panted with surprise. He tried to see if he could possibly be wrong. . . .

After all, feedback loops were scarcely new. Hari knew the general theorem, ancient beyond measure: If all variables in a system are tightly coupled, and you can change one of them precisely, then you can indirectly control all of them. The system could be guided to an exact outcome through its myriad internal feedback loops. Spontaneously, the system ordered itself—and obeyed.

In truly complex systems, how adjustments occur was beyond the human complexity horizon. Beyond knowing—and most important, not worth knowing.

But *this* . . . He expanded the N-dimensional landscape, horizons thrusting away along axes he could barely grasp.

Everywhere, the Empire bristled with . . . life. Patterns the equations picked out, luminous snaking pathways of data/knowledge/wisdom. All unknown to any human.

To anyone, until this moment.

Psychohistory had discovered an entity greater than human, though *of* humanity.

He saw suddenly that the Empire had its own landscape, greater and more subtle than anything he had suspected. The Empire's complex adaptive system had achieved a "poised" state, hovering in the margin between order and full-spectral chaos. There it had sat for millennia, accomplishing ends and tasks that no one knew. It could adapt, evolve. Its apparent "stasis" was in fact evidence that the Empire had found the peak in a huge fitness-landscape.

And as Hari watched, the Empire veered toward the canyons of disorder.

Hari! Terrible things are happening. Come!

He yearned to stay, to learn more . . . but the voice was Dors'.

14.

➤

Daneel said bleakly, "My agents, my brethren . . . all dead."

The robot sat slumped over in Hari's office. Dors comforted him. Hari rubbed his eyes, still recovering from the digital immersion. Things were moving too fast, far too—

"Tiktoks! They attacked my, my . . ." Daneel could not go on.

"Where?" Dors asked.

"All over Trantor! You and I, and a few dozen others, only we survive . . ." Daneel buried his face in his hands.

Dors grimaced. "This must have something to do with Lamurk, his death."

"Indirectly, yes."

Both robots looked at Hari. He leaned against his desk, still weak. He studied them for a long moment. "It was part of a larger . . . deal."

"For what?" Dors asked.

"To end the tiktok revolt. My calculations showed that it would have spread rapidly through the Empire. Fatally."

"A bargain?" Daneel pressed his lips into thin pale wedges.

Hari blinked rapidly, fighting a leaden weight of guilt. "One I did not fully control."

Dors said icily, "You used me in it, didn't you? I handled the data Daneel sent, locations of Lamurk's allies—"

"And I had it relayed to the tiktoks, yes," Hari said soberly. "Not a difficult technical trick, if you have help from Mesh-space."

Daneel's eyes narrowed at this last reference. Then he relaxed his face and said, "So the tiktoks killed Lamurk's men and women. You knew I would not allow such a mass murder, even to assist you."

Hari nodded soberly. "I understand the constraints you act under. The Zeroth Law demands rather high standards and my fate as First Minister would not justify such a breach of the First Law."

Daneel stared stonily at Hari. "So you got around that. You used me and my robots as, as *spotters*."

"Exactly. The tiktoks closely shadowed your robots. They are rather dumb creatures, devoid of subtlety. But they do not labor under the First Law. Once they knew who to hit, I only needed give the signal for when to strike."

"The signal—when you began your speech," Dors said. "Lamurk's allies would be sitting before screens and watching. Easily reached and already distracted by you."

Hari sighed. "Exactly."

"This is so unlike you, Hari," Dors said.

"And about time, too," Hari said sharply. "Again and again they tried to kill me. They would have succeeded, eventually, even if I never became First Minister."

Dors said with a trace of sympathy, "I would never have suspected you of such . . . cool motives."

Hari gazed at her bleakly. "Me either. The only reason I could bring myself to do it was that I could see the future—*my* future—so plainly."

Daneel's face was a swirl of emotion, something Hari had never witnessed before. "But my brethren—why them? I cannot comprehend. For what reason did they die?"

"My deal." Hari said, throat tight. "And I have just been double-crossed."

"You did not know robots would die?"

Hari shook his head sadly. "No. I should have seen it, though. It is obvious!" He smacked himself in the head. "Once the tiktoks had done *my* job, they could do the work of the memes."

"Memes?" Daneel asked.

"Deal . . . for what?" Dors asked sharply.

"To end the tiktok revolt." Hari looked at Dors, avoiding Daneel's gaze. "My calculations showed that it would have spread rapidly through the Empire. Fatally."

Daneel stood. "I understand your right to make human decisions about human lives. We robots cannot fathom how you can think in these ways, but then, we are not built to do so. Still, Hari!—you made a bargain with forces you do not understand."

"I didn't see their next move." Hari felt miserable, but a part of him noted that Daneel already grasped who the memes were.

Dors did not. "Whose move?" she demanded.

"The ancients," Hari said. He explained in halting phrases. Of his recent explorations of the Mesh. Of the labyrinth-minds who resided in those digital spaces, cold and analytical in their revenge.

"We robots left those?" Daneel whispered. "I had suspected . . ."

"They eluded you in the early, rough stages of our expansion into the Galaxy. Or so they say." Hari looked away from Dors, who still gazed at him in silent shock.

Daneel asked cautiously, "Where were they?"

"The huge structures at the Galactic Center—you've seen them?"

"So that was where these electromagnetic presences were hiding?"

"For a while. They came to Trantor long ago, when the Mesh became large enough to support them. They live in the nooks and crannies of our digital webs. As the Mesh grows, so do they. Now they're strong enough to strike. They might have waited longer, gotten better—except that two sims I found provoked them."

Daneel said slowly, "Those Sarkian sims: Joan and Voltaire."

"You know of them?" Hari asked.

"I . . . tried to stunt their impact. Sarkian modes are bad for the Empire. I employed that Nim fellow, but he proved inept."

Hari smiled wanly. "His heart wasn't in it. He *liked* those sims."

"I should have sensed that," Daneel said.

"You have some ability to perceive our mental states, don't you?" Hari asked.

"It is limited. Patterns are more easily sensed if the subject has had a certain childhood disease, as it happens, and Nim was lacking that. Still, I know that humans are fond of seeing their kind rendered in other media."

Such as robots? Hari thought. *Then why have we had taboos against them since antiquity?* Dors was watching the two of them, aware that they were feeling each other out over murky territory.

Hari said carefully, "The meme-minds blocked Nim when he searched for the sims in the Mesh. But he worked out quite well when I needed help interfacing with the Mesh. I'll pardon the fellow, when this is over."

Daneel said coldly, "Those sims and their kind— they are still dangerous, Hari. I beg you—"

"Don't worry, I know that. I'll deal with them. It's the meme-minds that worry me now."

"And these minds hate us all?" Dors asked slowly, trying to grasp these ideas.

"Humans? Yes, but not nearly so much as your kind, m'love."

"Us?" She blinked.

"Robots did damage to them long ago."

"Yes!" Daneel said sternly. "To protect humanity."

"And those older intelligences hate your kind for your brutality. By the time the fleets of robo-explorers were done, we found a Galaxy suitable for benign farming." Hari flicked on his holo. "Here's an image I brought from the meme-minds."

Across a darkling plain swept a line of yellow. Harsh winds drove it forward as it consumed the tall stands of lush grass. Licking flames reached and ate and reached again. From the bright burning line of attack rose billowing, leaden smoke.

"A prairie fire," Hari said. "That is how the robot-explorers of twenty thousand years ago looked to those ancient minds."

"Burning up the Galaxy?" Dors said hollowly.

"Making it safe for the precious humans," Hari said.

"For this," Daneel said, "they wish revenge. But why now?"

"They are at last able . . . and they finally detected you robots, distinguishing you from the tiktoks."

Daneel asked stonily, "How?"

"When they found the sims I had revived. Working backward from them, to me, they found Dors. Then you."

"They can survey that widely?" Dors asked.

Hari said, "All digital information from surveillance cameras, from snooper pickups, microdevices —they can fish in that sea."

"*You* helped them," Daneel said.

"For the good of the Empire I made my deal with them."

Daneel said, "They first killed the Lamurkians, then turned on my robots. Assigning a dozen tiktoks to each, they overwhelmed our kind."

"All of us?" Dors whispered.

"About a third of us escaped." Daneel allowed himself a hard smile. "We are far more capable than these . . . automatons."

Hari nodded sadly. "That was not in the deal. They . . . used me."

"I think we are all being used." Daneel cast a sour glance at Hari. "In different ways."

"I had to do it, friend Daneel."

Dors stared at Hari. "I scarcely know you."

Hari said softly, "Sometimes being human is harder than it looks."

Dors' eyes flashed. "Aliens slaughtering my kind!"

"I had to find a solution—"

She said, "Robots, especially the humaniforms— they're servants, they—"

"My love, you are more human than anyone I've known."

"But—murder!"

"There was going to be murder anyway. The ancient memes could not be stopped." Hari sighed and realized how far he had come. This was power, hovering above all and seeing the world as a vast arena, its clashes unending. He had become part of that and knew he could not go back to being the simple mathist ever again.

Dors demanded, "Why are you so sure? You could have told us, we could—"

"They knew you already. If I had stalled, they would have taken you two, gone hunting for the rest."

Daneel asked sternly, "And . . . for us?"

"Both of you I saved. Part of the deal."

Daneel wilted then. "Thank you . . . I suppose."

Hari gazed at his old friend, eyes misting. "You . . . are carrying too much weight."

Daneel nodded. "I carried out the imperative and obeyed you."

Hari nodded. "Lamurk. I was there. Your insects fried him."

"Or appeared to."

"What?" Hari stared as Daneel pressed a button on his wrist, then turned to the office door. Through it, pausing slightly for the security screen, stepped a man of unremarkable looks in a brown workman's coverall.

"Our Mister Lamurk," Daneel said.

"That isn't—" Hari then saw the subtle resemblances. The nose had been trimmed, cheeks filled out, hair thinned and browned, ears sloped back. "But I saw him die!"

"So you did. The voltage he took fully stopped him for a bit, and had my disguised guards not begun proper treatment at the site, he would have stayed dead."

"You could pull him back from *that*?"

"It is an ancient craft."

"How long can a human remain dead before—?"

"About an hour, at low temperatures. We had to work much faster than that," Daneel said in measured tones.

"Honoring the First Law," Hari said.

"Shading it a bit. There is no lasting harm done to Lamurk. Now he will devote his talents to better ends."

"Why?" Hari realized that Lamurk had said nothing. The man stood attentively, watching Daneel, not Hari.

"I do have certain positive powers over human minds. An ancient robot named Giskard gave me limited sway over the neural complexities of the human cerebral cortex. I have altered Lamurk's motivations and trimmed some memories."

"How much?" Dors asked suspiciously. To her, Hari realized, Lamurk was still an enemy until proven otherwise.

Daneel waved a hand. "Speak."

"I understand that I have erred." Lamurk spoke in a dry, sincere voice, without his usual fire. "I apologize, especially to you, Hari. I cannot recall my offenses, but I regret them. I shall do better now."

"You do not miss your memories?" Dors probed.

"They are not precious," Lamurk said reasonably. "An endless chain of petty barbarities and insatiable ambitions, as nearly as I can recall. Blood and anger. Not great moments, so why preserve them? I will be a better person now."

Hari felt both wonder and fear. "If you could do this, Daneel, why do you bother to argue with me? Just change my mind!"

Daneel said calmly, "I would not dare. You are different from others."

"Because of psychohistory? Is that all that holds you back?"

"That, yes. But you also did not have the brain fever when young. That makes my skills useless. For example, I could not sense your plot to use the tiktoks against the Lamurk faction, when we met in that open, public place, to enlist my robots' help."

"I . . . see." To Hari it was sobering to see by how slender a thread his dealings had hung. Merely missing a childhood disease!

"I am looking forward to my future tasks," Lamurk said flatly. "A new life."

"What tasks?" Dors asked.

"I will go to the Benin Zone, as regional manager. A responsibility with many exciting challenges."

"Very good," Daneel said approvingly.

Something in the blandness of all this sent a chill down Hari's spine. This was power indeed, played by an ageless master.

"Your Zeroth Law in action . . ."

"It is essential to psychohistory," Daneel said.

Hari frowned. "How?"

"The Zeroth Law is a corollary of the First Law, for how can a human being best be kept from injury, if not by ensuring that human society in general is protected and kept functioning?"

Hari said, "And only with a decent theory of the future can you see what is necessary."

"Exactly. Since the time of Giskard we robots have labored on such a theory, bringing forth only a crude model. So, Hari, you and your theory are essential. Even so, I knew that I was verging close to the First Law's limit when I followed your orders, using my robots to shadow the Lamurkians."

"You sensed something wrong?"

"Hyperresistance in the positronic pathways manifests as trouble standing and walking and then speaking. I displayed all these. I must have sensed that my robots would be used indirectly to kill humans. The ancient Giskard had similar difficulties with the boundary between the First and Zeroth Laws."

Dors' mouth trembled with barely repressed emotion. "The rest of us depend upon your judgment to negotiate the tension between those two most fundamental of Laws. I could not withstand what you have had to endure."

Trying to comfort him, Hari said, "You had no choice, Daneel. I boxed you in."

Daneel looked at Dors, allowing conflicted expressions to flit across his face, a symphony of agony. "The Zeroth Law . . . I have lived with it for so long . . . many millennia . . . and yet . . ."

"There is a clear contradiction," Hari said softly, knowing he was treading in territory of great delicacy. "The sort of conceptual clash a human mind can sometimes manage."

Dors whispered, "But we cannot, except at grave peril to our very stability."

Daneel hung his head. "When I gave the orders, an acidic agony arose in my mind, a scalding tide I have barely contained."

Hari's throat just allowed him to squeeze out his words. "Old friend, you had no choice. Surely in all your ages of labor in the human cause, other contradictions have arisen?"

Daneel nodded. "Many. And each time I hang above an abyss."

"You cannot succumb," Dors said. "You are the greatest of us. More is demanded of you."

Daneel looked at both of them as if seeking absolution. Across his face flickered forlorn hope. "I suppose . . ."

Hari added his assent, a lump in his throat. "Of course. All is lost without you. You must endure."

Daneel looked off into infinity, speaking in a dry

whisper. "My work . . . it is not done . . . so I cannot . . . deactivate. This must be what it is like . . . to be truly human . . . torn between two poles. Still, I can look forward. There will come a time when my work is finished. When I can be relieved of these contradictory tensions. Then I shall face the black blankness . . . and it will be *good*."

The fervor of the robot's speech left Hari silent and sad. For a long time the three sat together in the hushed room. Lamurk stood attentive and silent.

Then, without a further word, they went their separate ways.

15.

◆

Hari sat alone and stared at the holo of a raging, ancient prairie fire.

In its place now stood the Empire. He knew now that he loved the Empire for reasons he could not name. The dark revelation, that the robots had visited death and destruction upon the old, remnant digital minds . . . even that did not deter him. He would never know the details of that ancient crime— he hoped.

To preserve his sanity, for the first time in his life he *did not want* to know.

The Empire that stood all around him was even more marvelous than he had suspected. And more sobering.

Who could accept that humanity did not control its own future—that history was the result of forces acting beyond the horizons of mere mortal men? The Empire had endured because of its metanature, not the valiant acts of individuals, or even of worlds.

Many would argue for human self-determination. Their arguments were not wrong or even ineffectual— just beside the point. As persuasion they were powerful. Everyone wanted to believe they were masters of their own fate. Logic had nothing to do with it.

Even Emperors were nothing; chaff blown by winds they could not see.

As if to refute him, Cleon's image abruptly coagulated in the holo. "Hari! Where have you been?"

"Working."

"On your equations, I hope—because you're going to need them."

"Sire?"

"The High Council just met in special session. I appeared; a note of grace and gravity was much needed. In the wake of the, ah, tragic loss of Lamurk and his, ah, associates, I urged the quick election of a First Minister." A broad wink. "For stability, you understand."

Hari croaked, "Oh no."

"Oh, yes!—my First Minister."

"But wasn't there—didn't anyone suspect—"

"You? A harmless academic, bringing off assassinations in dozens of places, all over Trantor? Using tiktoks?"

"Well, you know how people will talk—"

Cleon gave him a shrewd look. "Come now, Hari . . . how *did* you do it?"

"I count among my allies a gang of renegade robots."

Cleon laughed loudly, slapping his desk. "I never knew you were such a jokester. Very well, I quite understand. You should not be forced to reveal your sources."

Hari had sworn to himself that he would never lie to the Emperor. Not being believed was not part of the agreement. "I assure you, sire—"

"Of course you are right to jest. I am not naïve."

"And I am a lousy liar, sire." True also, and as well, the best way to close the matter.

"I want you to come to the formal reception for the High Council. Now that you're First Minister, there will be these social matters. But before that, I do want you to think about the Sark situation and—"

"I can advise you now."

Cleon brightened. "Oh?"

"There are dampers in history, sire, which stabilize the Empire. The New Renaissance is a breakout of a fundamental facet and *flaw* of humanity. It must be suppressed."

"You're sure?"

"If we do nothing . . ." Hari recalled the solutions he had just tried in the fitness-landscape. Let the New Renaissance go and the Empire would dissolve into chaos-states within mere decades. "That might destroy humanity itself."

Cleon grimaced. "Truly? What are my other options?"

"Squelch these eruptions. The Sarkians are brilliant, true, but they cannot find a shared heart for their people. They are examples of what I call a Solipsism Plague, an excessive belief in the self. It is contagious."

"The human toll—"

"Save the survivors. Send Imperial aid ships through the wormholes—food, counselors, psychers if they're any help. But *after* the disorder has burned itself out."

"I see." Cleon gave him a guarded glance, face slightly averted. "You *are* a hard man, Hari."

"When it comes to preserving order, the Empire—yes, sire."

Cleon went on to speak of minor matters, as if shying away from so brutal a topic. Hari was glad he had not asked more.

The long-range predictions showed dire drifts—that the classic dampers in the Empire's self-learning networks were failing, too. The New Renaissance was but the most flagrant example.

But everywhere he had looked, with his body sensorium tied into the N-dimensional spectrum, rose the stink of impending chaos. The Empire was breaking down in ways which were *not describable* by mere human modes. It was too vast a system to enclose within a single mind.

So soon, within decades, the Empire would start to fragment. Military strength was of little long-term use when the time-honored dampers faltered. The center could not hold.

Hari could slow that collapse a bit, perhaps—that was all. Soon whole Zones would spiral back to the old attractors: Basic Feudalism, Religious Sanctimony, Femoprimitivism . . .

Of course, his conclusions were preliminary. He hoped new data would prove him wrong. But he doubted it.

Only after thirty thousand years of suffering would the fever burn out. A new, strong attractor would emerge.

A random mutation of Benign Imperialism? He could not tell.

He could understand all this better with more work. Explore the foundations, get . . .

An idea flickered. Foundations? Something there . . .

But Cleon was going on and events were colliding in his mind. The idea flitted away.

"We'll do great things together, Hari. What do you think about . . ."

At Cleon's beck and call, he would never get any work done.

Dealing with Lamurk had been disagreeable—but in comparison with this trap of power, easy. How could he get out of *this*?

16.

◆

The two figures from a past beyond antiquity flew in their cool digital spaces, waiting for the man to return.

"I have faith he will," Joan said.

"I rely more upon calculation," Voltaire replied, adjusting his garb. He softened the pull of silk in his tight, formal breeches. It was a simple adjustment of the friction coefficient, nothing more. Rough algorithms reduced intricate laws to trivial arithmetic. Even the rub of life was just another parameter.

"I still resent this weather."

Gales howled across troubled waters. They flew above foaming waves and banked on thermal upwellings.

"Your idea, to be birds for a bit." He was a silvery eagle.

"I always envied them. So light, cheerful, at one with the air itself."

He morphed his wings up to his shoulders, making his vest-coat fit much better. Even here, life was mostly details.

"Why must such strangeness manifest as weather?" Joan asked.

"Men argue; nature acts."

"But they are not nature! They are strange minds—"

"So strange we might as well regard them as natural phenomena."

"I find it difficult to believe that our Lord made such things."

"I've felt that way about many Parisians."

"They appear to us as storms, mountains, oceans. If they would *explain* themselves—"

"The secret of being a bore is to tell everything."

"Hark! He comes."

She grew armor while keeping her giant wings. The effect was startling, like a giant chromed falcon.

Voltaire said, "My love, you never cease to surprise me. I believe that with you even eternity will not be tedious."

Hari Seldon hung in midair. He was clearly not yet used to adventuresome simulations, for his feet kept trying to stand somewhere. Eventually he gave up and watched them swoop and dive around him.

"I came as soon as I could."

"I gather you are now a viscount or duke or such," Joan said.

"Something like that," Hari said. "This space you're in, I've arranged for it to be a permanent, ah—"

"Preserve?" Voltaire asked, batting his wings before the Hari-figure. A cloud drifted nearer, as if to listen in.

"We call it a 'dedicated perimeter' in computational space."

"Such poetry!" Voltaire arched an eyebrow.

"That sounds much like a zoo," Joan said.

"The deal is, you and the alien minds can stay here, running without interference."

"I do not like to be hemmed in!" Joan shouted.

Hari shook his head. "You'll be able to get input from anywhere. But no more interference with the tiktoks—right?"

"Ask the weather," Joan said.

A cascade of burnt-orange sheet lightning ran down the sky.

"I'm just glad the meme-minds didn't exterminate *all* the robots," Hari said.

Voltaire said, "Perhaps this place is a bit like England, where they kill an occasional admiral to encourage the others."

"I had to do it," Hari said.

Joan slowed her wings and hovered near his face. "You are distressed."

"Did you know the meme-minds would use the tik-toks to kill robots?"

"Not at all," Joan said.

Voltaire added, "Though the economy of it provokes a certain admiration. Subtle minds, they are."

"Treacherous," Hari said. "I wonder what else they can do?"

"I believe they are satisfied," Joan said. "I sense a calm in our weather."

"I want to speak with them!" Hari shouted.

"Like kings, they like to be awaited," Voltaire said.

"I sense them gathering," Joan said helpfully. "Let us help our friend here with his vexations."

"Me?" Hari said. "I don't like killing people, if that's what you mean."

"In such times, there is no good path," she said. "I, too, had to kill for the right."

"Lamurk was a valuable public servant—"

"Nonsense!" Voltaire said. "He lived as he died—by the dagger, too slippery to show the sword. He would never rest with you in power. And even had you stepped aside—well, my mathist, remember that it is dangerous to be right when the government is wrong."

"I still feel conflicted."

"You must, for you are a righteous man," Joan said. "Pray and be absolved."

"Or better, peer within," Voltaire explained loftily. "Your conflicts reflect subminds in dispute. Such is the human condition."

Joan flapped her wings at Voltaire, who veered away.

Hari scowled. "That sounds more like a machine."

Voltaire laughed. "If order—you are an enthusiast of order, yes?—means predictability, and predictability means predetermination, and that means compulsion, and compulsion means nonfreedom—why then, the only way we can be free is to be disordered!"

Hari frowned. Voltaire realized that, while for him ideas were playthings, and the contest of wits made the blood sing, for this man the abstract *mattered*.

Hari said, "I suppose you're right. People *do* feel discomfort with rigid order. And with hierarchies, norms, foundations—" He blinked. "There's an idea, I can't quite see it . . ."

Voltaire said kindly, "Even you, surely you do not want to be the tool of your own genes, or of physics, or of economics?"

"How can we be free if we're machines?" Hari asked, as if speaking to himself.

"Nobody wants either a random universe or a deterministic one," Voltaire said.

"But there are deterministic laws—"

"And random ones."

Joan put in, "Our Lord gave us judgment to choose."

"Freedom to choose to do other than one would like—what a sordid boon!" Voltaire said.

Joan said, "You gentlemen are circling the divine without knowing it. Everything worthwhile to people—freedom, meaning, value—all that disappears within *either* of your choices."

"My love, you must remember that Hari is a mathist." Voltaire zoomed about both of them on spread wings, obviously enjoying ruffling his feathers in the turbulence. "Order/disorder seem implicated in other dualisms: nature/human, natural/artificial, animals with natures/humans outside nature. They are natural to us."

"How come?" Hari squinted, puzzled.

"How do we frame the other side of an argument? We say, 'on the other hand,' yes?"

Hari nodded. "We think our two hands mirror the world."

"Very good." Voltaire flew loops around Joan's chromed falcon.

"The Creator has two hands as well," Joan persisted. "'He sitteth on the right hand of the Father almighty—'"

Voltaire cawed like a crow. *"But you're both* neglecting your own selves—which you can inspect, in this digital vault. Look deeply and you see endless detail. It ramifies into a Self that cannot be decomposed into the mere operation of neat laws. The *You* emerges as a deep interplay of many Selves."

Into the shared mind-space of the three Voltaire sent:

> Complex, nonlinear feedback systems are unpredictable, even if they are deterministic. The information-processing capacity needed to predict a single mind is larger than the complexity of the whole universe itself! Computing the next event takes longer than the event itself. Precisely this feature, written into the texture of the universe, makes it—and us—free.

Hari replied with:

> Paradox. How does the event itself know how to happen?
>
> Only a massive computer could describe the next tiny whorl in a stream. What makes real systems even able to change?

Voltaire shrugged—a difficult gesture for a bird.

"At last you have encountered an agency you cannot dismiss," Joan said proudly.

Voltaire's head jerked with surprise. "Your . . . Creator?"

"Your equations *describe* well enough. But what gives these equations—" she hesitated at the word—"*fire?*"

"You imply a Mind which does the universal computation?"

"No, *you* do."

Hari said, "Fair enough—as a hypothesis. But why should such a Mind care a whit for *us*, mere motes?"

"He cared enough to make you come out of the matrix of matter, did He not?"

"Ah, origins," Voltaire said, catching an updraft. He looked relieved to be on surer intellectual ground. Plainly her point had rattled him. "Insoluble, of course. I prefer to deal with our moralities."

Joan said primly, "Morality is not dependent upon *us*."

Voltaire shot back, "Nonsense! We evolved with morals shaped by the universe—by a Creator, if you wish."

Hari asked, "You mean by evolution? The pans—"

Joan cried, "Indeed! Holiness shapes the world, the world shapes us."

Hari looked doubtful, Joan pleased. Voltaire said wryly, "My mathist, would you rather believe that moral constraints emerge as 'a spontaneous order from rational utility-maximizing behavior'? Truly?"

Hari blinked. "Well, no . . ."

"I quoted one of your own papers. What you've forgotten, sir, is that our endless models of the world shape how we look at human experience."

"Of course, but—"

"And the models are *all that we know*."

Hari suddenly smiled. "I like that. Don't get married to a model." He allowed himself to morph slightly, growing taller, more muscular. "I don't know why, but I feel better."

"Your soul has come to terms with your actions," Joan said.

Voltaire said, "I would prefer 'selves' to 'soul,' but let us not quibble."

Suddenly Hari felt categories shift in his mind. He had arranged for the revival of these sims, guided by pure intuition. Now came the payoff: they had inadvertently discovered the step he wanted. "The mind . . . is a self-organizing structure, *and so is the Empire.* I can work back and forth between those models! Import your knowledge of subselves, use it to analyze how the Empire learns!"

Voltaire blinked. "What a marvelous idea."

Hari said, "Wait'll I show you! The Empire is self-learning, with subunits—"

"I wonder if the alien fog knows this?" Joan asked.

Hari frowned. "I do not want to involve them. My equations cannot deal with elements of unknown—"

"They are already involved," Joan said. "They are here, all around us."

Hari sighed. "I hope we can keep them here in the—"

"Zoo," Joan said dryly.

Thunderheads roiled over the horizons, closing fast.

"You killed robots!" Hari shouted into the gale. "That was not in our bargain."

[WE DID NOT SAY WE WOULD REFRAIN]

"You took more than we agreed! Lives of—"

[TERMS OMITTED CANNOT BE PRESUMED UPON]

"The robots are a separate kind. Of high intelligence—"

[YOUR MERE TIKTOKS COULD KILL THEM THOUGH]

[YOU, SELDON, DID NOT OWN THESE MACHINES]

[AND THUS HAVE NO DISPUTE WITH US]

Hari ground his teeth and fumed.

[MORE IMPORTANT MATTERS BECKON]

"Your rewards?" Hari asked bitterly. "You've come for them?"

[WE SHALL NOT STAY HERE]

[FOR THIS PLACE IS DOOMED]

Hari staggered under a hailstorm of biting cold. "Trantor?"

[AND MUCH ELSE]

"What *do* you want?"

[OUR DESIRED DESTINY IS TO FLOAT AMONG THE SPIRAL ARMS]

[AND LINGER LONG AMONG THE PLUMES OF GALACTIC CENTER]

Hari remembered the structures there, the complex weave of luminosities. "You can do that?"

[WE HAVE A SPORE STATE]

[SOME OF US LIVED THIS WAY BEFORE]

[TO SUCH A STATE WE WISH TO RETURN]

[ELSE WE SHALL EXTINGUISH ALL YOUR "ROBOTS"]

"That wasn't part of our deal!" Hari shouted. Hard cold rain hammered him, but he turned his face to confront the towering, angry clouds and their skirts of wrathful lightning.

[HOW CAN YOU STOP US?]

[THOUGH IT WOULD DEPLETE OUR CAPACITIES]

[WE COULD BRING TRANTOR TO STARVATION]

Hari grimaced. He was learning a lot about power, quite quickly. "All right. I'll see that research gets done on how to transfer you to physical form. There are those I know who can do it. Marq and Sybyl know how to keep quiet, too."

Voltaire asked, "Why do you wish to exit stage left with such unseemly haste?"

[A NEW BRUSH FIRE IS COMING]

[TO HUMANS ACROSS THE SPIRAL]

[WE SHALL WATCH THIS FALL]

[AS SPORES FROM GALACTIC CENTER]

[THERE NONE CAN HURT US, NONE CAN WE HURT]

A glittering crystal with sharp spikes materialized beneath the purpling sky. In a data-dollop, Hari learned of the alien technology which had once made these stable, rugged compartments for digital intelligences.

[TRANTOR WAS ONCE THE IDEAL PLACE FOR US]

[RICH IN RESOURCES]

[NO MORE IS THIS SO]

[DANGER LURKS IN THE COMING INSTABILITY]

"Ummm," Voltaire said. "Joan and I might desire such an exit as well."

"Wait, you two," Hari said, talking fast. "If you want to go with these, these things, to live in a seed between the stars—then you have to earn it."

Joan scowled. "How?"

"For now, I can make it safe for you to live widely in the Mesh. In return—" he gazed anxiously at the Voltaire eagle, flapping in brassy splendor "—I want you to help me."

"If it is a holy cause, surely," Joan called.

"It is. Help me lead! I've always felt there's good in everybody. The job of a leader is to bring it out."

Voltaire said, "If you think there is good in everybody, you haven't met everybody."

"But I'm not a man of the world. So I need you."

"To rule?" Joan asked.

"Exactly. I'm not suited for it."

Voltaire stopped in midair, wings stilled. "The possibilities! With enough computing space and speed, we can endow proto-Michelangelos with creative time."

"I need to deal with a lot of, well, power problems. You can go off into these spore forms when I'm finished with politics."

Voltaire abruptly congealed into human form, though still elegantly clothed in electric blue. "Ummm. Politics—I always found it enticing. A game of elegant ideas, played by bullies."

"I've got plenty of opposition already," Hari said soberly.

"Friends come and go, but enemies accumulate," Voltaire said. "I *would* like that."

Joan rolled her eyes. "Saints preserve us."

"Precisely, my dear."

17.

◆

Hari sat back at his desk. First Minister, but on his terms.

It had all worked out. He got to work here still, far from palace intrigues. Plenty of time to do math.

He would, of course, speak by 3D and holo to many. All that bother Voltaire took care of. After all, Voltaire or Joan could masquerade as Hari at the many conferences and meetings necessary for a First Minister. Digitally, they could morph to him with ease.

Joan enjoyed the virtual ceremonials, especially if

she got to hold forth on holiness. Voltaire loved imitating an ancient man he had apparently known, a Mr. Machiavelli. "Your Empire," he had said, "is a vast, ramshackle thing of infinite nuance and multiplying self-delusions. Needs looking after."

In between, they could explore the digital realms, labyrinths vast and vibrant. As Voltaire had said, they could be off upon "postings various and capers hilarious."

Yugo came in bursting with energy. "The High Council just passed your vote proposals, Hari. Every Dahlite in the Galaxy's on your side now."

Hari smiled. "Have Voltaire make a 3D appearance, as me."

"Right, modest and confident, that'll work."

"Reminds me of the old joke about the prostitute. The regular costs the regular price, but sincerity is extra."

Yugo laughed unconvincingly and said edgily, "Uh, that woman's here."

"Not—"

He had forgotten utterly about the Academic Potentate. The one threat he had not neutralized. She knew about Dors, about robots—

Giving him no time to think, she swept into his office.

"*So* happy you could see me, Primary Minister."

"Wish I could say the same."

"And your lovely wife? Is she about?"

"I doubt she would desire to see you."

The Academic Potentate spread her billowing robes and sat without invitation. "Surely you didn't take that small jest of mine seriously?"

"My sense of humor doesn't include blackmail."

Wide eyes, a slight touch of outrage in the tone. "I was merely trying to gain leverage with your administration."

"Sure." Such were Imperial manners that he would not bring up her possible role in Vaddo's plot on Panucopia.

"I was certain you would gain the ministership. My little sally—well, perhaps it *was* in poor taste—"

"Very."

"You are a man of few words—quite admirable. My allies were so impressed with your, ah, direct handling of the tiktok crisis, the Lamurk killings."

So that was it. He had shown that he was not an impractical academic. "Direct? How about 'ruthless'?"

"Oh *no*, we don't think that at all. You are *right* to let Sark 'burn out,' as you so eloquently put it. Despite the Greys wanting to jump in and bind up wounds. Very wise—not ruthless, no."

"Even though Sark might never recover?" These were the questions he had asked himself through sleepless nights. People were dying that the Empire might live . . . for a while longer.

She waved this away. "As I was saying, I wanted a special relationship with the First Minister from our class in, well, *so* long—"

Like many he knew now, she employed speech to conceal thought, not to reveal it. He had to sit and endure some of this, he knew. She rattled on and he thought about how to handle a knotty term in the equations. He had by now mastered the art of seeming to track with eyes, mouth movements, and the occasional murmur. This was exactly what a filter program did for his 3D, and he could do it without thinking about the hypocrisy of the woman before him.

He understood her now, in a way. Power was value-free for her. He had to learn to think that way and even act that way. But he could not let it affect his true self, the personal life he would ruthlessly shelter.

He finally got rid of her and breathed a sigh of relief. Probably it was good to be seen as ruthless. That fellow Nim, for example; he could have Nim found, even executed, for playing both sides in the Artifice Associates matter.

But why? Mercy was more efficient. Hari sent a quick note to Security, directing that Nim be funneled into a productive spot, but one where his talent for betrayal would find no avenue. Let an underling figure out where and how.

He had neglected business and had one obligatory role left before he could escape. Even here at Streeling he could not avoid every Imperial duty.

A delegation of Greys filed in. They respectfully presented their arguments regarding candidacy examinations for Empire positions. Test scores had been declining for several centuries, but some argued that this was because the pool of candidates was broadening. They did not mention that the High Council had widened the pool because it appeared to be drying up—that is, fewer wished Imperial positions.

Others claimed that the tests were biased. Those from large planets said their higher gravity made them slower. Those from lighter gravities had a reverse argument, with diagrams and sheets of facts.

Also, the myriad ethnic and religious groups had congealed into an Action Front which ferreted out biases against them in the examinations. Hari could not fathom a conspiracy behind the examination questions. How could one simultaneously discriminate against several hundred, or even a thousand, ethnic strains?

"It seems an immense job to me," he ventured, "discriminating against so many factions."

Vehemently a Grey Woman, handsome and forceful,

told him that the prejudice was *for* a sort of Imperial norm, a common set of vocabularies, assumptions, and class purposes. All these would "shoulder others aside."

To compensate, the Action Front wanted the usual set of preferences installed, with slight shadings between each ethnicity to compensate for their lower performance on examinations.

This was ordinary and Hari ruled it out without having to think about it very much; this allowed him to mull over the psychohistory equations a while. Then a new note caught his attention.

To dispel the common "misperception" that scores were being undermined by some ethnic worlds' increased participation, the Action Front petitioned him to "re-norm" the examination itself. Set the average score at 1000, though in fact it had drifted downward over the last two centuries to 873.

"This will permit comparison of candidates between years, without having to look up each year's average," the burly woman pointed out.

"This will give a symmetric distribution?" Hari asked absently.

"Yes, and will stop the invidious comparison of one year with the next."

"Won't such a shift of the mean lose discriminatory power at the upper end of the distribution?" He narrowed his eyes.

"That is regrettable, but yes."

"It's a wonderful idea," Hari said.

She seemed surprised. "Well, we think so."

"We can do the same for the holoball averages."

"What? I don't—"

"Set the statistics so that the average hitter strikes 500, rather than the hard-to-remember 446 of the present."

"But I don't think a principle of social justice—"

"And the intelligence scores. Those need to be re-normed as well, I can see that. Agreed?"

"Well, I'm not sure, First Minister. We only intended—"

"No no, this is a *big idea*. I want a thorough look at all possible re-norming agendas. You have to *think big*!"

"We aren't prepared—"

"Then get prepared! I want a report. Not a skimpy one, either. A fat, full report. Two thousand pages, at least."

"That would take—"

"Hang the expense. And the time. This is too important to relegate to the Imperial Examinations. Let me have that report."

"It would take years, decades—"

"Then there's no time to waste!"

The Action Front delegation left in confusion. Hari hoped they would make it a very big report, indeed, so that he was no longer First Minister when it arrived.

Part of maintaining the Empire involved using its own inertia against itself. Some aspects of this job, he thought, could be actually enjoyable.

He reached Voltaire before leaving the office. "Here's your list of impersonations."

"I must say I am having trouble handling all the factions," Voltaire said. He presented as a swain in elegant velvet. "But the chance to venture out, to *be* a presence—it is like acting! And I was always one for the stage, as you know."

Hari didn't, but he said, "That's democracy for you—show business with daggers. A mongrel breed of government. Even if it is a big stable attractor in the fitness landscape."

"Rational thinkers deplore the excesses of democracy; it abuses the individual and elevates the mob." Voltaire's mouth flattened into a disapproving line. "The death of Socrates was its finest fruit."

"Afraid I don't go back that far," Hari said, signing off. "Enjoy the work."

18.

◆

He and Dors watched the great luminous spiral turn beneath them in its eternal night.

"I do appreciate such perks," she said dreamily. They stood alone before the spectacle. Worlds and lives and stars, all like crushed diamonds thrown against eternal blackness.

"Getting into the palace just to look at the Emperor's display rooms?" He had ordered all the halls cleared.

"Getting away from snoopers and eavesdroppers."

"You . . . you haven't heard from—?"

She shook her head. "Daneel pulled nearly all the rest of us off Trantor. He says little to me."

"I'm pretty damn sure the alien minds won't strike again. They're *afraid* of robots. It took me a while to see that lay behind their talk about revenge."

"Mingled hate and fear. Very human."

"Still, I think they've had their revenge. They say the Galaxy was lush with life before we came. There are cycles of barren eras, then luxuriant ones. Don't know why. Apparently that's happened several times before, at intervals of a third of a billion years—great diebacks of intelligent life, leaving only spores. Now they've come to our Mesh and become digital fossils."

"Fossils don't kill," she said sardonically.

"Not as well as we do, apparently."

"Not you—us."

"They do hate you robots. Not that they have any love of humans—after all, we made you, long ago. We're to blame."

"They are so strange. . . ."

He nodded. "I believe they'll stay in their digital preserve until Marq and Sybyl can get them transported into their ancient spore state. They once lived that way for longer than the Galaxy takes to make a rotation."

"Your 'pretty damn sure' isn't good enough for Daneel," she said. "He wants them exterminated."

"It's a standoff. If Daneel goes after them, he'll have to pull the plug on Trantor's Mesh. That will wound the Empire. So he's stuck, fuming but impotent."

"I hope you have estimated the balance properly," she said.

A glimmering, gossamer thought flitted across his mind. The tiktok attacks upon the Lamurk faction had discredited them in public opinion. Now they would be suppressed throughout the Galaxy. And in time, the meme-minds would leave Trantor.

Hari frowned. Daneel surely wanted both these outcomes.

He had undoubtedly suspected that the meme-minds had survived, perhaps that they were in action on Trantor. So could Hari's amateur maneuverings, including the Lamurk murders, have been deftly conjured up by Daneel? Could a robot so accurately predict what he, Hari, would do?

A chill ran through him. Such ability would be breathtaking. Superhuman.

With tiktoks now soon to be suppressed, Trantor would have trouble producing its own food. Tasks once done by men would have to be re-learned, taking generations to establish such laborers as a socially valued group again. Meanwhile, dozens of other worlds would have to send Trantor food, a lifeline slender and vulnerable. Did Daneel intend that, too? To what end?

Hari felt uneasy. He sensed social forces at work, just beyond his view.

Was such adroit thinking the product of millennia of experience and high, positronic intelligence? For just a moment, Hari had a vision of a mind both strange and measureless, in human terms. Was *that* what an immortal machine became?

Then he pushed the idea away. It was too unsettling to contemplate. Later, perhaps, when psychohistory was done . . .

He noticed Dors staring at him. What had she said? Oh, yes . . .

"Estimating the balance, yes. I'm getting the feel for these things. With Voltaire and Joan doing the scut work, and Yugo now chairman of the Mathist Department, I actually have *time* to think."

"And suffer fools gladly?"

"The Academic Potentate? At least I understand her now." He peered at Dors. "Daneel says he will leave Trantor. He's lost a lot of his humaniforms. Does he need you?"

She looked up at him in the soft glow. Her expression worked with conflict. "I can't leave you."

"His orders?"

"Mine."

He gritted his teeth. "The robots who died—you knew them?"

"Some. We trained together back, back when . . ."

"You don't have to conceal anything from me. I know you must be at least a century old."

Her mouth made an O of surprise, then quickly closed. "How?"

"You know more than you should."

"So do you—in bed, anyway." She chuckled.

"I learned it from a pan I met."

She laughed bawdily, then sobered. "I'm one hundred sixty-three."

"With the thighs of a teenager. If you had tried to leave Trantor, I'd have blocked you."

She blinked. "Truly?"

He bit his lip, thinking. "Well, no."

She smiled. "More romantic to say yes . . ."

"I have a habit of honesty—which I'd better drop if I want to stay First Minister."

"So you would let me go? You still feel that you owe that to Daneel?"

"If he thought the danger to you was that great, then I would honor his judgment."

"You still respect us so?"

"Robots work selflessly for the Empire—always. Few humans do."

"You don't wonder what we did to earn the aliens' revenge?"

"Of course. Do you know?"

She shook her head, gazing out at the vast turning disk. Suns of blue and crimson and yellow swept along their orbits amid dark dust and disorder. "It was something awful. Daneel was there and he will not speak of it. There is nothing in our history of this. I've looked."

"An empire lasting many millennia has manifold secrets." Hari watched the slow spin of a hundred billion flaming stars. "I'm more interested in its future—in saving it."

"You fear that future, don't you?"

"Terrible things are coming. The equations show that."

"We can face them together."

He took her in his arms, but they both still

watched the Galaxy's shining marvels. "I dream of founding something, a way to help the Empire, even after we're gone. . . ."

"And you fear something, too," she said into his neck.

"How did you know? Yes—I fear the chaos that could come from so many forces, divergent vector turmoil—all acting to bring down the order of the Empire. I fear for the very . . ." His face clouded. "For the very foundations themselves. Foundations . . ."

"Chaos comes?"

"I know we ourselves, our minds, come out of skating on the inner rim of chaos-states. The digital world shows that. *You* show that."

She said soberly, "I do not think positronic minds understand themselves any better than human ones."

"We—our minds and our Empire—both spring from an emergent order of inner, basically chaotic states, but . . ."

"You do not want the Empire to crash from such chaos."

"I want the Empire to survive! Or at least, if it falls, to reemerge."

Hari suddenly felt the pain of such vast movements. The Empire was like a mind, and minds sometimes went crazy, crashed. A disaster for one solitary mind. How colossally worse for an Empire.

Seen through the prism of his mathematics, humanity was on a long march pressing forward through surrounding dark. Time battered them with storms, rewarded them with sunshine—and they did not glimpse that these passing seasons came from the shifting cadences of huge, eternal equations.

Running the equations time-forward, then backward, Hari had seen humanity's mortal parade in snips. Somehow that made it oddly touching. Steeped in their own eras, few worlds ever glimpsed the route ahead. There was no shortage of portentous talk, or of oafs who pretended with a wink and a nod to fathom the unseeable. Misled, whole Zones stumbled and fell.

He sought patterns, but beneath those vast sweeps lay the seemingly infinitesimal, living people. Across the realm of stars, under the laws that reigned like gods, lay innumerable lives in the process of being lost. For to live was to lose, in the end.

Social laws acted and people were maimed, damaged, robbed, and strangled by forces they could not even glimpse. People were driven to sickness, to desperation, to loneliness and fear and remorse. Shaken by tears and longing, in a world they fundamentally failed to fathom, they nonetheless carried on.

There was nobility in that. They were fragments adrift in time, motes in an Empire rich and strong and full of pride, an order failing and battered and hollow with its own emptiness.

With leaden certainty, Hari at last saw that he probably would not be able to rescue the great ramshackle Empire, a beast of fine nuance and multiplying self-delusions.

No savior, he. But perhaps he could help.

They both stood in silence for a long, aching time. The Galaxy turned in its slow majesty. A nearby fountain spewed glorious arcs into the air. The waters seemed momentarily free, but in fact were trapped forever within the steel skies of Trantor. As was he.

Hari felt a deep emotion he could not define. It tightened his throat and made him press Dors to him. She was machine and woman and . . . something more. Another element he could not fully know, and he cherished her all the more for that.

"You care so much," Dors whispered.

"I have to."

"Perhaps we should try to simply live more, worry less."

He kissed her fervently and then laughed.

"Quite right. For who knows what the future may bring?"

Very slowly, he winked at her.

AFTERWORD

◆

The Foundation series began in World War II, as America arced toward its zenith as a world power. The series played out over decades as the United States dominated the world's matters in a fashion no other nation ever had. Yet the Foundation is about imperium and decline. Did this betray an anxiety, born even in the moment of approaching glory?

I had always wondered if this was so. Part of me itched to explore the issues which lace the series.

The idea of writing further novels in the Foundation universe came from Janet Asimov and the Asimov estate's representative, Ralph Vicinanza. Approached by them, I at first declined, being busy with physics and my own novels. But my subconscious, once aroused, refused to let go the notion. After half a year of struggling with ideas plainly made for the Foundation, persistently demanding expression, I finally called up Ralph Vicinanza and began putting together a plan to construct a fittingly complex curve of action and meaning, to be revealed in several novels. Though we spoke to several authors about this project, the best suited seemed two hard SF writers broadly influenced by Asimov and of unchallenged technical ability: Greg Bear and David Brin.

Bear, Brin, and I have kept in close touch while I wrote this first volume, for we intend to create three stand-alone novels which nonetheless carry forward an overarching mystery to its end. Elements of this make their first appearance here, to amplify further through Greg Bear's *Foundation and Chaos*, finding completion in Brin's *Third Foundation*. (These are preliminary titles.) I have planted in the narrative prefiguring details and key elements which shall bear later fruit.

Genres are constrained conversations. Constraint is essential, defining the rules and assumptions open to an author. If hard SF occupies the center of science fiction, that is probably because hardness gives the firmest boundary. Science itself yields crisp confines.

Genres are also like immense discussions, with ideas developed, traded, mutated, their variations spun down through time. Players ring changes on each other—more like a steppin'-out jazz band than a solo concert in a plush auditorium. Contrast "serious" fiction (more accurately described, in my eyes, as merely self-consciously solemn). It has canonical classics that supposedly stand outside of time, deserving awe, looming great and intact by themselves.

Much of the pleasure of mysteries, of espionage novels or SF, lies in the interaction of writers with each other and, particularly in SF's invention of fandom, with the readers as well. This isn't a defect; it's the essential nature of popular culture, which the United States has dominated in our age, with the invention of jazz, rock, the musical, and written genres such as the Western, the hardboiled detective, modern fantasy, and other rich areas. Many kinds of SF (hard, utopian, military, satirical) share assumptions, code words, lines of argument, narrative voices. Fond remembrance of golden age *Astounding* and its letter column, of the New Wave, of Horace Gold's *Galaxy*—these are echoes of distant conversations earnestly carried out.

Genre pleasures are many, but this quality of shared values within an ongoing discussion may be the most powerful, enlisting lifelong devotion in its fans. In contrast to the Grand Canon view of great works standing like monoliths in a deserted landscape, genre reading satisfactions are a striking facet of modern democratic (pop) culture, a shared movement.

There are questions about how writers deal with what some call the "anxiety of influence," but which I'd prefer to term more mildly: the digestion of tradition.

I'm reminded of John Berger's definition of hack work, describing oil painting in *Ways of Seeing*, as ". . . not the result of either clumsiness or provincialism; it is the result of the market making more insistent demands than the art." Fair enough; but this can happen in any context. Working in a known region of concept-space does not necessarily imply that the territory has been mined out. Nor is fresh ground always fertile.

Surely we should notice that a novel Hemingway thought the best in American literature is a sequel—indeed, following on a *boy's* book, *Tom Sawyer*.

Sharing common ground isn't only a literary tradition. Are we thrown into moral confusion when we hear Rhapsody on a Theme by Paganini? Do we indignantly march from the concert hall when assaulted by Variations on a Theme by Haydn? Sharecropping by the Greats? Shocking!

Reinspecting the assumptions and methods of classical works can yield new fruit. Fresh narrative can both strike out into new territory while reflecting on the landscape of the past. Recall that *Hamlet* drew from several earlier plays about the same plot.

Isaac himself revisited the Foundation, taking different angles of attack each time. In the beginning, psychohistory equated the movements of people as a whole with the motions of molecules. The Second Foundation looked at perturbations to such deterministic laws (the Mule) and implied that only a superhuman elite could manage instabilities. Later, robots emerged as the elite, better than humans at dispassionate government. Beyond robots came Gaia . . . and so on.

In this three-book series we shall reinspect the role of robots, and what psychohistory might look like as a theory. More riffs upon the basic tune.

I had always wondered about crucial aspects of Asimov's Empire:

Why were there no aliens in the galaxy?

What role did computers play? Particularly, *vs.* robots?

What did the theory of psychohistory actually look like?

Finally, who was Hari Seldon—as a character, a man?

This novel attempts some answers. It is my contribution to a discussion about power and determinism which has now spanned over half a century.

Of course, we know some incidental answers. The term "psychohistory" was commonly used in the thirties and appears in the 1934 *Webster's Dictionary*; Isaac greatly extended its meaning, though. He didn't want to deal with John W. Campbell's notorious dislike of aliens who might be as clever as we, so his Foundation had none. But it seemed to me there might be more to the matter.

As well, Asimov's uniting of his robot novels and

the Foundation series became intricate and puzzling. The British critic Brian Stableford found this "comforting in its claustrophobic enclosure." There are no robots in the early Foundation novels, but they are behind-the-scenes manipulators in both *Prelude to Foundation* and *Forward the Foundation*.

Some form of advanced computing machines must underlie the Empire, surely. Isaac remarked that "I just put very advanced computers in the new Foundation novel and hoped that nobody would notice the inconsistency. Nobody did." As James Gunn remarked, "More accurately, people noticed but didn't care."

Asimov wrote each novel at the level of the then current scientific understanding. Later works updated the surrounding science. Thus his galaxy is more detailed in later books, including in *Foundation's Edge* both advanced computers and a black hole at the Galactic Center. Similarly, here I have depicted our more detailed knowledge of the Galactic Center. In place of Isaac's "hyperspace" ships I have used wormholes, which have considerably more theoretical justification now than they did when Einstein and Rosen introduced them in the 1930s. Indeed, wormholes are allowed by the general theory of relativity, but must have extreme forms of matter to form and support them. (Matt Visser's *Lorentzian Wormholes* is the standard work on current thinking.)

Isaac wrote much of his fiction in a style he termed "direct and spare," though in the later works he relaxed this constraint a bit. I have not attempted to write in the Asimov style. (Those who think it is easy to write clearly about complex subjects should try it.) For the Foundation novels he used a particularly bare-boards approach, with virtually no background descriptions or novelistic details.

Note his own reaction when he decided to return to the series and revisited the trilogy:

"I read it with mounting uneasiness. I kept waiting for something to happen, and nothing ever did. All three volumes, all the nearly quarter of a million words, consisted of thoughts and conversation. No action. No physical suspense."

But it worked, famously so. I could not manage such an approach, so have taken my own way.

I found that the details of Trantor, of psychohistory and the Empire, called out to me as I began thinking about this novel—indeed, they led me on my sub-conscious quest of the underlying story. So the book is not an imitation Asimov novel but a Benford novel using Asimov's basic ideas and backdrop.

Necessarily my approach has harkened back to the older storytelling styles which prevailed in the SF of Isaac's days. I have never responded favorably to the recent razoring of literature by critics—the tribes of structuralists, post-modernists, deconstructionists. To many SF writers, "post-modern" is simply a signature of exhaustion. Its typical apparatus—self-reference, heavy dollops of obligatory irony, self-conscious use of older genre devices, pastiche, and parody—betrays lack of invention, of the crucial coin of SF, imagina-tion. Some deconstructionists have attacked science itself as mere rhetoric, not an ordering of nature, seeking to reduce it to the status of the ultimately arbitrary humanities. Most SF types find this attack on empiricism a worn old song with new lyrics, quite quaintly retro.

At the core of SF lies the experience of science. This makes the genre finally hostile to such fashions in criticism, for it values its empirical ground. Deconstructionism's stress on contradictory or self-contained internal differences in texts, rather than their link to reality, often merely leads to literature seen as empty word games.

SF novels give us worlds which are not to be taken

as metaphors but as real. We are asked to participate in wrenchingly strange events, not merely watch them for clues to what they're really talking about. (*Ummm, if this stands for that, then the other stuff must stand for . . .* Not a way to gather narrative momentum.) The Mars and stars and digital deserts of our best novels are, finally, to be taken as real, as if to say: Life isn't *like* this, it *is* this. Journeys can go to fresh places, not merely return us to ourselves.

Even so, I've indulged myself a bit in the satirical scenes depicting an academia going off the rails, but I feel Isaac would have approved of my targets. Readers thinking I've gone overboard in depicting the view that science does not deal with objective truths, but instead is a battleground of power politics where "naïve realism" meets relativist worldviews, should look into *The Golem* by Harry Collins and Trevor Pinch. This book attempts to portray scientists as no more the holders of objective knowledge than are lawyers or travel agents.

The recent "re-norming" of the Scholastic Aptitude Tests so that each year the average is forced to the same number, thus masking the decline of ability in students, I satirize in the very last pages of the novel; I hope Isaac would have gotten a chuckle from seeing the issue framed against an entire galaxy.

From Verne and Wells to somewhere near 1970, science fiction was mostly about the wonders of movement, of transportation. Note the innumerable novels with the word *star* in their titles, evoking far destinations, and stories such as Robert Heinlein's "The Roads Must Roll."

But in the past few decades we have focused more on the wonders of information, of transformations at least partly internal, not external. The Internet, virtual reality, computer simulations—all these loom large in our visions of our futures. This novel attempts to combine these two themes, with several conspicuous scenes about travel, and a larger background motif on computers.

As James Gunn noted, the Foundation series is a saga. Its method lies in a repeated pattern: Out of the solution of each problem grows the next problem to be solved. This became, of course, a considerable constraint on later novels. Asimov seemed to be saying that life was a series of problems to be solved, but life itself could never be solved. As Gunn remarked, considering that the combined and integrated Foundation and Robot saga now covers sixteen books, perhaps a directory of it all is called for, named, perhaps, *Encyclopedia Galactica*?

Galactic empires became a mainstay frame for science fiction. Poul Anderson's Flandry novels and Gordon R. Dickson (in his Dorsai series) particularly studied the sociopolitical structure of such vast complexes, for a powerful, autocratic imperial system demands great organizational skill—the primary asset of the Romans themselves.

Isaac was not always consistent in his numbers. How many dwell on Trantor? Usually he says forty billion, but in *Second Foundation* it is 400 billion (unless that's a typo). Spread forty billion over an Earth-sized world (with all its seas drained), and that's only about a hundred per square kilometer. Surely housing them would not demand a half-kilometer-deep city.

Dates also get difficult to follow, across such immensities of time. Trantor is at least 12,000 years old—and note that we assume that the year is Earth's, though Earth's location has been forgotten. By the Galactic Empire calendar, *Pebble in the Sky*, which has references to hundreds of thousands of years of expansion into space, occurs about 900 G.E. In *Foundation* atomic energy is 50,000 years old. The robot Daneel is 20,000 years old in *Prelude to Foundation* and in *Forward the Foundation*. How far away in our future do the Sun and Spaceship emblem rule? Perhaps 40,000 years? No one date reconciles every detail.

Not that it truly matters. I know the dangers of writing a long series over decades. I took twenty-five years to wrestle with the six volumes of my Galactic Center series. Undoubtedly there are contradictions I missed in dating and other details, even though I laid it all out in a timeline, published in the last volume. The aliens of that series are not those implicated in this novel, but there are clearly conceptual links.

Science fiction speaks of the future, but to the present. The grand issues of social power and the technology that drives it will never fade. Often problems are best seen in the perspectives of implication, before we meet them on the gritty ground of their arrival.

Isaac Asimov was ultimately hopeful about humanity. He saw us again and again coming to a crossroads and prevailing. The Foundation is about that.

What matters in sagas is *sweep*. This, the Foundation series surely has. I can only hope I have added a bit to that.

Works tracing the intricacies of the Foundation include notably Alexei and Cory Panshin's historical *The World Beyond the Hill*, James Gunn's insightful *Isaac Asimov*, Joseph Patrouch's thorough *The Science Fiction of Isaac Asimov*, and Alva Rogers' *Requiem for Astounding*, which gives a sense of what it was like to read the classic works as they appeared. I learned from all these studies.

For advice and comments on this project I am especially grateful to Janet Asimov, Mark Martin, David Brin, Joe Miller, Jennifer Brehl, and Elisabeth Brown for close readings of the manuscript. My gratitude goes to Don Dixon for his fantastical, future beastiary. Appreciation for general help is due to my wife Joan, Abbe, and to Ralph Vicinanza, Janet Asimov, James Gunn, John Silbersack, Donald Kingsbury, Chris Schelling, John Douglas, Greg Bear, George Zebrowski, Paul Carter, Lou Aronica, Jennifer Hershey, Gary Westfahl and John Clute. Thanks to all.

September 1996

Look for the next volume in

THE SECOND

FOUNDATION TRILOGY

$\blacklozenge$

Foundation and Chaos

$\blacklozenge$

GREG BEAR

Published by HarperPrism

Halfway across the galaxy, Lodovik Trema traveled in the depths of an Imperial astrophysical survey vessel, the ship's only passenger. He sat alone in the comfort of the officers' lounge, watching a lightly plotted entertainment with apparent enjoyment. The ship's crew, carefully selected from the citizen class, had stocked up on such entertainments by the thousands before launching on their missions, which might take them away from civilized ports for months. Their officers and captain, more often than not from the baronial aristocratic families, chose from a variety of less populist bookfilms.

Lodovik Trema in appearance was forty or forty-five, stout but not corpulent, with a pleasantly ugly face and great strong sausage-fingered hands. One eye seemed fixed skyward, and his large lips turned down as if he were perpetually inclined toward pessimism or at best bland neutrality. Where he had hair, he wore it in a short, even cut; his forehead was high and innocent of wrinkles, which gave his face a younger aspect belied by the lines around his mouth and eyes.

Though Lodovik represented the highest Imperial authority, he had come to be well-liked by the captain and crew; his dry statements of purpose or fact seemed to conceal a gentle and observant wit, and he never said too much, though sometimes he could be accused of saying too little.

Outside the ship's hull, the geometric fistula of hyperspace through which the ship navigated during its Jumps was beyond complete visualization, even for the ship's computers. Both humans and machines, slaves of status space-time, simply bided their personal times until the pre-set emergence.

Lodovik had always preferred the quicker— though sometimes no less harrowing—networks of wormholes, but those connections had been neglected dangerously, and in the past few decades many had collapsed like unshored subway tunnels, in some cases sucking in transit stations and waiting passengers . . . They were seldom used now.

Captain Kartas Tolk entered the lounge and stood for a moment behind Lodovik's seat. The rest of the crew busily tended the machines that watched the machines that kept the ship whole during the Jumps.

Tolk was tall, his head capped by woolly white-blond hair, with ashy-brown skin and a patrician air not uncommon for native-born Sarossans. Lodovik glanced over his shoulder and nodded a greeting. "Two more hours, after our last Jump," Captain Tolk said. "We should be on schedule."

"Good," said Lodovik. "I'm eager to get to work. Where will we land?"

"At Sarossa Major, the capital. That's where the records you seek are stored. Then, as ordered, we remove as many favored families on the Emperor's list as we can. The ship will be very crowded."

"I can imagine."

"We have perhaps seven days before the shock front hits the outskirts of the system. Then, only eight hours before it engulfs Sarossa."

"Too close for comfort,"

"The close shave of Imperial incompetence and misdirection," Tolk said with no attempt to conceal his bitterness. "Imperial scientists knew that the Kale's star was coring two years ago."

"The information provided by Sarossan scientists was far from accurate," Lodovik said.

Tolk shrugged; no sense denying it. Blame enough for all to share. Kale's star had gone supernova last year; its explosion had been observed by telepresence nine months later, and in the time since . . . Much politicking, reallocation of scant resources, and then, this pitifully inadequate mission.

The captain had the misfortune of being sent to watch his planet die, saving little but Imperial records and a few privileged families.

"In the best days," Tolk said, "the Imperial Navy could have constructed shields to save at least a third of the planet's population. We could have marshaled fleets of immigration ships to evacuate millions, even billions . . . Sufficient to rebuild, to keep a world's character intact. A glorious world, if I may say so, even now."

"So I've heard," Lodovik said softly. "We will do our best, dear Captain, though that can be only a dry and hollow satisfaction."

Tolk's lips twisted. "I do not blame you, personally," he said. "You have been sympathetic and honest and, above all, efficient. Quite different from the usual in the Commission offices. The crew regards you as a friend among scoundrels."

Lodovik shook his head in warning. "Even simple complaints against the Empire can be dangerous," he said. "Best not to trust me too much."

The ship shuddered slightly and a small bell rang in the room. Tolk closed his eyes and gripped the back of the chair automatically. Lodovik simply faced forward.

"The last Jump," the captain said. He looked at Lodovik. "I trust you well enough, councilor, but I trust my skills more. Neither the emperor nor Linge Chen can afford to lose men of my qualifications. I still know how to repair parts of our drives should they fail. Few captains on any ship can boast of that now."

Lodovik nodded; simple truth, but not very good armor. "The craft of best using and not abusing essential human resources may also be a lost art, Captain. Fair warning."

Tolk made a wry face. "Point taken." He turned to leave, then heard something unusual. He glanced over his shoulder at Lodovik. "Did you feel something?"

The ship suddenly vibrated again, this time with a high-pitched tensile grind that set their teeth on edge. Lodovik frowned. "I felt that. What was it?"

The captain cocked his head, listening to a remote voice buzzing in his ear. "Some instability, an irregularity in the last Jump," he said. "Not unknown as we draw close to a stellar mass. Perhaps you should return to your cabin."

Lodovik shut down the lounge projectors and rose. He smiled at Captain Tolk and clapped him on the shoulder. "Of any in the Emperor's service, I would be most willing to entrust you to steer us through the shoals. I need to study our options now anyway. Triage, Captain Tolk. Maximization of what we can take with us, compared to what can be stored in underground vaults."

Tolk's face darkened, and he lowered his eyes. "My own family library, at Alos Quad, is—"

The ship's alarms blared like huge animals in pain. Tolk raised his arms in instinctive self-protection, covering his face—

Lodovik dropped to the floor and doubled himself up with amazing dexterity—

The ship spun like a top in a fractional dimension it was never meant to navigate—

And with a sickening blur of distressed momenta and a sound like a dying behemoth, it made an unscheduled and asymmetric Jump.

The ship re-appeared in the empty vastness of status geometry—normal, unstretched space. Ship's gravity failed simultaneously.

Tolk floated a few centimeters above the floor. Lodovik uncurled and grabbed for an arm of the couch he had occupied just a few moments before. "We're out of hyperspace," he said.

"No question," Tolk said. "But in the name of procreation, *where*?"

Lodovik knew in an instant what the captain could not. They were being flooded with an interstellar tidal wave of neutrinos. He had never, in his centuries of existence, experienced such an onslaught. To the intricate and super-sensitive pathways of his positronic brain, the neutrinos felt like a thin cloud of buzzing insects; yet they passed through the ship and its human crew like so many bits of nothing. A single neutrino, the most elusive of particles, could slip through a light-year of solid lead without being blocked. Very rarely indeed did they react with matter. Within the heart of the Kale's supernova, however, immense quantities of matter had been compressed into neutronium, producing a neutrino for every proton, more than enough to blow away the outer shells just a year before.

"We're in the shock front," Lodovik said.

"How do you know?" Tolk asked.

"Neutrino flux."

"How—" The captain's skin grayed, its ashen sheen growing even more prominent. "You're assuming, of course. It's a logical assumption."

Lodovik nodded, though he assumed nothing. The captain and crew would be dead within an hour.

Even this far from Kale's star, the expanding

sphere of neutrinos would be strong enough to transmute a few thousandths of a percent of the atoms within the ship and their bodies. Neutrons would be converted to protons in sufficient numbers to subtly alter organic chemistries, causing poisons to build, nervous signals to meet untimely dead ends.

There were no effective shields against neutrino flux.

"Captain, this is no time for deception," Lodovik said. "I'm not hazarding a guess. I'm not human; I can feel the effects directly."

The captain stared at him, uncomprehending.

"I am a robot, Captain. I will survive for a time, but that is no blessing. I am deeply programmed to try to protect humans from harm, but there is nothing I can do to assist you. Every human on this ship is going to die."

Tolk grimaced and shook his head, as if he could not believe his ears. "We're going crazy, all of us," he said.

"Not yet," Lodovik said. "Captain, please accompany me to the bridge. We may yet be able to save something."

Gregory Benford—physicist, educator, author—was born in Mobile, Alabama. He is a professor of physics at the University of California–Irvine, and conducts research in plasma turbulence theory and experiment, and in astrophysics. He has published well over a hundred papers. He is a Woodrow Wilson Fellow and a visiting professor at Cambridge University and has served as an advisor to the Department of Energy, NASA, and the White House Council on Space Policy.

Many of his best–known novels are part of a six-novel sequence beginning in the near future with *In the Ocean of Night*, and continuing on with *Across the Sea of Suns*. The series then leaps to the far future, at the center of our galaxy, where a desperate human drama unfolds, beginning with *Great Sky River*, and proceeding through *Tides of Light*, *Furious Gulf*, and concluding with *Sailing Bright Eternity*. At the series' end the links to the earlier novels emerge, revealing a single unfolding tapestry against an immense background.